*The*

# NIGHT

## PORTRAIT

## ALSO BY LAURA MORELLI

*The Last Masterpiece: A Novel of World War II Italy*
*The Stolen Lady: A Novel of World War II and the* Mona Lisa
*The Painter's Apprentice: A Novel of 16th-Century Venice*
*The Gondola Maker: A Novel of 16th-Century Venice*
*The Giant: A Novel of Michelangelo's* David

# *The*
# NIGHT
## PORTRAIT

### A NOVEL OF WORLD WAR II
### AND DA VINCI'S ITALY

## LAURA MORELLI

FIRST INTERNATIONAL EDITION

*Designed by Diahann Sturge*

*Part title image © Alik Keplicz/AP/Shutterstock*
*Chapter opener grunge grey background © Nataliia K/Shutterstock*

ISBN: 978-1-942467-49-6 Paperback, 978-1-942467-48-9 eBook, 978-1-942467-50-2 Hardback, 978-1-942467-51-9 Large Print, 978-1-942467-52-6 Audio

*For Max, and for all the others who work for good*

*The*

# NIGHT

## PORTRAIT

# Part I
## *War Machines*

# I

## LEONARDO

*Florence, Italy*
*February 1476*

A DARK SHAFT IN THE HILLSIDE. IN MY MIND, I SEE IT.

Down the long passage, a forgotten recess beneath the city's fortifications, I watch men loading charges of black powder.

The best laborers for this task, I think, mine coal by day. These men are used to toiling in the thin air, in the darkness, with the careful use of the torch and the pick. Their fingers and cheeks are permanently black, their breeches stiff with soil and char. For them, what better occupation than in the service of siege?

They are brave to advance in the darkness, their lights held high. Quietly, unsuspected, they unload black grit into the farthest recesses of the shaft. When they emerge, the cannoneer turns the wheel noiselessly on its cogs, moving the machine forward into the mine. Citizens scatter amid the chaos and explosions of spewing rocks. The enemy is soon in the attacker's clutches.

The design lives only in my imagination, of course. I must admit that. Still, I am compelled to put it to paper. These thoughts, these machines. They keep me awake long past the hour when the sun turns the Arno to gold and then sinks behind the hills. These contraptions fill my dreams. I awake in a sweat, desperate to trap the images on paper before they dissipate like first morning fog on the river's surface.

The fact is that I am surrounded by my old room, with its smoldering fire in the hearth, with precarious stacks of parchment sheaves on the table, with inkwells and their metallic fragrance, with oil lamps and their charred wicks, with an ever-shifting arrangement of lounging cats. I have secured the iron latch on my door to deter those so-called friends who might lure me to the taverns. They can have it all.

I have more important tasks at hand. If I don't capture them between the pages of my notebooks, they flit away like colorful moths just beyond the reach of my net.

Never mind that troublesome distraction of the panel on my easel. There lies my improficient attempt to capture the likeness of a merchant's homely daughter. But she glares at me from across the room. Dissatisfied, as she has every right to be. Her father has asked me to make her beautiful before he sends the portrait to a suitor in Umbria. My heart is not in it, if I am honest with myself, but I cannot argue with the remuneration. It keeps bread and wine on my table. Still, the tempera pigments on my poplar plank have long dried hard. I pull the drape over the portrait so that the girl's reproving gaze will no longer distract me. I am anxious to turn back to my drawing. If only I could convince a patron to pay me for my war machines instead of replicating his daughter's profile.

Then there are my own parts of my master's unfinished works. An angel and a landscape for a baptism of Christ. The monks have been pestering Master Verrocchio for months. A Madonna and child—uninspired, if I am honest with myself—for a noble lady near Santa Maria Novella. She has written me another letter asking when it will be delivered.

How can I afford these distractions when there is so much for me to capture from my own imagination? I turn back to my notebooks.

Why the tunnels? They will ask me, these men who think as much of war as I. But I have already thought of that. How the enemy might be surprised when their attackers emerge from the earth to overcome them! They will see that the shaft driving the machine allows it to turn seamlessly, effortlessly, into the tortuous shafts below ground, without making a sound. And when these mines are not being exploded, what treasures might be hidden there from those who might steal them, deep in the underground reserves where there is copper, coal, and salt?

We must keep our enemies close. Or so they say.

But what do I know? I am only one who imagines such fantasies and puts them to paper. One who believes that sometimes, art must be put in the service of war.

I pick up my silverpoint pen and begin to draw again.

# 2
## EDITH

*Munich, Germany*
*September 1939*

EDITH BECKER HOPED THAT THE MEN AROUND THE table could not see her hands tremble.

On any other Thursday, Edith would be sitting before an easel in her ground-level conservation studio, wearing the magnifying goggles that made her look like a giant insect. There, in the quiet, she would lose all track of time, absorbed in the task of repairing a tear in a centuries-old painting, removing grime built up over decades, or regilding an old, crumbling frame. Her job was saving works of art, one by one, from decay and destruction. It was her training, her calling. Her life's work.

But for the last half hour, the eyes of the most important men of the Alte Pinakothek, one of Munich's greatest museums, had been on Edith. They watched her unwind the straps from each binder and remove folios one by one, each one representing paintings in the private collections of families across Poland.

"The identity of the man in the portrait is unknown," Edith said, passing around a facsimile of a portrait by the Italian Renaissance painter, Raffaello Sanzio. Edith watched their eyes scan the likeness of a fluffy-haired man looking askance at the viewer, drawing a fur cloak over one shoulder.

Edith was glad she had traded her usual faded gray dress and conservator's smock for the smartest outfit she owned, a brown tweed skirt and jacket. She had taken the time to make sure her hair curled evenly on either side of her jaw-line, and the seams up the back of her stockings ran straight. The men gave her their undivided attention: the curator of antiquities, the museum board chairman, even the museum director himself, Ernst Buchner, a renowned scholar to whom Edith had never spoken directly before today.

"There have been several ideas about the identity of the sitter," she said. "Some even believe it may be the artist's self-portrait."

Edith was the only woman in a room full of the museum's executive staff. She wished they hadn't asked her to abandon the peace of her conservation studio, where, for the last few weeks, she had been working to restore a large battle scene by the sixteenth-century Munich artist Hans Werl. At some point in the 1800s, another conservator had overpainted the human figures and horses in the picture. Now, working at a painstakingly slow pace, Edith was removing the overpaint with a small piece of linen soaked in solvent. She was excited to see the brilliant pigments that the artist had originally intended emerge from the canvas, one centimeter at a time. She wished they would let her get back to work instead of placing her at the center of attention.

Her eyes moved nervously around the table and finally landed on Manfred, a longtime colleague and museum registrar. Manfred peered at Edith over his small, round glasses and smiled, giving her the courage to continue. He may have been the only one in the room who understood how challenging it was for Edith to speak in front of the group.

Manfred, Edith realized, was also the only one of her coworkers who knew something of her life outside the museum. He understood the difficulty she faced in caring for her father, whose mind and memory had deteriorated, day by day. Manfred and her father had been classmates at the Academy of Fine Arts, and it was Manfred who had facilitated a position for Herr Becker's diligent, studious daughter in the conservation department. Edith knew that if she was to keep her job, let alone find any success as a professional woman at all, she had to protect her personal life from the others. She clung to Manfred's reassuring smile to help still her shaking hands.

"A masterpiece," said the board chairman, handling the

facsimile of the painting by Raffaello Sanzio with care. "I see that the Czartoryski family had an impressive ambition to collect Italian paintings."

"Indeed." Edith, too, had been surprised to learn of the treasures locked away in castles, monasteries, museums, and private homes in the lands to the east. There were vast family collections, amassed over centuries, across the Polish border. Prince Czartoryski's family art collection alone served as a quiet repository of incalculable value.

And now, Edith was beginning to understand the point of all the hours, days, and weeks she had spent in the museum archives and library stacks. She had been instructed to pull together this research on paintings in Polish collections for the museum board. She didn't know why it hadn't become obvious before now. Someone wanted to procure these pictures. Who and why?

"And this is the last one," she said, pulling the final folio from the stack of images from the Czartoryski collection.

"The one we've been waiting for," said Herr Direktor Buchner, whose brows reached for the dark, wispy hair swept back from his high forehead.

"Yes," Edith said. "Around 1800, at the same time that Adam Jerzy Czartoryski purchased Raphael's *Portrait of a Young Man* from an Italian family, he also bought Leonardo da Vinci's *Lady with an Ermine*. He brought these paintings from Italy back home to his family collection in eastern Poland."

"And it remains there?" the antiquities curator asked, suspending his pen in midair as if it were a cigarette. The curator's old habit hearkened back to the time before the recent ban on smoking in government buildings; just months ago, Edith realized, the room would have been filled with smoke.

"No," Edith said, relieved that she had reviewed her notes before the meeting. "The *Lady with an Ermine* portrait has traveled often over the last hundred years. In the 1830s, during the Russian invasion, the family took it to Dresden for safekeeping. Afterward, they returned it to Poland but things were still unstable, so they moved the painting to a hiding place in the family palace in Pełkinie. When things calmed down, the family moved it to their private apartments in Paris; that would have been in the 1840s."

"And then it returned to Poland?"

"Eventually, yes," said Edith. "The family brought it back to Poland in the 1880s. It was put on public display then, to great fanfare. That's where many people first learned of the painting, and when historians began researching it. Several experts identified it right away as by the hand of da Vinci, and people speculated about the identity of the sitter. That's how it ended up"—she gestured to her stack of folios—"widely published and reproduced."

"Who is she?" asked Buchner, tapping his fat fingers on the tabletop.

"It is well accepted that she was one of the mistresses of the Duke of Milan, a girl named Cecilia Gallerani, who came from a Sienese family. She was probably about sixteen years old at the time that Ludovico Sforza asked da Vinci to paint her." Edith watched the facsimile of the painting circulate from hand to hand around the table again. The men pored over the girl's face, her bright expression, the white, furry creature in her arms.

"During the Great War, the painting came to Germany again," Edith continued. "It was held for safekeeping in the Gemäldegalerie in Dresden, but it was ultimately returned to Kraków."

"It is remarkable that the painting survived at all, given how often it circulated," Manfred noted.

"Indeed," said Herr Direktor Buchner, handing the facsimile back to Edith. She returned it to her thick binder and began to retie the straps. "Fräulein Becker, you are to be commended for your thorough background research in the service of this project."

"A senior curator could not have done a better job," the decorative arts curator added.

"*Danke schön.*" Edith finally exhaled. She hoped they would let her return to the conservation studio now. She looked forward to putting on her smock and starting on the stabilization of a French painting whose frame had been water damaged when it was placed in an unfortunate position under a plumbing pipe in a storage closet.

Generaldirektor Buchner stood. "Now," he said, taking a deep breath. "I have an announcement. In recent days, I have had a personal visit from Reichsmarschall Göring, who, as you may know, has been engaged by our Führer in the search for masterpieces like the ones we have seen here this afternoon. There is to be a new museum constructed in Linz. It has been fully funded by our Supreme Commander, who, as you know, has a personal interest in great art and its preservation. The museum in Linz, once it is complete, will be a repository for the safekeeping of all important works of art"—he paused to look around the table—"in the world."

There was a collective gasp. Edith let the idea sink in. Adolf Hitler had already opened the House of German Art, just a short walk away from her office. She and Manfred had gone to see the work of the officially approved contemporary sculptors and painters. But now . . . Every important work of art history in the entire world under one roof, all of it under the stewardship of the Reich. It was difficult—almost inconceivable—to envision.

"As you might imagine," Buchner said, giving life to Edith's thoughts, "this new vision of our Führer will be a massive undertaking. All of us in the art-related trades are being engaged as custodians in the service of safeguarding these works. As things become more . . . precarious . . . we must all do our parts toward this effort."

"But that's insanity!" the antiquities curator huffed out. "All the important works of art in the world? Germany will control the world's cultural patrimony? Who are we to be custodians of such a legacy? And who are *we* to take them from their current places?"

The room fell into nearly unbearable silence, and Edith wondered if the poor curator was already regretting his outburst. Edith watched Manfred press his pen firmly onto his page, drawing circular doodles, his other hand over his mouth as if to stop himself from speaking.

The museum board chairman broke the silence. "No, Hans, it is a worthy cause. I have good evidence that the Americans want to take valuable European paintings and put them in Jewish museums in America. On the contrary," he said, "the idea of a *Führermuseum* . . . it's ingenious. And anyway, you must realize that this is just a start. We are also making lists of important German artworks taken by the French and English in past centuries. Those works will be repatriated to Germany in due time."

Edith studied the director's face. Herr Buchner ignored the commentary, stood up, and calmly continued, though Edith thought she detected a twitch of the muscles at the base of his neck. "All of us will be receiving orders from officials at the *Braunes Haus*. We will be working with Germany's best artists, historians, curators, and culture critics. You will each be given jobs that match your specialty. Many of us, myself included, will be traveling afield to gather works to bring back to our storage rooms here, or to other German museums."

"But what about our work here?" Edith could not help but ask. "The conservation lab . . ."

"I'm afraid that our current projects will be mostly suspended. As for the museum itself, we have already begun rearranging our collections in storage to accommodate the works that will be coming to us, and we've secured additional space off-site."

"Where are we going?" asked the antiquities curator.

"We will be receiving our specific assignments later this week," the director said. "Fräulein Becker, I suspect that there is a very good chance you will be going to Poland." He gestured to the binders full of facsimiles that Edith had compiled.

Poland.

Edith felt her stomach seize.

"S-s-surely . . .," she stammered, "surely we could not be expected to . . ."

"How long?" a curatorial assistant cut Edith's question short.

Buchner shrugged, and Edith saw the twitch in his neck again. "Until our work is done. As long as it takes. We are at war."

The director then picked up his stack of folders, nodded, and exited the room. The stream of museum staff followed.

Edith filed out behind the line of men. Reaching the familiar door to the ladies' washroom, she pressed it open and sealed it behind her. She dropped her box of folios onto the floor, sat on the toilet seat, and pressed her face into her palms. She gasped for air, feeling as if she might faint.

Poland? Indefinitely? How would she manage? Who would care for her father? What about her plans to marry, finally, after so many years of hoping? Was she really being called to the front lines? In danger of losing her life?

After a few long minutes, Edith stood and splashed cool water from the tap onto her face and wrists. When she emerged from the washroom, she found Manfred pacing the hallway.

"Are you all right?" he whispered, taking her arm.

"I . . . I'm not sure, if you want to know the truth. Oh, Manfred . . ." She exhaled, stopping to press her back against the cool tiles along the corridor wall. "What news. I can hardly believe it." Her hands were still shaking.

"I think we are all in a state of shock," he said, "even those of us who . . . who have foreseen this outcome."

Edith squeezed Manfred's forearm. She had seen little of Manfred's life outside the museum, but she knew that he had been an organizer in a Munich group that was known for opposing nearly all of the Reich's policies, their ideas disseminated in weightless leaflets left on park benches and empty tram seats.

"You knew what they were planning?"

Manfred nodded, tight-lipped. "The Generaldirektor has already purchased several truckloads of pictures confiscated from Jewish collectors across Bavaria. If you don't believe me, come up to the third floor. There are so many pictures in my office that I can barely walk to my desk."

Edith felt her jaw drop. "I can hardly imagine it. But you . . . Where will you go?"

"I'll bet they keep me here to catalog whatever comes in. They need me. Plus, I am an old dog." He shrugged and mustered a smile. "It could be worse. Out of the line of fire. But you, my dear . . . How will you manage? Your father . . ."

Edith pressed her hands to her face again. "I have no idea," she said. "Heinrich. My fiancé. He is also being shipped out to Poland."

"Ah!" Manfred said, his eyes growing wide. "Then you are headed to the same place at least."

"Yes, but . . . *Heiliger Strohsack!*" she whispered loudly. "This was not what I was expecting."

"I wish I could say the same, my dear Fräulein Konservator," Manfred said. "You are too young to remember the beginnings of the last war. And here we are again. All the same, what can we do? When the Führer calls, we hardly have a choice. They will issue us conscription papers. Saying no is not an option unless. . . ."

Manfred gestured toward a window at the end of the hallway, one that overlooked the square where Jewish-owned shops had been forcibly closed or even burned in recent months. At this moment, Edith knew, Jewish families were boarding trams—either by choice or by coercion—that would resettle them in another place, that would consign them to a fate beyond her understanding. The Nusbaums, a couple who lived with their two young children in Edith's apartment building, had left weeks ago. In the ground-floor corridor, under the sharp eye of their doorman, Edith had watched Frau Nusbaum piling worn leather bags and grain sacks full of their most precious belongings into a rickety barrow.

Edith knew that Manfred was correct in saying that refusing the Führer's call was not an option, but her mind raced, looking for a way out of the predicament. Was it too much to ask, to return to her conservation studio, to her humble apartment, to her father, to a new life with her husband?

"Well," said Manfred, mustering a tight grin. "Poland! Perhaps there is a silver lining. You will get to see all those masterpieces you've studied all this time."

# 3

## EDITH

*Munich, Germany*
*September 1939*

EDITH WAS STRUGGLING WITH THE LOCK ON HER apartment door when she heard her father shriek.

The fine hairs on the back of her neck tingled, and a jolt like a live tram wire ran down her spine. She had never heard that wrenching sound come from his mouth before. She rattled the door with all her force.

"Papa!"

Finally, the key clicked and the door opened. Edith nearly fell into the apartment. She dropped her shoulder bag, spilling the art books and folders she had brought home from work. Bookmarks and handwritten notes fluttered and spun across the worn, wooden floor. Edith rushed down the hallway, toward the loud voice of a radio broadcaster announcing that German troops had crossed the Vistula River in southern Poland. In the front room, she found her father seated in his chair, lashing out with his lanky arms and legs toward the slight woman looming over him.

"Herr Becker!" Elke, the woman who cared for her father while Edith was at work, struggled to grasp the old man's forearms. Her hair had come loose from its pins at the crown of her head. Her face was a contorted grimace. Edith's father's long legs lashed out again, stiff and unco-ordinated, toward Elke's shins.

Then the smell of urine and excrement came over Edith, and she felt her heart sink.

"He refuses to walk to the toilet!" Elke finally let go of Herr Becker's forearms and turned toward Edith. "I cannot get him to leave that chair!"

"It's all right," Edith said, trying to steady her voice. "Let me talk to him."

Elke threw up her hands in exasperation and retreated to the kitchen. Edith strode across the room and switched off the radio, silencing the ranting announcer.

"Papa." Edith knelt on the rug before her father's chair, just as she had when she was a little girl, hungry for an-other one of her father's stories about counts and duchesses from long ago. The floral patterns on the arms of the chair had worn pale and threadbare, the cushion sagging and now surely beyond salvage. Edith did her best to ignore the stench.

"That woman . . ." her father said, his eyes wide with uncharacteristic rage, cloudy orbs rimmed in yellow. From the kitchen, Edith heard water running, followed by the loud clang of pots.

Coarse white hairs protruded from his chin. Edith imagined that Elke had been struggling with her father for hours. It was becoming a daily occurrence, Herr Becker's refusal to partake in the simplest tasks, from putting on a clean shirt to shaving. Getting him in the bath was close to impossible; in recent weeks he had developed an inexplicable fear of water. Edith felt pity for Elke, at the same time that she was frustrated that no one in the ever-changing group of caregivers that Edith had hired understood how to coax her father to cooperate. It required a high level of patience with a dose of trickery, Edith had to admit.

From the crease between the cushion and the frame of the chair, Edith excavated Max, the ragged, stuffed dog that had belonged to Edith as a child. Now, Max was her father's constant companion, its white fur matted and stained irreparably.

"It's all right, Papa," Edith said, putting her palm securely on his forearm, with its thin, lined skin marked with darkened spots. With his other hand, her father grasped the ragged animal tightly to his side. Behind them, the Swiss clock ticked loudly. Messy stacks of art books lined the walls, slips of paper haphazardly sticking out of each volume. Dusty, yellowed pages of scholarly catalogs and journals her father had once devoured now stood abandoned.

"Shall we get you cleaned up? I have a feeling that you might have a visitor."

Her father's eyes lit up as he digested her white lie, and Edith felt a pang of guilt slide across her gut. None of her father's friends were coming to visit. When her father no longer recognized their faces and could not recall their names, one by one, they dwindled away. Edith had watched wordlessly, powerless to stop it.

Her father no longer tracked time, but Edith knew that months had passed since their last visitor, with the exception of Edith's fiancé, Heinrich. And even that was about to stop. Heinrich would soon be boarding a train for Poland, assigned to a newly formed infantry division of the Wehrmacht. As soon as the invasion of Poland had been broadcast across the radio and newspapers less than two weeks ago, Edith had held her breath and begun to pray, but Heinrich's official orders had come anyway.

But Edith didn't want to think about that now.

In the bathroom, Edith ran her hand under the tap until the water warmed. She would never have dreamed that the barrier of modesty between father and daughter would have fallen away so completely. What else was she to do? When the caregivers she hired inevitably gave up trying to wrangle her stubborn father, who else but his only daughter would care enough to loosen his trousers, to blot a damp cloth across his shoulders, to carefully run a razor across his jaw? Edith's mother had been gone nearly five years now, and in moments like these, she missed her more than ever.

*"Guten abend!"*

Edith poked her head out of the bathroom doorway long enough to see Heinrich enter the apartment, greeting Elke as the stout nurse departed in a blur of blue raincoat and hat.

As much as her heart surged to see her fiancé, it also sank at Elke's abrupt departure. Tomorrow there would be a visit to the agency and another search for a nurse so that Edith could continue her work at the museum and put food on their table.

Heinrich pecked a brief kiss on Edith's lips. "What happened in here? It smells like a farm."

Edith pressed her face into Heinrich's neck and drank in his scent for a long moment. "I'm going to get him cleaned up now. I'm sorry. I don't know whether Elke ever got to preparing dinner. Have a look in the kitchen."

The voice of his daughter's fiancé in the hallway had lured Herr Becker from the front room. Now, the old man braced himself against the doorjamb, his trousers sagging, a sideways grin on his face.

"Greetings, soldier!" Heinrich smiled at his future father-in-law and rushed to steady him. Edith watched her father endeavor to give Heinrich a firm handshake. "Looks like you're in for a good shave from this lovely lady. Lucky man!" With gratitude and relief, Edith watched Heinrich steer her father successfully to the bathroom door.

Edith did her best to clean up Herr Becker, showing him as much patience and compassion as she could muster. When they emerged from the bathroom, her father dressed in clean pajamas, Edith saw that Heinrich had moved the soiled chair to air out by an open window and had brought a bowl of fruit and bread from the kitchen to the dining table. He was picking up the papers and books that she had spilled by the apartment door.

For a moment, she watched Heinrich kneeling over her satchel in the dim light of the entryway, a calm beacon in the storm. He was wearing the gray cotton collared shirt that brought out the sky gray of his eyes. She could hardly bear the thought of standing on a station platform, watching him wave to her from a small train window in a newly pressed field tunic.

"I'm sorry there is no dinner," she said, kneeling beside him to pick up the last sheets of paper from the floor.

"We have bread. We have fruit. We have muesli, reheated from this morning, but healthy all the same. More than many people have, surely."

Edith helped her father sit in his usual chair at the dining table and put a piece of bread in front of him. Finally, she took a deep breath and relaxed. She sat at the table and began peeling an apple with a worn knife.

"What's all this paper?" Heinrich asked.

"Research," she said. "They've asked me to compile a dossier of old master paintings in Polish collections. You remember I was telling you about all the library visits I've made in the past weeks? I had to give a presentation today to the director."

"Herr Professor Dokter Buchner?" Heinrich raised his eyebrows.

"Yes." Edith felt her stomach constrict as she thought about the room full of men, the Führer's museum, the news that she had no idea how to break to Heinrich and her father.

"I thought they kept you locked up in the back storerooms with a paintbrush and chemicals," Heinrich said.

She nodded. "Yes. It's not my usual place, but Herr Kurator Schmidt asked me to do it. He said I have special knowledge of Italian Renaissance paintings. You know I am happy to stay hidden away in my little scientific department, not standing before an audience."

Heinrich leaned back in his chair and thumbed through one of the large illustrated volumes that Edith had brought home from the museum library. Edith watched him nervously, wondering how to find the words to tell Heinrich and her father. How on earth would she break the news? When Heinrich reached a bookmarked, full-page color facsimile of a woman holding a small white creature, he stopped.

"Leonardo da Vinci," Heinrich read the caption. "*Portrait of a Lady with an Ermine.*" He looked up at Edith. "What's an ermine?"

Edith shrugged. "Ladies in the Italian Renaissance kept a variety of exotic pets. An ermine is something like a ferret."

"No," her father interjected, raising a crooked finger. "There is a difference. Ferrets are domesticated. Ermines are wild. Their fur turns white in the winter."

Heinrich and Edith looked at each other, then laughed aloud at Herr Becker's assessment. Edith's heart surged whenever a spark of clarity flickered in the fog, when her real father came back to her, if only for a fleeting moment.

"*Bravo*, Papa. I had no idea," Edith said, but the flicker was gone, and her father had returned to spooning watery muesli into his mouth. "That's one of my favorite pictures," Edith said. "Da Vinci painted it when he was still a young man, before he became well known."

"A strange creature," Heinrich said, tapping the picture with his finger, "but a beautiful girl."

This was what she would miss most, Edith thought, sitting with her father and Heinrich, talking of art. She wanted to hear her father's lessons again, random shards of information he pulled from the dusty corners of his brain, left over from years of teaching art history at the university, volumes of historical facts that he had transmitted to his daughter along with a passion for art. Was it too much to ask? She just wanted a laugh with her father and to eat a meal with the man she loved. She did not want to have to cobble together yet another caregiver to help her nearly helpless papa. And above all, she did not want to count the days left until Heinrich boarded a train. She pushed it to the back of her mind, stood, and began to clear the table.

Heinrich moved another armchair near the window and settled Herr Becker so that he could watch the lights begin to flicker from the apartment windows lining the edge of the park. He retrieved Max from the floor and pressed the old, ragged stuffed dog into Herr Becker's lap. Then Edith heard Heinrich talking softly to her father, telling him about something funny that had happened at his father's grocery market, just off the Kaufingerstrasse. She knew her father wouldn't remember any of it after a few minutes, but no matter. The next time Heinrich visited, his kind, familiar face would be enough to lure her father from his chair.

Not long ago, Edith would have sat with her father after dinner, listening to his impassioned opinions of current events, his critique of the greed and corruption of government officials. Edith wondered if her father had any inkling of what was happening beyond the walls of their apartment now. Continued reports of corruption. The dismantling of synagogues. The confiscation of businesses and apartments belonging to Jewish neighbors. The heightened surveillance by their apartment block leaders, who seemed to record her every move. The swift, unexplained departure of two staff members from the museum. Non-German books pulled from libraries and burned in the streets. New laws that would punish anyone who listened to a foreign radio broadcast.

Most of all, she worried about the disappearance of the little boy at the bottom of the stairway. Edith used to look for the Nusbaums' son every morning as she left for work. She'd find him sitting in the hallway with his pens and paper. She would stop to greet him and he would show Edith what he'd drawn that day. She would compliment him and tell him to keep drawing. But one day, he was gone, along with his innocent face and his fastidious drawings. The rest of his family were gone, too, simply walking away with the coats on their backs and a wobbly, wheeled cart.

While she did her best to stay focused on the details of her work and home life, Edith felt deeply troubled about how Munich had changed in recent months. More than that, she missed her father's commentary on current events, which might have provided her with a compass to help navigate her way through the disturbing events that swirled around them.

"Edith?"

She turned to see her father's wide, shiny eyes set on her, as if he had just recognized her face after not having seen her for a long time.

"Yes, Papa!" she said, laughing.

He held out Max the dog. "I believe this is yours."

Edith stared down at the button eyes that her mother had sewn and resewn many times over the years. Max had occupied her bed as a child, then was cast aside as Edith grew into a young woman. When her father had rediscovered Max one day, shortly after her mother died and he began to decline, he had latched on to it like a beloved pet.

"Max," she said, stroking the stuffed animal's matted fur. "But I wouldn't want to lose him." She pressed him back into her father's hands. "Will you take care of him for me?"

Her father settled the ragged stuffed dog back in his lap. "All right," he said, deflated.

"I love you so much, Papa," Edith said, squeezing her father's hands. She tried hard not to let her voice crack.

When her father began to doze off in his chair, Edith joined Heinrich in the kitchen. He dried the dishes with a frayed rag and stacked them on the wooden shelves above the sink. "She's not coming back, is she? The woman in the raincoat?"

Edith sighed. "I'm afraid not. I have to call the agency first thing in the morning. The problem is that he has become so stubborn! They are supposed to be professional nurses, but they don't know how to coerce him into doing the most basic things! I don't know what to do."

Edith felt Heinrich's hand on her back. She stopped and bowed her head, pressing her forehead to Heinrich's chest. She felt his hands go to her hips and rest there. For a few long moments, they stood there, holding each other.

"I have no right to burden you with this when you have

bigger things to worry about," she said. "I'm sorry." Edith pressed her face into his cotton shirt and felt his lean, hard chest under her forehead. She inhaled his clean, male scent as she listened to the clock tick loudly in the hallway. How would she break the news that he was not the only one with official orders?

"Edith . . ." he began softly. "They have given me a date. I have to report to Hauptbahnhof Station in two weeks." He must have felt her body freeze under his grasp; he paused. "I just want you to know that, whatever happens . . ."

"Shh," she said, pressing a finger to his lips and shaking her head, her light brown curls hitting her cheeks. "Not yet. Can we just make this last for a bit longer?"

# 4

## CECILIA

*Milan, Italy*
*December 1489*

**"THERE IS A LIVE ONE. I CAN FEEL IT CRAWLING."**

"Where?"

"Just there. Behind my ear."

Cecilia Gallerani felt her mother's thick, calloused fingertips slide through her dark strands, unraveling the twists. Her mother pinched her frayed fingernails along the length of one hair, yanking so hard that Cecilia bit her lip. She heard her mother swish her hand through the small bowl at her side, a mixture of water and vinegar with small, white nits floating dead on the surface.

"Did you get it?"

An exasperated cluck. "It was too fast. Will you sit still?"

A slow ache was working its way across Cecilia's forehead. How many hours had they been sitting by the light of the window? Through its frame, Cecilia's almond-shaped eyes scanned the layer of cold fog that had settled in the inner courtyard. She watched a dove flutter from the bare branches to a high windowsill overlooking the empty, symmetrical footpaths below. Such a strange place, this hard, wintry stone palace, with its fortified towers and armsmen pacing the upper galleries. So far away from the blindingly sun-filled squares and raucous, bustling streets of home.

As their carriage had rolled through the streets of Milan the afternoon before, Cecilia had watched the flat, vapid landscape suddenly turn to a jumble of fine buildings and crowded streets. The slow crawl through the crowds afforded momentary views of the spiky white spires of Milan's cathedral under construction. She had caught fleeting glimpses of the city's women, their long braids wrapped in silk and transparent layers of veil, men with fur-lined leather boots reaching to the knees and their breath sending vapors into the cold air. Cecilia had marveled at their odd Milanese tongue, a dialect that sounded clipped and harsh, at the same time that it flowed from their lips like a song. She grasped a few familiar words, but they spoke too quickly for her to understand the meaning.

At long last, they had reached the Castello Sforzesco on the outskirts of the city. Guards armed with spears and crossbows had lowered the bridge over the moat, and their horses' hooves had echoed through the tunneled gatehouse into the fortified inner courtyard.

"*Aya!* I feel it moving again."

Another *tsk* of exasperation. Her mother ran the comb roughly through a tangle. "Honestly, Cecilia, I hardly see the point. All this hair will be shorn within a few days."

"That is not decided." Cecilia felt the familiar squeeze of discontent across her stomach.

It made perfect sense. Of course it did. Her eldest brother, Fazio, their mother's greatest pride, as well as their father's namesake and successor, had laid it out in clear, logical terms. He had already made arrangements with the Benedictine sisters at San Maurizio al Monastero Maggiore. Cecilia should consider herself fortunate to have such an opportunity, they told her. It was only through her brother's position as a Tuscan diplomat to the court of Milan, a position that their father was never able to reach even after years of service as a petitioner at the ducal court, that the possibility was open to Cecilia at all. It's what had brought them to this wintry palace in the first place.

"Soon enough," said her mother, half under her breath. Cecilia caught sight of her mother's brown hand and forearm, as thick as one of the piglets in their courtyard back home in Siena. Cecilia felt a veil of shame and embarrassment cover the two of them sitting at the window. It was laughable, her stout, sun-speckled mother sitting here among the pale, elegant ladies of the ducal palace. What place did the two of them have here? In Siena, they held their heads high, the wife and daughter of a petitioner at the court of Milan. But here, in this northern palace, the seat of His Lordship's domain, Cecilia and her mother passed for little more than peasants. She felt certain that she could see the women in their silk gowns snickering at them behind their gloves and fans.

How quickly her fate had turned.

Only a season ago, her future had looked entirely different. She and Giovanni Stefano Visconti were set to wed, an arrangement that had been in place since she was barely old enough to take her first steps. It was a perfect solution, her father had said, to marry their youngest, the only girl, to the Visconti, a Milanese family with a noble legacy and ties to the Sforza ducal family. Giovanni himself was nothing so remarkable, little more than a lopsided grin of a boy not yet turned to man. A dusting of freckles spread across his nose, and the wide shoulders of his father's overcoat hung from his lanky frame, but Cecilia had been at peace with the safety and security of marrying into a respected family. The two had already had a ring ceremony to commemorate the commitment, as perfunctory and devoid of emotion as it was legally binding. But Cecilia felt secure, content even, with the arrangement. She was accustomed to being in the company of boys and men, anyway. She had grown up in the chaotic tussle of a house with six brothers. Spending the rest of her days inside a cathouse of a convent sounded like the dullest possible fate.

But only months after her father was in the ground, the magnitude of her brothers' foolishness had come to light.

There was no more hiding it. Together, her brothers had frittered away Cecilia's dowry, squandering it on ill-advised investments, dice games, and drink. Once things were out in the open, Giovanni Visconti's father had burned the marriage contract in front of her brothers' own eyes at the gates to their farm.

After that, there was a letter dispatched to her eldest brother, Fazio. Within a few days, Cecilia and her mother were loaded into a small carriage rattling north toward Milan, where Fazio had promised to make things right.

"But I don't see why I must go to the Monastero Maggiore," Cecilia said. It came out like a childish whine and Cecilia immediately cringed. Her mother yanked a little harder than was necessary.

"*Aya!*" Cecilia clasped her palm to her scalp.

"You should count yourself fortunate to have such a chance, Cecilia. We have already been over this. The cloister is the perfect place for a girl like you," her mother said firmly, ignoring her daughter's yelp and letting another twist fall from the pile of hair on top of Cecilia's head. Cecilia had heard the arguments; she was intelligent, fluent in Latin, knew how to write poetry and play the lute. She came from a respected family. As if she read her daughter's mind, Signora Gallerani added, "You will be able to do all those things you love—reading and writing and playing music. And you will be a woman of purity and high regard."

"Then I might find myself a highborn husband right here in this castle instead," Cecilia said. She had made sure that her brothers had signed not only her marriage annulment but also attested to her maidenhood before she had departed for Milan. She knew that she was considered a great prize as a wife; the beauty of Fazio Gallerani's only daughter and her purity were whispered about in Siena. "Surely I could use my talents to hold court in a great house instead of behind the convent walls, where I will have no audience."

Her mother crossed her arms across her broad chest and shook her head. Then she let out a sharp laugh that made her midsection jiggle. "What pride! Where did my daughter get such high ideas? If your father were alive, he would take a switch to your legs."

A soft knock fell on the door, then her brother's face appeared.

"My ladies," Fazio greeted them with a brief bow, and their mother's face lit up. She dropped the comb onto the inlaid table alongside the bowl of vinegar and dead lice, then clapped her hands together and pressed her palms to her eldest son's cheeks.

"My beauty," she said, stroking her son's face as if he were a favorite horse. Cecilia had to admit that her eldest brother, at twenty-six years old and ten years her senior, had indeed grown into a handsome, capable man worthy of more than their father's legacy at the court of Milan.

"They are ready for us at the midday meal," Fazio said.

"Santa Maria!" Signora Gallerani exclaimed, swiftly returning to Cecilia's back and weaving her hair into a tight braid. "Those blasted pests have caused us to work too long." She quickly tied the end with a leather strap. Cecilia felt the braid thump down the length of her back.

"Fazio," Cecilia said. "If I must live here in Milan, then I want to stay here in this palace instead of a convent."

She heard her mother let out a guffaw. "She continues to talk nonsense," she said, picking up the comb and waving it at Cecilia as if threatening to beat her with it. "We must get her out of this overblown pile of stone as soon as possible." She cast her eyes to the gilded and brightly painted decoration in the coffered ceiling above their heads.

Fazio laughed. "Whatever do you mean, girl?"

Cecilia looped her hand through the crook of her brother's arm. "Surely you, with your high rank here, are in a position to find me a husband."

"A husband!"

"Yes," she said, patting his hand. "One with a large house and a court full of people, full of poetry and music." She did not dare to say it out loud, but the truth was that she also saw herself richer, cleaner, more elegant, just like the women she glimpsed outside the window, those whose lives she only imagined.

Cecilia saw her brother's face waver, and then he exchanged a wary glance with their mother.

"But it is already arranged with the sisters," he said, his brow furrowing.

"Fazio, you know well that I could be one of the most sought-after brides in our region. Plus, you owe me a new husband after what happened with the last one!"

For a few long moments, silence hung thickly in the air.

"*Vergogna*!" her mother broke in. "Prideful girl!" Her mouth had formed a deep scowl. "Your brother owes you nothing! He has already done more for you than you deserve. Besides, you will see. After only a few days with the sisters, you will understand that the convent is the right place for you, Cecilia. I have already told you—I have already told the prideful girl, Fazio—you will get to do all those things you love. And most of all, you will be a woman of purity and high regard. You will bring our family honor and you will pray for your father's eternal soul on behalf of all of us."

Her brother, a skilled diplomat, stepped sideways. He offered his remaining arm to his mother and steered the two women toward the door. "Shall we go eat? Rice again, I'm afraid, but I saw the cook adding pomegranate arils and citrus. I'm famished."

Beaming at her son, their mother finally took his arm.

But no sooner had Fazio opened the door to the corridor than he stopped short, pressing the women behind him. A small crowd was making its way toward them from the end of a long corridor. As the cluster of courtiers approached,

Cecilia watched her brother bow in deference. She and her mother attempted to follow his example, casting their eyes to the intricate patterns on the floor. Cecilia heard the hiss of silk across the marble and could only catch fleeting glimpses of velvet gloves and slippers, silk hose, polished buckles, transparent sheaves of black lace, ribbons of green and gold.

The man at the front of the crowd stopped, and the crowd circled behind him.

"Fazio Gallerani," the man said. From behind her brother's back, Cecilia could only see that the man was stout and black-haired, with a voice so deep that it sounded as if his mouth was full of pebbles.

"My lord," her brother said, his head and shoulders dropping still lower in deference to the man.

"You have brought guests," he said, the deep voice and his Tuscan words with their Milanese accent both strange and beautiful to her ear.

"Guests? Oh no, my lord. Just my mother and my little sister. They arrived last night from Siena."

"Let us greet them, then."

A few long, silent moments passed. Cecilia watched her mother stare down at her dress, where red earth was still caked to the hem and under her fingernails. She did not move from her place behind her son's back.

Cecilia pushed her way in front of her brother, where she found herself standing face-to-face with a man who could be no other than the lord of Milan. Though at least twice her age, Ludovico il Moro stood eye to eye with Cecilia. His face was angular but mostly invisible behind a richly oiled black beard. His breast was covered in velvet and metal, each finger adorned with a colored gem. The front of his doublet hung heavy with jangling emblems, the sounds heralding his arrival as if he were a prized beast. He raked his dark eyes over Cecilia, then held her under a penetrating gaze for a few more long moments. Was he waiting for her to bow?

But Cecilia did not bow. She only met his dark gaze and smiled.

# 5

# LEONARDO

*Florence, Italy*
*December 1476*

**A SODOMITE.**

Is that all I have become? The sum of my work? The reward for my years of tutelage under Master Verrocchio? The sum of my gifts in designing siege machines and other useful contraptions for men of war?

My father won't speak on my behalf; he never has gone out of his way to protect his bastard son, and why should he now? And my uncles only tell me that I must be more careful about who I befriend. They say I am naïve, that I have much to learn of the ways in which noble families of Florence are accused for no good reason. But I am old enough to know that all it takes is for a cruel, jealous person to slip an anonymous accusation into the letter box of the Signoria to send a man to the gallows.

They will never prove anything, of that tailor, of the

goldsmith, or of me. They cannot produce evidence for anything that was scratched out on that piece of parchment and slipped into the Mouth of Truth in the middle of the night. And as for Saltarelli, that young profiteer who prompted the whole thing, I hope the Officers of the Night find him. The rumors about him being more than an artist's model may be true, but in the end, it is little more than jealousy that sparked this fiasco. If Saltarelli knows what's good for him, he will have left Florence before another denunciation is passed into the *tamburo* at the Signoria.

But now I see that the time has come for me to depart Florence, too. Two accusations in as many years. I am not as naïve as my uncles think.

Surely, beyond the city, there is honorable work. There are men who will pay for my talents, for my contraptions, for my vision. They will put a roof over my head and food on my table.

Far to the north of here, they are already at war. The men of Pavia, Ferrara, Milan. Especially Milan, where not even churches are safe. Milan, where we hear that Duke Galeazzo Sforza has just been stabbed to death in the Basilica of Santo Stefano during high mass. And now, his little boy, Gian Galeazzo, barely old enough to lift a crossbow, carries the burden of the duchy. If anyone needs my assistance with war machines, it's the poor little Duke of Milan.

No one need know of the unfolding events here. My drawings speak for themselves. I need only find people with connections far beyond Florence. Men in power who will advocate on my behalf. The right letters of introduction from the right men.

The fat tabby leaps onto my writing table and nearly spills the glass well of indigo ink. I run my hand over her gray stripes and feel the contented rumble in her throat as the beast urges her bony head against my palm. Then the cat narrows her golden eyes to slits and I ask her the inevitable question.

Who will grant my safe passage out of Florence?

# 6
# DOMINIC

*Normandy, France*
*June 1944*

DOMINIC'S SHAKING FINGERS FIDDLED WITH HIS helmet's chin strap and he dug down deep for an ounce of courage. *It's about time,* he told himself, a refrain repeated for months before he arrived here. *I'm here to do a job after all; here to fight for something. We should have stood up to his madness long before now. How many lives might have been saved if the Americans and English had deployed troops months ago? Years ago?*

He found himself running his fingers across the light stubble on his jaw. Dominic hated the feeling of having his hands idle. He was desperate for something to do with his nervous energy, something to think about that wasn't being crammed shoulder to shoulder with thirty-five other men on the Higgins boat. Each undulating wave propelled them closer to the beach—and the enemy. Each man crouched in that hull was fighting his own internal battle to ignore the cold perspiration, pushing the fear down somewhere deep inside.

*Let's get this done*, he thought. *Let's do the right thing, the just thing, so that we can all go home.*

The sky was as gray as the sea; mist muffled the world around them so that even though Dominic knew there were thousands of other men aboard scores of landing craft all around them, it felt as though this little platoon was all that stood between the Nazis and the lives they strove to protect. As though only their little platoon would land on Omaha Beach and alone, face their fate.

Not quite alone. The shadow of a plane overhead chilled the air.

Instinctively, Dominic reached between the buttons of his fatigue shirt, only to feel a pang of longing when his fingers brushed against a ball chain and two dog tags. They had made him take off his Saint Christopher medal at basic training back in Fort Leonard Wood, Missouri. He had stored the medal inside a zippered pocket of his leather wallet, resolving that it would be safe there until the day he could finally exchange his dog tags for his beloved Saint Christopher.

How soon would this be over? Dominic closed his eyes, feeling the kiss of spray on his cheek, and dreamed his way back to a bright day that now felt another lifetime and a world away.

Swede Hill. Greensburg, Pennsylvania.

It had been Dominic's whole world for twenty-two years. He had grown up there, in the bosom of the only "wop" family among the Swedes and Irish. At least that's how people referred to the Bonellis, some jokingly, some with derision in their eyes.

Dominic thought of his mother, who had latched that Saint Christopher at his neck, stood on tiptoe to kiss his cheek, and put on a brave face.

*Just come back to us,* amore.

He had met Sally there, seen his first child born there, too. His little Cecilia. Watching them wave good-bye was the hardest damned thing Dominic had ever had to do.

But Dominic knew what it felt like to be the target of prejudice, and besides, he had an important mission. He wasn't about to duck away from doing his part. Dominic had been following the headlines in the *Pittsburgh Post-Gazette* with his morning coffee for some three years now. The Nazis had stolen personal property and raped the country-side of Europe. They had murdered hundreds of thousands of innocent people, most of them for nothing more than being Jewish. For two years, the newspapers had been reporting on the many thousands corralled in death camps across Germany, Austria, Poland. More than a million in Poland alone, he had read. Dominic couldn't understand how anyone could stand by and do nothing. The Americans should have acted long before now, Dominic thought, and he knew many of his fellow soldiers felt the same.

Even though saying good-bye to his wife and daughter was the hardest thing Dominic could imagine, all the same, he and all the men around him were committed to face the enemy, to shut down Hitler's machine. And now, finally, after months of training, they were ready to land on the beach. Ready to set things right in the world again.

*Let's do this thing*, he thought, trying to still his trembling fingers.

A sudden wave caught the landing craft; a jarring bump and a splash of icy spray on Dominic's face brought him back to the present. His medal was gone, even the photographs of Sally and little Cecilia taken from him, but he had to believe that God was with him regardless. Wasn't he?

The dog tags jingled against his chest as he shifted his weight, trying to relieve his numb feet. The twin plates of metal held only the most basic information: Bonelli, Dominic A. Social Security number. Blood type O. Catholic. Just the essence of him, stripped of the details that made him human.

This was how the army saw him. A number. Cannon fodder. One of thousands of faceless men in colorless uniforms, packed like cattle into the claustrophobic landing craft. Dominic found himself twisting and untwisting the chain of his dog tags, rubbing them together. His hands felt empty again. Idleness before a mad rush.

At home, his hands had never been still. When he wasn't

shoveling coal in the mines below Pittsburgh, he was rocking his baby girl and singing to her in his rough voice; sometimes nonsense ditties he invented on the fly, sometimes old Sicilian songs his *nonna* had taught him but no one understood anymore.

Cecilia hadn't cared. She had loved them all, cooing as she stretched her chubby hands toward his face. And when Cecilia was asleep and the house was filled with the sound of opera turned down low on the radio, he'd grasp a charcoal stick and sit sketching as Sally washed the dishes. He often thought of doing a landscape or a still life, but every night he ended up sketching the perfect lines of her hair, the curves of her body. The newest, a swelling of her belly filled with the promise of a second child. He kept looking up at her as he drew, but he knew it wasn't necessary; Sally was imprinted into his mind's eye, indelibly stamped into the fabric of his soul.

Especially her smile. It had captured his heart on an afternoon three years ago when he'd been walking up the hill toward home after work in the mines. He had spotted her in her parents' garden orchard, picking apples. It wasn't easy to win Sally's heart. At first, she had refused to be impressed by his silly banter, refused to fall for his nagging, refused to be captured. She fussed at him and told him to get lost, but Dominic detected a smile beneath the sass. Dominic's grandfather advised him that persistence would always win, and he was right. Dominic kept stopping at the corner on his way home until one day, she finally shared an apple freshly picked from the tree.

The fierce cry of his commanding officer brought Dominic back to reality. As the men around him scrambled to ready themselves for landing, Dominic's heart fell through his boots. He looked up and saw the gray expanse of Omaha Beach thrown open before them; the mist and the drizzle enfolded it in wispy shrouds that hid the sinister enemy he knew must be lying in wait behind the dunes. He dropped his dog tags and laced his shaking fingers together to mask their tremor. The distant pop-pop of rifles somewhere was already making his heart beat faster; he knew that each of those soft cracks was the sound of death coming for one of the men on the beach.

"God help us," gasped the soldier beside him. He saw the boy's hands trembling, his bolt-action rifle shaking between his fingers.

His commander's voice rang out again. "We're off, boys!"

Operation Neptune.

Dominic watched his commander's face, his lips moving, but the looming shadow and deafening roar of a plane engine drowned the rest of his words.

Dominic unlocked his fingers and grasped the barrel of his rifle. Beyond the rim of the boat, the beach was a mass of disembarking men and gunfire. It didn't look like an organized assault; to Dominic, it looked like chaos. Already, muzzle flashes lit up the mist.

Dominic watched the hinged ramp of the landing craft creak open, then suddenly, it crashed down, a rush of cold water hissing inside. A desperate war cry tore from the throats of the entire platoon. Shoulder to shoulder, they rushed forward.

# 7

## LEONARDO

*Florence, Italy*
*April 1482*

THE BEST DESIGN FOR A BATTLESHIP, I THINK, IS ONE with a ramp that lowers from the mouth of the boat. A sort of landing craft. A boat with a hinged ramp that might open upon landing, spilling soldiers onto the ground to take their enemies by surprise.

Like most inspired ideas, it comes to me in the middle of the night. I barely have time to sketch it on paper before jogging across the bridge to the walled sculpture garden inside the palace of the Medici.

Now, I watch Lorenzo il Magnifico run the palm of his hand over his stubbled cheek, the thin line of his mouth tight and contemplating as his knowing, intelligent eyes scan my torn page. My lord must appreciate how such a craft might serve useful against the Pisans. Surely, for all their supposed prowess at sea, they have not come up with such a design.

I do not want to sound ungrateful, for I count myself lucky to have the favor of His Lordship's attention at all. But I no longer hold on to any hope that Il Magnifico will give me a commission for a war machine. He will not save me a place at his table. He will not pay me a stipend or even grant me a commission. Permission to sketch ancient statuary in the peace of his garden is all I have earned after years of trying. At this point, all I can hope for is a word from His Lordship that might find me a patron far away from here.

"Yes," Il Magnifico tells me, putting the parchment back in my hand. "I see how a warship with this ramp design might be advantageous. But not in Milan. How would you convey the value of this idea to a man born in Lombardy, a man who rules a vast, landlocked spread of flat wheat fields and rice paddies as far as the eye can see?"

He has a point. After all, Ludovico Sforza, the one they call the Moor, has seized control of the court of Milan without the slightest need for a boat. All he has done is poach his enemies—his own relations—one by one. He even pushed out the young boy-duke's own mother and her closest, most trusted political and military advisers. And now, Ludovico Sforza is Regent of Milan—a duke in practice if not in name.

"We must make sure that Florence stays in alliance with Milan," Il Magnifico tells me. I scramble to follow him down a long corridor adjacent to his lush garden filled with ancient statues pulled from the dirt around Rome. "Ludovico Sforza has proven himself a powerful force," His Lordship says. "Any fourth son who manages to overtake his older relations is not to be taken lightly. We must watch him."

"I might go to Milan on your behalf," I offer. "See this court from the inside. I could keep you informed, my lord."

Il Magnifico slows his hurried pace, then stops for a few long moments to examine the tender bloom of a white lily. For a moment I fear that he might pinch off the fragrant, dew-speckled flower of this *giglio*, the symbol of our city, but finally, he lets it spring back on its stalk. "Yes," he says. "You along with others. We will organize a retinue of diplomats and court entertainers. You will make a gift to Ludovico the Moor from our Medici family."

I pause to think. "An armored carriage. Or perhaps a wheel-powered catapult. My lord?"

"No," he says. "A musical instrument. You are gifted with the lyre."

"A lyre."

He nods, his thin lips firm in decision. "Bring me a design."

"But, with respect, my lord, the Regent of Milan might have need of defensive designs rather than musical instruments. You have said yourself that the Venetians plot against Ludovico il Moro from the east; from the north, the French. They even plot against him from inside his own palace. I have heard that his own court physicians mix poison for his closest relations—"

A small wave of the hand and I am silenced.

"You will follow a retinue of diplomats and musicians to Milan. My men will see to the arrangements. I will make sure you have a letter of introduction. You have only to make the lyre."

"And for defensive designs . . ."

"If you want to elaborate on your skills for Ludovico il Moro, then you may attach your own list of qualifications."

# Part II
## *A Thing of Beauty*

# 8

## CECILIA

*Milan, Italy*
*January 1490*

**HER SONG BEGAN WITH A PLAINTIVE NOTE.**

Cecilia felt the first sound start low in her chest. A wobble; she fought to steady her voice. The sound grew, rising up as it began to take life. Then, it expanded into the space of the great audience hall of the Castello Sforzesco.

Cecilia could not bear to meet any of the pairs of eyes trained on her, those of a dozen or so visitors from outside the palace, dressed in finery like Cecilia had never imagined. Instead, her eyes trailed a length of ivy snaking along the gray, rough-hewn stones and red bricks of the window ledge. Beyond the window, Cecilia glimpsed the dank waters of the moat and one of the palace gates, where a man with a feathered helmet was patrolling on horseback. Far below this high floor of the castle, Cecilia imagined that there might be a labyrinth of passages used to defend it, if ever the palace came under attack.

Cecilia reached for the next line of the song. She sensed the familiar feeling of emptying her chest of air at the same time that she filled the air in the room with her voice. She concentrated on the formation of the words. Surely they could hear the pounding in her chest as much as the bright sound from her lips?

If she had had more time to prepare, she could have accompanied herself on the lute or the lyre, Cecilia thought. She had spent many hours playing and picking out notes to her own ear. But this is not how things would be done at the court of Milan. Marco, the court musician, did his job. He played effortlessly, watching Cecilia with a warm expression, letting his fingers pluck the strings of his lute as if with little thought.

Buoyed by Marco's calm assurance, Cecilia dared to look into the crowd now. Her eyes landed on her brother, with his rapt expression, his frank smile. She tried to avoid looking at her mother, whose eyes were cast to her fingers fidgeting in her lap. Cecilia continued to sing each line with greater precision and power.

She would never have such an audience in a convent, Cecilia thought, or anywhere else for that matter. This was her one opportunity to work her way into the life of this palace, into another life altogether. Her one chance to escape inevitable imprisonment, of unthinkable tedium, behind the walls of a convent. One chance to avoid spending the rest of her days with a needle and thread alongside her mother, who would only spend the rest of *hers* criticizing Cecilia's stitches. One chance to win the heart of a man who might transform her life with a wave of his hand. As long as she kept him captivated, that is. But Cecilia knew how to talk to men, how to advocate for her desires. *I have to make this work,* Cecilia thought as she reached the last line of the song. *This may be my last opportunity to make something substantial of my life.*

In the long moment of dead silence that followed the last note, her brother nodded his quiet approval. Marco pressed his palm to the lute strings to quiet them, then smiled at Cecilia. Then, suddenly, a deafening roar of applause filled the chamber. One of the men cried, *"Brava!"* A few of the palace guests stood and called out more verbal bursts of approval.

Only then did Cecilia find the nerve to set her eyes on Ludovico il Moro, seated in the center of the group. His chin lifted high, his expression was nonetheless difficult to interpret. His jaw was set and squared, but his dark eyes did not leave Cecilia's face. Then, she detected one corner of his mouth rise.

Cecilia felt something like intoxication, bliss, fill her now. The sound of applause began to quell but the feeling stayed. She took a small, unpracticed curtsy.

*This is it,* she thought to herself. *I've done it. This is what I was meant to do. My family. They will see. This palace. This court. This man. All of it is within my reach.*

# 9
## DOMINIC

*Northern France*
*August 1944*

IN DOMINIC'S DREAM, SALLY STOOPED OVER A BASKET, pulling out a damp sheet with the businesslike strength that Dominic still found astounding in her petite figure. Her hair was tucked neatly behind her ears as she shook out the sheet and swung it onto the long piece of twine they had tied between two trees.

"Hello, ma'am," Dominic said, taking off his cap. He pulled her close, smudging sweat and coal dust down the front of her dress.

"You need a bath," she said in her crisp Irish accent, a fake scowl on her freckled face. Then she pressed the length of her body against him to kiss him with a passion that set him on fire.

Waking was like having shards of ice pushed through his heart. Dominic stirred to the harsh reality of the bottom bunk, his thin body separated from the metal frame by what seemed like half an inch of dirty mattress. He lay there, rendered motionless by agony for a few moments, then gazed listlessly at his surroundings. All around him, his comrades were smoking, nibbling on rations, lying on their beds and staring at the gently moving canvas ceiling of the tent. The floor was already damp with rain. Had it only been a few hours since they had pitched it? Perhaps they'd have the luxury of staying in the same place for a few days this time. Dominic had lost track of where they were now. France, Belgium—some forsaken corner of wet and war-torn Europe. He was weary of it already, at the same time marveling that he was still alive, that he had survived the brutal landing on the beaches and the intense gun battles that had ensued.

None of the others were paying him attention. Judging by the soft snoring coming from the top bunk, Paul Blakeley, the lanky private from San Antonio who had been commissioned with Dominic in a Military Police unit at Camp Glenn and shipped off to Normandy, was asleep. Dominic rolled over to his little knapsack and pulled out a scrap of paper he'd scavenged from outside the officers' tent. It had been crumpled up and tossed to the ground, but despite the fragments of a telegram printed on one side, to Dominic it was pure gold. He'd also scrounged a stick of what passed for charcoal from a smoldering forest they'd passed a few days ago. And now, finally, he could bring the two together.

There was no question of what he would draw. The charcoal stick was forming her familiar curves on the paper before he could even ask himself the question. He drew her the way he loved her best, curled on her side in bed, her loose hair a tangle against the back of her neck. Even in black and white, in his mind, he could see the burning color of Sally's hair on the pillow.

Suddenly, a grubby hand came down and grasped roughly at the paper. Instinctively, he snatched his hand back, but a tiny tear appeared in one corner and he reflexively let it go.

"Well, have a look at this!" boomed a coarse voice. "Who is this sizzling lady?"

Dominic rose to his feet, face burning. Private Kellermann was a towering mass of a man, with the thick shoulders and manner of a rhino. He held the sketch up to the light and laughed, the sound rolling out of him on a tide of vulgar intentions. "She's a beauty, Bonelli. Don't you want to share?"

Dominic's fingers curled into fists. The idea of Kellermann's eyes on even a fleeting likeness of his wife set his blood on fire. "Give it back," he said.

But the other soldiers were already gathering around; a sweaty, smelly horde of half-starved men who hadn't seen a living woman in months, and Dominic's lifelike portrayal of his wife was more than enough for them. Hooting and yelling, they passed the sketch between them, and with each grubby thumbprint that stained the page, Dominic's blood rose. Wolf whistles pierced the air as Dominic rushed from one man to the other, snatching at the precious sketch, but his slight frame kept him just out of reach of it as they passed it back and forth above his head.

"Jump, Macaroni!" one man's voice howled. "Jump for your lady!" Dominic brushed off the all-too-familiar slur.

Finally, Kellermann had the picture again, and he waved it easily and tauntingly above Dominic's head, leaning back against his bunk. "You heard the man, Macaroni!" he cackled. "Jump!"

Before Dominic could respond, the motionless lump that had been lying in the top bunk sprang suddenly to life. Paul's hand flashed out from under the blankets and swiped the paper clean out of Kellermann's hand in one brisk movement. Turning indignantly, Kellermann opened his mouth to protest, but when Paul sat up, he thought better of it. While Dominic's bunkmate spoke with a Texan twang, his great height and clear blue eyes spoke of some Scandinavian ancestor that had chewed on shields in a berserker rage on Viking longboats a thousand years ago. The expression in his face warned Kellermann that he'd think nothing of doing something similar right now.

"Enough." Paul didn't speak much, but when he did, men listened. The group of men dispersed in bits and pieces until only Dominic was left, arms folded, staring

Kellermann in the eye even though he had to tip his head back to do so. "That's his wife, man. Stop it."

There was a moment of icy silence between them, then Kellermann let out a scathing belly laugh. "Enjoy your little art project, wop," he growled. "We'll be off fighting a war." He slouched off, turning his broad back only to spit on the floor a few feet from Dominic's boots.

Seething, Dominic turned back to his bunk. Paul held out the drawing to him. "Thanks," Dominic said, taking it back, surprised at how much his voice was shaking. He smoothed the paper between his rough fingers.

The silence stood heavy and painful. Paul pushed it gently aside. "It's a really good picture," he said quietly, his Texas twang softening the thick air between them. Paul had been a stalwart comrade ever since they'd ended up as bunkmates in boot camp. He was one of the few of their platoon who had survived the decimation on those grim beaches of Normandy. Paul's sturdy good humor had made their slow advance over the devastated landscape less impossible. For all his size and quietness, Paul had quick hands and a quicker mind; the speed with which he'd plucked the drawing from Kellermann's hands was echoed in card games and tricks by candlelight. Those moments were few and far between, not because they didn't have idle time but, Dominic figured, because their spirit for games had been crushed on those beaches, all those weeks ago.

"I never knew you could draw, Bonelli," Paul said.

Dominic shrugged, one-shouldered, then stood and began tidying the thin blanket on his bunk. "I've drawn since I was a little kid. I would have loved to go to art school, to find a teacher, but what could I do? I had to start working in the mines just after ninth grade. Then there was Sally, and the wedding, and Cecilia . . . and the war." He touched his neck where the Saint Christopher medal was so conspicuously missing. "I just draw here and there when I've got a little spare time. Helps me relax, you know?"

Dominic realized that for all the time he and Paul had spent together since boot camp, they had only shared snippets of their lives back home. And yet, Dominic marveled, their time together in the face of ever-present threats had bonded them as if they had been together their whole lives. War could do that, Dominic supposed.

Paul had not spoken much of his family. Dominic knew that he had had little time for his father. The old rancher had fought in the Great War and come back broken; he had spent more time looking at the bottom of a bottle than at his son, and his family had suffered for it. Paul's mother had wrestled five boys through the years of the Depression on a cattle ranch that was falling apart. It had been all she could do to feed the boys, let alone give them affection. Paul barely mentioned them. But he often mentioned Francine. He never once described the girl he loved as beautiful; but the look she put on his face certainly was. The mention of her name had lit him up from the inside out. Dominic knew the feeling.

"You always draw your wife?" Paul asked, his pale legs now dangling from the bunk above.

"Usually," Dominic admitted, a smile creeping onto his face despite himself. "It's always one portrait or another, though. I've drawn most of youse guys and slipped the pictures into my letters to Sally so that she can see what you look like." He grinned.

"Sneaky. I knew I had to look out for you!" Paul joked. "Who's your favorite artist?"

Dominic shrugged again. "I used to go down to the library when I was a kid to look at paintings in books. The old masters—Rembrandt, Rubens, you know. But Leonardo da Vinci was always my favorite. I suppose he'd have to be, being Italian and everything."

"Ever been to Italy?"

Dominic shook his head. "My parents couldn't wait to get out of there and make a new life in America. I guess they're more American than Italian, really—they've got a full-size photograph of me in my uniform with a giant American flag." He huffed out a laugh, then smoothed his hand down the front of the stained and tattered remains of his uniform, now a ratty shadow of the splendor that had been photographed that day. "I'd love to visit there someday, though. It would be something to see those masterpieces in real life."

The bunk creaked as Paul flipped onto his back again, his voice growing muffled. "Someday you will, I reckon."

Dominic wished he could share Paul's optimism. He couldn't emulate it, but he was grateful for it. Moments of peaceful conversation about anything other than war had been few and far between. Dominic had lost count of how many skirmishes they'd been in; each time his survival seemed even more like a miracle. Had Dominic's little unit made a dent in the war against the Nazis? Had they made any difference at all? Even after all these weeks of narrow misses, he wasn't sure. He only knew he had to keep going, had to keep focused on their mission to win this war. His officers complimented him on his sharpshooting skills and dedication to protecting other soldiers, but he knew that the only reason he was still here was luck. And perhaps the prayers of his mother, all the way back home across the ocean.

"Attention!" A sharp word from the door of the tent brought every soldier to his feet as automatically as machine-gun fire. They stood neatly side by side, feet together, arms by their sides, bodies as straight as their exhausted muscles could make them. An officer walked into the tent, the glittering badges on his shoulders marking him as a major. There was utter silence but for the squish of his boots in the mud that had pooled on the floor of the tent.

The major strolled down the twin lines of men, examining the names embroidered on their uniforms.

"Blakely!" he cried.

Then, his eyes settled on Dominic.

"Bonelli!" he boomed.

"Sir!" Dominic saluted.

"I hear you're a good cover." The expression in the major's dark eyes was unreadable. He quirked an eyebrow. "Come. We have a job for you. Don't want to keep the commander waiting."

# 10

## CECILIA

*Milan, Italy*
*January 1490*

**"COME. YOU MUST NOT KEEP HIS LORDSHIP WAITING."**

Cecilia's underarms raged as if a dozen bees were stinging her skin at once. Reluctantly, she raised her arms in the air again. Wearing only her sleeveless linen chemise, Cecilia let Lucrezia Crivelli, the dressmaid, fan her underarms with fluttering hands. Around Cecilia's bedchamber, a dozen gowns in silk, satin, and velvet lay across every surface.

"*Aya*! What's in this?" Cecilia huffed out three strong breaths, staving off the pain.

"A little quicklime, some arsenic, pig lard. A few other secrets. A favorite recipe of His Lordship's mother. Not much longer," Lucrezia said. "You're supposed to say two Our Fathers."

"Our Father, who art in heaven . . ." Cecilia began,

but her voice trembled. She shivered in the frigid air and squeezed her eyes shut against the stinging.

"Get used to it. His Lordship doesn't like his women with hair on their bodies."

Cecilia opened her eyes wide now and stared at Lucrezia, a girl about Cecilia's age who was tasked with attending Cecilia and helping with her hair and dress. She examined the girl's wide, brown eyes to see if she might be teasing her. "Really? Nowhere on the body?"

Lucrezia shook her head. "We'll do your *pòmm* next. Keep going."

Cecilia didn't know any Milanese words, but she could guess which body part might be up for the next depilation. She squeezed her eyes closed again, pushing through the cold and the nearly unbearable stinging. She got through the prayers, spitting them out as quickly as she ever had. While she prayed, Lucrezia dabbed at Cecilia's underarms with her fingertips.

When Cecilia completed her Our Fathers, Lucrezia went to the hearth, where a pot roiled over the fire. She dipped a cloth into the water with tongs, then wrung it out and placed the steaming fabric under Cecilia's arm.

"*Aya!*" The cold was replaced with scalding heat. Lucrezia roughly wiped away the vile mixture from both underarms, taking the hair out with it from the roots. At last, Cecilia let her arms, nearly numb, fall to her sides. She grasped a brown velvet mantle from a nearby chair and slung it over her shoulders. She brought her fingertips to her underarms, where the bare, raw skin throbbed but was undeniably smooth and hairless. The stinging, lingering but more tolerable, continued as Cecilia walked to the bed. She ran her palms lightly over the pile of dresses. Green satin. Purple velvet. Red silk with black lace and gilded wire threaded through the neckline.

"They are so beautiful," Cecilia said. In fact, the dresses were the most beautiful things Cecilia had ever seen.

"Castoffs. You'll need them altered to fit you. You're a scrawny thing," Lucrezia said, pressing her hands into Cecilia's waist so hard that Cecilia flinched. Lucrezia shrugged. "We just pulled these from the wardrobe of the last mistress."

A long pause. "The last mistress?"

Lucrezia nodded.

"What happened to her?"

"Oh!" A nervous laugh. "She didn't last long."

"Why not?" Cecilia studied Lucrezia's face again to see if she might be setting herself up to be the butt of a joke.

"His Lordship tired of her quickly," Lucrezia said, her voice suddenly sad in a way that, to Cecilia, sounded anything but sincere. "If you want to know what I think, it's that she talked too much. Whatever the case, His Lordship's . . . diversions . . . are usually brief anyway. Only little Bianca stayed behind."

"Bianca?"

"Poor little bastard child." Lucrezia shook her head. "She is a beauty, though. Hair as black as midnight. Just like her father's."

Cecilia flopped into a chair next to her bed and pulled the mantle tightly around her shoulders. Had she stepped into waters that might close quickly over her head? She wondered how many other important things she did not know.

A knock at the door. Lucrezia ushered in a gray-haired woman in a chambermaid's dress. The maid uttered something to Cecilia in Milanese dialect, then bowed her head and extended a folded parchment with a wax seal. Cecilia recognized her brother's elegant handwriting on the parchment but she hesitated. It was the first time anyone had ever bowed to her, and besides, Cecilia had no idea what the maid had said. The old woman met Cecilia's eyes and smiled. Lucrezia stepped in and took the letter from the maid's hand, then gave it to Cecilia. "A letter for His Lordship's flower."

# II

## EDITH

*Munich, Germany*
*September 1939*

EDITH BRACED HERSELF AGAINST A METAL DOORFRAME as the train whistle sounded and the wheels screeched. She pressed herself against the window and watched the twin onion domes of Munich's Frauenkirche recede into the dusk.

For weeks, Edith had been preparing herself to watch Heinrich board a train for Poland. She had pictured their farewell a thousand times, Heinrich handsome, tall, and lean in his uniform. She imagined herself running along the platform, pressed into a crowd of women as the train pulled out of the station.

Never did Edith foresee that *she* would be the one fastening up the buttons on a starched field jacket that had been cursorily modified to fit a woman's shape. That she would be the one boarding the huffing train for Kraków, watching from the window while Heinrich ran along the platform waving, growing smaller as the train pulled eastward from Hauptbahnhof Station. Now she was the one holding conscription papers. There was no refusing the call. Her orders were little more than a signed, stamped shred of paper, a single folio that had the power to change her entire life. Maybe even to take her life, if she were one of the unlucky ones.

Behind her back, Edith heard a low whistle, a catcall that made the hairs on the back of her neck rise.

"*He*! Klaus, they have skirts here!" the soldier yelled over his shoulder to someone in the line behind him.

"Excuse me, madam," the man said mockingly as he squeezed past Edith standing by the train window, pressing himself against her back more closely than necessary as he pushed through the narrow train corridor.

She refused to honor his vulgarity with a reaction, but her nerves were ruffled. Edith moved away from the fresh air in the window. She opened the door to a passenger car and made her way down the center aisle. The train car was filled with men, most wearing the same field jacket as her own, others in civilian clothes. She glanced beyond them, struggling to keep her emotions in check. She knew her eyes had to be red, her cheeks puffy. She felt their gaze on her as she hurried down the aisle, managing her large bag.

In the stifling air of the sleeping car, Edith finally exhaled. It was tightly spaced with two stacks of bunks, empty. All the other cars like this were filled with five or six soldiers.

Being a woman, they had assigned her one to herself. Edith pressed herself into one of the lower bunks and turned her thoughts again to Heinrich.

*Please tell me that you are not already taken.*

Edith smiled even now through the blur of tears, thinking of Heinrich's first words to her, two years ago, at a Bavarian festival in a popular Munich beer garden.

"Pardon me?" she had said to the tall stranger who pushed through the crowd of revelers, the handsome man with the lock of blond hair over his brow who dared to be so forward.

"You're a beautiful woman," he had said. "I only hope that someone has not already stolen you away so that the rest of us might have a standing chance."

She'd laughed at him, admiring his audacity. Edith had always considered herself as plain as a kitchen mouse and had come to accept that she may spend her days as a spinster at her father's side. The mere thought of Heinrich still had the power to make her stomach flutter, even when she conjured images of their first few headlong days together.

It was a daring beginning, but even after getting to know each other over months, Heinrich had truly won her heart. And when he came to her father to ask for his daughter's hand in marriage, Edith's heart had been forever his. Heinrich knew that her father may not even remember his name, but all the same, he had treated him with respect and tenderness.

"Yes," her father had said, and she knew that in that moment, there was not only clarity in his mind, but happiness in his heart.

A sliver of dim light remained outside the narrow window, but Edith was too filled with nervous energy to settle in her bunk. Instead, she stood again, turned her canvas bag on its side, and pulled out a small notebook. She stared at the blank page. Should she write a letter to her father? Would he understand where she had gone? Would he remember her at all?

Her neighbor, Frau Gerzheimer, had seemed more than willing to help. Edith held out hope that Frau Gerzheimer would have what it took to convince her father to cooperate. She trusted that Heinrich would stop by after working at his father's store to make sure everything was all right, before he, too, had to board a train. And she prayed that the agency would send a relief nurse as soon as possible. The last thing she wanted was to see her father sent to a sanatorium where he might wither away.

Unable to find the words to say to her father, Edith put the pen to the paper and started a letter to Heinrich, but all she could think to write was how much she already missed him. Edith and Heinrich were heading separately to Poland, both pawns in a game that had grown larger than themselves. Names whispered to block leaders for the slightest suspicion. Jewish neighbors—men, women, even innocent children like the little Nusbaum boy—led from their homes in dark silence, amassed, corralled, and shifted like human game pieces on a great chessboard. And boys no older than fourteen, marching in uniform, their voices echoing in the streets.

*Today, Germany is ours / tomorrow, the whole world.*

Edith, Heinrich, and thousands of others across the Reich, she imagined, felt helpless, or too afraid of the consequences, to resist.

Would they find each other after their arrival in Poland? What would they find when they returned home, if they returned at all?

Edith hoped that the act of writing might calm her nervous stomach, might relieve some of the trepidation about what lay ahead. Instead, it only unleashed a flurry of unanswered questions in her mind. How had events escalated to this degree so quickly? Why couldn't she, like Manfred, have foreseen what the museum directors were planning? And how had she—a lowly conservator toiling quietly in a basement conservation lab—been thrust into the middle of this conflict?

Edith felt her heart sink as the answer to the last question crystallized in her mind.

*Because I am the one who brought their attention to these paintings.* She felt like an idiot for not recognizing beforehand what she was being asked to do. For not understanding what it might mean and what might be the consequences of her seemingly benign research project in the museum library.

Edith pulled out the binder of folios she had made of the art the museum directors wanted to safeguard. She unwound the straps and began shuffling through the pages again. Surely these paintings only made up a small portion of what the Czartoryski family owned.

When Edith reached the reproduction of da Vinci's *Lady with an Ermine*, she paused. *I am to blame for putting all these pictures at risk*, she thought. *It's my fault that we are on our way to take these pictures from the Czartoryski family. My entire adult life has been dedicated to saving works of art. And yet, in one moment, in the name of doing my job, I have endangered some of the most priceless works of art in the world.* Was there a way to undo the damage she had done?

The clack of the train wheels and the short bursts of steam set the pace for Edith's racing thoughts. Outside the window, the treetops rushed by, a blur of shadows.

Edith's mind searched for an answer, a way to save da Vinci's *Lady* and the other pictures that she had put unintentionally in the line of fire. But as the ragged outlines of the trees disappeared and the sky began to turn black, Edith only felt the weight of despair like a stone on her chest. The paintings, too, had been cast like dice into a game that had spiraled out of her control, a series of events that Edith now felt powerless to stop.

# 12
## CECILIA

*Milan, Italy*
*January 1490*

CECILIA HAD UNLEASHED A SERIES OF EVENTS THAT
she would be powerless to stop. That's what her brother had
meant, even if he had written it in more eloquent language.

She fingered the broken seal on the parchment her
brother Fazio had sent, a missive letting Cecilia know that
their mother had arrived safely back home in Siena. Cecilia
wondered how long it would take for her mother to speak
to her again, if she would hear from her at all, ever.

Cecilia's mother had understood that the moment when
her brazen daughter had not bowed but dared to step forward and bare her teeth to Ludovico il Moro in an un-
abashed smile, there was no turning back. The Regent of
Milan would claim her for his own. No one was in a position to stop him, especially not a portly Sienese widow in a
dirt-caked dress. In the end, Cecilia pitied her mother, for

there was nothing for her to do but scream, break a plate, rattle away in a carriage, and leave the Castello Sforzesco behind in a cloud of fog and mud.

Cecilia could laugh about it now, she supposed, now that her mother was far distant from the palace. And Cecilia did laugh a little, quietly to herself. There was little else to do as she sat waiting for Ludovico il Moro, running her palms across the slippery silk dress. He should have been here long before now, but she imagined that he had other things to do than come visit her in her new bedchamber.

Ludovico surely was occupied, consulting with his military and political advisers. From her bedchamber window, Cecilia had seen diplomatic liveries cross the courtyard, flying the colors of Ferrara and Mantua. As Regent of Milan, Ludovico faced constant threats from Venice, Cecilia's brother had told her, and from the French king's army. Even from his own nephew. Ludovico had already sent his nephew's closest advisers to the gallows, the dressmaid Lucrezia had told Cecilia as she brushed out her hair in the candlelight. When you were that powerful, the girl told her, *anyone* might be your friend one moment, and then your enemy the next.

So Cecilia waited. She had already gone over every inch of the bedchamber several times. There were so many books. A cabinet held stacks of folios stitched together with linen threads, long cords of vellum, and leather bindings. Some of the volumes were covered with stiff pasteboards and hinged spines. She had spent hours poring over the brown ink on parchment. She even found a lady's book of secrets, a sort of recipe book with beauty concoctions like the one she had endured under Lucrezia's insistence to remove every last hair on her body. She had looked and looked again at the painted images on the wall, paintings that brought to life the stories in many of those books— ancient tales of love, betrayal, battle, death, redemption. She had picked up each glass vial and gilded box on the table, watched the morning fog roll across the gardens outside the window, and tried on every dress of silk and velvet hanging in the wardrobe. She had let herself disappear into the piles of woolen and silk bedding and curtains draped around the high bed. From the open window, the aroma of rice cooking in diced onions and butter wafted into the room.

"My daughter is going to the convent. It is already decided!" Her mother's words filled her head again, unbidden. "Otherwise, she goes back to the country with me. That is the choice."

"And what will happen to her there?" Fazio had said. "If I had been home with you, maybe things would have been different, but as it stands, thanks to my brothers, she no longer has a dowry to marry her to a decent family. She will be nothing more than a country peasant. A spinster. Here she will be given riches and status. It is not forever, Mother."

"And what convent will want her after she has lost her virtue?" her mother had challenged, her hands on her hips. "No man has touched her! You know it as well as I do."

"I know it sounds strange," Fazio had said, pacing before the window, "but being His Lordship's *inamorata* will afford Cecilia a higher status than she has now. Even the nuns will respect it."

Cecilia had watched as her mother's round face reddened. "I refuse to leave my daughter here, with that . . . that little pompous ox." She gestured as if to measure Ludovico il Moro's stature with her hand. "He is too sure of himself, is he not? He will use her and throw her away. And then what will we have to show for it?"

Cecilia had begun to feel red anger swell inside of her own chest. How dare they act as if she was not in the room? How dare they act as if she was still a silly child with no thoughts of her own? She could, and would, make her own decisions.

"I am staying here," Cecilia had said quietly.

"You will be a whore!" That was when her mother had thrown the plate, shattering it against the tiles.

"No, Mother," Cecilia had said, as calmly as possible. "I will be a lady. I will be the head of this castle. You will see." For a moment, she had seen an expression like pity on her brother's face, but she couldn't fathom why.

Her brother had told her that, after her vocal performance, Ludovico Sforza had been determined to bring

Cecilia into his household. That there was something about Cecilia that he could hardly put into words. There was no deterring him on the matter.

Fazio had laid out Cecilia's choices in clear terms. There were only two ways to stop His Lordship's orders, he had told her. Cecilia could decide to preserve her maidenhood and return home with their mother, a choice that Cecilia could hardly bear. She could join the sisters at Monastero Maggiore, an even less desirable outcome in Cecilia's eyes, even though her mother and her brother begged her to consider it again. But if she decided to stay in His Lordship's care, Fazio told her, then there was no reversing the decision. And, he added, she would have to live with the consequences. At that point, there was little her family could do to help her and anyway, it was out of their hands.

But to Cecilia, only one thing mattered. Ludovico Sforza, Lord of Milan, wanted *her* and he could give her everything she ever wanted. In one second, he could transform her from a penniless country girl into a *duchessa*. At least she imagined so.

"I am staying," Cecilia had whispered.

That was it. The turning point. And now here she stood, clad in silk in this beautiful bedchamber. There was no doubt in her mind that she was right where she was supposed to be. They would see.

At last, the door creaked open and Cecilia stood. She was ready, but the moment His Lordship entered the room, she felt her resolve waver. As much as she was resolute in her decision, she suddenly felt nervous being with him alone in this room. After all, he was a stranger. She could not show the turbulence that roiled through her veins.

Slowly, he walked toward her. She watched his eyes flicker in the lantern light. "It was a good decision to stay," he said. "I can assure you that you will be adequately rewarded."

"I was honored by your offer," Cecilia said, casting her eyes to the floor.

His Lordship approached close enough so that she could smell the dank scent of his hair and beard. He took another calculated step toward her, closer than any man who was not her father or brothers had ever come. Then he set his eyes on her. They were as black as coals, so dark that she could not make out the pupils. She felt her stomach flutter as if it were full of moths. Their faces stood at the same level.

"You are a lovely woman," he whispered in his deep voice, thick with its Tuscan tongue, tinged with the strange Milanese accent. She felt his hot breath near her neck and she fought against the tingle that ran up her back.

Cecilia cleared her throat. "I am also learned," she said, taking a step back. There was still a quake up her spine, making her feel unsteady and unsure, but she did not want him to perceive the power he held over her. "Maybe you have heard."

She thought she detected a teasing smile cross his face,

but it was difficult to tell in the shadows, under the thick beard. The idea that he might be mocking her infuriated her, and she took another step back.

"Tell me more," he said. She felt his fingertips grasp her hand, then move lightly up the silk sleeve of her dress. His eyes burned hot and focused.

"So much to tell." She hoped he could not hear her voice waver. She wished that she had had even a little of the diplomatic training of her brother; only now did she realize that she did not know what to reveal and what to withhold. She was only sure that it was important to know the difference. "I can read and write in Latin. My father made sure that I had a good tutor. The best one in Siena. I can calculate numbers. I write verses. I can sing—you already know that. And I play the lute and the lyre. I play other stringed instruments, too, well, a little bit . . ." Was she already talking too much? Lucrezia had warned her.

Ludovico listened halfheartedly. His hand was gathering together the heft of her skirt, pulling it up toward her thigh.

"Is it true what I've heard? You still are virtuous? No man has touched you before?" His voice rose barely above a whisper.

Cecilia swallowed that truth like a stone and nodded. Of course this was why she was here. This is what a mistress did, why she was allowed to stay here in the castle with all these beautiful things at all. It had been her decision.

She swallowed hard again, then mustered her courage. "How . . . how much will you wager that I am smarter than any woman of this castle? Smarter than any mistress you have had before me?"

He barked a loud laugh. "I hope you are," he said, but then she felt his hot breath on her neck, his beard against her jaw. She closed her eyes; she could not help it. His mouth seared her skin with heat as his hands continued their way up under her skirt.

"I . . . I want to be the lady of this castle," Cecilia gasped the words out as his fingers found their way under her skirts and to the linen ties of her undergarments. She knew what was about to happen to her and in a moment of clarity, she realized that she didn't want to just be a mistress. Before he could have her, before he could use her up and throw her out, she wanted his word.

"I want to be your wife," Cecilia blurted.

A deep, rich laugh reverberated from his core. He pulled away and looked her in the eyes. There was something there more than fire, more than a burning, but Cecilia, in her inexperience, did not understand it fully.

"My dear girl," he said. Then he pushed her toward the bed and turned her roughly onto her stomach.

# 13

# DOMINIC

*Eastern Belgium*
*September 1944*

DOMINIC STARED OUT OF THE OPEN SIDE OF THE quarter-ton truck as it rumbled through the countryside. Countryside was the wrong word, he thought. Once, this part of Belgium must have been beautiful. Even now, in the treetops, the fragments of autumn pushing through the warm blanket of late summer held the promise of coming splendor. But the landscape was marred by the still-smoking remains of little villages. Dominic's heart tightened at the sight. The earth was scarred and blackened in places, fields trampled by tank treads, shell casings, and scattered pieces of equipment strewn everywhere. An orchard stood in tattered ruins, the charred branches of fruit trees twisted and broken against the blue sky.

Paul Blakely tightened his hands on the wheel as they drove into the rubble. The truck crawled through the main street of what was, until recently, a village. Only its church steeple was left, teetering precariously on its half-ruined foundation. The cross at its tip was a brave and tragic silhouette that made Dominic's fingers itch to sketch. But the rest of the town was anything but picturesque. Blackened shells and broken walls were all that remained of the houses and shops that had once lined this street. The truck detoured around a fallen lamppost and labored through the pockmarked road.

"Man, would you look at that . . ." Paul sat at Dominic's side, gazing ahead to the wasted landscape, the strap of his helmet swinging with the motion of the truck. Dominic shifted his rifle, wishing he could lay it down, but this territory remained unfriendly. He had to be ready for action at any moment. Now, three months after landing on Omaha Beach, watchfulness had become automatic. His nerve endings felt frayed and electrified, ever on high alert. He wondered if he would ever lose the feeling that there were enemies stalking him.

Before he sent Paul and Dominic off with the empty deuce-and-a-half truck, a Military Police transportation officer had briefed them on their mission. "This new assignment is something different," he had said. "You two will still be on security detail. But you'll be part of a squadron of men with a unique job. Yes, we're fighting Nazis, but we're also trying to preserve as much as possible of this culture that's so damned bent on destroying itself." He gestured at the ruined landscape. "There are important buildings, monuments, and works of art everywhere you look. This war could be the end of all of it—priceless stuff, master-pieces we need to try to save at the same time that we're trying to save our own asses."

Dominic had leaned forward, his interest piqued. In his determination to beat the Nazis, to simply survive and go home to his family, he hadn't considered the war's impact on art and architecture.

"So we're supposed to avoid damaging old churches and other monuments," the officer had gone on. "That should be clear enough. But we're also looking for paintings, sculptures. This regime has been stealing works of art all through the war, carrying them off to be displayed in their houses like trophies."

"You mean they're keeping them for themselves?" Paul had asked.

"Yep. Our intelligence is telling us that some of the highest-ranking Nazis are even hanging up da Vincis inside their own homes." He had paused, and Dominic let that sink in. For years, he had been reading the news reports of the horrors of the Nazi death camps, of Hit-ler's unceasing determination to take over the world. He felt stupid that he had not considered that they were also taking whatever they wanted, raping the countryside for treasures that they had no right to take—even priceless works of art.

The officer had continued. "Some things have already been destroyed, either by the Nazis or even by us. Accidentally, of course. Let's face it, some destruction is just unavoidable, right? But the president has created a commission called the Monuments, Fine Arts, and Archives Program—the MFAA. Monuments Men."

"Monuments Men . . ." Dominic said.

"Mostly museum folks, art historians, people who know about that stuff. Our mission is to protect these works and to get them back from those Nazi bastards so that the works can be returned to their rightful owners after this fiasco is behind us."

Dominic could hardly believe his ears. How could the American president be worried about paintings and sculptures when thousands of people were losing their lives? But at the same time, he couldn't deny his wonder. "You mean these . . . Monuments Men . . . are just focused on saving art? How are they doing that?"

The officer shrugged. "There's no guidebook for this stuff. We are looking at aerial photos, marking churches, bridges, monuments to be saved. And we're going inside to see what's left, what we can salvage. We've already found a bunch of important paintings and portraits, especially, some by the great masters—Rembrandt, Titian, big guys."

Dominic sat back abruptly, awed. Faced with the prospect of possibly seeing some of those masterpieces, he couldn't help but feel a thrill of excitement. He thought of da Vinci's works bombed out and destroyed by the war, or hanging in Hitler's palace, and bile rose in his throat.

"So your job, fellas, is to protect these Monuments Men," the officer had continued. "They put themselves at risk daily. They go into some dangerous places to get that art back—and you two are here to watch their backs while they do their jobs. They've been waiting for MPs—and especially transport—for weeks now. We finally got the authorization."

Ahead, on the scorched horizon, the gray encampment seemed almost as much of a blemish as the bombed-out buildings; rows of drab and uniform tents stood between watchful tanks. Paul switched off the truck's engine, and rifles still held close, he and Dominic disembarked. Soldiers lounged between the sagging tents, their dirty uniforms smelling of unwashed men and gunpowder. At the sight of the truck, several of the men stirred, looking at Dominic and Paul with hopeful expressions. The ground was trampled and littered with shell casings and cigarette butts. Like all encampments, it was a mixture of strict discipline in the tight lines of the tents and messiness in the posture of the exhausted men. But to Dominic, it was beginning to feel more and more like home.

An officer approached but spared no pleasantries. "It's about time you got here," he said. "That's your commander. Captain Walker Hancock." He turned and walked into the encampment. Exchanging a brief glance, Dominic and Paul followed.

Even from a distance across the dreary camp, Dominic could see that Captain Hancock was as out of place as a mare among mules. Tall and lithe, his uniform draped elegantly over his lean frame. He looked like he should have been wearing a suit and swirling a glass of sherry instead. His piercing blue eyes were watchful as Dominic and Paul followed the officer over to him.

"Hancock's not just a soldier," the officer told them as they walked. "He's some kind of famous sculptor, too."

The educated, refined man seemed utterly incongruous here in this bitter and charred landscape, but with a shock, Dominic realized that he must have been commissioned as well.

The officer stopped and saluted; Dominic and Paul followed suit. "New men for the security detail, sir."

Hancock turned and studied the men. Seeming to register the large white MP stamped on their helmets, he nodded. "Good," he said. "We'll need more of them as we move toward Aachen." He drummed his fingers on the barrel of his weapon; Dominic could imagine them grasping a chisel. "Get them settled in."

"Yes, sir." The officer turned to lead the men away, but Dominic's curiosity was getting the better of him.

"How will you go about finding these works of art, sir?" he blurted. He looked at the officer as he spoke, too nervous to meet Hancock's eye, but the men all knew to whom the question was directed. Hancock merely quirked his other eyebrow and turned away.

The officer saved Dominic from his embarrassment. "A bunch of professionals in Europe and the US have been working on this thing ever since the war started," he said. "Museum curators and such. They've been using their own research to make lists of these works and maps for where we might . . ."

The officer's words were lost in a thunderous sound that electrified Dominic's whole body. Bullets tore into the nearest tent, sending canvas flying in all directions. Shouts and gunfire filled the encampment and, in slow motion, Dominic saw Hancock turning, saw machine-gun fire tearing into the ground ever closer to him.

By sheer instinct, Dominic lunged forward and threw his short frame into Captain Hancock. He felt earth splatter on his boots from the spray of bullets, curled himself determinedly around the commander, and rolled behind the cover of the giant rubber tire of their two-and-a-half-ton. Bullets whined as they ricocheted off the hub. Dominic gripped his rifle, waited for a break in the thunder and returned fire, his gun kicking back against his shoulder. He emptied the magazine until he heard a scream and the gunfire abruptly ceased. A few long moments stretched, followed by the shuffle of boots, and then silence.

Panting, Dominic lowered his gun. As the smoke cleared, Dominic saw two German uniforms, bodies lying still at the edge of the encampment. Some Americans groaned among the tents, too, other men hurrying to their aid through the clearing smoke. Dominic was relieved to see Paul's tall frame sprinting toward the injured soldiers.

Captain Hancock was sitting up, brushing dirt from his uniform. There was a smear of mud across his cheekbone. He studied Dominic, wide-eyed.

"Are you hurt, sir?" Dominic asked, reloading his rifle and stepping cautiously out from the cover of the tire. The encampment had the burnt, smoky smell of recently discharged guns, mixed with the salt tang of blood, a smell Dominic had come to know and hate. But both Americans who had been shot were stirring and swearing. Good news.

"No." Hancock crawled out from behind the tire. Dominic extended a hand and pulled him to his feet. Hancock returned his grip and met his eyes, his face suddenly splitting into a dazzling smile. He squinted at the name on Dominic's uniform.

"Bonelli, huh?" He pumped Dominic's hand with a tight grip. "Welcome."

# 14
## EDITH

*Pełkinie, Poland*
*September 1939*

THE HELMET ON EDITH'S HEAD HAD BEEN MADE FOR a man. It nearly covered her eyes, and the metal rattled against her skull along with the rumble of the Kübelwagen's tires over the rocky terrain.

While she was compiling the facsimiles for the museum director and board, Edith had looked up Pełkinie in a dusty atlas pulled from the shelves of the museum library. She had never heard of it before, but she ran her finger across the map to a small village in far eastern Poland, near the Russian border. The Czartoryski family had had a country estate there for years, she had read. And now, Edith was pressed into the rear seat of the beige car along with two armed soldiers, heading straight for the Czartoryski estate itself.

She squeezed herself in as tightly as possible. She felt grateful to have claimed a seat by the deep sill of the vehicle, from which she could watch the Polish countryside unfold around her. The sun had risen around the time that the train arrived in the Kraków station, but Edith had yet to glimpse its rays. Instead, the landscape was cast in a gray haze, a combination of cloud cover and the dust from the rubble alongside the roads and the dirt kicked up by the Kübelwagen's knobby tires. As they followed a bend in the road, Edith caught a glimpse of the rest of the long convoy of German vehicles behind theirs. She could not see the end of the line. She had heard that the *Feldgendamerie* had already secured the Czartoryski home. Did they need so many more soldiers?

For a while, the view flattened out into a series of fallow fields with a long, straight train track that ran parallel to the road. Edith heard a low train whistle, then turned her head to watch the train cars pass. The train should have easily overtaken the convoy, but for some reason, it was rolling slowly, a long chain of old, rusted-out cattle cars laboring along the track. When the train finally began to keep pace with the Kübelwagen, Edith caught sight of a small hand waving listlessly from one of the narrow, dusty windows in the side of the boxcar. After a few moments, the hand was replaced by the drawn face of a young woman, her eyes dark and sunken.

Edith felt a jolt slice through her as her heart sank. She recalled the Jewish families walking toward the train stations of Munich, their most precious possessions collected in pillowcases, small containers, and shopping bags. Was this train headed to a detention camp? The train finally picked up speed and the hand disappeared from the window. Edith dropped her eyes to her folded hands in her lap, knowing she would never forget the woman's face, the haunted, sunken eyes.

The car finally turned into a long path lined with formal gardens and tall, manicured spruces. At the end of the path, Edith spied the grand, sand-colored palace. Pełkinie. Edith recognized its long, symmetrical façade of pilasters and windows from the books in the museum library.

It was a relief to step out of the car, where she had felt like a prisoner even though she was wearing the same uniform as the men in the vehicle. The men in the convoy proceeded to the palace in formation, squeezing Edith between them. She removed the bothersome helmet.

"Fräulein Becker." An officer sliced his way into the formation, easily picking her out. "Lieutenant Fischer," he said, his hands wound behind his back. "I am gratified to see that you have arrived safely. Come. They are waiting for you inside."

Edith walked quickly behind Lieutenant Fischer as he snaked through the dozens of soldiers and through the central doorway of the house. Inside, there were more soldiers moving furniture and fixtures. Edith rushed to keep up, her surroundings a blur of gilding, crystal, polished wood, silver, and richly colored upholstery.

"We found the pictures in a secret room in the oldest part of the house, the part beneath the old watchtower," Lieutenant Fischer said, and Edith followed him up a wide staircase into the diffuse light. "The door was hidden behind a piece of furniture."

With each step, Edith thought about the family members who had abandoned their home for their own safety. She pictured the family living here, the children running through the vast rooms, laughing, chasing one another down the long corridors. She could imagine the adults, riding horses through the lush forest, picnicking on the lawn, gazing at the stars at night, living their lives in peace.

"The family . . ." she said, feeling a wave of trepidation. She did not know how to phrase her question.

The officer shook his head. "They had already fled before we arrived. The Gestapo is trailing them."

A strange mixture of shame and relief washed over Edith. She personally had assembled the catalog of this family's known paintings. Edith was responsible for the theft of some of the world's most valuable works of art, the ransacking of this estate, and the confiscation of everything inside it. In the process, she had put people's lives at risk. What if she refused to continue to help? Would her life be at risk, too?

Edith feared that she might vomit. She had never meant to send anyone into exile. She certainly didn't want to have anyone killed. It was her fault they were not here anymore, she realized. But as she took in the vast scale of this operation—an entire convoy of armed vehicles, dozens of soldiers, officers, and military police—Edith realized it was too late. She was fully engaged in a conflict that was much bigger than herself, whether she had intended it or not.

Would the family get far enough ahead, or find refuge before the Gestapo found them? Until they could return to their home? An image of the sunken eyes of the woman on the train seared through Edith's mind.

"They must have judged us idiots," Lieutenant Fischer said, his eyes lighting up with self-satisfaction. "It was obvious that the narrow door had just been patched. The mortar was still wet."

"A wall?" Edith asked.

He nodded. "They hid a lot of the things in an old room that you can access only through a narrow door hidden behind a cabinet. Made it appear like it was simply a wall. But it was poorly done. Our men found it within a matter of minutes."

Edith felt a chill run down her spine.

Lieutenant Fischer turned a corner and an elegant sitting room stretched out before them. The room was cluttered with dusty furniture covered in sheets and tarps, neglected goods stored over many years. A half-dozen military police staff milled around idly among the disorder. The officer led Edith to a hole in the back wall, where bricks had been hastily removed.

"We received the information about this location from a Polish bricklayer, the one who walled up the door. He tried to keep it a secret, but he was not able to keep the truth from us." Lieutenant Fischer gave her another thin smile.

A series of long tables had been set up around the room, each stacked with decorative items and wooden crates. On one table, two sets of paintings were stacked on top of each other. Edith wondered if the men knew how valuable these paintings and artifacts were. It seemed to her they had been careless in their movement of the items.

"I don't know much about art," Fischer said to Edith, "but it looks like a museum here to me." He addressed the guards. "The lady is a specialist from the Alte Pinakothek in Munich. Let her have free access to examine the works. She will decide what is to be loaded for transport." The men stepped aside and Edith moved forward. Her hands shaking, Edith reached down and touched the frame of the first painting on top of the stack, a small landscape darkened by centuries of dust.

"I assume you know your duties here. I'll leave you to your work," Fischer said. "Just one more thing, Fräulein Becker." He reached for her arm and lowered his voice. "Be careful about who you share information with. Our forces are easily taking the cities, but there are Polish resistance groups throughout the countryside."

Resistance. What did that mean, exactly? Edith's heart began to race in her chest.

Lieutenant Fischer seemed to read her mind. "They are more organized than our commanding officers in Germany realize. Someone might try to contact you or get information. It might be someone you think you should trust. Don't be fooled by a handsome face, fräulein. Watch what you say and to whom."

Suddenly, a muffled voice emerged from one of the large crates at the back of the room.

*"Heiliger Strohsack!"*

Everyone turned. A short soldier, his helmet and uniform coated in dust, emerged from the stacks of crates and gilded frames. Between his hands, he balanced a rectangular package wrapped in paper, its edges torn to reveal a section of a gilded picture frame.

"Look what I found!"

# 15

## LEONARDO

*Florence, Italy*
*May 1482*

BEYOND THE GATES OF FLORENCE, I FEEL THE CAR-
riage wheels shudder into the ruts of the road. I steady the
wooden crate that bumps against my thigh.

Finally. After years of trying to gain favor at the Medici
court, of trying to find a supporting patron, after years of
holding my breath for fear of another accusation, I am leaving Florence behind for better prospects.

Buried deep inside one of the rocking mule carts behind us lie trunks full of notebooks, paintbrushes, charcoal, pens, pigments. Silken hose, gowns and caps of satin,
linen undergarments, and my favorite cape of purple velvet.
Milan is cold, they tell me.

I watch the gray-haired man seated across from me on
the plush, embroidered cushions, one of Lorenzo il Magnifico's notaries. His mournful eyes watch the towering

clay dome of our cathedral grow smaller outside the carriage window. Alongside me, my young and beautiful friend, the singer Atalante Migliorotti, hums a tune under his breath. Il Magnifico has chosen well, I think. Surely we will impress the court of Milan. They say that the Milanese try to emulate our Florentine language and dress.

I have insisted on bringing a small notebook and a fresh stick of charcoal into the carriage so that I might sketch any sights that capture my fancy along the journey. And the crate. Of course, the crate. I have devised a wooden container filled with straw to transport the lyre, Il Magnifico's diplomatic offering to Ludovico il Moro, Regent of Milan. I must not let it out of my sight.

The lyre itself is a wonder, if I do dare to compliment myself. I cast it in pure silver, in the form of a horse's skull. It will accompany Atalante's voice perfectly; we have already spent hours rehearsing together and have even practiced before the Medici women. And if the Lord of Milan asks me to play it, how could I refuse?

Along with the lyre, the crate also holds Il Magnifico's letter of introduction on my behalf. Extraordinarily important. Disappointingly brief.

I cannot stop myself from sighing aloud. If I am to win any important commissions among the court of Milan, I must elaborate on my abilities. I turn to my notebook, where I have penned a letter. I have scratched out passages and rewritten them. Hopefully, by the time we reach the gates of Milan, the list of my offerings will be complete:

*To the Most Excellent Lord of Milan, Ludovico Sforza*
*From your most humble servant, Leonardo da Vinci, in*
   *Florence*

*Most Illustrious Lord,*

*Having sufficiently seen and considered the achieve-ments of all those who count themselves masters and ar-tificers of instruments of war, and having noted that the invention and performance of the said instruments is in no way different from that in common usage, I shall en-deavor, while intending no discredit to anyone else, to explain myself to Your Excellency, showing Your Lordship my secrets, and then offering them to your complete dis-posal, and when the time is right, bringing into effective operation all those things which you might desire.*

*In part, these shall be noted below . . .*

*1. I have plans for light, strong, and easily portable bridges with which to pursue and, on some occasions, flee the enemy; and others, sturdy and indestructible either by fire or in battle, easy and convenient to lift and place in position. Also means of burning and destroying those of the enemy.*

*2. I know how, in the course of a siege, to remove*

water from the moats and how to make an endless variety of bridges, covered ways and scaling ladders, and other machines necessary to such expeditions.

3. If, by reason of the height of the banks, or the strength of the place and its position, it is impossible, when besieging a place, to avail oneself of the plan of bombardment, I have methods for destroying every rock or other fortress, even if it were founded on a promontory, and so forth . . .

4. I have also types of cannon, most convenient and easily portable; and with these I can fling small stones almost like a hailstorm; and the smoke from the cannon will instill a great terror in the enemy, to his great detriment and confusion.

5. And if the fight should be at sea I have many machines most efficient for offense and defense; and vessels which will resist the attack of the largest guns and powder and fumes.

6. Also, I have means of arriving at a designated spot through mines and secret winding passages constructed completely without noise, even if it should be necessary to pass underneath a moat or river.

7. Also, I will make covered chariots, safe and unassailable, which will penetrate the enemy and their artillery, and there is no host of armed men so great that they would not break through it. And behind these, the infantry will be able to follow, quite uninjured and unimpeded.

*8. Also, should the need arise, my lord, I will make cannon, mortar, and light ordnance of very beautiful and functional design that are quite out of the ordinary.*

*9. Where the use of cannon is impracticable, I will assemble catapults, mangonels, trebuchets, and other instruments of marvelous efficiency not in common use. In short, as the variety of circumstances dictate, I can contrive an endless number of items for attack and defense.*

*10. In times of peace I believe I can give as complete satisfaction as any other in the field of architecture, and the construction of both public and private buildings, and in conducting water from one place to another.*

*11. Moreover, work could be undertaken on the bronze horse, which will be to the immortal glory and eternal honor of the auspicious memory of His Lordship your father, and of the illustrious House of Sforza.*

*12. Also I can execute sculpture in marble, bronze, and clay. Likewise in painting, I can do everything possible as well as any other, whosoever he may be.*

*And if any of the abovementioned things seem impossible or impracticable to anyone, I am most readily disposed to demonstrate them in your park or in whatsoever place shall please Your Excellency, to whom I commend myself with all possible humility.*

# 16
## CECILIA

*Milan, Italy*
*June 1490*

CECILIA OPENED THE SONNET WITH A CONFIDENT burst of air from her lungs. Just as her new singing tutor had shown her, she pushed all the air from low in the pit of her stomach.

*Così del tuo favore ho qui bisogno . . .*

She held the last note, setting her gaze on the broad window and to the vista beyond. The scent of summer was so thick in the air that it was nearly sickening, like the odor of flower stems that have been left to turn to slime in a vase. Above the sill, a bumblebee looped in drunken spirals, gorging itself on the red flowers spilling over the edge.

Even though there were only a handful of people in the room during this practice, Cecilia endeavored to sing as if the audience hall were full of courtiers. She took a deep breath, listened for the cue on the harp, and found her way to the next line.

*Però mostra a Mercurio, o Anfione,*
*Che mi 'nsegni narrare un novo sogno . . .*

She had improved, Cecilia thought. She wished that her brother were here, that he had not been dispatched on one of His Lordship's missions far afield from Milan. She knew that Fazio would be proud of her, would heap praises on her new talents that were being developed under the tutelage of Ludovico il Moro's court poet and musicians. And, if she were truthful with herself, she knew that Fazio's presence would give her the courage she needed right now, practicing and preparing herself to sing before Ludovico, his court, and a room full of strangers.

Cecilia's gaze rested instead on the court poet, Bernardo Bellincioni, a gray-haired man seated behind Marco at his harp. Bernardo's eyes were bright and earnest, and Cecilia saw that his lips moved almost imperceptibly, mouthing the words of the song. He could not stop himself. He had written the words to this sonnet, and many others, himself. She hesitated, but Bernardo urged her with a small gesture. "Continue, *cara.*"

With Bernardo, Cecilia had spent hours delving into poetry, music, literature. In spite of the fact that Bernardo was old enough to be her grandfather, he was the closest thing to a friend that Cecilia had found in the ducal court. Together, Cecilia and Bernardo had composed a few bits of verse and song, the expert pleasantly surprised by Cecilia's talent, and Cecilia enthralled by the beauty of his words and his practiced skill of arranging them together with little more than a fast scribble of his quill.

"Now stop," instructed Bernardo, and Cecilia watched him scratch out a few lines on his parchment, whispering to himself as he adjusted words and rhymes as he went. "Give me a few moments," he said.

Cecilia moved away from her page of music and to the window to breathe the heavy, flower-scented air. At the window sat Lucrezia Crivelli. Cecilia imagined that Ludovico, if he thought of such things, figured that Lucrezia might be a friend for Cecilia, but the girl was not interested in any of the things that Cecilia loved. She did not give the first thought to music, poetry, or myth. She seemed only to care about the clothing and manners of the court. When she wasn't busy torturing Cecilia with the latest beauty treatment pulled from a book of women's secrets, Lucrezia spent hours fanning herself by the windowsill or idly pulling a colored thread through her embroidery.

But Cecilia had no interest in spending her days as an idle courtier. She wanted more. She wanted not only to surround herself with talented musicians, poets, and writers like Bernardo; she wanted to be one, too. If she could prove her real worth to Ludovico il Moro and his court, then she wouldn't be just another new plaything who shone brightly for a season, then just as quickly lost her luster. If she could demonstrate her literary and musical skills enough to entertain and delight Ludovico's guests, then surely he would see the advantages of keeping her at his side for many years to come.

"His Lordship doesn't care for the harp," Lucrezia whispered, barely loud enough for Cecilia to hear, but out of earshot of Marco, the court musician.

Cecilia digested Lucrezia's assessment, and then wondered what else she didn't know about Ludovico's peculiar tastes. If she was to be more than His Lordship's plaything, she thought, she had better find out fast.

# 17
## DOMINIC

*Outside Aachen, Germany*
*October 1944*

ON THE HORIZON BEYOND THEIR ENCAMPMENT, Dominic made out a stream of dust, then heard the rumbling of engines. Paul stirred from a fitful nap, his back propped against his rucksack in a small patch of yellowed grass. The soldiers readied their rifles for a skirmish, but when the small convoy came into view, the trucks were all American deuce-and-a-halfs.

Dominic and Paul watched Captain Hancock's lean frame stroll up to the vehicles as they came to a halt. The leading truck's passenger door opened and a stocky man disembarked, his mustache as sharply clipped as his expression.

"Sir!" Captain Hancock saluted. Dominic and Paul exchanged glances and followed suit.

"At ease, Hancock," said the new soldier. His stripes

marked him as a lieutenant commander. Hancock gestured toward the higher-ranking officer. "Lieutenant Commander George Stout," he said to the men. "He's our boss." Dominic took in the tall, dark-mustached lieutenant commander.

For two weeks, Dominic and his fellow soldiers had paced nervously around this camp, watching the city of Aachen burn from a distance. The landscape was little more than a smoldering pile of stone. By night, the sky glowed. By day, the soldiers watched columns of smoke rise into the air. The renowned center of art and culture—Charlemagne's capital—was reduced to just another bombed-out city hulking on the horizon, like the coals of a campfire discarded by some careless giant.

While they waited, Dominic had sketched quick portraits of his fellow soldiers on whatever scraps of discarded telegrams, food wrappers, or other surface he could find. When Paul had caught Dominic making a quick sketch of him as he washed out his canteen at a rusty spigot, he finally agreed to pose for him. "For God's sake, just don't tell anyone," Paul had said as Dominic laughed. "Ain't never wanted to be some kind of artist's model." The jab had constituted a small kind of acceptance, and it had given Dominic the shot of levity he needed to keep going. To keep waiting. And to keep drawing.

Over days, a gaggle of American and British journalists had gathered, squatting around the relative safety of the encampment like scavengers following a dying animal. They had not been able to secure transportation to the front, and everyone seemed disappointed when Dominic and Paul had arrived in only one two-and-a-half-ton truck. There wasn't enough space for everyone. So the soldiers and journalists returned to waiting and watching the aftermath of the battle. But now, with a line of trucks on the edge of camp, perhaps they could finally get moving.

Dominic shifted his weight where he stood guard, the cumbersome heft of his rifle dragging on his shoulder. His sore feet echoed his sore psyche. Then the commander nodded at Dominic. "You guys have waited around long enough." He jerked his head toward the vehicles. "Let's go."

Paul was tasked with driving Lieutenant Commander Stout in their truck, marked in large white "Military Police" letters and now standing at the front of the line. Dominic piled into the back of the next vehicle alongside a group of soldiers already inside the truck bed. They shifted over to make room; a few of the men had to hang on to the outside of it. Dominic scooted over to give more room and bumped into a short soldier huddling in the corner.

"Sorry," he said automatically, glancing up.

To his surprise, pinched feminine features stared out at him from under an army helmet. She squatted awkwardly there, staring big-eyed at the swarm of armed men inside the Jeep, but there was a fire in her eye that made him cautious to offend her.

"What'cha staring at?" she asked, a sharp Brooklyn accent in her voice.

"Sorry, miss." Dominic felt himself blushing. "I didn't realize—"

She silenced him with a waved hand. "Josie Garrett, *New York Times*."

Dominic raised his eyebrows. "You're a reporter?"

"Yep. Been following Stout and his men for weeks now. You have him to thank for your transport to the front."

The truck's engine turned over with a sputter and Dominic swayed with the familiar motion of reversing and turning around; Josie put out a hand, catching herself on the wall to keep her balance. Dominic felt a pang of pity as he grasped his weapon tighter.

"So what's the news?" he asked.

Josie produced a small stenography pad from the front of her army greatcoat, a few sizes too big. "Well, a sculpture by Michelangelo was stolen in Bruges, that much I can tell you." The very name Michelangelo seemed as incongruous in a conversation about a war mission as her petite frame in the back of an army truck.

"They stole a Michelangelo?" Dominic felt his jaw drop. If the Nazis thought nothing of slaughtering millions of innocent people, then he guessed they thought nothing of stealing a famous work of art.

Josie nodded, rifling through her notes. "And a whole bunch of other stuff from nearly every country in Europe.

They've even stolen a Leonardo da Vinci and a Raphael in Poland. They're telling the Germans that the Allies are hiring Jewish art experts to steal everything of artistic value. Supposedly we're shipping it all back to the US for private collectors. A big fat lie, of course. The whole point of the Monuments Men's mission is to send art back to its rightful owners here in Europe. We're not taking anything back home with us."

Dominic shook his head. "I had no idea. So what are they looking for in Aachen?"

She gestured toward the forward truck, as if they could see Lieutenant Commander Stout in the passenger seat, alongside Paul. "Well, now that the bloodbath is behind us, he's hoping there's something left in the church. It used to be the capital of the Holy Roman Empire. But we don't know if there's anything left at this point." Josie shrugged. "All we know is that they're going to salvage everything they can. Other teams of Monuments Men have been trying to preserve the works too." She scanned her notes again. "They're spread out across France and Italy. They've even been sandbagging the Ponte Vecchio in Florence. My colleague reported on it earlier this week."

"That's a waste of time, if you ask me," opined another man sitting opposite them. "Protecting the monuments isn't our job. We're just here to salvage what's left, and to move what we can to safer places. Trying to protect those buildings is pointless."

"Pointless or not, that's the plan," said Josie. "The Allies have drawn detailed aerial maps to protect other monuments, too."

Dominic stared dully out at the rubble of the landscape as they trundled nearer to the burning city of Aachen. He knew that the count of American dead in the Battle of Aachen had been in the thousands, but that there were many more German casualties on top of that. The fight had been bitter and thousands of German prisoners had been taken, according to the intelligence reports they'd received while they watched the city burn, helplessly, from their encampment. And in the territories to the east, millions of people had already lost their lives at the hands of the Nazis. At this point, what did some paintings and old buildings matter?

As much as Dominic appreciated art, he valued people more, and he wondered how Sally would feel if she heard that he'd been killed defending some painting or sculpture. Thousands of lives. How far would the ripple of grief spread? In the face of that, what did this mission matter? At least, in his old platoon, he felt like he was doing something to push back the enemy. Now, Dominic felt his optimism begin to dim in the face of the useless waiting, the cleanup after a pillage.

"We're also getting intelligence reports about stolen art repositories within Germany," Josie went on, shooting the other man a glance that brimmed with New York attitude. "Stout's keen for the liberation to be done with so that we can get to it. He's on the phone all the time, trying to get more men together so that we can go after it. All that stuff the Nazis stole has to have gone somewhere—if we can get to their hiding places, then we can get it out and send it home."

"There's precious little left of home if you ask me," murmured a soldier sitting beside them. Staring out at what was left of Aachen, Dominic had to agree. Not for the first time, he thanked God that Sally and Cecilia were safe in Pittsburgh, and he prayed that the war would never spread that far. He wondered how many of the rightful owners of these works were even still alive.

The acrid smell of the bombed-out city grew stronger in their nostrils. Awed by the sheer scale of the destruction, everyone in the truck fell into deep silence. The narrow trolley track that they were following was the only road in passable condition for the first few miles. The truck struggled and bumped through ruts and holes. Wires hung from the trolley ties. As they headed nearer to the city center, the track was lined with townhomes. Dominic could still see the remnants of their former glory: a section of sandstone wall here, a marble statue in a garden there, a fragmented façade standing cracked and worn with the house number askew beside the charred remains of the doorframe. In the industrial areas of the city, there were no more standing walls, only heaps of rubble, the fragments of lives and dreams torn and thrown down mercilessly to the earth. Apart from their convoy, the city was nearly abandoned. Its beauty was reduced to a flat, eerie wasteland. The farther toward the city center they went, the fewer windows were intact. Finally, the houses were nothing but shells. In one of them, a bookshelf stood on its side, half destroyed; paper rustled in the wind as books lay scattered over what remained of a wooden floor.

Josie, who had been scribbling frantically in her notebook, gave a soft gasp and pointed. "Oh."

Dominic followed her finger to a heap of rubble as they passed. It was a shoe: a tiny, crocheted thing that he could imagine being lovingly crafted in the hands of some doting grandmother. Now it lay bloodstained and covered in soot and plaster dust in the middle of the street. One of the truck's tires had crushed it into the dirt.

"Look at that," said one of the other soldiers, pointing upward. Dominic looked up and saw, with a shock, a building still standing: some grand old church, its façade pockmarked by gunfire, but its steeple still standing proudly aloft. As they neared the oldest part of the city, more and more churches appeared through the smoke, all of them old and half preserved. Dominic realized that these had to be the work of the Monuments Men's maps. If not for them, surely these churches would have been razed to the ground like the rest of the city—like the townhomes belonging to innocent civilians who hadn't asked for this war that had destroyed their lives.

"Are there survivors?" he asked in a hushed voice.

An officer sitting near them shrugged. "Most of the

civilians were evacuated. As for the rest, I suppose they're hiding in their cellars. If there are any still alive."

Dominic thought of families hiding down there in the dust and darkness, cowering closer together as they heard the trucks rumble overhead. Why was this convoy moving toward some old buildings when there were human beings down there who needed them? He stared out at the remnants of Aachen. Suddenly, the gun in his hands felt like a ton of stone.

They'd all believed that they might be heroes. They'd all thought they were fighting for something: freedom and justice, the liberation of innocent people, the prospect of peace someday so that their children would never have to face the same horrors.

But as he journeyed across the sea and across the European continent, with every day that passed, Dominic was starting to wonder if he made any difference at all. What did art matter, and what did his own opinion matter? Both, he thought, seemed expendable. He shut his mouth and his mind, stared glassily at the canvas wall of the truck, and rode on in bitter silence.

Beside him, Josie scribbled in her notepad, a furiously paced shorthand. For all the times he searched and longed for scrap pieces of paper, Dominic thought, even if Josie tore out a fresh sheet and handed it to him, there's no way he could find it within himself to write or draw anything. Not now.

# 18
## CECILIA

*Milan, Italy*
*September 1490*

FROM LUDOVICO IL MORO'S BED, CECILIA WATCHED A flock of swallows make frenzied loops outside the window. The sheets were still clammy from the lazy hours they had spent there after the midday meal.

Ludovico stood and wrapped a sheet around his waist. From a bowl on a small table, he plucked a pomegranate. One of the kitchen staff had scored lines along the sides of the red fruit to make it quicker and easier to peel. Cecilia wondered how and where they had managed to find such a luxury so early in the season.

"Our guests should be returning soon from the hunt," he said, glancing out of the window. "I hope you have prepared something entertaining for them tonight."

Cecilia nodded. She was getting more practiced at not talking unless Ludovico asked her a direct question, and she could only surmise that it had its desired effect. In recent weeks, Ludovico had showered her with gifts. A beautiful new velvet gown with a gilded neckline. A string of black onyx beads long enough to wrap around her neck twice.

"Master Bernardo's new sonnet," he said.

"Yes." Cecilia propped herself on her elbow. "But I thought you didn't like the harp."

He turned to her and one half of his mouth turned up in a grin. "Who told you that?"

She met his gaze. "I don't recall."

"It's true that I prefer the sound of the lyre to accompany vocal compositions," he said. "There is no more beautiful instrument, to my ear."

"Then I'll remember that for the future," she said.

Ludovico smiled now and returned to the bed. "My flower . . ." He pressed his face into Cecilia's neck and the roughness of his beard sent a tingle down her spine. "The truth is that everyone wants to hear your beautiful voice, no matter what the accompanying instrument."

"Then you are satisfied with my work."

Ludovico chuckled low under his breath. Then he grasped her long, untidy braid. She watched him wind it around his fist and pull her to him as if by a rope. "Very satisfied," he said.

"Hopefully the guests will be satisfied as well. With the music."

Ludovico rose again and threw open the shutters. "My

dear," he proclaimed loudly, "your reputation has already spread across Lombardy and beyond. In no time, the name of Cecilia Gallerani will be spoken throughout the land."

Then, Ludovico flopped in a chair and began to peel the pomegranate. Cecilia lay back and watched him extract the plump arils from the center of the fruit as blood-red juice trickled down his hand. A hungry, lustful smile. Then Cecilia watched him press the sweet, ripe fruits to his tongue, letting the bitter, hollow rind fall to the floor.

# 19
## EDITH

*Pełkinie, Poland*
*September 1939*

THE GIRL'S EYES WERE INTELLIGENT AND ALMOND shaped, gazing toward the light as if she were distracted by a flock of birds beyond the windowsill. In her arms, she cradled a white, furry creature the size of a newborn baby, its beady, glasslike eyes focused in the same direction as the girl's.

Edith had read earlier scholars' assessments that Cecilia Gallerani was dressed *alla spagnola*, with her velvet gown, open-armed blue mantle, and square neckline trimmed in a band of gilded embroidery. A small cap and black band held a nearly transparent veil with a scalloped edge across her forehead. Cecilia's sleek hairstyle was shown in the fashion of the day, parted down the middle and arranged in a long braid bound in a silk casing. A string of onyx beads fell across her breast and was wrapped a second time around her slender neck in an artful arrangement.

Edith ran her finger carefully across the surface. She was already noting the small imperfections, marks of damage that she alone could perceive, thanks to her years of training and experience. A fine craquelure of dried paint had textured the surface of the picture, no doubt the result of dramatic changes in temperature and humidity as the picture, painted on a walnut panel, had been ferried over countless miles along with the Czartoryski family in past decades. Did anyone else see the brown overpaint that made it appear as if her cap were an extension of her hair? That, surely, was the result of a misunderstanding by a later restorer. And the black background, though dramatic in its effect, was surely not original. Da Vinci must have envisioned a distant landscape similar to the one in his famous *Mona Lisa*, Edith thought. However, some restorer a hundred years ago must have covered this background with black varnish, perhaps to mask some earlier damage to the painting.

But the picture was so much more than the sum of these parts. How many people had had the opportunity to stand before this beautiful portrait of the young woman who might have been the mistress of an important ruler of fifteenth-century Milan? To gaze upon the hand of Leonardo da Vinci himself? Edith had set her eyes and hands on so many paintings of the Renaissance era, but this portrait left her in awe. As much as she hated being torn away from her family and her work in Munich, she had to admit that standing before this picture was a dream come true.

Edith's heart had nearly stopped when the soldier had pulled the picture from a crate in the back of the walled-up room. She recognized that it was an old panel, probably from the Renaissance, even from the back. The frame was likely made in the eighteenth century, a hefty construction of gilded wood. She knew the size and recognized the walnut panel typical of Italian paintings of the late 1400s. Still, she held her breath until the soldier turned it around for everyone to see.

Now, Leonardo's *Lady with an Ermine* lay flat on a table in the once-secret room of the Czartoryski Palace. Many of the important pieces reproduced on the folios of Edith's catalog lay stacked around her: Rembrandt's *Landscape with the Good Samaritan*, Raphael's *Portrait of a Young Man*, all the paintings that Edith had presented to the museum staff, and many more.

Over the course of a few days, Edith had spent nearly all her time in the windowless, vaulted space, documenting and assessing the valuables the family had tried to hide before they fled. Two soldiers were stationed to help her handle the large paintings, furniture, and other heavy pieces, and to guard the extensive collection of antique jewelry against temptations from other soldiers. Even though Edith was awed by the careful selection of priceless objects in the family's collection, the work must be tedious and dull for these men, she thought. They spent hours waiting around for Edith to finish writing down her copious observations. In addition to the paintings that Edith had already cataloged back in Munich, the family's collection included vast amounts of furniture, drawings, bronzes, coins and medals, priceless jewels and gems. It would take many hours for Edith to examine and inventory everything in the collection.

The men's idle bantering formed the background of Edith's concentration on the works of art and her wondering if Heinrich might have arrived in Poland with his unit by now. They complained about Polish food, about the language, about boredom. They would be reassigned to points eastward, they said, once more troops arrived in the region. The men had tried to make conversation, to question Edith about her work at the museum, her personal life, about how she had gotten here, but Edith did not want to open herself to their examination.

They had also told Edith that there were Polish prisoners being held upstairs. Lieutenant Fischer's words rang in her ears: *resisters in the countryside.*

As she worked, Edith's stomach remained twisted in knots, wondering where the Czartoryski family had gone, and if they had managed to escape capture.

Finally, one afternoon, her answer came.

"Fräulein Becker."

She turned to see Lieutenant Fischer coming down the stairs. He approached the table where Edith was examining surface cracks in a small seventeenth-century German still life, dark with age and neglect. For a few long moments, he raked his eyes over the picture. Then he turned to Edith.

"I have been told to instruct you to make a selection of twelve or so of the most valuable works here," he said. "The men may help you repackage them for safe transport."

"The pictures are being transported? What about the family?"

"It did not take long for the Gestapo to find the prince and his pregnant Spaniard. They have been taken into our custody."

Edith felt her chest heave. "They were arrested? But what will become of them?" The weight of despair closed in around her again, and the room became a tunnel rimmed in black. Would she be responsible for the fate of the family's most prized possessions, but also for their own safety, maybe even their lives? Would Edith bear the blame for the fate of the young prince and his wife? Even their unborn child?

"That is no longer any of our concern," Fischer continued. "I have directions from SS Oberführer Mühlmann. He is the newly appointed Special Commissioner in Charge of Safeguarding Works of Art in Eastern Occupied Lands. Dr. Mühlmann has just arrived in Poland and has sent orders to you."

"Orders." The word came out as a nearly breathless whisper.

Lieutenant Fischer nodded. "Oberführer Mühlmann

wishes to examine the most valuable pieces from this collection personally. He is en route to another of the Czartoryski residences near Jarosław."

Edith wondered how she might choose only ten or twelve pictures from the carefully curated Czartoryski collection. Cecilia Gallerani's lively face caught Edith's eye, and she focused on it, trying to steel her nerves.

"We will come for them in the morning, so you may start your selection and packaging immediately. And you are to accompany us to Jarosław," Lieutenant Fischer said. "I would advise you to choose wisely. Oberführer Mühlmann has asked for you directly."

# 20
# LEONARDO

*Milan, Italy*
*September 1490*

**"HIS LORDSHIP HAS ASKED FOR YOU DIRECTLY."**

So says the young page, out of breath after sprinting from the ducal castle at the edge of the city. He has sped to my lodgings in the Corte Vecchia, and up the ever-narrowing staircases to the rooftop.

It is from this fortified rooftop that I'm determined to make a man fly. For months now, I've been working on the contraption, for the first time turning a lifetime of dreams and drawings into reality. I have filled stacks of pages with images of lightweight wooden frames that might hold a passenger. After studying and drawing the wings of pigeons, bats, and dragonflies, I have settled on those of a hawk, which, I judge, should allow the craft to soar and hover better than the other designs. With the help of two carpenters, we have constructed the passenger frame of a lightweight wood coated in balm. We are building the armatures for the wings, which will be covered with fine Milanese silk stretched across them.

But now the young boy, perspiring, has come to lure me away from my workshop, my little factory, to the ducal palace and to the audience hall of Ludovico il Moro. "His Lordship has sent orders," the boy says. *Orders.*

It has taken seven long years for Ludovico il Moro to put me on a salary, to feed me and house me in this crumbling old pile of stones overlooking the city's main square. I have everything I desired. Room to live and work. A place at his table. That is the good news. The bad: Like everyone else on His Lordship's accounts, I am now beholden to the man. When Ludovico il Moro beckons, I must drop everything else. Every last one of my projects.

"What," I ask the boy, "is the nature of His Lordship's request?"

"A portrait," the boy says.

Ah. At last, a portrait. It was only a matter of time. I have anticipated that His Lordship might ask for me to replicate his image. In my mind, I have already imagined how I might portray his square jaw. The slick, black hair that falls over his broad forehead. His Lordship has already shown me the portraits he's had made by other painters' hands. I will not show His Lordship in profile. Not only is it an old-fashioned and unnatural image, but I have already given thought to a different composition that might serve to soften Ludovico il Moro's hawklike nose.

Or is it possible, I wonder, that His Lordship has decided to have me paint his nephew, the young Gian Galeazzo instead? After all, the boy is the rightful Duke of Milan in name, if not in practice. I have seen the youth a few times when he has been called to Milan from the fortresses of Pavia or Certosa. There, I am told he is kept as little more than a well-treated prisoner. And when he visits here in the Corte Vecchia, Gian Galeazzo Sforza slinks waiflike along the corridors and takes his meals in his private rooms. Surely the boy feels the burden of his father's legacy, if not his father's reputation for pulling apart the limbs of those who crossed him, or having his enemies, still breathing, nailed into their coffins. Setting aside any of his father's sadistic pleasures, the boy must feel the weight of his responsibility to his people. But with his long, fine curls and pallor, the little duke appears more like a fallen angel than a ruthless sovereign of an entire duchy. The subject of a portrait commissioned by his uncle and regent, Ludovico Sforza? Probably not. In fact, I do not place my bets on the poor boy's prospects at all.

"*Subitissimo*," the young page tells me. "His Lordship wants you to come right away."

I look at my flying contraption, nearly finished, lacking surely only a few more days of work. How could I bear to break away at this point?

I have not yet heard of Ludovico il Moro, like his older brother, delighting in peculiar tortures of his own design. Nonetheless, anyone would be stupid to cross him. During the short years in which I have made Milan my home, I have done nothing save for plying myself into the good graces of His Lordship and the other men of the court. I have gilded and painted a large sculpted polyptych in the church of San Francesco Grande, no more than a cog in the wheel of a team of sculptors, woodworkers, and painters. An annoyance, to be sure, but it led to more commissions. I finished no less than two versions of the *Virgin of the Rocks*, and got to design a few buildings, several hydraulic machines, and even a new kind of silk loom.

His Lordship finally conceded to my proposal for an enormous equestrian statue, a monument to Ludovico's late father. I have already drawn the horse's head and designed the metal armatures that will form the preparatory model. We will start with a clay model while I think about how to go about casting the enormous piece in bronze.

To be fair, I have also had plenty of time and space to build some of the contraptions from my notebooks. The castle courtyards and a long disused audience hall provide the perfect factory of ideas. I have even lured a few men to work as assistants.

But right now, the page tells me, "His Lordship really wants a portrait of his mistress. The new one. *Subitissimo.*"

I hesitate. A new lady?

There was another mistress, not long before my arrival in Milan, but His Lordship must have lost interest, for she is nowhere in sight. Only a little girl, a black-haired beauty named Bianca, is left behind in the ducal castle as a testament to this tryst.

And now, a new lady. A mistress worthy of a portrait.

Before me, a ragged piece of silk flaps idly from the half-assembled frame of one of my flying machine's wings. I am on the verge of getting this right, at last. We might see a man take flight over the central square of Milan. I stifle a sigh; the messenger is watching me.

Must I stop work on this contraption, all for the sake of this distraction, of painting a young girl in the grips of Il Moro?

But no one has asked my opinion on the matter.

"Grant me a few minutes to prepare my drawing things," I tell the page. "Tell His Lordship that I am coming."

# 21
## CECILIA

*Milan, Italy*
*October 1490*

"THE PAINTER HAS ARRIVED, SIGNORINA. I HAVE SEEN him leave his horse with the grooms at the gate."

Cecilia looked up from her small volume, a compilation of Latin verse, to find Bernardo Bellincioni, poet to the court of Milan, peering into the library. Bernardo came to where Cecilia was sitting by the window. Her new white puppy, a precious gift from Ludovico, curled in her lap.

"Aristotle," he said, gesturing to her parchment pages. "A good choice."

She nodded. "Stay with us," she said, squeezing the poet's hand.

"It would be my pleasure, signorina, if it meets with his approval. Master da Vinci and I . . . we are acquainted, from back home."

Over weeks, Cecilia and the court poet had shared many

hours together in the peace of the castle library. It brought Cecilia comfort to hear his familiar Tuscan tongue, especially because her brother Fazio was often away on diplomatic business and she lacked for companionship. The women in the castle, whether chambermaid or courtier, were all occupied with bleaching their hair with horse urine, comparing the latest adornments on their shoes, and sharing gossip of quarrels and attachments, all petty subjects of little interest to Cecilia. With Bernardo, she relished the hours of good conversation over common interests.

Bernardo was the only one who recognized her true potential value to the court, Cecilia thought, certainly more so than His Lordship himself. Since that first night when Ludovico il Moro had taken her virtue, Cecilia had continued to advocate for her own high position in his court. She read him lines of poetry, pieces of ancient philosophy, Bernardo's words ready to put to music. Sometimes, Ludovico brought her out of her private chambers to sing a song, recite a poem, or charm his guests with a story or a tune on the lute. But more often, he only patted her face as if she were a lapdog, then left her to her bed. Cecilia would pull the wool up over her naked body and try to stave off the feeling of emptiness that swelled in her chest.

As the bedding cooled, the heat of her lover dissipating into the night, she would lie awake, wondering how things might have ended differently. What if she had gone to the Monastero Maggiore, had proved her value there, had preserved her virtue? What if her silly brothers had not lost her dowry and she was a wife in the country, with land and a brood of children?

It was futile to dwell on the possibilities.

To be sure, Ludovico valued Cecilia, just not in the way she had envisioned for herself. He lavished her with every gift and luxury she could imagine, from dresses to gilded trinkets. A fine horse, the best of a breeder from the Dolomite mountain range, stood waiting for her in the stable. Violina, the docile white puppy that had brought her to tears of joy when Ludovico had presented it, now settled into a warm circle in her lap. Cecilia marveled at the beauty of it all. Her childhood home in Siena, with its chipped crockery and mended undergarments, seemed nothing more than a story heard long ago.

And now, a portrait. Ludovico had engaged an artist, Master da Vinci of Florence, to capture his mistress in paint.

Still, sitting for a painting, though an honor, sounded like the dullest possible way to spend an afternoon. But with Bernardo with her in the library, at the least she could continue her studies and their engaging conversations.

As it turned out, Master da Vinci was anything but dull. He strode into the room adorned in a green velvet cloak, fastened together at the neck with a jeweled clasp, and light green hose emerging from shoes with elaborate leather cutwork. His dark hair and copious beard flowed from underneath a sagging velvet hat. Behind him, a valet and chambermaid swayed under the heft of the painter's leather bags.

Leonardo and Bernardo greeted each other with kisses on both cheeks and a strong clasp of the shoulders. Then, the artist fell to the floor on one knee, grasping Cecilia's hand in both of his. "Your talents are already being praised across the land, signorina. But now I see that no one who has spoken so highly of you has done justice to your beauty."

"You are kind." Cecilia blushed.

"It will be my challenge—and my privilege—to preserve your beauty in paint for future generations. Besides," he said, "we Tuscans must stay together in this gray city."

Cecilia decided immediately that she liked Master Leonardo. She took a seat in one of the two armchairs, the one nearest the bright window, while Bernardo perched himself on the window's ledge to look out upon the neat rows of trimmed junipers in the courtyard below. Her dog settled in her lap, wheezing almost imperceptibly. Cecilia ran her palm over his bony head. The painter fished out a few leaves of parchment and a long stylus from one of his bags.

"I thought you were going to paint me?" she asked.

"Indeed. But we will begin with preparatory sketches. It will take some time."

Cecilia nodded and relaxed in the chair, where she could watch Master da Vinci work. She had never been painted before and had never even met a painter, but as far as she could tell, Master da Vinci did not look like one. His clothes were impeccable. If she met him on the street, she might take him for a nobleman. He did not even have stains on his fingernails.

"Do you paint every day?" she asked.

"No," he said quickly. "Haven't painted anything for months. That's not why I'm here."

Bernardo stepped in. "His Magnificence has engaged Master da Vinci as a military engineer."

"An engineer?" Cecilia asked.

"Bridges," the master said. "Catapults. Trebuchets. Siege vehicles. Machines that might even attack from the air. That has been my trade of late. It's what brought me here to begin with."

"There are so many threats to the duchy?" Cecilia asked, squirming in her chair.

"Men of Il Moro's standing always find themselves threatened, *cara*," he said, his eyes soft. "But to answer the question you originally posed, yes, I offer my services as a painter in times of peace. But more often than not, men like Ludovico il Moro find themselves at war."

"And Master da Vinci, therefore, finds himself employed." Bernardo smiled.

"Correct, signore." Leonardo smiled, too, and pointed his silverpoint pen in Bernardo's direction. Then he began to run it carefully over the page, shifting his brown eyes up occasionally to watch Cecilia as she caressed her dog's soft ear. "And I am at His Lordship's disposal for anything that needs design or visual display, like the upcoming nuptials."

"A *matrimonio?*" Cecilia asked. "Who is getting married?" For a few long moments, the only sound was the soft purr and scraping of a pigeon under an eave near the window. From her peripheral vision, Cecilia saw Bernardo squirm uncomfortably at the windowsill, crossing his legs and rubbing his palm over his mouth.

Master da Vinci's face blanched. "The daughter of the Duke of Ferrara," he said haltingly. "Beatrice d'Este." Her name came out as a whisper.

Heavy silence fell again over the room. Cecilia felt her heart begin to pound, and heat rose to her cheeks as the pieces began to coalesce in her mind.

"Cecilia," Bernardo broke the silence. "Surely you knew? His Lordship has been betrothed for many years already, as you were yourself."

"I am an idiot," Master da Vinci said, rushing to kneel at Cecilia's side. "My poor, innocent child. I should have taken more care. Forgive me for being a brute. There can be no doubt that you are the light in His Lordship's eyes. That is plain to see. Why else would he have wanted to immortalize you with a picture by my own hand?"

Cecilia struggled for words. How could she have been so naïve? Of course a marriage would have been arranged long ago for a man like Ludovico Sforza. Why hadn't she seen it, or thought to ask? What made her think that she had the slightest chance to be the lady of this castle? Beside her, Leonardo da Vinci stared at her with huge, sad brown eyes.

"You are not an idiot," she said, placing her hand on his to reassure him. "I am. I'm just a stupid country girl. Not sure why I thought I might be the duchess of Milan."

"*Cara mia . . .*" Bernardo stepped forward to console her. "Surely you have not allowed our master to take your heart as well as your virtue?"

Cecilia had to stop and think about this. Bernardo had a way of putting things in stark light. Did she love Ludovico? The question lingered heavy and unanswered in the air.

All she knew was that things had become quickly complicated. Her lover, her keeper, her master—he would marry another woman. It had been decided long before Cecilia darkened the doorway of the Castello Sforzesco. This Beatrice d'Este, daughter of the Duke of Ferrara, was the perfect match. Of course she was. Of course she would be the head of this castle. She would be the one to entertain their guests, to assemble painters, poets, musicians. She would be the one who might, if the stars aligned, win Ludovico's heart.

For the first time since arriving in Milan, Cecilia wasn't sure about anything. And her own feelings for Ludovico were complicated by a secret that she had not shared with anyone else. She was carrying his child.

# 22
## LEONARDO

*Milan, Italy*
*November 1490*

CECILIA GALLERANI'S DAYS IN THE DUCAL PALACE OF Milan are numbered. Surely she knows it?

The girl is naïve. Intelligent, yes. Beautiful, yes. But naïve. She had even seemed surprised to hear of Ludovico's betrothal to Beatrice d'Este. No one thought to inform the poor girl? Does she even see that her own dressmaid, Lucrezia Crivelli, is angling to take her place?

In my sketches, I've tried many different turns and shifts of the head. And I've tried to capture the mixture of intelligence and naiveté that I observe in Cecilia's face. There must be a way to portray the vivacity, the immediacy of life that anyone feels in her presence. Surely it is part of what drew Ludovico il Moro to her bed.

But no. Something is not right. I scribble out the image and crumple the page. I've been working on the composition for days, but I don't have it yet.

I set down my drawings and walk to my bedchamber window. The Corte Vecchia is an old residence but like an aging beauty, it has its charms. From the fortified rooftop and from the windows of my suite of rooms, I enjoy a glorious, unencumbered view of Milan's cathedral in progress, the ducal castle on the edge of the city, and on a clear day, the foothills of the Alps.

But today, there is no vista. Fat, wet snowflakes fall from a gray sky. If I could catch one on the black sleeve of my cloak, I might see—only for a fleeting moment—perfect symmetry, a unique design of our Creator, captured in ice. And then, just as I might begin to trap the most complex and perfect of God's designs in my mind, it would disappear from view, leaving only a dark, wet stain on my sleeve.

Cecilia's days are numbered, I think, drumming my fingers on the cold, stone windowsill and trying to think of a new way, a novel way to make her live through paint on panel. And I must figure it out quickly, before Il Moro changes his mind. A woman like Cecilia Gallerani must know that she comes into the ducal palace going out. The only question is, when? And more importantly, how? What will become of this girl?

I watch the heavy snowflakes drop down into the gated precinct of the cathedral workyard below my window. The workyard is filled with slabs of pink-veined white marble shipped on barges from the Alpine lakes along manmade canals dredged only for this purpose. The building must have been under construction for at least a hundred years before my arrival, I think. For the years I've been in Milan, those marble slabs have never moved. At the rate it's going, I imagine that the building might not be finished a hundred years from now.

I observe the first spikelike spires completed along the buttresses of the building, a strange style I am told is common in France. If the construction continues along this design, I think that the building might one day resemble a great ice palace. Along with many others, I myself have proposed a design for an octagonal central cupola of the building before Ludovico il Moro. But Il Moro hardly seems interested. Instead, all he can think about is lovely Cecilia.

Cecilia.

I turn away from the window, away from the perfect proportions of architecture and snowflakes, and back to my sketches.

Master Verrocchio taught us that painting is the imitator of all works of Nature. My picture must resemble the girl as she is in life. That is certain. Ludovico il Moro may not be well informed on matters of painting, but a resemblance will be the least of his expectations. And it is also certain that Cecilia Gallerani is already perfect in her own right.

But perfection and beauty lie not only in Nature, but in proportions, in the composition of a perfect harmony, in the perfect placement of the body and the head on the panel.

The perfect placement of the features of her face. Time will destroy the harmony of female beauty; that is also certain. But by painting Cecilia Gallerani, by capturing her beauty today, I will preserve it for eternity. And the viewer—now or in the future—may derive pleasure from the depicted beauty as much as from the living beauty.

His Lordship is smitten in a way that he has never been before; that's what Bernardo the poet has told me. It is easy to see Il Moro's obsession. There is something about Cecilia that is hard to put into words. A liveliness of spirit, an intelligence that is matched by any man at court. A few more marks on my page, and the outline of Cecilia's lips take shape. For a moment, I think she might speak or sing.

# 23
## EDITH

*Pełkinie, Poland*
*September 1939*

A PORTRAIT OF FLEETING BEAUTY, OF FROZEN perfection that had endured through the centuries. Edith braced the wooden panel of *Lady with an Ermine* against her drab green uniform skirt as she watched the Czartoryski Palace grow smaller in the distance. She could not let anything happen to the portrait. She had done enough already.

The driver of the light cargo truck, a boy who looked too young to have been sent to war, had invited Edith to sit in the front seat, but she had declined. She preferred to secure the painting against her leg as the rugged vehicle rattled out of the manicured, lush grounds of the palace and onto the main road.

Under normal circumstances, Edith would have insisted that a work like a portrait by Leonardo da Vinci, as well as the dozen other paintings she had selected as the best of the

Czartoryski collection, be packed in custom-made wooden crates made for carrying such works of incalculable value. But there was no such thing here.

Besides, she refused to let the picture out of her sight. It was the least she could do, she thought, for its rightful owners—the Polish prince and his pregnant wife—who were now in the hands of the Gestapo. Edith was filled with shame as she pressed the picture to her side.

In the secret room, she had instructed a handful of soldiers how to carefully pack each picture in layers of canvas tarps. She had personally inspected each package as it was loaded into the back of the truck. Each was tagged with the full identifying information. But with da Vinci's work, Edith did not want to take a chance. She positioned herself in the back seat, laying the wrapped portrait flat beside her as the truck lugged across the rutted road.

The land unfolded into vast expanses of forested hillsides and cultivated fields. Flocks of birds flew over the drooping stems of dying crops, diving, then corralling, then swarming up into the sky again.

*Resisters in the countryside.* Were they being watched? Edith scanned the landscape. In the distance, she glimpsed a few thatched-roof farmhouses, but there was no smoke in the air and she saw no one.

"All those packages in the back of the truck are pictures?" The driver turned his head briefly back toward her.

"Yes," she said.

"Where are they going?"

"For now, Jarosław. Later, I think that they may be . . . safeguarded . . . in other locations."

From under the driver's seat, Edith spied the corner of a newspaper. She leaned down to grasp it, spreading it across her lap. *Deutsche Lodzer Zeitung,* its black Gothic letters announced in bold across the top. The German-language newspaper of Lodz, Poland.

Edith read the headline: 120,000 POLES MARCHING IN GERMAN CAPTIVITY TODAY.

An image of Heinrich seared through her mind. Had he arrived in Poland? Was he part of this massive operation of capturing prisoners across the country?

Instinctively, Edith turned to look out the window of the vehicle again, as if she might catch a glimpse of him. But there were no people outside, only endless rolling hills with the hint of autumn color in their leaves. In a great field, hundreds of sunflowers were dying. They had turned their faces to the sun for one last time, and now the stalks stood angled and leaning, their heavy flower heads drooping and brown, dropping seeds to the fields.

"You have encountered . . . resisters . . . here?" Edith asked tentatively.

"Who, the Poles?" the boy driver asked, then shrugged. "Sure. They're out there. The Home Army. The People's Guard. Sometimes just zealous farmers with guns. That's why we wear these," he said, knocking on the top of his metal helmet. He looked back, taking his eyes off the road for another brief second. "You some kind of lady *Kurator?*"

"I suppose I am, something like that," said Edith, unable to suppress a grin. No one had ever called her that. "I am more of a *Konservator* than a curator. I restore old paintings, bring them back to life."

Edith wished that she knew more about Kajetan Mühlmann, the man who had called for her to bring him the best works uncovered at Pełkinie. He must have been highly regarded by the Party, or he would not have been put in such a position as Oberführer. But Edith had learned in her years of museum work that positions of authority were often doled out unfairly; his rank might not mean that he was qualified or would have her own professional interests at heart. She was prepared to distrust him.

It was nearly noon by the time the car pulled into the entrance of another grand home, not a palace like the one in Pełkinie, but a large, fine private residence nonetheless. The gravel drive in front of the house was filled with Nazi soldiers and officers, plus a dozen or so armored vehicles and trucks. She followed the soldiers up the wide staircase to the front door, carrying the painting under her arm, unwilling to let go.

The soldiers led Edith down a long hallway lined with tall, open windows spanning from side to side. The corridor led to an elaborate ballroom decorated with gilded molding and marble sculptures.

From the other side of the room, a great hulk of a man stepped toward her.

"Herr Dokter Mühlmann." One of the soldiers snapped his heels together and saluted the large man, whose broad shoulders and juglike jaw made him look like he belonged on an athletic field rather than in a museum office.

"Fräulein Becker. Thank you for coming," the man said in a distinctive Austrian accent. "Generaldirektor Buchner from the Alte Pinakothek has spoken highly of you." He extended his hand to Edith.

"Oberführer Mühlmann," she said, surprised at his soft, clammy grasp.

"Please," he said. "Call me Kai." His mouth spread into a thin line. In spite of his intimidating stature, Kai Mühlmann had a gentle voice. "You may not realize it yet, but you have already done much to help our effort. You have made my job with the Czartoryski collection simple." He grinned wider.

Edith felt the muscles around her shoulders tighten at the persistent thought of the fate of the prince and his wife but she was having a hard time steeling herself against Kai Mühlmann. He seemed mild-mannered, intelligent, and modest, and his Austrian accent added a certain charm. She let down her guard a little.

Behind them, several soldiers were bringing in the paintings that Edith had carefully wrapped in tarps. She watched them stack them against a wall.

"I don't know what else I could have done," Edith said. "My career . . . my life . . . has been dedicated to preserving paintings."

A nod of satisfaction. "So I have heard. I've done some research on you. Top of your class at university! The only woman to reach such a level. I am proud of you and I don't even know you yet."

Edith had to laugh. "Thank you."

"So," he said, "I am curious about the piece you have chosen to handle yourself? I noticed the others have all been brought in a truck while you were left to guard this one."

"I wasn't left to guard it," Edith corrected. "I wouldn't be able to protect this myself as they have not issued me any weapons. I chose this one because I want to make sure nothing happens to it."

"I cannot wait any longer, then. Let's have a look," Kai said.

Edith watched him carefully loosen the string that secured the loose tarp around da Vinci's portrait of Cecilia Gallerani. He laid the picture flat on the large marble surface of a table, then opened it. For a long, few silent moments, Edith watched Kajetan Mühlmann lean his palms against the table, taking in every detail of the richly oiled surface, of the girl's lively expression, of the turn of the sitter's body, and that of the strange creature in her lap.

Finally, he looked up at Edith with a smile that revealed a row of straight teeth. He nodded his approval.

"I am delighted that you have brought this masterpiece to me directly. It shows your good judgment that you chose to safeguard this particular piece with your life."

Edith could see the honesty on his face and in his words. She felt a little better, knowing that she wasn't the only art specialist in Poland who knew the importance of these pieces.

"I feel that this picture is the first modern portrait," she ventured. "Da Vinci has gone beyond the traditional strictures of representing sitters in profile or as idealized figures. Here, he has captured the duke's mistress as she probably really looked in life."

Edith watched Kai's eyebrows raise, and he examined the picture again with the new light of Edith's assessment. Then, he set his eyes on her. "I can see that you will be a valuable member of my scientific team."

"Scientific team . . ."

Kai nodded. "I already have a group of art experts based in Warsaw, and I am now putting together a team based in Kraków to cover the south. We will be . . . paying visits . . . to private collections like the ones you've already seen. And churches. Monasteries. Universities."

Edith felt a chill run up her spine. She wouldn't be so dumb this time.

"You are taking works of art."

Kai's eyebrows arched. "We are preserving works of significant interest to the Reich. We are creating a catalog of

Poland's finest artworks. The catalog will be presented to the Führer himself, who, as you may know, takes a personal interest in the history of art."

Edith fell silent, letting the information sink in. She was already responsible for the plunder of one family's art collection, and maybe even their capture by the Gestapo. Would she be forced to do it again? Did she have a choice? If she refused, what might happen to her? To her father?

As if he read her mind, Kai continued, "Your job, Fraülein Becker, will be to divide the newly safeguarded works into three categories: first selection, second selection, and third. *Wahl III* represents objects of representational purposes—silver services, ceramic pieces, carpets, and the like. Those in the category of *Wahl II* are pieces that, while not necessarily worthy of the Reich but of good quality, will be fully inventoried and stored. *Wahl I*, our first selection, will be photographed, documented, and carefully conserved. *Wahl I* will represent the finest masterpieces of Polish collections. No doubt this one"—he ran his fingertip along the ornate edge of the gilded frame and his eyes over the face of Cecilia Gallerani—"will be at the top of the list."

Edith protested. "But these works don't belong to the German government. They belong to museums, churches. To families . . . Prince Czartoryski and his wife . . ."

"No longer," he interrupted. Edith watched the muscles of his square jaw tighten. "In our care, these works will be studied, appreciated, preserved for future generations. If we leave them here, in the hands of Polacks, well . . . they face certain destruction. I'm sure you can appreciate that they are safer in our hands."

"But they belong to museums, to private owners," Edith insisted. "One might argue that many of these works cannot be assigned a monetary value. All the same, no money has changed hands. No legal transfer of the goods has taken place."

She thought she saw Kai's thin smile waver, but he said, "I'm afraid that's not the way the initiative is being carried out and between you and me, I would advise you not to repeat that assessment to anyone else." He turned his attention back to da Vinci's *Lady*.

Edith fell silent, feeling the burden of her role in the Czartoryski family's arrest fall over her again. "The paintings won't be kept in here, will they?" Edith asked, watching the men teeter under the awkward heft of a large Dutch landscape.

Kai shook his head and turned to Edith again. "No. This particular estate is a security risk from threats outside the house, and besides, our commander does not want to assign an officer to every window; they have more important jobs. As you know, there is also the risk of exposure from the sun on hot days. So this is only a holding place. You and I will be repacking a handful of the best works to take to Kraków."

"Kraków . . ."

"Hans Frank is our newly appointed governor-general of Poland. He is expecting us tomorrow. He will personally view our selections there, a handpicked group of pictures representing the best of Polish collections. I understand that Governor Frank is nearly as educated and passionate about art as our Führer."

"What does he want to do with them?" she asked, protectively reaching her hand toward the frame of da Vinci's portrait.

Kai shrugged. "I suspect that we will be returning with everything to Berlin."

Edith felt her heart surge. Was she going home? Already? "And we are going with them?" she asked.

"We won't want to let these treasures out of our sight, will we? You are playing an important role in the mission to safeguard these works of art, Fräulein Becker. You are a brave and intelligent woman."

Edith thought she saw his face turn pink but ignored his comment, no matter if it was offered humbly. Instead, she searched the reflective, patterned marbles in the floor, feeling a jolt of excitement pass through her. She was going home. Yet her elated feeling abruptly dissolved when she realized she would be back in Germany just as Heinrich's unit reached the front lines in Poland. She wasn't going to see him even if he passed through. She did her best to ensure the disappointment did not show on her face.

Kai carefully rewrapped the portrait in the protective paper, "One of our men will show you to your quarters upstairs. They will serve you a meal around 19:00 hours. They can hardly lure the dogs to the stove here in Poland, I'm afraid. Little more than pigs' feet and rotting cabbage. The good news is that we'll be back to German food soon enough. You should be ready to leave for Kraków with me at daybreak tomorrow."

He lifted the newly wrapped masterpiece off the table. As she watched him tuck the picture under his arm, Edith tried to formulate words. Her mouth opened but nothing came out. A group of nearly a dozen soldiers, who had suddenly appeared out of the shadows, fell in behind him.

Mühlmann then turned toward Edith, clicked his heels together, and reached out one hand, his palm facing down.

"*Heil Hitler,*" he saluted.

He turned and walked out of the ballroom with the painting hugged tightly to his side, leaving Edith standing alone underneath a gigantic crystal chandelier. It shuddered slightly as the last soldier in the line closed the door.

# 24
## DOMINIC

*Aachen, Germany*
*October 1944*

INSIDE THE CATHEDRAL OF AACHEN, THE SILENCE was absolute but for the crunch of gravel underneath boots as Hancock led the way inside. Dominic and Paul followed closely behind, Josie wedged between them.

In spite of the Monuments Men's best efforts, Dominic could see that Aachen Cathedral had been reduced to little more than a shell. Gaps and holes in the vaulted ceiling allowed shafts of sunlight, filtered by smoke, into its once-majestic interior. Part of one wall had been destroyed, the broken stone crushing one row of pews. A single tapestry, inexplicably left behind, stirred in the breeze that blew in through a ragged hole in the wall.

Then, Dominic heard it. A shuffling noise, somewhere near the pulpit. Before he could think, he swung his weapon around and took aim. The group sprang at once to tight alertness, guns raised. There was a frozen moment and Dominic heard the sound again, this time paired with a loud gasp.

"Come out with your hands up!" Paul shouted.

Dominic fixed his eyes on the pulpit, finger on the trigger, bracing himself for the burst of noise that would signal the start of yet another gunfight. But when the occupant of the pulpit emerged, it was with raised hands first. It was followed by a balding head and then, trembling in the sad tatters of his stained robe, the vicar of Aachen.

Dominic lowered his weapon. The old man clambered out to stand before them, as skeletal and shaky as his church. His robes were covered in fine gray ash that puffed to the floor when he moved, his dark eyes sunken and glassy with trauma. He said nothing, merely staring at them in mute capitulation.

"It's all right." It was Paul who spoke first, putting away his gun. "We're not here to hurt you."

The vicar did not look reassured. "Please," he said, his voice fragmented, shaky with fear, thick with a German accent. "There is nothing left here for you. Just be going."

"We're not going to take you prisoner," Paul said. He took a step nearer and held out a hand. "Are you injured?"

The vicar's eyes darted from one man to the other as they all lowered their weapons. "No," he stammered.

"Have you been here the whole time?" asked Dominic.

"Of course. I could not leave the church. My holy duty. I

stayed there—under there." He gestured toward the pulpit. "It was so loud. The walls were all falling down." He gazed around the cathedral, and his eyes filled with tears. "I just stayed like this." He lowered his shaking hands to his head and clasped them over his ears, screwing his eyes tightly shut, his face crumpling into an expression of abject terror.

Paul and Josie led the vicar to one of the aisles and sat him down there. Hancock dug in his pack for a canteen and some of his rations. He handed them to the skeletal older man, who introduced himself as Vicar Stephany. He ate in ravenous gulps; he had been hiding since the shelling started days ago, he said, too scared to come out even now, when they could still hear the distant whistle and thud of shells.

With no apparent threat to them now, Dominic turned, staring around the church some more. The cluster of medieval buildings must once have been majestic, but now it was little more than a strange skeleton of stone and glass. Great shards scattered the floor in different colors. He wondered how many centuries those mighty walls and beautiful windows had stood intact, and felt a pang of frustration and regret that he'd only arrived in time to see them destroyed.

On the altar of the church lay the finned figure of an unexploded bomb. It rested upside down, its sleek shape speaking of motionless menace. The aisles were filled with scattered objects left behind by citizens and soldiers who had sought refuge there before the bombing; books, toys, a broken ceramic cup, a woven sack with the name of a bakery printed on it. They must have thrown everything down and taken flight. A child's doll lay draped across the back of one of the pews, its button eyes staring at the ceiling. Dominic hoped its owner was alive to miss it.

"If you are being kind," Vicar Stephany was saying, "then why are you here? The soldiers, they tell me the Americans are here to destroy. What do you want?"

"We need your help, Vicar," said Hancock.

Stephany tilted his head, uncomprehending. "*My* help?"

"Yes. We're looking for the works of art that used to be in your church. You said there was nothing here for us to take . . . did you mean it's all gone?"

Stephany lowered his head. "Yes. It has all been taken."

"Taken?" said Hancock. "By whom?"

"The soldiers. The German soldiers." Stephany's mouth pulled down at the corners. "They take all the relics of Charlemagne, all precious things, that have been in the treasury for more than a thousand years. And other things—priceless. Priceless." He raised a shaking hand to his mouth. "They take it all and they leave the church and me here to be bombed."

"Did they say where they were taking it?" Hancock's tone was gentle.

"No. They just say that it is being saved from the Americans." His eyes were agony. "But you have been kinder to me than my own people."

"We're not here to take the art, Vicar," said Hancock. "We want to get it back and return it to its rightful owners. To you. They've got no right to steal it."

Stephany's eyes widened, then glistened in the dust-filled light. "It belongs to the cathedral. It always has. Hundreds of years. I was supposed to take care."

"There was nothing you could have done to stop all those men." Hancock laid one of his sculptor's hands on Stephany's knee. "We're going to do our best to get it back."

Tears filled Stephany's eyes and spilled over, washing clean pink lines through the ash on his face. He grasped Hancock's hand in both of his, his emaciated frame shaking with sobs. "I not do my job to protect it. Please," he begged. "Please. Bring it back."

Dominic stared, trying to comprehend what Stephany was going through. He had just survived a bombing that had killed hundreds—thousands—of people, almost including himself. Yet he was worried about the treasures that had once graced his cathedral.

Perhaps, Dominic considered, this mission did matter after all, at least to this poor man trapped under his pulpit.

The sound of footsteps at the door brought Dominic sharply back to reality; he spun, gun raised, only to lower it immediately when he recognized Stout and his retinue arriving. The lieutenant colonel's eyes scanned the group, resting on Stephany and Hancock. "Anything?"

Hancock shook his head. "There's nothing left here, sir.

Nothing except for him." He patted Stephany's shoulder. "He says that German soldiers have already carried off all the works that used to be here."

"At least they're not destroyed," said Stout.

"Yes, but they soon will be." Hancock shrugged hopelessly. "If we don't know where they are, there's nothing we can do to protect them from being bombed."

"On the contrary." Stout pulled a piece of paper from the inside of his jacket. "I just got a lead from Intelligence."

Hancock took the list and scanned it quickly, eyebrows rising. "German museum personnel, sir?"

"Exactly. Their names, roles, and whereabouts—if they are known." Stout nodded as Hancock started passing the list around. "Somebody on this list might tell us where some of the repositories of stolen art are. Hopefully we can get to at least some of the stuff in time."

Dominic stood on tiptoe to scan the list over Paul's shoulder. *Edith Becker, conservator, Alte Pinakothek in Munich, current whereabouts unknown*, he made out on the paper.

"There might be a few solid leads here, sir," said Hancock, grinning.

Before Stout could reply, there was a piercing whistle that made every fiber of Dominic's body spring to alertness. The scream of the shell sent them all scattering for cover. Yelping, Vicar Stephany flung himself under a pew. Paul and Dominic dove under the remnants of an arch, and the next moment, the shell struck the street just outside the church. The explosion rocked the floor, the sound of it making Dominic's ears ring. Stout was yelling, but Dominic couldn't hear his orders over the chaos. The next shell struck so close that it knocked Dominic to his knees, curled protectively around his rifle. He scrambled to his feet and hurried into the aisle, taking a quick glance around for his unit; Paul was at his side, other servicemen emerging from the pews with grim expressions. Journalists and officers took refuge under pews, arches, and doorways inside the church.

Dominic thought of Stephany, curled up for days under the pulpit, hands clapped over his ears, waiting for it all to be over. But Dominic knew he could never do that. He knew what his job was even before Stout ran into the aisle, beckoning them forward. He had to throw himself headlong into that chaos. So, raising his weapon, Paul's heavy footsteps behind him, he ran out into the square.

Time stood still in the heat of the skirmish. Dominic's focus was razor-sharp and etched in slow motion on facing the next Nazi uniform that appeared in the dusty haze, dodging the next bullet. The deafening sounds of the fight melted away until the shots from his rifle were a dull pop-pop in his ears. The enemy had taken refuge behind a heap of rubble opposite the church, and Dominic fired on every place where he perceived bullets. Smoke veiled the air and choked his lungs; he saw sprays of powder flying up where his bullets punched into the rubble, feeling a stab of both regret and relief every time the spray of gray ash became a spurt of blood and yet another enemy fell with a scream. He had stopped counting how many men he'd killed. He just fought and hoped he would survive and drew himself closer with every breath to destroying this evil once and for all, closer to going home to Sally.

It could have been thirty seconds. It could have been thirty minutes. Near the end of it Dominic was huddled against a huge stone that had fallen, whole, from the cathedral wall; he braced his gun against it and fired and fired and fired at the silhouettes of the Germans on the heap of rubble opposite.

And then, it was over.

Silence.

Dominic cautiously emerged from behind the stone. He glanced back toward the cathedral to see if the others were all right. Stout was crawling out from behind the cover of an arch, his weapon still smoking.

It was only then that he saw Paul.

His friend lay spread-eagled across the floor at the portal of the church, a dark red stain spreading out across his chest. His gun lay in a limp hand, and blood mixed with the ash beneath him. His eyes were closed.

"No!" Dominic threw down his weapon and ran toward his friend, tears choking him. He fell to his knees, heedless of the warm blood that soaked through his uniform, and seized Paul by the shoulders. "Blakely. Blakely!"

The blond lashes fluttered, and Paul opened his eyes. His face was gray and twisted with agony, his breath coming in rapid, shallow gasps that rattled in his throat. He dropped his gun and one of his huge hands clasped Dominic's arm.

"Bonelli," he groaned.

"Stay with me, Blakely." Dominic tore at Paul's uniform, trying to find the ghastly wound that was causing all this bleeding. "You'll be okay. We'll sort you out." He glanced around wildly. "Medic! We need a medic!"

"Bonelli. No." Paul groaned and lifted his head. "Dominic, man. Look at me."

Dominic met his friend's eyes. Despite the agony on his face, his eyes were blue and peaceful as a summer sky; they stared with piercing intensity. Paul took another breath, choked slightly, and gritted his teeth to ride out a wave of pain before he could speak. A smile seeped into his features.

"Keep drawing, my friend," he whispered. Then his eyes fluttered shut, and his strength seemed to leave him. His head lolled back, helmet thumping into the dirt.

"Blakely!" Dominic shook him. "Blakely!" He grasped at his friend's throat, feeling for a pulse he knew wouldn't be there. "No! NO!"

"Bonelli." It was Hancock's touch on Dominic's shoulder. "It's too late. There's nothing we can do for him."

"No!" Dominic yanked his shoulder out of Hancock's

grip. "Don't leave him here. We have to—he has to—" He choked on his own words, his vision blurred with tears.

"He's gone, Bonelli." Hancock gripped his arm.

Less than an hour before, two other servicemen had sat alongside Dominic in the back of the rumbling truck. Now, the same two men came forward with a tarp. Speechless, Dominic watched the men wrap Paul's body and carry it inside the cathedral.

# 25
## CECILIA

*Milan, Italy*
*November 1490*

**FROM THE CORRIDOR LEADING TO THE PALACE** kitchens, Cecilia caught sight of His Lordship's illegitimate daughter. It could only be, Cecilia thought. Little Bianca. The girl was about seven or eight years old, with black ringlets framing her round, fair cheeks. She sat at a large, rustic table in the kitchen, rolling dough with her hands. Cecilia had never seen the girl before; only heard about her. She presumed that she spent her days in the palace nursery with her tutors. Cecilia pressed her back against the wall in the corridor and watched the girl for a few long moments.

The smell of stewing veal shanks wafted through the corridor. Cecilia's mouth watered. It was hours until the next meal, but she was starving all the time now, it seemed. The life growing inside her demanded to be fed. She thought she might be able to ask the cook for something small, or perhaps snitch something herself from the palace pantries.

She had to find a way to tell Ludovico that she carried his child, she thought, before he figured it out for himself. But now, with the new knowledge that His Lordship had been long betrothed to Beatrice d'Este of Ferrara, Cecilia hardly knew what to say to him at all. She'd spent the last few days feigning sickness, sticking to her bedchamber and hoping that Ludovico would leave her alone long enough for her to find the right words, the right questions to ask. What could she do or say that would make him back out of his agreement with the Duke of Ferrara and take Cecilia for his wife instead? And what would happen to her when her pregnancy became known? She feared that Ludovico might immediately toss her out with the kitchen refuse, or even that someone might slit her throat in the middle of the night. She had not told anyone about her condition. Would Ludovico keep her child here under his roof, but banish Cecilia to some unknown fate? Where was this little girl's mother, anyway?

But one thing frightened Cecilia even more than being banished from the palace, even more than being stripped away from her child: she feared that she might not survive the birth at all. She had seen two of her own aunts go to the World to Come just as their newborns emerged into this one. She had seen the blood, had heard the last cries of the mother along with the first cries of the baby. It happened every day that women sacrificed their own lives as they gave it to others. As much as she wished she could unburden herself to someone, she could hardly face the truth herself. And the truth was that she was terrified.

At last, her hunger got the best of her and Cecilia stepped into the kitchen. The girl sensed Cecilia's presence and she looked up from her messy project. Cecilia scanned the kitchen—its dark, cavernous space cluttered with metal pots, dishes, rags, and old wooden furniture. It was empty. The girl only blinked at Cecilia, her pale blue eyes wide and fringed with black lashes.

"You are His Lordship's daughter."

The girl nodded, then returned to her work.

Cecilia approached the table and pulled out a chair. "I'm Cecilia."

"I know," said the girl.

"What are you making?"

"It's bread with raisins and orange." The girl was wearing an apron three times too big for her, perhaps given to her lovingly by one of the cooks.

"I would like to taste it. It looks good." Cecilia smiled.

"It is. It will be. After Cook bakes it for me."

"Can I try?"

Bianca said nothing but pushed a ball of dough across the table to Cecilia.

Silence stretched between them. Cecilia pressed the warm dough between her fingers and struggled to ask the one thing she wanted to know more than anything. No one else was in the room and Cecilia had to take advantage of the opportunity, she thought, because it might not come again.

"Your mother . . ." Cecilia hesitated. The girl looked up now, setting her pale blue eyes on Cecilia. "Where is she?"

## 26
## DOMINIC

*Aachen, Germany*
*December 1944*

DOMINIC SAT ON A ROCK OUTSIDE A TENT FLAP AND tried to draw the mother of his babies. For a long while, he stared at the blank piece of paper in the waning evening light. A nice piece of paper. A real one. A lined sheet that Josie had torn from her little steno book and had handed to Dominic before she left Aachen to join some journalists following another unit at the front.

A few strokes of the pencil, but the image wouldn't come. Dominic didn't want to consider the worst, that he had already forgotten what Sally looked like. How could that be? But her face seemed fuzzy and out of focus in his mind. His heart ached.

Dominic tapped the pencil on his knee and tried to think of what else to capture, what might help him warm up to a drawing of Sally, but his mind was a jumble of images. The tip of little Cecilia's upturned nose. Exploding sand at Omaha Beach. The cold, overwhelming darkness of a Pennsylvania coal mine. Paul Blakely splayed out before the doors of Aachen Cathedral, his chest soaked in red. Dominic set the pencil and paper down on the rock then stood up, clasped his hands behind his head, and paced back and forth in the dirt.

Behind him, snippets of German conversation filled the air. The tent was just one of hundreds housing German refugees who were doing their best to survive amid the unimaginable devastation. For three months, Dominic's unit had picked their way across the region to refugee camps and nearly ruined museums, seeking out any remaining art professionals who might be able to help them locate and protect priceless works of art. But many of these artists and museum staff proved to be mostly silent—perhaps afraid of what might happen to them if they said anything at all. Others were already long gone—fled to the still-enemy territory east of the Rhine.

Vicar Stephany had traveled along with the unit, doing his best to rally his fellow German refugees into helping find the art he cherished. But those efforts had had little effect. They'd found nothing; the blank expressions on the refugees' faces told Dominic that they were beginning to despair of finding value in life itself anymore. Far from the cheering crowds of overjoyed citizens welcoming their American saviors that the propaganda promised, the

Germans remained wary. Who could blame them? Half starved and fearful, they had little reason to trust the Americans. Dominic understood that liberation was going to be more complicated than he'd expected.

"Bonelli! Load up!" Dominic saw several of the men of his unit loading a truck near the drive into the camp. He saw Hancock helping an older man, a German museum worker, up into the truck. They'd found the old man half dead in a tent with walls so thin that Dominic could see daylight filtering through them; but the man had been alive enough to tell them that he was a retired art specialist, and he wanted to help. That had been good enough for Hancock. At least their foray into this camp had been more fruitful than the last.

Dominic slung his bag over his shoulder and ambled toward the truck. He left his fresh piece of paper and pencil sitting on the rock.

# 27
## EDITH

*Western Poland*
*October 1939*

EDITH STUDIED KAJETAN MÜHLMANN AS HE DOZED fitfully in the plush, upholstered seat of the swiftly moving train.

Even in the vulnerable state of sleep, he was difficult to read. Edith watched patches of filtered light skirt across the wide planes of Kai's face, illuminating coarse stubble in need of a razor. With his broad forehead and shoulders, and juglike jaw, Edith imagined him at home in a boxing ring. If she had passed him on the street, she would have never identified him as an art historian. But Mühlmann had risen high enough in the profession to be entrusted with personal transportation of priceless works of art. And clearly, he was a Party sympathizer. No one who wasn't would have been put in the role of SS Oberführer.

What was she doing here?

For a moment, Edith felt as if she had been pushed onto the stage of a surreal play, as if she was living inside of a dream. The smooth chug of the train pulled them forward, the lulling calm of the engine drawing them ever nearer to Kraków. In other circumstances, it might have been easy to nod off, but Edith's nerves were too frayed to sleep.

It was a far cry from the train ride that Edith had taken from Munich to Kraków, rattling along in a bare sleeping car, little more than barracks. Now, Edith and Kai occupied the first-class cabin of an elegant Pullman that they had all to themselves. The two dozen paintings that they had selected were carefully wrapped and secured, stacked carefully among the velvet-upholstered seats, tasseled draperies, and cherry tables of the luxury train car. In the glass-front cabinets, heavy silver serving pieces made a pleasant jangle as the wheels of the train clacked along at a steady pace.

At either end of the train car, a *Feldgendarm* was stationed, each with a machine pistol holstered at his waist. Edith watched the men's lean silhouettes darken the glass as they paced the narrow strip between the smoothly purring train cars. She supposed that they were positioned there to keep the Pullman and its contents secure, but Edith felt anything but safe in this strange, altered reality.

Kai's eyelids fluttered open and he fell into a fit of deep coughing. Edith quickly looked away, studying a grove of maple trees whose leaves were beginning to turn golden. Had he seen her watching him?

"After we unload the pictures in Berlin, you could return to Munich," he said, clearing his throat. His voice was low and thick, drawing the vowels out in his distinctive Austrian manner. Edith's heart quickened, and she wondered if he had really been asleep, or whether he had sensed her watching him all along.

She nodded but said nothing, watching the deserted Polish landscape tick by outside the window. In the distance, Edith could make out curls of smoke rising into the air, a smoldering pile. A farm? A town?

Her brow must have been visibly knotted because Kai pressed her. "Won't you be happy to go home?"

Edith nodded and met his gaze. "Oh yes. It's just . . . There is a chance that my fiancé Heinrich may pass through on his way to eastern Poland. I expect that he will be here within a few days. Or perhaps he is here already. I thought I might have a chance to see him, if only for a moment." She shrugged. "Silly of me to think . . ."

Dr. Mühlmann nodded, then rubbed his palms together as if warming them. "Difficult." A shadow crossed his face, and his mouth pulled into a grim line.

"It was just a hope, that's all."

"Nothing wrong with hope," he said. "But things will not be the same when he returns. Your fiancé will be a changed man. You must prepare yourself that things will be different. That *he* will be different. I saw it happen to my friends who served in the Great War."

Edith didn't want to think about that. She wanted her Heinrich back. Could Kai sympathize with wanting to resume their lives the way they were before?

Dr. Mühlmann pressed his lips together. "You have your family in Munich?" he asked.

"Just my father, and some distant cousins," she said. "My papa is an old man now, frail and weak. He was once a well-known professor at the Academy of Fine Arts, but he no longer remembers even the smallest things. I worry about him every minute that I am away. It has been challenging to find a reliable nurse . . ." She forced herself to stop. Had she shared too much?

"Well," he said, and his mouth turned into a thin line again. "I hope you get home soon to see your father."

"So do I," said Edith, meeting his eyes. "This is no place for art historians."

Kai chuckled, which brought on another fit of coughing. He recovered, saying, "Yes. I wrote my dissertation on Baroque fountains in Salzburg. I never set out to be the Special Representative for the Protection and Securing of Artworks in the Occupied Eastern Territories." A tight grin spread across his face.

"But there must be something we can do to stop it?" Edith felt her voice waver. "Surely there is a better way to ensure the safety of these works." She gestured to the crates secured among the plush, upholstered seats.

Kai ran his broad hand across the stubble of his chin,

considering. "I assure you that these works are much safer in our possession—and within the confines of Germany—than they will ever be out there." He gestured to the bleak landscape outside the train window. "Poland will soon be reduced to rubble; that should be obvious to you. Also, fräulein, although I do not dispute that you have already made an important contribution, you must realize that this initiative is much bigger than you and me. We play but a small role."

"But . . ." Edith interrupted. "We could have intervened before . . . before the prince and his wife . . . before these pictures were stripped from their owners in such a brutal manner! Did they have to leave Poland in the hands of the Gestapo?"

A shadow seemed to pass over Kai's face, just like a storm cloud suddenly blocking the sun. Edith paused and regretted sharing her assessment. Could Kai have her arrested? Killed, even?

He seemed to read her mind. "Governor Frank," he said, "will not hear anything of the sort and I strongly advise you, fräulein, to keep such assessments to yourself. Very little of what happens in Poland escapes Governor Frank's eyes and ears. There may be . . . unintended consequences. Consider yourself warned."

A long pause stretched out between them and Edith wondered if anything at all was in her power to change.

"May I ask you something?" Edith said, leaning forward

in her seat. "Do you believe in what you—in what we—are doing?"

Kai hesitated. Edith watched his eyes flicker toward the silhouette of one of the guards at the end of the train car. Then he leaned forward, too, met her gaze, and lowered his voice. "We are at war, fräulein. We are charged with confiscating and sequestering enemy property; that is our job. And as I have already pointed out, we are ensuring that these works survive for future generations. Apart from that, our own personal views matter very little."

Edith watched another shadow pass over Kai's face, aging him years in just a few seconds. The train whistle let out a shrill cry. They passed into a tunnel, and the interior of the train car fell into blackness.

# 28
## DOMINIC

*Aachen, Germany*
*January 1945*

NOT LONG AGO, THE SEURMONDT MUSEUM MUST HAVE been splendid. Dominic observed the grand staircase running through the center of the building, the colonnades of the atrium, the vaulted ceilings painted to resemble the sky with mythical creatures floating above his head. Now, just like the many other old buildings he'd seen in the past months, the museum stood in ruin. Even inside, frigid gusts of wintry air blew through the weave of Dominic's fatigues, chilling him to the bone.

Judging by the unhappy expression on Captain Hancock's face, this latest walk through another art collection was a disappointment. Dominic kept one eye on his surroundings for possible threats as he watched his commander pull open the drawers of a hulking, dirt-covered desk in one of the museum offices, looking for any clues as to the whereabouts of the Seurmondt's masterpieces. Dominic stepped over broken bricks and powdered plaster from the gaping hole in the wall to reach the other side of the room, where two men were exploring the contents of a file cabinet.

A thick spread of dust was settling on everything, and not just from the battle. Fall had slipped into winter; Dominic knew that, outside the museum, the landscape around them was reduced to rubble covered with a sparkle of ice. A few sheets of paper fluttered out into the breeze, mingling with the snowflakes that blew in through the hole.

Across the room, Captain Hancock spun into the nearest dust-covered office chair. He pulled open a drawer and yanked out a stack of notebooks; he grabbed the nearest one and began to flip through it. Dominic's legs felt leaden; he wondered where Hancock found all his energy.

"They have to have taken them somewhere, maybe even somewhere close by," Hancock said.

Instead of responding, Lieutenant Commander Stout slammed the cabinet drawer shut. It shuddered, and a scattering of shell casings and snow slid off the top. The three men looked up simultaneously at the gaping hole in the ceiling of the office. It had punched through the floors of the building, leaving a tattered array of splintered wood and crumbled stone all the way up to a circle of gray sky.

A knock on the doorjamb heralded the arrival of another MP to relieve Dominic so that he could slink off to wolf down his tin of C-rations. As he wandered into an adjacent gallery, Dominic saw evidence of the hot battle that had taken place between the Allied forces and the Germans. Whole galleries and corridors were filled with debris. Many darkened pictures, pieces of ceramic, and small sculptures were still standing here and there, but for all their combing through the wreckage, they'd found no evidence of the major masterpieces this museum was supposed to house. Abandoned bits of equipment were scattered in the elegant passages where the upper class of Aachen had spent many a peaceful evening enjoying the centuries-old art that had disappeared. Gaping spaces and bare hooks on the walls counted the missing pictures.

The gallery's floor had once been polished to a mirror finish. Now, it was cracked by war and scratched by the heavy boots of the soldiers who had dumped themselves and their belongings around the floor. The cold gnawed at Dominic's gut; when he pushed the door open and stepped inside the gallery, he was greeted with the smell of cooking soup. Despite himself, he took a deep breath and smiled. Somehow, Vicar Stephany could make even their meager and tasteless rations smell like a real meal.

"Dominic!" The vicar was bent over a pot on the little campfire he'd cobbled together out of bits of wreckage. "Come! Sit. Eat. You look frozen."

While Stephany concocted an unlikely meal in an unlikely place, two servicemen and the German art professional whom they had located in one of the refugee camps were examining the few pictures still hanging on the gallery's walls. One of the men scribbled furiously while the German called out details for a hastily documented catalog.

Dominic sank his weary body down onto his pack and gratefully accepted the bowl that the vicar offered. He spooned up a mouthful of hot soup and relished the warmth as it slid down his throat.

Stephany's transformation from the gaunt, shaking man they'd fished out of the cathedral wreckage was startling. At first the officers had resisted his attempts to follow them; but later, realizing the value of having a native German on their side—especially one so personally invested in the recovery of stolen art—they had relented. Now, Stephany seemed like a new man. His skeletal face had filled out into an enthusiastic, ruddy visage with an easy smile. He traveled everywhere with the unit, praying over them and occasionally attempting to sprinkle the grubby troops with holy water. Those who were not as practiced as Dominic grumbled, calling him a crazy old man, but everyone appreciated his sunny presence—and his talent at reviving army rations with scraps of food picked up along the way.

Dominic glanced across the room at the German museum worker they'd located in the refugee camp. Stephany followed Dominic's gaze. *"Ach,"* he said, spooning up another bowl of soup. "He is getting better." He limped over to the old man and proffered the bowl, speaking rapidly in German. Wide-eyed, the old man took it and sipped tentatively. A smile spread across his features, and he turned back to the giant ledger lying on the floor beside him with more enthusiasm, eating the soup as he turned the pages looking for evidence of where those masterpieces might have gone.

Stephany's gesture of kindness reminded Dominic of Paul. A pang of agony shot through him so powerfully that nausea rose in his stomach. He set the bowl down, his appetite gone, and stared sightlessly at the floor. Every night he saw the agony in Paul's eyes, the cracked quality of his voice as he choked out his last words: *Keep drawing.* And every day, when he sat to one side at meals, when he faced the gunfire among the other men, when he listened to the unfamiliar breathing of the man in the bunk above him, he missed Paul a little more.

When would the longing cease? Dominic closed his eyes against the pain and hugged himself, sick of yearning for people he loved. He did his best to hold out hope of seeing Sally and little Cecilia again. Would he ever hold his new baby?

As for his own drawing, he hadn't put pencil to paper since Paul died. He just couldn't bring himself to do it. It was for art that his best friend's life had been sacrificed. Hancock had begun to receive intelligence reports about possible hidden stashes all over Germany and even farther east. And Hancock and Stout were crazy enough to risk everything for their quest. But was it really worth it?

Stephany had been watching Dominic. He spoke gently, prompting him out of his reverie. "You are Italian, yes?"

Dominic looked up, relieved that his thoughts had been interrupted. "Pittsburgh, actually. But my parents came over from Italy."

"You know Leonardo da Vinci?"

Dominic smiled despite himself, still feeling a stirring at the name of the grand master. "Of course. One of my favorites."

Stephany beamed. "We keep looking. Before long, we find one."

Dominic chuckled at Stephany's assessment. At least one of them remained optimistic, he thought.

"You are troubled," Stephany said, setting his bright eyes on him.

"What?"

Stephany gestured with his spoon. "I see that something disturbs you."

Dominic hesitated. "Lots of things about this war disturb me, Vicar."

"Yes. But you also saw your friend killed," said Stephany gently. "Not an easy thing."

Emotion boiled in Dominic's chest. Suddenly, he wanted to scream and punch something, but he swallowed and kept his voice under control. "I just wonder if it's worth it," he said. "I know you really want your church treasures back. But is it worth Blakely's life—and the lives of all the others who have been lost?"

Stephany paused, reflecting. "I understand. Mr. Blakely. He was not wanting to come on this mission?"

"I mean . . ." Dominic swallowed. "Blakely was resolved to go wherever he was sent, I think. Isn't that what we signed up for? And he believed the Monuments Men's mission was important. Look. I think it's great that these guys are trying to save something for humanity and all," Dominic said, gesturing toward Hancock, "but I don't see how it's worth putting even one life at risk, much less . . . millions. You have heard, Vicar, of what Hitler's troops have done in Poland? Millions of people massacred in the ghettos, sent to work camps for no reason. How is that possible? And yet . . ." Dominic huffed out a breath. "Here we are, sitting on our asses in some godforsaken museum. Sorry," he said, pulling at the roots of his hair.

But Stephany remained unfazed. "Yes. An evil unseen for generations. I know." He turned to face Dominic, his eyes intent and serious. "But let me ask you something, my friend. If we were looking for a store of food or something else that would keep us alive, would it be worth it?"

Dominic frowned. "I guess so."

"And if you stay alive through the war, what will you do when you go home?"

"I'll kiss my wife and babies." Emotion rose in Dominic's throat. "I'll go back to work in the mines. And . . ." He paused, remembering the happiest times of his life: sketching Sally as she washed the dishes. "And I guess I'll start drawing again, one of these days."

"See there." Stephany touched his shoulder, smiling. "We have already lost so much. We cannot lose what we love, too." He gestured at the men inventorying the pictures left stacked against the wall. "Imagine a world without art, without music, dancing, without the things we do not really need. It would not be a world worth living in."

Dominic felt his heart lighten a bit. He picked up his soup again, half listening to the men writing down a description of one of the few paintings left on the wall.

"Market scene," said the old German, as the serviceman scribbled in his notebook. "Seventeenth-century German, possibly an imitator of Altdorfer . . ."

A serviceman entered suddenly from one of the staircases leading down to the lobby, holding a huge book. "Is Hancock here?"

"I'm here." Hancock spoke behind Dominic, making him jump. "What is it, Private?"

"A museum catalog, sir. Look."

Dominic and the others clustered around the serviceman as he knelt and opened the book on the floor. The neat lines of text were marked up in red and blue pencil.

Hancock flipped through the book, giving muffled exclamations of excitement. "This is what we were looking for!"

Stephany and the art professor leaned over Dominic's shoulder to see. The professor waved his arms and gabbled in rapid German; Stephany had to ask him twice to slow down before he could translate. "He says we will find many paintings like this," he said. "This is an official register. Village schools. Courthouses. Cafés. Other places where paintings and sculptures might be stored."

"But look at that." Hancock tapped a notation at the bottom of the page with his finger. "My German isn't perfect, but I see the word 'Siegen' in there."

"Yes," said Stephany. "It says that some of the most important objects have been taken to a mine there."

"But that's all the way on the other side of Germany, across the Rhine," said Hancock, dismayed. "I can't imagine these pictures would have survived that journey intact." Dominic looked up at the commander's furrowed brow. Perhaps this meant that they could just clean out Aachen and then be done with this crazy mission.

But Hancock raised his head, plastering his smile back onto his face. "Anyway," he said, "it will be a long time before we make it that far."

Dominic's shoulders fell. As much as he would have loved to see a painting by Leonardo da Vinci in person, he wanted to go home more. He had no desire to pick his way through the devastation all the way across Europe.

Dominic felt Vicar Stephany squeeze his shoulder, and he turned to see the old man's winning grin.

"I tell you, we will find these treasures. You see, my friend? There is hope."

# 29
## EDITH

*Kraków, Poland*
*October 1939*

**THEY HEARD THE ROARING ENGINES OF THE ARMORED** vehicles first.

Edith watched Kai Mühlmann pace nervously from one side of the Jagiellonian Library reading room to the other. He stopped before a Dutch painting depicting a lush still life and chewed on the ragged edge of his fingernail. His face was dire, his wide jaw set and his mouth frozen in a thin line. He stopped to adjust the angle of an easel, then began to pace the room again, lacing his fingers tightly behind his back. In the background, they heard vehicle doors slamming, and the tread of boots in the library vestibule.

All afternoon, Edith and Kajetan Mühlmann had supervised the unloading and display of the two dozen paintings they had accompanied on the train from Jarosław. The great reading room of the Jagiellonian Library now resembled an art museum rather than a repository for rare books. The works Mühlmann had judged the best of those confiscated from Polish collections were now exhibited around the room.

The Great Three. That's how Mühlmann had begun to refer to the three most valuable works pulled from Polish collections—Rembrandt's *Landscape with the Good Samaritan*, Raphael's *Portrait of a Young Man*, and da Vinci's *Lady with an Ermine*. In addition to those pictures, now prominently displayed, there were a handful of masterful landscapes and portraits, all of them, *Wahl I*. First tier.

The priceless paintings were carefully placed to take advantage of the diffused, natural light emanating from the windows high up in the ceiling coffers. Around them, the walls were lined with thousands of books, extending some three stories high, accessible by a series of angular staircases and precarious ladders.

The reading room smelled as if it were in the process of slow decay, everything covered in layers of dust. Still, apart from the painting conservation studio, there was nowhere Edith would rather be than a library of crumbling books. In other circumstances, she would have relished spending the day here, wending her way up the stairs to pull long-neglected volumes off the shelves. It would be a thing for a peaceful time, for a daydream. For now, she had to keep her head down and follow orders. What choice did she have? She would be home soon enough. That's what Kai had promised her on the train.

As the doors of the library opened, Edith positioned herself beside Mühlmann, who had finally stopped his pacing. They waited.

Soon, a line of officers in long coats filed into the reading room, pistols strapped prominently around their waists. Edith watched Kai brush lint from his uniform. The men saluted in Kai's direction. If they took note of Edith at all, they showed no sign.

In the midst of another swirl of men in uniform, a great buzzard of an officer, his field coat heavy with decoration, strode into the room. His hair dark and slicked, his nose a ridged beak, the man raked his dark eyes like a bird of prey across the reading room. Edith took a step back into the shadows, pressing her body between two easels.

*The new governor of Poland*, she thought. Hans Frank. It could only be.

"*Sieg Heil!*" The man extended his arm, saluting Kai.

Kai returned the gesture. "Governor Frank." For a few moments, the men stood face-to-face, both broad-chested, preening birds, their jaws set and their eyes locked. As they raised their right hands in the gesture of Nazi unity, Edith had trouble recognizing Kai, the opaque yet gentle-mannered art historian she had begun to know.

After the formal greeting, Hans Frank's manner softened. He offered his right hand to Kai, pumping it vigorously. "My friend," he said. "How gratifying to find you here." Frank was close enough to Edith that she could smell the strong aroma of soap and pine. His black hair was raked back against his head as if he had used shoe polish to manicure it.

Kai gestured for Governor Frank to follow him toward the first painting they had placed on an easel, a small eighteenth-century French painting that showed a view of an idealized landscape, a classical temple in a lush setting. A small group of soldiers followed, and Edith was left to stand alone.

Was she invisible? She hesitated, unsure whether or not to draw attention to herself.

She watched the governor run his dark eyes over Raphael's *Portrait of a Young Man*. He was rapt, she could see. Kai held his full attention, giving Governor Frank details about where and how the pictures were located, and what made them worthy of preservation under the Reich.

A few of the soldiers idled at the doorway to the reading room, looking bored. Another few straggled behind Kai and Hans Frank, listening to Kai's description of the paintings. One of the soldiers reached out to a small portrait as if he were going to run his fingers down its surface. Edith stepped forward, ready to stop him, but he hesitated, put his hands behind his back, and then continued on.

"We do not know the identity of the sitter," Kai was explaining to Governor Frank, "but some believe that Raphael may have painted it as a self-portrait."

Edith felt a flash of envy, that feeling she always experienced when she heard someone who held the confidence and talent to share their knowledge. It was one of her father's gifts, the ability to make the viewer really "see" the work in a way they hadn't before. Her heart ached that his brilliant mind had been degraded in such a cruel way. Her heart leapt a little as she clutched onto the hope that she would soon see her father.

Governor Frank gazed intently at each painting, nodding his admiration. Finally, he stopped in front of the *Lady with an Ermine*. Kai paused, giving him a moment to absorb the picture. The way the governor was looking at it made Edith squirm. It was a hungry, consumptive look, the look of an obsessive collector. She had seen it many times among collectors and would-be collectors as they browsed the galleries at the Alte Pinakothek.

"It is considered the first modern portrait," Mühlmann began. "Da Vinci has not painted her in profile as portraits had been painted before, or as an idealized woman of mythical status."

Edith's heart began racing in her chest as she heard her own words come out of Mühlmann's mouth. Was he taking credit for her knowledge of the picture? She felt a streak of heat across her face and neck. How dare he take ownership of her own research, knowledge he may not have known if she had not fed him these very words?

Mühlmann continued. "Instead, da Vinci has gone

beyond tradition. He has captured the duke's mistress as she probably looked in life . . ."

"Where did you find this?" Frank interrupted, a demanding tone in his voice.

Kai stammered to a stop, seemingly annoyed to have been stalled in the middle of sharing his newfound knowledge. "Our own Fräulein Becker found it in a stash the Party obtained from the Czartoryski Palace."

"Fräulein Becker," the governor said.

Kai raised a hand to motion for Edith to join them. She stepped into the light.

The governor turned his dark eyes to Edith now. Greed. Yes, that was it, that look on his face. She cringed inside, wishing that she could fade back into the shadows.

Edith gathered her nerves. "We found it hidden in a secret room of the family palace at Pełkinie, walled up behind brick and mortar."

"Forgive me," Kai said, gently reaching for Edith's elbow. "May I introduce Edith Becker? She came to us from the Alte Pinakothek in Munich," he said, "highly recommended by Generaldirecktor Buchner for her experience in Italian Renaissance painting, and especially in conservation. Graduated in the top of her class from the Academy of Fine Arts."

Hans Frank took her in with his dark eyes, and Edith wished that Kai would stop heaping praise on her. Now, a few of the soldiers were also watching her. Just as she had back in that museum meeting room in Munich, somehow she had made herself the center of attention.

Governor Frank nodded. "I am impressed, fräulein." He took her hand in greeting, gripping a little more firmly than she would like. "You may know that it was our Führer's greatest dream to attend the Academy of Fine Arts in Vienna, and I myself considered a career in art before my father pressed me on to law school. I look forward to having many conversations with you."

"Thank you." She met his gaze, hoping that he would not feel the clamminess of her palm. Her instinct told her to pull her hand away, but she did not want to give this boorish man the satisfaction of having rattled her composure. She held on until he finally let go and spun around on his heel. He addressed Kai again.

"*Sehr gut*! I am pleased," he said, and she saw Kai's mouth spread into a thin line that looked more like a grimace than a smile.

For a few long, silent moments, Governor Frank strode around the room again, running his careful gaze over the little exhibition. Then, he stopped and pointed a long finger at three paintings. He addressed the soldiers following him. "This one, this one, and this one." Edith felt all the hairs rise on the back of her neck. Raphael's *Portrait of a Young Man*. Rembrandt's *Landscape*. And da Vinci's *Lady with an Ermine*.

The Great Three.

"These will stay with me in Kraków," he said to Kai. "You may take the rest to Berlin." He dismissed the other pictures with a quick flick of his hand. The soldiers moved into action. Edith watched as one young soldier grasped the frame of the Raphael and pulled it from the easel.

"Wait!" Edith cried. Without thinking, she rushed forward and grasped the forearm of the soldier with the painting in his hands. Under her grip, the soldier froze. For Edith, time seemed to stand still. Would they listen to her now that she had been the center of their focus? Would she have any say in the matter at all? But the soldier turned away from her and all the men in the room turned their attention to Hans Frank instead.

"You cannot just take them!" Edith cried, feeling her chest tighten and heave. "They don't belong to . . . us. They were all part of the Czartoryski family's own collection. Their ancestors purchased these pictures in Italy two hundred years ago . . ."

She watched Kai's face blanch. "*All* these paintings are to be crated for transport to Berlin, sir. We have orders." Kai stepped in front of Edith, shielding her view of Governor Frank with his broad shoulders. He was protecting her, she realized.

Frank stepped forward, contemplating. "Well," he said, "the rest of them may go to Berlin. These . . . selections . . . belong here. They were already in Polish collections, and they may stay here." The soldiers made a move again.

"It isn't possible, Governor Frank," Kai interjected. "These paintings . . . They have all been slated to be safeguarded in the new museum the Führer is building. He will have the most valuable and priceless artifacts, paintings, statues, and other items from all around the world on display there . . ."

"I am well aware of the museum plans," Frank interrupted, waving his hand in dismissal again. "I myself have been intimately involved. But what does not appear in Berlin will not be missed." Frank gestured for another soldier to lift Rembrandt's *Landscape with the Good Samaritan* from the easel. The man jumped into action.

"Hans . . ." Kai reached out for Frank's forearm. Edith surmised that Kai must have a long relationship with Governor Frank if he dared to address him by his first name, dared to touch him, unsolicited. Kai lowered his voice, seemingly out of earshot of the soldiers. "It's Göring."

For the first time, Edith saw Governor Frank hesitate.

Göring. Hermann Göring? The leader of the Party? The name seemed to give Hans Frank pause. For a few long moments, the governor scratched the bridge of his beaklike nose.

Kai continued. "Göring knows about them already, Hans. He has personally signed for the paintings to come to Berlin. He has seen facsimiles. He has seen the inventories that we have prepared. He is expecting a da Vinci, a Rembrandt, a Raphael, others. If we are to hold anything back here in Poland, then someone will have to answer to him. I do not wish that person to be me. I am sure you can respect that, sir."

Edith felt nervous for Kai. She wouldn't want to fight the governor. And she would not want to have her own credibility scrutinized by the likes of Reichsmarshall Göring.

Frank finally nodded, his mouth turned into a deep frown. "I see."

Kai continued. "I assure you that they will be well secured. Fräulein Becker and I will accompany them personally to Berlin by armored train. We have troops assigned specially to our train convoy. Do you see? Returning them to the Reich is the only way we can ensure that these masterpieces will be safeguarded. Things are more . . . unstable here at the front," he said. "I don't have to tell you that." His voice trailed off.

The governor turned toward Edith now and his mouth spread, a thin line. "Miss Becker," he said. "I hope we get the chance to talk further next time I see you."

In spite of herself, Edith returned his civility with a silent glare.

Governor Frank turned and marched toward the door. The soldiers rushed to formation, following his retreat.

As the men exited the library, air seemed to flow back into the room for the first time. Edith felt a wave of relief wash over her. She could not stomach the thought of Frank walking out the door with da Vinci's *Lady* in his grip. It had been difficult enough to watch Kai take it from her own hands.

Once they heard the rumble of the engines outside, Edith let out the breath she'd been holding and let her shoulders slump. "Thank goodness. There's no telling how that might have come out if you were not brave enough to speak up."

All the color seemed to have drained from Kai's face. "I had no choice, Edith. How am I to go back to Berlin without all the promised pieces? I would be shot." He paused, and Edith realized that he was not exaggerating. "Göring is not an easy man. When he gives an order, it is to be done, without question. The same as if it came from the Führer himself. There is no excuse I could have invented to explain why these pictures weren't with us." He ran his palms over the top of his skull.

"I do not envy you. I would not want to get in between those two men."

"No," Kai said, shaking his head vigorously. "Exactly what I was trying to avoid. I cannot afford to leave anything on the list behind here in Poland. Especially not in Frank's hands."

"Then I am glad the governor didn't continue to push."

Kai began to return the velvet drapes over each picture, protecting their delicate surfaces. They would spend the next day supervising their crating and reloading onto the train, this time bound for Berlin.

"We are pressed into service, but what business do we have in these machinations of war?" Edith saw Kai's brow wrinkle. Behind his opaque exterior, she could see that he was rattled. "As you said yourself, Edith, this is not a place for art historians."

While Kai managed the larger Rembrandt, Edith walked over to the easel with da Vinci's *Lady*. Carefully, she lifted the picture by the frame and laid it flat on a large tarp spread out on a nearby table.

*Oh, lady*, she said silently to the girl in the picture. For a moment she stared into Cecilia Gallerani's lively eyes as if she expected her to respond. *It seems you've attracted the attention of a greedy, obsessive man. A man who can change your fate with the flick of his wrist.* Edith hesitated. *Well*, she continued silently, *maybe you know what that's like? But the truth is that it's* my *fault that you are in this mess. I'm sorry. And I promise you, I will do whatever is within my power to get you out of it.*

# Part III
*Hidden from View*

# 30
## LEONARDO

*Milan, Italy*
*November 1490*

**WHY DO SOME WOMEN INSIST ON ENTANGLING THEM-**
selves with obsessive men? Dangerous men. Men who do
not deserve their attentions. As in Florence, so too in Milan.

I ponder the question while I push the delicately speck-
led quails' eggs to one side of my plate. I have already informed His Lordship's kitchen staff that I do not consume
the flesh of animals, nor even their eggs. But they persist.
Perhaps one of the dishwashers or chambermaids might
pluck them off my plate when it goes back to the kitchen.
All for the better. I only want to make sure that I do not
offend His Lordship by refusing to eat them.

But Ludovico il Moro is not watching me.

At the head of the table, His Lordship is tearing par-
tridge flesh from a spiky bone, his eyes focused across the
room. I follow his gaze to Lucrezia Crivelli, the girl who

attends to Signorina Cecilia. Lucrezia stands in a small clutch of ladies-in-waiting, their backs against the wall, ready to respond to the smallest need of the ladies at the table. But Lucrezia and the other ladies-in-waiting have made themselves anything but invisible. They are brightly adorned as if gemstones come to life—sapphire, ruby, emerald. Lucrezia herself appears like a bright flower in a dress the color of a ripe tomato. She has entwined a matching bright ribbon into her dark braid and colored her cheeks.

I have never understood the Milanese court's taste for these vulgar colors. My eyes turn upward to the painted vaults of the dining hall. The ceilings of each public room in His Lordship's palace are garishly colored, frescoes hastily turned out by a team of painters chosen on the basis of their low bid rather than on merit. I might propose to His Lordship to do something entirely different, given the opportunity.

In many ways, I think, Lucrezia Crivelli is the opposite of dear Cecilia, at least in the way I have decided to portray her. She will be fashionably but modestly clothed in a silk shernia draped over one shoulder. She will wear her newest velvet gown, the one with the square-necked bodice and a pattern of knots. Cecilia has told me that the dress was a gift from His Lordship, along with a long string of onyx beads to offset her pale skin. I have sketched her hair in two heavy swaths, pulled tightly along her cheeks. The overall effect will be one of elegance, of understatement, the very opposite of this castle's cheaply painted ceilings and walls.

I watch Ludovico il Moro's black beard come to life as he chews. His gaze has not strayed from Lucrezia. With his beadlike eyes and nose like a beak, he resembles a great bird of prey, and I cannot help but think of the hundreds of drawings I have made of hawks in preparation for my flying machine. And then, I see that Lucrezia recognizes his gaze. She smiles, a shy yet comely grin.

I must complete this portrait of Cecilia Gallerani as quickly as possible, I think, for in this place, things might change at any moment.

# 31
## CECILIA

*Milan, Italy*
*November 1490*

"YOU MUST TAKE CARE NOT TO TRUST PEOPLE WITH your whole heart. They may not always have your best interest in mind, even if they seem kind on the surface."

Cecilia heard Master Leonardo's words, but she didn't fully listen. She kept thinking about what His Lordship's bastard daughter had told her in the palace kitchen. Her mother had gone to a convent, the girl had said. She knew little of her mother, the girl had told Cecilia, matter-of-factly; only what she wrote in letters Bianca received on her birthday, on her saint's day, or at Christmas.

Cecilia's heart ached. What would become of her and her own child? Would they be torn apart, the child trapped behind the walls of this castle and Cecilia trapped behind the walls of a convent? She did not know how to reveal her secret, the consequences of which loomed large, frightening, and unknown.

Cecilia's thoughts were interrupted by the sight of three armed *condottieri* coming through the castle gates on muscular black horses. Their armor reflected the sun and the colored plumes on their helmets must have made them visible from a long distance, Cecilia thought. Hardly a way to sneak up on anyone. She expected hired mercenaries to be more subtle.

All morning, Cecilia and Leonardo had enjoyed the fresh air of the castle courtyard, where Master da Vinci told her they might take advantage of the natural, filtered light that would make for a more beautiful portrait. He had brought a stack of sketches in a leather portfolio. He pulled out a fresh page and began to draw, but, with a troubled look on his face, he held his pen in midair and paused.

"You see, *cara*? Even within these castle walls, some people feel . . . threatened. His Lordship himself must actively defend not only his territories but his own life."

Cecilia tried her best to take Master Leonardo's words into good conscience. She knew that Master Leonardo was intelligent, that he knew things of all manner of subjects, of matters far beyond the castle walls. When she had asked, he had shown her his notebooks, full on both sides of each page with a strange, left-reading, backward handwriting that she failed to interpret. Treatises on military machines and hydraulics, he had told her. On optics, on anatomy, even on the flight of birds. Drawings of Madonnas, of saints. Of beautiful, angelic-looking young boys.

"And His Lordship's nephew. He is also a threat?" she asked.

Leonardo huffed. "Especially young Gian Galeazzo. He is only a boy but he is still the Duke of Milan," he said, lowering his voice to a whisper. "Between you and me, I fear what might happen as he grows old enough to take matters—" Leonardo stopped himself, looking behind him instinctively to see if anyone might overhear their conversation. "But you, my dear. You yourself are in a position of relative power right now, as His Lordship's companion," he continued, "whether you realize it or not. Someone might try to take something from you, or perhaps withhold it. As I said, I advise you to watch those closest to you."

But Cecilia felt anything but powerful. Instead, she feared for her life.

# 32
## DOMINIC

*Bad Godesberg, Germany*
*March 1945*

HERR WEYRES WAS A SHADOW OF A MAN, HIS EYE sockets dark and haunted. He shivered under a threadbare blanket on a kitchen chair, his gaze darting around the room, focusing on each American in turn as they clustered around him. Dominic imagined that the war must have reduced Weyres, who said he had once been an architect and an assistant to the provincial art conservator, to this shivering bundle of nerves.

"You're telling me the lists were all lost?" Hancock asked.

"All of them," Weyres said. Behind him, a hefty woman—Weyres's distant cousin, who'd been giving him shelter—cursed in German as the stove sputtered and struggled in the icy wind. The men hardly fit into the little kitchen. They filled the bare room with a forest of tall soldiers. The woman's house had been half bombed. Shattered glass lined the window frames; the tattered remnants of curtains had been drawn fruitlessly over the empty holes, fluttering in the desolate wind. She attempted to relight the fire under the copper pot that sat on the stove, trying to heat water for powdered coffee. The soldiers barely spared her a glance as Captain Hancock spoke to Herr Weyres.

"All of them," Weyres repeated, drawing the blanket a little closer over his shoulders. "Burned in the bombings or torn apart by my own people." Freezing rain pelted through a hole in the roof that gaped like a missing tooth. Dominic huddled a little deeper into the collar of his greatcoat, watching Herr Weyres's hollow eye sockets. "Why would they take and destroy their own culture?"

The look on the old architect's face had become all too familiar to Dominic and the others over the past few weeks as they followed the trail of Allied victories east. First Cologne, and then Bonn had fallen, both arduous battles. Dominic continued to want to be on the front lines, where the real warriors were, he believed. Where he could make a real difference. Instead, Dominic and his unit brought up the rear. They had never been far behind the front, seeking out as many museum and university professionals as they could, ticking names off a list in the smoldering aftermath of each battle. A tedious, soul-rending slog.

Most of the time, they came up empty. The individuals they sought had fled, were hiding, or, if they had chosen to stay, were certainly dead. But Captain Hancock, with the enthusiastic support of Vicar Stephany, persevered; the few professionals they had managed to find had been able to give them some information. Word of the Monuments Men—and of those few works of art they had been able to uncover—was beginning to spread underground through war-torn Germany. Gradually, a few people with information became more willing to speak to them. A few had even come forth of their own accord.

While their stock of recovered works of art grew slowly, Hancock's list of art repositories was reaching into the hundreds. At every opportunity, he located a secure telephone line to make calls to Allied commanders on the front.

Bonn had given them their strongest lead yet. The home of Count von Wolff-Metternich, a leading Konservator of the Historical Monuments Commission, the city had promised to yield a gold mine of information. Dominic had spent so many hours following Hancock and the others through the all-too-familiar desolation, combing around for any sign of Metternich. But his university office had been razed almost to the ground. Dominic remembered most vividly the desk, or rather, what was left of it; the flagstone that had fallen on it in the explosions had not so much crushed as splattered it. Papers and splinters had lain in all directions. The Konservator himself, it turned out, had fled east—behind enemy lines, where Dominic's unit wouldn't dare to go, at least not yet.

Starting, however, with a pay slip found among the

rubble and continuing with painstakingly slow sleuthing work, the trail had led them here to Bad Godesberg and this relic of a house. And to Herr Weyres, the Konservator's assistant, hiding in his cousin's kitchen.

The cousin, one of those splendid German women who had somehow managed to maintain her strapping figure despite the ravages of war, bustled between the soldiers with steaming mugs in her hands. She elbowed them aside as if they were little more than naughty children, tutting and clicking her tongue. "There," she said, stumbling over the English as she held a mug out to Weyres. "Warm. Be thanking this good young man." She turned to Dominic and gave his cheek an affectionate pat. Dominic felt his face flush as two of the servicemen struggled to stifle a chuckle. Weyres had looked so pathetic huddling there, he'd felt compelled to offer him his ration of powdered coffee. It was cheap and brackish stuff, but it was worth something in this bone-chilling air.

Herr Weyres brought the mug close to his face and savored the steam as if it was the most inexpressible luxury. He took a huge gulp, choked a little, and spluttered as his cousin pounded him on the back.

"So you have no record of where any of it went?" Hancock prompted him, drumming his long fingers on the kitchen table; it stood on three rickety legs, the fourth a pathetic stump.

"*Ach*, no, no, that is not what I said." Herr Weyres wiped

his bristly mustache and clasped the mug in both hands, his shivering subsiding. "To start, I was writing down a list of the repositories in a small ledger book. I kept it hidden in a metal compartment on the side of our fireplace. I thought that no one would find it there, connect it to me. We had some small resistance groups in town. I did not have enough courage to join them, but I thought that maybe, sometime, I would have an opportunity to hand over my ledger book to the leaders of that group. Maybe they would be able to recover the works, or at least help prevent them from being destroyed. But then, someone whispered my name to the authorities. I heard they were coming to find me."

Dominic could hardly believe his ears. This man had risked his life for a handwritten list of artwork?

Herr Weyres continued. "As quickly as I could, I lit a fire in the hearth. And I threw the ledger book on the flames. By the time the Gestapo arrived, there was no longer any evidence. I was lucky."

"And so the lists are destroyed," Hancock said, his shoulders falling.

"No, I still have them."

"What do you mean?" Hancock said.

"I still have the lists of the repositories. All here." He reached up and shakily tapped his head with one finger. "Maybe not all of it, but much. I had a feeling about these men who were taking my collection, so I tried to remember."

"Can you tell us?"

"Of course." Herr Weyres took another sip. "You bring the art back to my museum, to my people." He gestured as if writing in the air. "You must bring paper, yes?"

Hancock plucked a notebook and pencil out of his coat pocket. "Fire away."

At surprising speed, Weyres began to rattle off a list of repositories all over Germany, so fast that Hancock's writing grew drawn-out and scrabbled in his attempt to keep up. He covered three pages on both sides before finally, as suddenly as he'd begun, Herr Weyres stopped. He took a long pull at the bitter coffee and then sat staring at Hancock for a few seconds.

"That is all I remember. There can be one or two that I have forgotten."

"This is brilliant." Hancock pushed his back against the chair and huffed a sigh of relief. "We can do a lot with this. Thank you, sir." He rose, prompting the rest of the unit to prepare to leave, shuffling toward the door. Hancock extended a long hand to the old man. Herr Weyres clasped it in both of his own, staring intently into Hancock's eyes.

"You will find the art in all manner of strange places, *Amerikaner*. Look in places you cannot imagine. Castle dungeons, monasteries, bank vaults, restaurant storage rooms, hotel rooms, school gymnasia, even beneath ordinary homes. But what you really want is in Siegen." His grip tightened so that Dominic saw the blood leaving

Hancock's fingers. "There, below the citadel, is a copper mine. You will find the greatest treasures there."

Siegen. Hancock nodded at the name they had come across in Aachen.

The men stepped outside into the icy rain, which pounded hollowly on Dominic's helmet. His head felt the same: empty, shallow, a shell. He knew "the greatest treasures" had to refer to Charlemagne's relics, perhaps even other lost masterpieces. But while he felt a pang of relief that dear old Vicar Stephany was one step closer to the possibility of seeing his beloved treasures again, after all the death and destruction, Dominic could summon no emotion at the thought of art anymore.

*Keep drawing*, Paul had said. Right now, the distance between himself and home yawned ever greater. But Dominic knew that with this hastily scribbled list of art repositories, Hancock would move ever eastward with a renewed sense of purpose. They would be busy for a long time.

If he was in this for the long haul, Dominic thought, then he might as well get on board. Men like Weyres were putting their own lives on the line to save works of art. And maybe Stephany was right. They must not only live. They must find something to live for.

Dominic resolved that as they headed eastward, if he were to come out of this war with any ounce of sanity, he must hang on to the idea that art made life worth living. His life depended on it.

# 33
## EDITH

*Munich, Germany*
*November 1939*

ART MAKES LIFE WORTH LIVING, HER FATHER HAD always said. Edith tried to hang on to the idea that she had done her best to care for some of the most precious works in the world, to atone for having once put them in danger.

"Make way."

Edith stepped aside as two men managed an unwieldy canvas—an expansive landscape darkened by time— through the middle of her conservation studio. As they passed, Edith noticed the layers of dust that had settled into the crevices of the ornate, gilded wooden frame.

All that mattered, she told herself, was that her father was safe and as well as could be expected under the care of a new home nurse. For that, she was ever grateful.

But to Edith's dismay, her normally quiet conservation studio had been commandeered as a station for classifying and prioritizing paintings brought in from far afield. She had looked forward to a return to her work and her peaceful laboratory, but the room had been transformed into a thoroughfare, with the few staff members left at the Alte Pinakothek managing the organization, cataloging, and storage of the new works pouring in from across Europe.

Paintings were stacked by the dozens against all the available wall space. Someone had moved her gloves, varnish removers, canvas patches, and neutralizers from the shelves to her desk, which was now piled with unopened mail, books with flagged pages, and teetering stacks of paper. The once-orderly shelves were now a cluttered display of bronze clocks, small sculptures, ceramic pieces, textiles stacked in disarray.

Edith's dismay was only tempered by the fact that her friend Manfred was one of the few left behind. Manfred and his two assistants were now spending their days in the museum's loading docks, equipped with a large camera and small tags to label each work that arrived. The museum had engaged two dozen laborers, strong men who spent their days unloading armored vehicles onto the museum's loading area. "There are new works by Holbein, Cranach," Manfred said, a tinge of excitement in his voice.

"Manfred," Edith lowered her voice to a whisper and closed the door to her conservation laboratory. "Do you understand the magnitude of what is happening? We are being conscripted to strip the entire continent of its most valuable works of art. We are taking family heirlooms—people's most valuable possessions. And they are going directly into the hands of Party leaders!"

Manfred blinked, his eyes wide behind his round spectacles. "I am aware of it, my dear."

Edith blinked back. "You are?"

Manfred nodded. "Since you know more than most, I will share a secret with you. I am in contact with our colleagues in museums in Italy, France, and England. We communicate through channels that are . . . undisclosed. It is not only the museums that are being stripped, my friend. Personal collections—especially those of the Jews you see being corralled to the trains—are also being confiscated, not only here in Munich but all over Europe."

Edith's hands flew to her mouth. "My God, Manfred . . . What can we do?" Her words were muffled as she voiced her dismay.

Manfred continued. "We may not be able to stop the events that are already in motion. They are . . . larger than us. And rapidly moving. But at least we can document everything we see, everything we touch, everything we know. We are compiling complete records of each work of art—where it came from, who it belonged to. One day, when this is all behind us, we hope to be able to get the works back to their rightful owners."

Edith took in the information. "And the Generaldirektor?" she asked. "He knows about this?"

Manfred shook his head. "I believe that before, Dokter Buchner's intentions were honorable. But now . . . he feels compelled to please the Party; Munich is held to a higher standard than even the rest of Germany. We have been at the center of the German Day of Art and many other cultural exhibitions. Besides, he is also trying to secure our building from air raids. So what can he do?" Manfred shrugged. "Our city is the headquarters of the Nazi Party. And I would not dare tell him what I know now. It is much too dangerous."

To what lengths would her other colleagues go to protect themselves? Now that Edith had had a taste of what safeguarding works of art meant, she wondered how many other German art professionals would lie, steal, and plunder if it meant saving their own lives, if not gaining attention from the Party leadership?

She perched on the edge of her desk, reeling from this newfound knowledge of Manfred's mission and role. She struggled to imagine her mild-mannered friend as a cog in a great wheel of resistance, allied with museum professionals across Europe against Germany's interests.

Manfred reached for Edith's hand. "Now that you are back, perhaps you will join us in this effort." He paused. "You are your father's daughter, after all."

"What about my father?"

Manfred squinted. "How much has he told you about his efforts after the Great War ended?"

"Almost nothing," Edith said, searching her memory. "He has always said that people are easily misled, especially at the beginning. I don't know much more than that."

Manfred laced his fingers behind his back and began to pace, staring at the floor tiles. "You may not recall the uprisings in our city in 1918. You were young then. Many of us in Munich wanted to ensure that we never allowed that history to repeat itself. Your father was inspired, I think—we all were—by the sailors and munitions workers who organized strikes, and those soldiers who were brave enough to desert their barracks to demand peace instead of continued violence."

Manfred continued. "Your father helped a group of students who wanted to print leaflets denouncing the corruption they saw in the different levels of government. He knew I was doing something similar with my associates. But your father had to be extra careful; there were—and still are—mostly supporters of the Party inside the universities. They managed to leave the leaflets in places where they would be readily seen: dropped in the corridors outside of lecture halls, affixed to the insides of lavatory doors, even tucked secretly into students' book satchels."

"My father did this?"

Manfred nodded. "He helped arrange the printing of the leaflets. He felt that it was important. As I said, we have already lived the consequences of men who want to aggrandize themselves at a cost that puts so many lives at risk."

"And it's happening again!" Edith cried. "Manfred," she said. "If you could have seen it. General Frank . . . He wanted to keep a Rembrandt, a Raphael—even the da Vinci!—for himself."

"Governor Frank? You have seen him yourself?"

"He tried to take the *Lady with an Ermine* right out of our hands!"

Manfred's face blanched. "Edith," he said, "my God. I feel pity for anyone who comes in contact with that man. Do you know what he has done? So many innocent people have lost their lives in Poland; Frank is the one issuing the commands. Edith, I worried for your safety every day. And I don't doubt that they have stripped away anything at all of value from homes across the country. You will never read anything about any of this in the news reports. Most people are ignorant of it."

"But Manfred . . . It's *my* fault those pictures are now at risk. You were there during my ridiculous presentation right here in this museum. How could I have been so naïve? How did I not see how the information would be used? How they would make me a pawn?"

"You must not blame yourself. This conflict is much larger than you. The British newspapers are saying that General Frank has issued a decree for the confiscation of all Polish property. *All* of it—think about that, Edith. The Brits are reporting on the numbers of people Frank has already had executed or sent to the camps. That is why it is more critical than ever before that we act. And now, Edith, you have special knowledge of the situation in Poland—"

A knock on the door. Manfred paused in midsentence.

"Forgive me. Perhaps I have said too much. I must get back to the loading docks; they must be looking for me already," Manfred whispered. He squeezed Edith's hand. "Think about it, my friend. You know more than most of us. And you would be an asset to our effort."

Manfred slipped through the doorway as a messenger boy entered the conservation studio, his bag slung across his torso and hanging to his skinny knees.

"Is there an Edith Becker here?"

"I am Edith Becker," she said.

"Telegram for you, fräulein," the boy bent forward to hand the envelope to Edith, then turned on his heel.

She stared down at the envelope.

EDITH BECKER, KONSERVATOR

ALTE PINAKOTHEK

MÜNCHEN

It was marked from Berlin. Edith pressed her lips together, her heart jumping in her chest. Was this a message about Heinrich? With shaking fingers, Edith tore the thin paper enclosing the message. She read it, then blinked hard and read it again.

OFFICES OF KAJETAN MÜHLMANN DESTROYED BY FIRE AFTER AIR RAID. YOU ARE HEREBY INSTRUCTED TO MEET DR. MÜHLMANN IN THE DIRECTOR'S OFFICE AT THE ALTE NATIONALGALERIE IN BERLIN ON DECEMBER 1 TO PREPARE FOR PAINTINGS TRANSPORT FOR KRAKÓW. OFFICIAL ORDERS.

## 3 4

## CECILIA

*Milan, Italy*
*December 1490*

**"LET US REPEAT IT ONCE MORE."**

Bernardo paced the library, a sheaf of vellum in his hand. Cecilia cleared her throat, and began again:

*Perchè le rose stanno infra le spine:*
*Alle grida non lassa al Moro e cani . . .*

While Bernardo paced and Cecilia recited the lines of the newly composed sonnet, Cecilia felt Master da Vinci's eyes on her. His preliminary drawings complete, the master had set up his easel and a small, foldable table that held pots of pigment as well as a collection of long-handled brushes tipped with the hair of horses, weasel, and fox. Still, Cecilia was puzzled to see that more often than not, the painter used the brush to apply pigment to his own thumb or fingertip, then he carefully applied the thinly diluted color with his finger to the panel. He never went over the same part of the panel twice in one day, letting each soft layer of paint dry before applying the next. So far, only her face had begun to emerge in any detail.

This work was exceedingly slow. They had long abandoned the idea of Cecilia sitting before the window. Sitting still seemed impossible, she thought, especially now. She was filled with nervous energy about the new life growing inside her body. And today, more than any day since she had arrived in the Castello Sforzesco, she was filled with elation, for Ludovico knew she carried his child, and he was happy.

To Cecilia's great surprise, Ludovico had already guessed that Cecilia was pregnant. And an even greater shock: he had delighted in the news. As her midsection expanded, he told her, so did his admiration for her. When she lay naked and exposed with him, he put his hands on the small swell of her middle, his child inside of her, and he told her she was as beautiful as a flower. Cecilia looked into his face and saw that his joy was as intimate as it seemed pure.

As relief and hope began to overpower the weeks of dread, Cecilia worked to bolster her place in Ludovico's court with renewed energy. Ludovico had asked Cecilia to perform a suite of rhymes, sonnets, and songs for a group of dignitaries who would visit the castle in two days' time. Bernardo had paced the room with her until late into the night, correcting her pronunciation, adjusting the nuances of her diction, softening her Tuscan accent, and making small changes to the verses of poetry on his page as they practiced aloud.

Cecilia had the impression that Leonardo da Vinci preferred his subjects to sit still, but he had adapted his practice to follow her as she moved in step with Bernardo across the polished tiles. Perhaps, she thought, the painter still felt guilty about breaking the news of the duke's marriage before she discovered it in a more decent fashion. He did not complain about her movements. And working on the performance was a welcome distraction for Cecilia, who was becoming more uncomfortable. She wondered if anyone else had suspected the blooming life inside her.

As she came to the end of the poem this time, Leonardo smiled widely. *"Brava!* The best version yet. They will be captivated."

Cecilia made a small curtsy. This was the best part of her day, in the happy companionship of these two creative men.

"The old French ambassador is difficult to impress," Bernardo said. "I have seen it myself. And he has been known to fall asleep as soon as he is seated for a performance. But I feel that this one will at least keep him awake, if not entertain him."

"The French ambassador?" Cecilia asked. "Why is he coming?"

Bernardo said, "His Lordship is attempting to align himself with King Charles of France."

"To what end?" Cecilia asked. "Why would anyone want to become entangled with the French?"

"You may be an educated young lady," Bernardo said, "but you have much to learn about politics. Aligning with King Charles will earn him greater authority, and the duchy greater security."

"Yes," Leonardo mused. "And the French have an impressive—and well-organized—army. I might endeavor to offer my services as a military engineer."

Everyone, Cecilia thought, was elbowing for their own position at court. If she was honest with herself, Cecilia was doing the same. She worked hard to earn the applause and compliments of visitors to the Sforza court. Nothing filled her with light and joy as when a room full of guests exploded in applause after one of her performances. Was she vain for craving the attention, the approval of these strangers? Was it the same for Leonardo, when he earned compliments for completing a painting or one of those strange contraptions of his?

Whatever the case, Cecilia had worked hard to charm every visitor to the ducal court. And her lilting voice, not to mention her careful accompaniment on the lute and her uncanny ability to recite verse, had seemed to impress. It made her proud to know that others found her work so satisfying, and when she saw the look in Ludovico's eyes each time she charmed someone new, she knew it was work-ing. As much as Cecilia felt the uncertainty of her status in the core of her gut, she had to admit that Ludovico held a certain passionate pull on her. She craved his approval, his assent.

"Your hands, I don't know . . ." Leonardo gestured for Cecilia to take her seat, resuming the position she took in the portrait. "The dog, perhaps. Can you put her in your arms?"

Cecilia lifted Violina from the floor and settled the dog's warm, plump mass into her lap as she sat in the chair. Vio-lina looked expectantly at Cecilia with beadlike eyes, then flattened her ears as Cecilia ran her palm over the dog's small, round skull.

"A traditional symbol of fealty," said Bernardo.

"No!" Cecilia said. "Not a dog."

"No dog?" said Leonardo, suspending his brush in midair. "What then?" Cecilia tapped her finger on her chin. It seemed silly but it was an important question, she knew that. Cecilia only knew that the idea of the dog in her lap didn't sit well with her. Somehow, the word *fealty* grated at her.

"No, I don't think a dog will do."

Leonardo stared at her from behind his easel. "Well, something then. Did you have another idea?"

"How about . . . another animal?"

She saw Master da Vinci's eyebrows raise.

"Another animal? But the dog seems to be the better symbol for this picture. Loyalty is traditionally expected for such a portrait."

Cecilia nodded. "But there are other animals people keep as pets. Cats. Birds. Mice. Ferrets."

"Or an ermine," said Bernardo, raising a finger like an ancient orator. "In Greek, *gale*. *Gale*. Gallerani . . ."

"Yes!" cried Cecilia. "Gallerani! My family name. His Lordship can never forget who I am."

"I hardly think that is a risk, signorina," the painter said.

For a long moment, Leonardo looked at the painting in progress. Cecilia was certain he was about to argue and possibly paint the dog anyway. But instead, he ran his palm over his beard as if it helped coax the nuances from a complex idea.

"The ermine," he said. "Its coat turns white in the winter so that it may be better hidden from the enemy. They say that, faced with a hunter, the ermine would rather die than soil its beautiful white mantle. It is therefore a symbol of purity. It can also be a sign of fertility. Even pregnancy."

Cecilia watched the artist's cheeks turn pink in embarrassment when he realized what he had just said. The three of them sat in awkward silence as the painter pondered the problem. He did not want to offend her, she was sure.

"But," Cecilia said, "think of it! The King of Naples himself honored His Lordship with the Order of the Ermine. This will so please Ludovico. I am certain of it." Suddenly his face lit up and she saw that familiar enthusiasm that she had grown to enjoy. Quickly Leonardo began to sketch the requested ermine on a piece of vellum at his side.

"My dear, you are nothing short of brilliant."

Back in their rhythm of subject and painter, Leonardo and Cecilia settled into their comfort again. She ran her hands over Violina's white head while Leonardo worked out the ermine on the piece of parchment.

The door to the study opened and Cecilia turned to see Marco, the duke's official court musician, rush into the room, his unruly locks of hair falling over his eyes.

"Have you heard the news?" he asked, nearly tripping over Master da Vinci's collapsible table cluttered with pigments and brushes. "Happiness! A remarkable celebration is upon us! The date has been set for the marriage between Our Lord and the lovely Beatrice at the Castello di Pavia."

Cecilia swallowed hard.

"A spectacular winter celebration!" he cried. "Fewer than thirty days away. There is so much to be done!"

# 35
## EDITH

*Munich, Germany*
*November 1939*

ON THE BROAD AVENUES BORDERING THE PARK, enormous flags bearing swastikas were being hung in advance of a military parade. A winter celebration.

"You walk fast."

Edith suppressed a grin. "I'm sorry, Papa. We are in no rush."

Edith grasped her father's arm as he shuffled down the sidewalk. In the other arm, her father clenched Max, the matted, stuffed dog, tightly to his side. She slowed her pace, trying not to think about that small telegram, another slip of paper that would, once again, change her life. In two days, she would be leaving home again, back into the line of fire. How could she tell her father?

Winter had arrived in a blast of cold wind that rattled the windows and bent the brittle limbs of the trees lining the park. Across the Isar River, men in uniforms were filling the streets, marching in formation as the people of Munich looked on from their windows.

In the time that Edith had been away from home—mere weeks that seemed like a lifetime—the city of Munich had transformed into the capital of the Nazi world. Everywhere, tremendously sized flags flapped and men in field jackets and greatcoats lined the streets. Tanks blocked some of the main thoroughfares to allow for frequent parades. Around the city, preparations were being made for works of German painting and sculpture to be carried through the streets as the citizens chanted and sang patriotic songs.

In spite of the fanfare, Edith knew that during her weeks in Poland, there had also been an attempt on Adolf Hitler's life. According to the newspapers, the Führer had stepped down from the speaker's podium at a popular beer hall when a timebomb exploded, narrowly missing its target but killing eight others standing nearby. To Edith, the tanks blocking the main streets of Munich seemed less of a show of patriotism and more of a show of defense.

No matter the strange atmosphere of her home city and its bitter temperatures, Edith had vowed to get her father walking outside as much as possible. She knew it was good for him, and she could not bear to think of how she had found him upon her return.

When Edith had arrived in Munich, she was dismayed

to find that her father was gone from their apartment. In her absence, he had been entrusted to the care of a sanatorium on the outskirts of the city. Her neighbor, Frau Gerzheimer, had apologized profusely, but needed to prioritize the care of her own sick mother, who had come from the countryside so that her daughter could care for her.

At the sanatorium, Edith had found Herr Becker slumped in a chair in a dim room, his clothes and teeth dirty, more rawboned and frail than when she had left just weeks ago. He looked like a hunched-over child, clutching his stuffed dog tightly to his side.

Edith quickly signed his discharge papers and secured a nurse from the sanatorium: a middle-aged, auburn-haired hen of a woman named Rita who had worked for some three decades with elderly who had turned forgetful.

"Better you should take your papa home as soon as possible," Rita had whispered to Edith when she arrived to find her father. "They have instructed us to cut back on food for patients like him. It's not right. The numbers of deceased here are increasing. There are many empty rooms here now. No one dares to ask questions. If he was my own father, I would have taken him home long before now." Edith saw Rita's eyes filled with fear.

"Are you free to work with us directly?" Edith had whispered, out of earshot of the other nurses. "Please . . . come home with us. I will make it worth your while."

Now, Edith gave Rita a much-deserved break. Edith and

her father walked another long, slow stretch of the park, watching the last of the autumn leaves swirl and skip across the paths toward the pond. The walkway opened onto a grove of trees along the water's edge. Edith led her father to a park bench and settled herself next to him.

She took the daily newspaper, the *Völkischer Beobachter*, from the crook of her arm. Rita had told Edith it was important to read to patients who no longer remembered the past; it helped stimulate their minds, she said, sometimes even helped them recall memories. Besides, Edith was constantly poring over the papers for news of Prince Czartoryski and his wife, feeling anxious for what had become of them.

Edith scanned the headlines. GERMAN SOCIAL DEMOCRACY WILL CONQUER ENGLAND'S MONETARY DOMINANCE. TIME TO CLEAN UP THE JAPANESE MESS. THE FÜHRER REVEALS HIS LATEST SECURITY PLAN.

"NO MORE MORAL HYPOCRISY," Edith muttered another headline out loud.

"Moral hypocrisy . . ." her father repeated. "Ha! *Arschlecker!*"

"*Arschlecker*, indeed, Papa," she said. Her father's uncharacteristic profanity struck her as suddenly hilarious. The two of them sat on the park bench for a minute, laughing so hard they could hardly catch their breath. She suspected that her father didn't have any idea of what the headline was about, or why they were both laughing so hard, but who cared? When was the last time the two of them had had a spontaneous laugh?

"Papa," she said, dabbing her eyes. "I need to ask you something. Something important. Do you remember working with students at the university, during the Great War? Helping them with a printing project?"

She paused. Her father did not respond, but his laughter died away.

"They were trying to influence the other students to do the right thing . . ." Edith looked over her shoulder self-consciously. "Do you remember anything about that?"

Silence.

Edith sighed. How she wished her father could share something she could hold on to, some bit of paternal wisdom that might help her see more clearly what was in her power to control—and what was not.

"I have something to tell you, Papa." Edith searched for the right words. "I have to go away again for a while. You remember that I work at the Alte Pinakothek, right?" Her father continued to stare at her blankly. "The art museum?"

Edith waited for a spark of recognition that never came. She continued. "I have to go to Berlin, and then back to Kraków, to take care of some important, very valuable paintings."

Her father looked out at the barren trees. "Hhmp," he acknowledged.

"It's not my choice, Papa, I have official orders. They

want me to . . . safeguard these works before they are destroyed. You have always taught me that life is nothing without art. Remember?"

Her father seemed to be working hard to process what she was telling him. "Edith," he said. She grasped his hand in relief.

"Yes, Papa."

He turned his eyes on her. "*Wehret den Anfängen.*"

Edith recognized the flash of clarity. "Beware the beginnings." Her stomach fluttered.

When she saw her father's jaw begin to rattle with cold, Edith helped him up to begin their slow walk the few blocks home. Frost coated the bare branches of the trees along the park paths. Newly fallen leaves curled under the weight of the white coating, making a jagged pattern on the gravel pathways that wended their way back to their block. They passed the dusty, neglected doorway to the Nusbaums' apartment, and Edith's heart sank. Her mind flickered with the image of the many trains she had seen in recent weeks, heading east. She wished she had known back then, could have urged them to flee. If only she could have foreseen all of it, she thought.

In the apartment hallway, Edith hung her coat and opened a drawer in the table where the shiny black telephone sat. Inside the drawer were two letters she'd received from Heinrich. The first was dated the day after she first left for Poland. The other was dated a few days afterward.

She had read and reread them dozens of times. It had been almost a month now and she had no idea where he was. He had been safe then, but what about now? Was he keeping warm? Was he secure? Alive? Her heart ached for him. She lowered herself into the chair by the desk and read through both letters once more with tears in her eyes.

The stack of mail also included all the letters she had written home to her father while she was in Poland. None of them had been opened. Her heart sank. Weeks had passed, and her father had not heard from her. When Frau Gertzheimer had taken him to the sanatorium, had he wondered where she was? Had he remembered that he had a daughter at all?

In the kitchen, Edith heard Rita talking to her father, describing her process for making beef and cabbage soup. Edith felt her heart fill with gratitude for Rita's presence. She could not imagine what might have happened if her father had stayed in the sanatorium, nor could she imagine what Rita had told her about the numbers of disabled dwindling there.

In her sparse bedroom, Edith packed a few necessities into a leather bag for the train ride to Berlin. The telegram had only given her the basics—Kai Mühlmann's office had been destroyed but he must be all right if he was calling her to meet him. It hadn't said whether anyone else was hurt or whether anything had been salvaged. What had happened to da Vinci's *Lady*? Edith couldn't imagine the possibility that the picture might be damaged or destroyed. If that happened, Edith would never forgive herself as long as she lived. No. It was her job to save works of art, not to put them at risk. But would she put her own life at risk for a work of art? While she pressed her warmest gloves down on top of her few pieces of clothing, she pondered Manfred's proposal. How far would she go to save a painting?

What would her father have done? She only wished he could tell her.

# 36
## EDITH

*Kraków, Poland*
*December 1939*

AS DAWN BROKE, EDITH WATCHED THE ONION-SHAPED towers of Wawel Castle come forth into the light. She felt the train car sway into the curve following a promontory of the Vistula River, where a thin blanket of snow outlined the water's edge. The sound of freezing rain was like small bullets, pelting the metal roof of the sleeper car.

She stood and stretched. Her entire body felt wrung out and achy. She had forfeited a night's sleep on the train, tossing on the narrow, hard bunk and watching the shadows of the trees clip by against the night sky. Finally, she had dozed fitfully to the rocking of the train in the darkness, her hand resting on the wooden crate that held da Vinci's *Lady with an Ermine*.

The picture was packed in the proper way now, thanks to the work of a fellow conservator at the Alte Nationalgalerie back in Berlin. It stood encased in a wooden crate made especially for it, with a sturdy leather handle for easy carrying. Edith took some consolation in knowing that the picture would be transported more safely this time; she trusted herself more than she trusted the soldiers who knew nothing of handling this treasure.

"It wasn't easy," Mühlmann had told Edith as he escorted her to the Berlin train station in a black Mercedes with a uniformed driver. From the back seat, the crated painting wedged between them, Edith had examined Kai's haggard face. "Governor Frank made an argument that the pictures we brought from Kraków were state property," he had told her. "He demanded that all of them be returned to Poland. Immediately."

Edith had felt herself sink down into the leather seat as she considered the audacity, the greed of this man to demand a Rembrandt. A Raphael. A da Vinci. Many other priceless works. All for himself. At the same time, Edith was not sure that taking the masterpieces back to Germany had made them any safer than they would have been in Poland. *It was only a stroke of luck that had kept the pictures from being destroyed in that air raid on Berlin*, Edith thought. Mühlmann told her that he had moved the pictures into the Kaiser Friedrich Museum just days before bombs began to fall from the sky.

But now, only the *Lady with an Ermine* was once again in her care. Edith had gripped the leather handle of the crate as the darkened apartment windows of Berlin had clipped by outside the car window. "And the others?" she had asked.

"Don't worry; they're safe. The curator at the Dresden Gemäldegalerie is personally seeing to their care in their storage vaults. They've already been tagged for the Führer's museum in Linz."

But of all the pictures he demanded, Mühlmann had told her, Frank only succeeded in securing the return of the da Vinci. The governor negotiated for more than just *Lady with an Ermine*, though. He wanted Edith to deliver it to him personally. "Only this painting," Mühlmann had told her, patting the top of the wooden crate as they had pulled into the circle before the Berlin train station. "And only you."

Stepping out of that car with her bag in one hand, the crated painting in the other, was one of the hardest things Edith had ever had to do. Kai had stood awkwardly before her, seemingly unsure if he should shake her hand or embrace her. Instead, he clasped his hands behind his back and bowed slightly in her direction. "You should be proud of your contributions, Edith. Safe travels."

But now, watching the dawn bring the hulking outlines of Wawel Castle into focus outside the train window for the second time in three months, Edith felt anything but proud. She felt dirty instead, soiled by her conscription into the effort of stripping personal belongings from their rightful owners and putting them into the hands of an evil man. Her heart sank.

What could she do? She could not afford to question or seem to defy the orders of Governor Frank, not if she valued her life. That much was clear. He had already been responsible for the death of scores of people; Edith imagined that he might consider her dispensable, too, in the end.

Edith thought of her father, and of Manfred, working quietly behind the scenes to turn the course of events in the last war. Surely there must be a way to stop this seemingly insane stripping of art across Europe. Who would help her? Surely Kai Mühlmann had the right connections and a seemingly genuine care for art, but she could never ask for his help. He had already made it clear to her that she was only to follow orders if she wanted to return home alive.

*Resisters in the countryside.* How could Edith find them? And where?

The train slowed into Kraków station, its whistle exhaling like a long-suffering sigh. Edith stood. On the train platform, a sheaf of newspaper lay discarded, wadded into a battered ball. Edith watched it skirt and skip among the icy drifts, until it finally fell lifeless into the pit where the train wheels creaked to a stop.

# 37

## CECILIA

*Milan, Italy*
*December 1490*

AFTER HER PERFORMANCE FOR THE LATEST GATHER-
ing of guests, Ludovico held Cecilia tightly to him as they
watched wavering patterns on the ceiling above the bed,
made by shifting waters in a small pool in the gardens below
her private chambers.

"You have become more than the woman you once
seemed, a woman who might help me legitimize my position in the face of those who oppose me."

Cecilia propped herself up on her elbows to look into
the black wells of Ludovico's eyes. "Well, I did inform you
that I wanted to rule this castle." He buried his face in her
neck then and ran his palm over her budding midsection.
She wondered if he knew that this was why she worked so
hard on her poetry and her vocal practice, why she had
learned how to smile perfectly, and how to hold herself as a

courtly lady. She wanted to be the woman of the castle and had known she needed to prove herself as valuable. And if she were to believe his words, then she was doing exactly as she had hoped. Surely, Ludovico saw how valuable she was now.

But in her mind, Cecilia began to count the nights that he came to her, realizing that, in spite of his apparent admiration, their trysts were becoming less frequent. Sometimes it was as if he was insatiable to her and she had learned how to take her own pleasures from him. But he was coming for her less and less often and it had frightened her. On the nights when she lay alone in her bed, those words he'd spoken—of how important she was becoming to him and to his court—seemed like a dream. She began to wonder what else she could do to keep herself in the good graces of this man whose whims cast the form of her fate.

# 38

## EDITH

*Kraków, Poland*
*December 1939*

AS EDITH STEPPED INTO THE VAST COURTYARD OF Wawel Castle, she searched her mind for what else she could do to protect herself against this man whose whims seemed to cast the form of her fate.

Though she had spent time inside two fine Polish palaces in recent months, nothing prepared Edith for the massive scale of Hans Frank's official headquarters at Wawel. A dozen SS soldiers marched her into the giant courtyard, with three stories of symmetrical arches open to the gray sky. It reminded Edith of one of the Italian Renaissance palaces that she had studied at university. Against the tremendous, flapping flags with Nazi swastikas, the freezing rain had transformed into small snowflakes, which drifted into icy puddles on the great stones. Men with machine guns stood stationed under the arches, looking down into the courtyard as she marched forward with the soldiers, up a wide, stone staircase.

The men accompanied her through a dizzying maze of corridors and courtyards, wending up broad, stone staircases. She let one of the young men carry her bag of belongings, but she insisted on carrying the portrait of *Lady with an Ermine* herself, gripping the leather strap on the wooden crate with a gloved hand.

Incongruously, at the top of the stairs she passed three children playing with marbles in the hallway, rolling them back and forth and delighting in the pretty colors they cast on the ground in the icy light. She admired their matching ensembles, green and gold *lederhosen* with yellow shirts underneath. Their curly blond hair made it almost impossible for her to know who was a boy and who was a girl. The older two, who looked close to the same age, passed the transparent spheres back to the younger one, a beautiful, clear-faced girl of about four years old.

Edith followed the men down the hall until the soldier in front of her stopped at a tall wooden door, undoubtedly the private offices of the governor-general. On either side stood an armed guard, as still as tin soldiers. The man in the front of Edith's group extended his hand in salute, and one of the tin soldiers sprang to life, opening the door so that Edith could enter.

Behind a desk that seemed many times too large for its purpose, Edith recognized the now familiar, hawklike profile of Hans Frank in the dim light. At the sound of the door, Governor Frank raised his head and set his black eyes on her. He stood.

"Fräulein Becker," he boomed, and he spread his arms wide as if he expected her to embrace him. She did not want to move too close. She only hoped she could hold her tongue long enough to make it back home safely. Edith nodded curtly. She noted that he was no longer looking at her, but that his eyes rested on the wooden crate in her hands.

"Please," he said after a moment, "call me Hans. We are fellow Bavarians in a strange land, after all. Besides, I have a feeling that we will be seeing a lot of each other, so all the better to dispense with the formalities up front, don't you agree?"

Edith nodded curtly again but refused to repeat his first name.

"I was about to make myself a drink," he said. "What can I offer you?"

"Nothing, thank you."

Hans shook his head and looked directly at her. "Polish vodka is surprisingly palatable. But I suppose that, after such a journey, you might prefer coffee instead." Frank gestured to one of the soldiers standing near the door. "Have Renate bring Miss Becker a coffee." The soldier clicked his heels and exited.

Frank went to the bar cart near the window and began

to pour clear liquid out of a decanter. He glanced again at the crate.

"I am eager to see her again," he said. To Edith's dismay, Frank grasped the leather handle from Edith's hand. He placed the crate on his desk. "Open it," he said to one of the soldiers standing at the door. The man sprang into action.

"I understand that you are an expert in Italian Renaissance works of art, Fräulein Becker?"

"I have worked to restore the work of artists of many eras and places," she said. "Memling, Friedrich, many others."

He swallowed nearly all his Polish vodka in one swig and then looked at her directly. "Then I see that we have many interests in common. And that you have a good eye."

Edith felt the hairs on the back of her neck stand on end.

"You have demonstrated a talent for identifying and locating important, worthy paintings," he continued. "Only first-rate. Nothing degenerate."

"I believe that all art is worth preserving." She met his gaze.

"That is why I have requested that the director of the Alte Pinakothek let me have you for a while."

Edith was rendered nearly mute. Let him have her?

How could she explain that she had duties back home? And yet what choice did she have? She had never felt so pressured, so on the brink of fearing for her life. If not her life, she could be tortured or . . . she shuddered, refusing to allow the word to form in her mind. *I would be shot,* she had heard Mühlmann say. And what had Manfred told her? Frank had decreed the confiscation of all Polish property. And he had already sent untold numbers to the detention camps.

Behind them, the soldier had managed to open the crate holding the *Lady with an Ermine*. As soon as Frank spotted the painting carefully packed inside, he set down his drink and moved to look more closely. He leaned forward, his hands clasped behind his back, as his eyes ran over the girl in the painting. Then he turned to look at Edith for a few long moments.

"You will help me hang it," he said. He lifted the painting from the crate and took it to the other side of the room.

The soldier moved a stepladder near the wall opposite Frank's desk. Frank gently put the painting down. On a nearby table, a small hammer and nail stood waiting. Frank handed both to Edith. She hesitated, feeling the heat of the men's eyes on her.

Seeming to move in slow motion, she climbed the stepladder and tapped the nail gently into the wall above a radiator. The soldier lifted up the picture and handed it to Edith. Carefully, she leveled the frame. Frank took a few steps backward, looking proudly at his newest acquisition.

Edith felt her legs tremble as she descended the ladder, but she forced herself to face Frank. "You cannot just . . . just take it," she said quietly.

Frank stared at her for a few long moments and she held

her breath. But then he only chuckled, shaking his head. "No, my dear. I didn't take it. *You* did. And now, the Führer has gifted it to me, as a token of his esteem."

Edith sucked in her breath. Yes, she had taken the picture. It was undeniable. All the same, he was patronizing her. Surely Hitler had more important things on his mind than pictures?

"We have to guard this one carefully, no? I spend all my time here. My guards are always outside. There is no better place than here for such a beautiful work of art. No one will take it. It will be safe under my personal care."

"Such a painting is not replaceable," she said. "And the radiator . . . It will make the paint crack."

Frank looked perturbed and she realized she'd overstepped her bounds. "It will be secure here. You have done your duty, you do not need to worry about it anymore. Come. Sit with me."

He walked forward with a stiff pace to a table by the large window. He pulled a chair out for her to sit and took her coffee cup from her hand. She had not taken a sip.

"Let us refill this with something more suitable. Make yourself comfortable . . ."

She sat down hard and pressed her lips together as he went to the bar and made them both another drink. Her head was already swimming a little, the result of nerves and the lack of sleep. She turned her head to look at the portrait again. The girl seemed to call out for her help, Edith thought, her eyes seeming a little more desperate and sad than before. What could she do to save her this time?

Frank came back and set the glass down in front of her. Then he sat and took a sip of his drink, looking at her over the rim.

"Please, fräulein, tell me how you came to be so prominent in the Munich art world?"

She took a sip of the strong concoction, hoping it would calm her. "I don't hold a prominent position at all," she said. "I only work in a simple conservation studio . . ."

"But you graduated top in your class at the art academy, Mühlmann has told me."

She hesitated. "My father taught me about art when I was young; he taught me that art makes life worth living. And after that, I wanted to learn everything I could about preserving paintings." She looked warily again at the priceless masterpiece by Leonardo da Vinci, now hanging over a radiator.

Frank nodded. "You will be an asset to the future of this empire. I intend to let the Führer know my opinion of your work, which, as you might have guessed, is highly favorable."

Frank raised his glass in a toast, then leaned toward Edith, so close that she could smell the tangy metal of his breath.

"I am eager to see what other treasures you might find for us."

# 39
## DOMINIC

*Bonn, Germany*
*March 1945*

DOMINIC CAREFULLY PASSED UP A PAINTING WRAPPED
and padded in canvas tarps to another soldier standing
on the flatbed of the Jimmy. The other soldier handled it
with reverence, sliding it to rest beside a stack of similarly
wrapped artwork. It was the last of several dozen pictures
recovered from the basement of a university library in Bonn.

The pictures safely secured, Dominic hopped up into
the back and crouched beside them, clasping his rifle between his knees in a pose that had become all too familiar.
Another soldier slammed the tailgate closed and slapped
his hand against the back of the truck to signal the driver.
Dominic stared blankly out the back as the truck trundled off, swaying between two other servicemen. He barely
knew their names. One or two of them had attempted to
reach out to him, as starved for companionship as he was;

but none of them were gentle Paul, and especially, none of them was Sally. He shunned them all, retreating into a ball of silence as desolate as the landscape around them.

The truck made its slow and laborious way through the debris and out into the countryside, heading eastward, toward enemy territory, toward Siegen, and whatever treasures might be hidden there. The road was pitted and uphill, but it was the only one that was open for them to use; all the others still fell under heavy fire. Even this one was covered in ruin, and the occasional dark stain on the earth bore testimony to the price that had been paid to open it.

At least the truck in front of them carried the closest thing to a friend that Dominic still had: Stephany. The old vicar had met up with them again in Bonn, determined to be present when they arrived at Siegen. Hancock had tried to dissuade the vicar from joining them because of the obvious dangers of trekking through territory still under fire, but Stephany would have none of it. He was going to Siegen whether Hancock liked it or not, and it would have taken more than a mere American army to stop him from seeing if his beloved cathedral treasure was hidden there as promised.

As the cover of town receded, Dominic felt exposed in the hilly countryside. He stared out at the rolling horizon, scanning for the barrels of enemy guns that he knew still had to be out there, hidden just over the crest of a hill. Wisps of smoke marked the sky in places, the remnants of battles still raging not far away. He clasped his rifle a little tighter, an uneasy feeling stirring in his gut.

Someone was watching them.

The next moment, the air ripped with gunfire. Dominic threw himself to the floor of the truck bed as holes exploded in the canvas tarp that covered them, punching into a priceless canvas, gunpowder spraying into the air. Without thinking, Dominic grasped the edge of a wooden frame and pressed the canvas down into the bed of the truck. The man beside him screamed and rolled, blood from his shoulder splattering hot on Dominic's cheek. Dominic pressed himself to his belly as the truck screeched to a halt.

He tumbled out, using the truck as cover, swinging his rifle to seek the enemy. There. The hilltop bristled with gun barrels and muzzle flashes. Dominic's stomach sank into familiar dread as he fell into the old routine. Filled with terror, he squeezed the trigger and his rifle twitched and jerked in his hands.

"Bonelli!"

Hancock's scream came just in time. Dominic ducked instinctively and felt heat on his right arm. He glanced down at his shoulder, barely comprehending, seeing the rip in the cloth and the healthy flesh just beneath. His closest call yet. Perhaps the next one would send him the same way as Paul, and he would never hold his beautiful wife and little girl again. He would never see his new baby. The thought of his family set his soul on fire. He threw himself back to his feet and fired with an accuracy born of desperation. One by one, the line of German soldiers fell as his every bullet met its mark. The last few, seeing the line of death growing nearer to them, hugged their rifles to their chests and fled back over the rise.

Silence fell. Dominic tried to peer through the veil of smoke. Finally lowering his gun, he saw that his hands were shaking. He turned toward the rest of the convoy, all staring at him, even Hancock. A niggling thought penetrated the white noise of his mind. *Stephany.* He swung his rifle back onto its shoulder strap and stepped over the body of his fallen comrade as respectfully as he could, walking to the truck immediately preceding his, where he pulled back the canvas.

Stephany was crouched on the floorboard, curled up as tightly as his body could compress itself, his hands clapped over his ears. Dominic's heart broke as he realized that this was how the vicar had spent the entire Battle of Aachen, cowering beneath his pulpit. His lips moved in a string of sotto voce German that Dominic knew had to be prayer. He moved his hand to Stephany's shoulder. "Vicar. *Stephany.* It's okay."

By degrees, Stephany uncurled, his eyes piercing Dominic's with raw terror. His face was drained of blood, and his glazed expression said that he was back there in his beloved cathedral, stripped of its treasures, as the bombs fell. Dominic squeezed his shoulder. "You're safe. They've gone."

Stephany clutched Dominic's wrists in trembling hands and stared into his eyes. "Why do they do this? Why all the killing?" he cried hoarsely. "My own people."

Dominic wished he could ask those same questions out loud. Instead, he gave Stephany the closest thing he could to a smile. "There's still time to go back to Bonn, you know. You don't have to come to the mines. You'd still get your art back if we find it there."

Stephany was shaking his head before Dominic could finish. "No, no. I come. The end." His eyes flashed with determination. "They will not take everything from me."

"Come on!" Hancock yelled. "Let's get out of here."

It was a long, slow day of crawling through the countryside, pausing to take cover whenever they saw movement on the hilltops. Somehow, they managed to avoid another skirmish. It was only as dusk fell and they moved into the cover of a dense forest that they managed to pick up speed. Dominic carefully laid each painting flat in the bed of the truck, examining each one for bullet holes or other damage.

Exhausted, Dominic leaned against the side of the truck, the familiar weight of his rifle pressing against his knees as they rocked deeper into the night. The firefight had pocked holes in the brown paper wrappings of the paintings. Dominic leaned his head back and watched the headlights of the truck behind them shine through the holes and reflect on the gilded frames. The sight was surreal, a speck of beauty that did not belong in this wasteland of death and destruction.

As the sun set, the truck rumbled across a bridge, and Dominic looked out to see the wide, sparkling expanse of the Rhine. They headed east, toward Siegen.

# 40

## CECILIA

*Milan, Italy*
*January 1491*

**"TIGHTER."**

Cecilia grasped the stone mantel of the hearth as Lucrezia Crivelli pulled the strings of her stays tightly around Cecilia's burgeoning middle. She did her best not to cry out in agony.

"Signorina, your middle has grown," Lucrezia said. "There is little more I can do. What a pity." The insincerity in her voice made Cecilia's scalp tingle.

January. Halfway through her pregnancy, and there was no more hiding it. Cecilia had bloomed with child and the growth was only going to become more apparent. It was no longer a secret; everyone in the castle whispered about Cecilia's growing midsection. But Cecilia had sent word to Ludovico that she would visit him in his chambers—the first time she had ever requested such a meeting with His

Lordship herself. Now, she did her duty to look as much as possible like the young, charming mistress who had earned her a place in the palace to begin with.

It took all her strength to stand upright in the constricting garment. Cecilia swayed into the marble corridor, as dizziness filled her head and trepidation welled into her breast. Would he listen to her, consider her pleas? Or would he want to take her just before he exchanged gold rings with Beatrice?

For weeks, the castle had fluttered with activity. Banners of blue, red, and gold arms flapped in the courtyards, proclaiming the alliance of Ferrara and Milan. Servants bustled down the corridors, dusting cobwebs and corners of the hallways and stairs. The smell of apple cakes wafted from the kitchens on the lower floors, where the cooks timed the rotations of the sandglass carefully before removing their edible masterpieces from the brick ovens. There they chopped onions, parsley, and beets until the juice turned their fingertips and palms blood red. The horses in the stable were brushed, slicked with oil, and shod with new irons from the blacksmith's forge.

Cecilia did her best to ignore the details, but through the whispers of the servants and the ladies that Ludovico insisted on sending her as companions, she learned that the wedding ceremony had blossomed into something bigger than just a conjoining with Beatrice d'Este. It would be a double celebration, at the same time joining Beatrice's younger brother Alfonso to Anna Sforza, the sister of Ludovico il Moro's nephew.

In the flurry of nuptial preparations, His Lordship had retreated behind the closed doors of his own private chambers. Even Leonardo, whose job it was to orchestrate the staging of the wedding, had quickly abandoned Cecilia's portrait. She was left again to the solitude of her books and her dog. Cecilia had insisted on her normal routine in the library, where she practiced her recitations and the lute with Bernardo. But it was only through a daily leap of imagination that she was able to ignore the marriage preparations around her.

She dismissed everyone who tried to engage her, everyone except for Bernardo the poet and eventually her brother Fazio, who had returned to Milan from Tuscany just in time for the wedding. He had lifted her into his arms and laughed, then run his hands over her middle, wide-eyed with wonder. And it was only Fazio who had the power to allay Cecilia's fears that she might be cast aside or dead before the marriage took place.

"Nonsense, Cecilia," her brother had said, squeezing her hands. "You are perfectly healthy and the joy of His Lordship's life. You will remain so. I am certain of it."

Now, Cecilia tried to corral some of her brother's confidence as she dared to rap on the door to Ludovico's private chambers. She heard his deep voice rumble that she should enter.

She drew in a deep, sharp breath when she saw Ludovico adorned in layers of fine velvet, silks, and metal insignia. In spite of herself, the vision of him ready to wed stabbed at her heart. She forced herself to stare at the floor.

"My beautiful flower." He brought one palm to her cheek and wrapped another around her middle. She felt the metal rings strapped across his chest press into her bodice.

"Ludovico."

"I know that I have not visited you in some time. All the same, you bring me joy."

For a few moments, Cecilia allowed herself to close her eyes and breathe in his heady scent of perspiration masked with *acqua vita*.

"You must visit the stable later today," he said quietly, running his palm up one side of her neck. "There is a new mare from Callocci Stables in Umbria. She is the pick of the mating season. My equerry will acquaint you with her. I will leave you to give her a name."

"I am indebted to you once again, my lord," Cecilia said, but she did not meet his eyes.

It was only the latest of the fine gifts Cecilia had received in past weeks, while Ludovico remained behind locked doors. There had been exotic fruits delivered to her rooms, so sweet they were like eating the finest desserts; gilded boxes that flickered in the lantern light; colored stones that hung heavily against her breast; and fine webs of pearls for her hair. There were strings of glass beads, and

ribbons of transparent blue to weave into her braids. There
was a black cap, made of organza, fashionable among the
women of Milan. And now, another horse. The closer to
the wedding, the more frequently the gifts were presented
to her. But Ludovico himself remained absent.

Outside the window, Cecilia heard the rattle of carriage
wheels on the stone pavement. There was not much time.

"Ludovico." Cecilia straightened herself in her dress, her
hand once again finding its way to her middle. She took a
deep breath. "I would make you a better wife."

He smiled at her indulgently. "My flower," he said again,
taking her hands in his. "You already have my heart. And
you have played games with my mind, so much so that I
have already postponed this . . . event . . . not once but
twice." He sighed heavily and wagged a finger at her as
if scolding her. "All the same, Cecilia, I cannot delay any
longer. And you know that the strength and security of the
duchy rely on my alliance with Ferrara."

Cecilia shook her head. "No. I do not know that. Tell
me one thing that Beatrice d'Este can do that I cannot.
I have spent countless hours entertaining your guests with
food, drink, and conversation. I have recited sonnets for all
the important people who have set foot in your court. I have
even sung a ridiculous song for the ambassador of France!"

Ludovico muffled a laugh.

"And"—her voice fell to a whisper—"I am carrying
your son."

Ludovico's finger lightly tipped her chin up to him and he brushed his lips against hers. The kiss was sweet, tender, and filled with the first inkling of passion. She felt her body open to him. But then, he broke the kiss and only touched his forehead gently against hers.

"I am sorry."

"But why? I know you feel it between us. I know there is more to what you feel for me than simply what takes place behind our chamber doors." Cecilia's heart was beginning to race as she realized that she may lose the battle.

Ludovico sighed and walked to the window, looking down at the carriages that had assembled below the blue and gold banners of the court of Ferrara.

"Because this marriage is not simply a marriage. I am obliged."

"But it isn't right. I am the one who deserves it."

Ludovico came close to her and ran his hand down her arm. "My beauty. You are deserving of so much more than that. I am not leaving you. I promise. I will still come to you. You will have land. Honor. A wet nurse. Servants to help you. Every possible thing you should need. I will keep you here in the palace, tucked away where the two of us will not be disturbed. You will not lose me."

Cecilia felt her lips begin to quake. She had always been so careful to mask her emotions in front of him, but this had become too much.

"Please," he said, stepping back as her shoulders began

to crumble. "You must understand the position I am in." Cecilia felt that she could no longer form a word without crying.

From the window, Ludovico looked down into the courtyard as lines of *condottieri* in their finest armor marched up the stairway into the castle. Then, Cecilia watched Ludovico's polished leather boots move toward the door. As his hand reached for the latch, she took a deep breath and found her voice.

"Ludovico!" It came out loudly as if she were calling him from a great distance. He stopped in his tracks and whirled around to face her. She had never raised her voice to him, but right now, hot desperation rose in her throat.

"You must take *me* as your bride instead! Go out there and tell everyone. You are in charge, after all. It is *your* decision. No one else's."

For a long moment, they held each other's gaze. She watched his black eyes flicker in the light. Then, she saw the lines on either side of his eyes crinkle, and the side of his mouth rose in a half smile.

"My dear girl."

# 41
## EDITH

*Outside Puławy, Poland*
*March 1940*

**WAHL I. WAHL II. WAHL III.**

First Rate, Second Rate, Third.

The harsh rake of light from the desk lamp illuminated stacks of ledgers and inventories. Farther away, in the shadowy recesses of the basement storage room, unknown treasures awaited her inspection. Over the past weeks, Edith had identified a small picture by the Dutch painter Anthony van Dyck. And there were more stacks of paintings, sculptures, rugs, and furniture lying in wait for her examination. There were also scores of smaller pieces—silver services, glass and crystal, brass.

*Wahl I. Wahl II. Wahl III.*

Edith had started thinking of them in colors: green, blue, red.

And photographs. Hundreds, maybe thousands, of

photographs. Nameless faces stared out at Edith in the shadows as she sat alone with her pen and a blank ledger page. Photographs in frames, in boxes, in albums, loose.

Yet another Polish estate. This time, she did not know the name or the exact location of this once-fine country house, nor did she know what had become of its owners. The belowground level—now transformed into Edith's workspace—had been set up for the collection and sorting of property stripped from private owners across Poland. Edith was only glad that Hans Frank had chosen a location far from Wawel Castle. Far from Frank's own offices. Far from Frank himself.

Edith was so relieved to have been assigned far away from Frank that she didn't even mind being the only woman lodged along with a houseful of men. The upper floors had been transformed into barracks to house Nazi officers. Once the men learned that Edith's fiancé was one of them, that he too was deployed on the Polish front, they treated Edith with respect. They also shared stories about their own wives, girlfriends, sisters, and mothers they had left behind in Germany.

Edith was assigned to a sparse former servants' quarters off the kitchen, where the smells of stewed meat and pastry filled her room. She and the officers were fed from a large ground-floor dining room staffed by three Polish matrons who had been coerced into housekeeping and kitchen duty. The women whispered among themselves as they rolled dough or chopped onions and carrots. Edith had tried to be friendly with the only other women in the building, but she quickly discovered that the kitchen ladies were not only extremely guarded but also understood no German. Edith spoke no Polish, so she soon gave up trying to make a friend or even have a conversation beyond crude hand gestures if she needed something.

All day long, Edith sifted carefully through each item that came through the doors. Three repositories. One for valuable items, one for those of some interest, and another for objects of little value. For months, the goods had continued to pour into the rooms without ceasing. Once-empty palace rooms had begun to fill, and they had moved into adjacent rooms.

Edith was only a little surprised by the variety of items that came through her hands. Oriental carpets, silver candelabras, bronze clocks, small sculptures, porcelain of Meissen and Sèvres, entire silver table settings. Some of the items were watches, sentimental tokens, toys, or small baby mementos made of silver or brass. They were useless to the Führer. But they were priceless to the family that lost them. *Wahl III.* She notated their descriptions in a thick ledger that stood on a wobbly wooden podium under a single, high window.

Edith was not alone in this nearly impossible effort; Frank had assigned her three assistants. Two were enlisted German soldiers assigned to Edith based on their brawn rather than any experience with art. Karl and Dieter spent their days unloading trucks and bringing things into the lower-level storage rooms. Jakub, a slight, gray-haired Polish man and former schoolteacher, had been conscripted to the German effort to translate for the officers upstairs. Occasionally, Jakub helped Edith decipher Polish documents and written material that came off the trucks.

Since her arrival in Poland this second time, Edith had been issued a cotton and canvas skirt, field jacket, and shiny leather loafers. She was not much to look at, she thought, but Frank had insisted that his staff wear German uniforms, and anyway, it helped Edith blend in among the men.

But then one day, as a group of soldiers collected around the dining tables for the evening meal, Edith recognized a familiar face.

"Edith?" the man stared across the table at her, his spoon suspended in midair.

"Franz!" It had been at least ten years since Edith and Franz Klein had shared the same classroom in Munich. Franz had grown into a tall, broad-shouldered man with a chiseled face, but with the same green eyes and space between his front teeth that she recognized from long ago. Years later, she saw him occasionally at the same beer hall where she had first encountered Heinrich.

"You do remember me!" he said.

"Of course," she said. "You were friends with Heinrich." At her fiancé's name, Edith's heart ached. "He is with the Wehrmacht, Eighth Army."

"Eighth? They are moving through the area," he said.

Hope surged into Edith's chest. "Then you must let me go with you into the field. It has been so long since I have seen him."

Franz huffed. "Take you with us? Edith, you do not want to leave this place to go out there," he said, gesturing toward the front door. "Not if you value your life."

Though he continued to refuse her insistence that he take her out with the soldiers, Franz often stayed at the estate for days at a time as he traveled across the Polish front. When he arrived, he came downstairs to visit with Edith and share what news he could. Yes, he told her, there were prison camps being set up in the countryside nearby. Yes, trainloads of Jews and other undesirables were being unloaded inside their newly made, high walls, protected by barbed wire. At the same time, trainloads of German civilians were being unloaded in towns across Poland to repopulate the new territory with German blood.

Protected within the basement storerooms and idyllic grounds of the estate, Edith struggled to imagine this enormous sorting of people, just beyond her sight. At night, she slept fitfully as her mind filled with images of sorting. *Wahl I. Wahl II. Wahl III.* Green. Blue. Red. Everything and everyone was being judged, valued, divided into categories that would determine their fate.

When Franz was away from the estate, Edith peppered the soldiers with more questions about what was happening outside the estate grounds, and if they could give her news about Heinrich. She asked if anyone knew what had happened to Prince Czartoryski and his pregnant bride. No one could tell her, but all the same, the soldiers began giving her news freely. They became relaxed, friendly with Edith. She knew they had left women behind at home, and they welcomed her conversation when she emerged from the depths of the house and stepped out into the once-manicured gardens for a breath of cold air.

In the evenings, Edith wrote to her father. With each letter and no response, she became more anxious that he wasn't receiving them. She'd put her trust in Rita and hoped that he was being cared for. She prayed with everything in her that he had not had to return to the sanatorium.

In addition to her copious inventory recorded in the leather-bound ledger, each week Edith prepared a report that detailed works she deemed most valuable. These reports were handed over to one of the soldiers billeted upstairs. The *Wahl I* list was dispatched directly to Kraków. In her mind, Edith imagined Governor Frank running his finger down the list of each week's inventory, hungry for Edith to locate another treasure for his collection.

In return, each week a shipping order would be returned to Edith. She and her assistants packaged each work for transport. She watched Karl and Dieter haul the items out to the gravel path at the entrance to the palace, labeled for storage units, museum offices, warehouses, and other locations in Berlin, Munich, Dresden, Nuremberg, or some other undisclosed hiding place within the confines of the Reich. Governor Frank wasn't the only one benefiting personally from these luxury goods, Edith realized. Other high-ranking Nazi officials received shipments directly to their homes. Meticulously, Edith recorded each item and its destination in her ledger.

Occasionally, there was an order to package a certain high-value item for Wawel Castle. She hadn't heard anything about the *Lady with an Ermine* and as far as she knew, it still hung above the radiator in Hans Frank's office. She shuddered to think it was in the hands of such a vile man. She prayed that this would all be over soon, but she felt powerless to return the painting to its original place with the Czartoryski family, if they were even still alive.

After dinner in the barracks kitchen, Edith would find a quiet corner to read the German newspapers, usually weeks old, that the soldiers procured. Edith found the German papers filled with nothing but stories about the success of Hitler's campaigns, glorious accounts of German expansion into neighboring lands. In the background, the Polish women chopped vegetables, washed pots and pans, bantered back and forth in whispered tones.

One article reported that works of art were being safeguarded across Europe to ensure that they did not fall into the hands of Jewish collectors in America. Edith guffawed in response. Faced with the staggering quantities of the personal belongings piling up in stacks around her, Edith could no longer hold on to the illusion that she, Kajetan Mühlmann, or any of her colleagues were in the business of safeguarding anything at all.

*Wahl I, Wahl II, Wahl III.*

All of it was at risk instead.

And, Edith knew, nothing was going to the Jews, in America or anywhere else. It was only being stripped away from them instead, along with their freedom and maybe even their lives. She could not ignore the evidence before her eyes. Everything reported in the news articles was a lie. What else was happening outside the walls of the estate that was not being reported? Edith could not begin to grasp the enormity of it. All she knew was the works of art were not falling into anyone's hands but high-ranking Nazi officials like Governor Frank.

And Edith had to face the fact that *she* was part of the giant network that enabled these men to aggrandize themselves, at the expense of so many innocent lives. She had not placed a hand on anyone, nor had she acted from a place of malice or prejudice. She had only been following orders.

But now, Edith realized, following orders did not absolve anyone from being connected to something criminal. Cowardly. Evil. There was no judge, no jury, no one to indict her. Instead, jurisdiction, Edith realized, lay only with her own conscience.

# 42
## LEONARDO

*Milan, Italy*
*January 1491*

CARRYING A STACK OF BOOKS FROM THE SHELVES TO the table, I notice something small and nearly weightless flutter to the floor.

I bend to retrieve it from the floor of my dusty bedchamber. It is one of the earliest sketches I made of Signorina Cecilia, one that shows her in profile, with the gentle slope of her high forehead and the trace of her nose. How different the picture looks now compared to this preliminary thought.

At first, I had one of my boys prepare the walnut panel with gesso and arsenic paste to deter boring insects. For months, the panel stood on the easel, waiting for me. Blank.

I then began the full-size cartoon that formed my working model. On a large swath of parchment, I worked out the turn and pose of her body, the bare outlines of the distant landscape behind her. For the hands, I used an idea from a previous portrait, sketched separately and attached with a dot of rabbit glue. When finalized, I pricked the outlines with holes, and then pounced the holes with charcoal dust to make an outline on my panel, just as Master Verrocchio taught me when I was barely old enough to grind pigments.

A new kind of portrait. There is no reason to show a subject in profile anymore. That is better reserved for coins and medals. Yet painters have been doing it for years, even, or perhaps especially, at the court of Milan. One has only to look at the latest court portraits of His Lordship and his own father, God rest his soul.

But this portrait of Signorina Cecilia is different, I think. A new kind of portrayal that the Milanese court has never seen.

I turn to the latest page in my notebook and examine my latest arrangement of her left hand and the ermine. I have positioned her body not to show her status—in the end, what status does this girl really have?—but rather, as she looks in life. Yes. I must endeavor to show Cecilia as His Lordship sees her—lively, intelligent, a young girl with the power to captivate an entire room full of people accustomed to such entertainments. It is also how I see her. Her true nature.

For though Cecilia Gallerani is no duchess, she is something more than just a girl with a dog.

## 43
### EDITH

*Outside Puławy, Poland*
*March 1940*

CARRYING A HEAVY LOAD OF BOOKS FROM A BASEMENT
storage room to her desk, Edith noticed something small
and nearly weightless flutter to the floor.

She moved the stack to her desk, shifting cluttered
papers and a large bronze clock out of the way. An old
lamp sat in one corner of the desk. She reached over and
turned the small knob until a harsh pool of light flooded
the desk. Edith turned to find what had fallen to the
floor: It was a square, black-and-white photograph with
ragged edges.

She leaned down to pick up the picture. A little girl with
a dog larger than her, both of them seated on what looked
like the front stairs of an apartment building, stared back at
Edith. The girl's dark hair fell across her forehead in tousled
locks, her smile wide and unencumbered. The dog, for its

part, flashed its own smile, a long tongue hanging from its mouth.

Edith flopped down in her desk chair and took a deep breath. She stared into the girl's dark eyes for a few long moments. What had happened to this smiling girl and her big dog?

The picture had fallen from a large, leather-bound album. She began to shift the clutter so that she could pull it out. A few stray pictures slipped from the book and landed on the floor by her feet.

Edith's stomach tightened, but she dared to look. A sober-looking woman in a wedding dress with a long, lace veil that hung to the floor. An elderly couple, someone's grandparents, seated stiffly for the camera in their starched clothes. Another picture that might be the smiling girl, now grown into a woman, her hair cropped tidily at her chin, her face now somber.

Suddenly, the cold room seemed to flush with heat. Everything in the basement appeared to lurch toward Edith—the stacks of books, photos, the jumble of candelabra, rolls of rugs, fur coats, and unending stacks of personal belongings. All of it seemed to teeter and topple upon her at once, as if she sat at the center of a swirling vortex that pulled everything down into its black heart.

Edith turned the picture of the little girl and her dog over. She could not face the girl's smile, her blatant innocence. Up to now, Edith had tried only to capture the information about each work, not to think too deeply about the families themselves. She hadn't let herself. She had her own family to worry about. She just wanted to be separated from the tragedy, even as her own hands pawed through their belongings—their beloved china, their wedding pictures, their history, their lives. Edith took some deep breaths to stem the harsh swell that rose in her throat.

She switched off the light and the room was cast into dim shadows. She didn't want the soldiers or Jakub to see her like this, on the verge of a breakdown. Edith closed her eyes, struggling to get her wits back. She counted to ten in her mind. She was glad she was alone. If any of the men saw her that way, they might be less likely to trust her judgment in the future.

She scanned each stack in front of her, shadows stretching out behind each one in the dim light of the basement. Her breath came and went rapidly as she thought about the enormity of the situation. She had been here for months, going through dozens of stacks each day, each stack representing a family. Sometimes two or three stacks all came from the same place. Possessions families had gathered over the years.

Her heart sank as she thought about the myriads of displaced families as a result of the war and the machinations of the Wehrmacht. People had either fled, were captured, or were killed. Jewish men, women, and children corralled into camps just beyond the confines of this very estate.

*Beware the beginnings*, her father had said.

Edith thought about Franz and the other men upstairs, about Heinrich. They seemed like decent, intelligent, moral men. She considered herself similar in many ways, just a regular German citizen trying to keep her head down until this whole thing ended. So how had they acquiesced to serving something so far-reaching, so deeply evil?

Was it too late to do something? Was it too late to take some action, however small, that might help return life to the way it was before? That might save one work of art? One life?

Edith stood. A pale luster of moonlight illuminated the podium with her large ledger. From the back of the book, she tore a handful of blank pages, taking care not to make noise.

She did not know how she would get this information out, or who might help her, but she resolved to start. Someone had to figure out how to get these things back to their rightful owners, to save and return what was important and meaningful of their lives. *Why not me?* Edith thought of her father, printing pamphlets. Such a simple act, yet if everyone were brave enough to do something small, wouldn't it make a difference, in the end?

Edith turned to the first page of the book and began to copy her inventory, line by line. Item. Description. Destination. Original owner.

## 44
### CECILIA

*Milan, Italy*
*April 1491*

**WOULD SHE MAKE A DIFFERENCE, IN THE END?**
Cecilia sat on her bed and contemplated the question while she listened to Bernardo the poet read his latest composition:

> *. . . the more lively and beautiful Cecilia is,*
> *The greater will be your eminence in the future.*
> *Be thankful therefore to Ludovico, or rather*
> *To the genius and hand of Leonardo the painter*
> *Which allows your image to endure for posterity.*

But the larger the poem made her seem, the smaller Cecilia felt. She ran her palms over Violina's full belly. The white dog was stretched down the length of her legs, dormant, its ears spread out over her knees, its paw pads resting on Cecilia's bulging midsection. From her spot on her high, platform bed, Cecilia watched the dog's eyes open and close lazily, alternately sleeping and waking to peer at Bernardo as he paced back and forth before Cecilia. Bernardo continued:

*Everyone who sees Cecilia Gallerani—even if too late*
*To see her in life—will say: that suffices for us*
*To understand what is nature and what is beauty.*

". . . what is nature and what is *art*," said Master da Vinci, holding his brush in the air as he spoke.

"You are correct on that count, my friend." Bernardo scratched out a word on the parchment with his pen. ". . . what is nature and what is art," he said. "Much improved."

The nuptials concluded and the guests long gone, the Castello Sforzesco had returned to its quiet rhythm. The only difference was that Cecilia was now holed up in her own private chambers instead of the library. Yes, she was cast aside. But if she was honest with herself, she was not completely dissatisfied with this arrangement, as she had no desire to encounter Ludovico's new wife in the corridors. Beatrice d'Este of Ferrara, by the servants' accounts, was a girl Cecilia's own age, and of remarkably similar appearance, with the exception that she had unparalleled taste in clothing. In no time, she was sure to set the fashions for all the ladies in the house, if not for the entire duchy of Milan.

With his mistress little more than a prisoner in her own suite, Ludovico had consented to Cecilia's request to have some of her favorite volumes transferred from the library to a cabinet in a small sitting room at the threshold to her bedchamber. It was there that Leonardo and Bernardo met each day to continue their creative pursuits, and where Cecilia did her best to keep the court ladies and servants away. She requested a particularly quiet chambermaid twice a day to tend to the fire and tolerated Lucrezia Crivelli's double-edged banter only as long as it took for her to fasten the tight buttons up the back of her dress and to oil the soles of her feet.

With his elaborate decorations put away and the rotting flowers thrown out, Leonardo had returned to the portrait. And Bernardo was now composing a laudatory poem in praise of the picture—and in praise of Cecilia herself. Cecilia realized that as much as she had dreaded the thought of sitting for long hours before the artist, she relished their private jokes, their conversations about literature, ancient stories, and the meaning of symbols and images. She could not imagine how empty her days would have felt without these two fellow Tuscans by her side.

"I shall begin again," said Bernardo, clearing his voice. He held the paper out with an extended arm. Cecilia watched him squint at the large, looping script he had captured on the page:

*. . . Nature, who stirs your wrath, and who arouses your*
*envy?*
*Nature: It is Master da Vinci, who has painted one of your*
*stars!*
*Cecilia Gallerani, today so very beautiful, is the one*
*Beside whose beautiful eyes the sun appears only a dark*
*shadow.*
*The poet: All glory to you, Nature, even if in his portrait*
*She seems to listen rather than talk . . .*

A knock at the door interrupted Bernardo's recitation.

Cecilia recognized her brother's face poking into the room. The lace sleeve flourished as he waved. He cleared his throat.

"Excuse the interruption, signori." Fazio's eyes flitted toward the portrait, and Cecilia saw Master da Vinci place his body in front of it as if to shield it from view, at the same time that the painter smiled at her brother. "Our Most Excellent Lord requests to know the status of the portrait. And of Master Bernardo's verses."

"We are working on them now," Cecilia said, grimacing as the baby kicked her swiftly in her side. She pressed her palm to her middle and arched her back. The baby had become active in recent days, sending stabbing pains through her back and thighs. As Cecilia squirmed, Violina trotted, tail wagging, toward Fazio. The dog pressed her stomach to the ground, cowering in submission to Fazio's hand on her head. Cecilia wished that she, too, could crawl into the comforting embrace of her brother, that he might be able to give her some assurance that everything would be all right, in the end. But she would never want to appear so vulnerable to Master da Vinci and to Bernardo. They were counting on her.

"My poem will be a mere distraction compared to Master da Vinci's portrait, but we will be ready," said Bernardo.

"I had hoped to see the likeness of my own sister before the crowds assemble to break down the gates of the palace," Fazio teased. "It seems that Master da Vinci's name is on everyone's lips in Milan. People are clamoring to see his work after having witnessed his talent for decorative programs. After this party, I am certain that everyone in this city will want a picture painted by Leonardo da Vinci!"

Master da Vinci took a curt bow. "I am flattered."

"It is true," Fazio said. "An unseen number of guests have accepted His Lordship's invitation."

Cecilia stood awkwardly, pressing her bulk before her and setting her slippered feet on the stone floor. She approached her brother. "Fazio, you are sure that Ludovico wants me there? It is strange, I think."

"Don't be ridiculous!" said Fazio. "The portrait is of *you*, my lovely. It would be strange if you were tucked away in this chamber while everyone is gawking at your likeness."

"Your brother is correct," Bernardo said.

"Besides," Fazio continued, "one of the seamstresses is finishing a new dress for you to wear to the portrait's unveiling. His Lordship himself requested that she make one that more . . . suits your current condition." Fazio waved an unsure hand across Cecilia's burgeoning form.

She nodded. "Good. I might play the lute with no problem but I can hardly sing with my laces strapped so tight." Cecilia looked down and ran her hands over her stomach. "And . . . Beatrice?" she asked warily.

Fazio shook his head. "His Lordship's secretary has assured me that while you all are entertaining guests at the unveiling, Beatrice will be in a carriage on her way to Ferrara with her sisters-in-law. We made sure that she had business to attend to there."

Cecilia felt her shoulders drop in utter relief. "*Madonna mia.* Thank you," she said to her brother, grasping his hand.

"My pleasure," he said. "I am a diplomat, after all, though I must admit that this type of thing is outside my usual course of business."

Leonardo had gone back to painting, making small, careful adjustments with his brush and thumb. Fazio took advantage of the opportunity to glance at the portrait. Cecilia watched his hand fly to his mouth as he examined it.

"*Complimenti*, Master," he said. "You have captured my sister's beauty—and her stubbornness."

Cecilia swatted her brother's arm. "Not very diplomatic of you, Fazio!"

Her brother sniggered. "Well, the part about capturing your likeness is the truth. I only see one mistake."

"A mistake?" Master da Vinci asked.

"Just one," said Fazio. "That's not a very good likeness of Violina."

"It's not supposed to be Violina!" Cecilia exclaimed, swatting at her brother again.

"Then you have a weasel I don't know about hidden somewhere in this bedchamber?" he asked, pretending to hunt under the bed for the creature.

"It's not a weasel, it's an ermine."

"The ermine," Leonardo said, "out of moderation, never eats but once a day; it will rather let itself be taken by a hunter than to take refuge in a dirty lair, in order not to stain its purity."

"And," Bernardo added, "do not forget that the King of Naples bestowed the honor of the Order of the Ermine on His Lordship not so long ago."

"Good," Fazio said. "Then His Lordship will be even more pleased with the portrait. And my sister, your admirers will be ready for you."

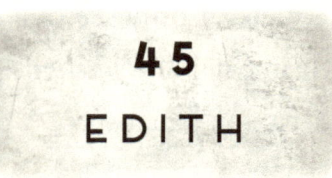

**45**

# EDITH

*Outside Puławy, Poland*
*December 1940*

IN THE POCKET OF HER FIELD JACKET, EDITH HELD
the one letter she'd received from home. For months, she'd
kept it neatly folded there. Now, the edges were tattered, the
creased lines set. But as she trundled along in an armored
car alongside Franz and several other soldiers, she pulled
the letter from her pocket and read it again:

*Dear Edith,*

*I trust that this letter, along with the others I have
sent, has found its way to you. We do not hear from you,
and we do not know if you are trying to reach your father.
We do not know your location. I continue to write, hoping that you will receive at least one of our messages.*

*Your father continues on as usual. His appetite is good.*

*He has a fondness for my Stollen and fried potatoes. I try to walk with him in the park as much as he will allow, but mostly, he likes to stay in his chair looking at the trees from the window. He does not call your name but I think he is looking for you.*

*My colleagues at the sanatorium report more and more patients gone to God every day. The policies. Well. I dare not share too many details, for fear that this letter may not reach you at all. Suffice it to say that I am grateful for an opportunity that pulled me—and Herr Becker—away. I will do what is in my power to keep your father from returning there. We hope you will return home soon.*

*—Rita*

For a few moments, the letter transported her back home, far away from the reality of eastern Poland. Edith scanned the desolate fields through the car window. Beyond the peace and order of the estate gardens, the countryside was a great panorama of hell. Where was Heinrich?

Franz Klein had relented finally to Edith's insistence that he take her off the estate grounds. He had told her that there was a small chance he could take Edith to the encampment where Heinrich's regiment was positioned. And now, Edith's heart lifted with hope at the thought that she might be just a car ride away from Heinrich. Did he know that she was looking for him?

But as they moved farther away from the villa and into the Polish countryside, Edith felt a jarring pang of cruel irony twist at her gut. Her villa, her basement office, the beautiful gardens of the oasis she occupied in the middle of the chaos, had kept her sheltered from the true effects of war. Since Edith's arrival just months ago, it had become impossible to make out towns, villages, government buildings, even restaurants or stores. Now, squeezed between three soldiers in the back of an armored car, rumbling out of the palace grounds and onto the main road, Edith saw that structures that once dotted the landscape were little more than broken masses of stone, thatch, and tile. She wondered how many people were out here, hiding in the loft of a barn, or tucked away in a root cellar under a smoldering ruin of stone. How many innocent families had hidden away to avoid incarceration in the camps?

And the people, the families who were the rightful owners of all the things gathered in the palace basement—all those who were listed on her copious inventories—where were they? Had they already been rounded up? Forced into detention camps? Killed?

She thought about her secret inventories, the ones she kept stuffed under her mattress at night. Was there some way that her list of stolen objects could make a difference? Were any staff left inside the Polish museums? Would there be anyone who could help her salvage the works of art? Would anyone be left to return the works to, in the end?

After her repeated requests to learn what had happened to Augustyn Józef Czartoryski and his wife, Dolores, the rightful owners of da Vinci's *Lady with an Ermine*, Jakub was able to share good news with Edith. Through diplomatic channels, they had been granted exile to Spain, Dolores's home country. Edith felt relief wash over her to think that the family was safe, and that she didn't have to bear the burden of guilt for their arrest. She wished that she had some way to contact them, to tell them that their precious collection was at least safe, if no longer in their home. But the knowledge that they had escaped the clutches of the Gestapo gave Edith the courage to keep going.

The convoy slowed to a crawl. They were passing an encampment where Polish insurgents had been rounded up. A line of bedraggled men stood behind a tall barbed-wire fence, watching the convoy. In the distance, smoke curled into the sky. A chill ran over Edith. She couldn't take her eyes away from the distraught, hopeless looks on the faces of the Polish men wandering around. They were much too thin and their clothes were little more than rags. Would they survive the winter?

Edith wondered why the convoy had slowed to a near halt. Were they giving her an eyeful of the ragged men? Were the soldiers taking pleasure in the appearance of the Polish prisoners?

Edith pulled in a deep breath and held it for a moment.

She had become an expert at holding a neutral face. It was the safest way, the only way, to exist in a world where she had little choice. She didn't want the men to see her as a weak woman underneath the hard façade.

Suddenly, behind them came a loud explosion. Edith jumped in her seat and then the broad hand of one of the soldiers sitting by her pushed her down to the floorboard. She heard a spray of gunfire. Bullets whizzed overhead, making her heart leap into her throat.

"Stay down, fräulein!" the soldier hissed at her.

For a long moment, all she heard was ringing in her ears. Then, suddenly, they were attacked by noise from all directions. Chaos. She couldn't hear what the soldier with her was yelling. He was on his knees and straightening up just enough to see over the seats in the car, extending one hand to indicate she should stay there.

Edith kept her head down until the noise and chaos cleared. She looked up in time to see the soldier lift his hand into a thumbs-up sign. She pushed herself off the floor.

The door hinged open, and the men piled out. Suddenly, there was the sound of thudding boots on the gravel. Soldiers ran up and down the road, looking for anyone who was wounded.

"Are you all right, miss?" the soldier asked. "Are you hit or hurt?"

"I'm okay." Surely they could hear her heart pounding?

Without another word, he ran in the direction of the

commanding officer. Edith opened the door and put one foot on the ground.

The Polish insurgents who had fired at their car were now lined up on the side of the road, most of them on their knees. Those who refused to kneel were shot first. She watched the men fall, holding in her shock.

She scanned the line. There were eleven men lined up there, two of them already on the ground dead, shot through the forehead. Had they escaped from the encampment? Were they trying to rescue prisoners? The men in the encampment had looked helpless. And these men were little more than walking corpses, their eyes sunken, their bodies skeletal, their clothes ragged and covered in ash, anger and desperation in their eyes.

Edith waited and watched, unmoving, trying to keep her eyes from the line of men about to be executed. She heard the German soldiers yelling at the insurgents. None of the men responded. They were on the ground, their hands behind their heads, their eyes down. None of them looked up, though Edith could hear the soldiers demanding that they do so. She heard the soldiers laughing at the Polish men, hurling vile insults.

One of the soldiers paced back and forth in front of the nine men. Some noise to the left made Edith turn and look. Two more German soldiers approached, a struggling Pole between them. They were gripping his arms and shoved him toward the line of his countrymen. He stumbled a bit, kicking up some dust. He spun around and tried to tackle the soldier who had shoved him and was immediately shot by the other one.

Edith closed her eyes. She heard the Pole hit the ground.

"Stop it!" Edith screamed, but her voice seemed lost in the chaos.

Without another warning, the soldier who had almost been tackled walked down the line of insurgents, shooting each one in the head.

"Stop—please!" Edith had to turn her head away. The insurgents didn't look like they were physically strong enough to pose any threat to the German soldiers. They were executed as if they were animals. Each one who dared to look straight ahead or into the eyes of the German soldiers had hatred embedded deeply there, easy to detect, though it was mixed with the familiar look of desperation.

Edith retched. Her Heinrich. Was he among those shooting these helpless, sick, poor people?

Edith looked down at her hands, balling them up into fists. Was she any different from these men with guns? After all, she was aiding in the looting of homes all across Poland and the rest of Europe. The men jumped back into the armored car. Edith felt dirty, not wanting to sit beside any of them.

"There is more fire ahead, sir," another soldier told the driver. "Turn around. The insurgents may have planted mines in the road. You have to go back."

Edith felt the driver turn the car around sharply, tires lurching in the ruts in the road, and they headed back to the quiet estate.

During the ride, Edith's ears rang with the aftershock of the gunfire, and she was filled with horror. She kept thinking about what Kai Mühlmann had told her: that Heinrich would not be the same man when he returned. What kind of man would he be? What kind of man could stand in front of those helpless prisoners, look them in the eye, and execute them? And what kind of woman would she be, if she were lucky enough to make it out of this situation alive?

# 46

## CECILIA

*Milan, Italy*
*May 1491*

WHAT KIND OF WOMAN WOULD SHE BE, CECILIA
thought as the midwife ran her palms over Cecilia's bulging midsection, if she were lucky enough to make it out of
this situation alive?

Cecilia studied the fading, colored faces painted in the
vaults above her bed, waiting. The midwife was a gray-haired, serious-looking woman with cold, smooth hands.
She worked slowly, reading her body as if Cecilia had potential as a racehorse: poking, prodding, listening, watching for signs.

Even if she did survive the birth, Cecilia thought, surely
her days in the ducal palace were numbered anyway, unless
she continued to defend the position she had earned, continued to prove her worth to Ludovico. And if she were sent
away instead, what then? Perhaps none of it mattered in the

end. Every few days she saw a little blood. At first, she had waited and wished it away. But when it only continued, she had finally confided in Lucrezia, and the midwife had appeared.

Finally, the midwife stood and regarded Cecilia with a lined brow. "The next few weeks are the most critical," she said. "You have already seen blood. If you see it again, you must stay in bed. You must not get up for any reason. Understood?"

Cecilia nodded, thinking of her vocal practice in preparation for the next string of events planned in the castle. "And how do I make sure that the birth goes . . . as planned?"

But the midwife only pursed her lips. "I do not want to tell you a lie, my lady. No two births are the same. There is no guaranteed outcome. Ultimately, nature will take its course; I am only an instrument. Another midwife might give you false assurances, but I only tell the truth." The woman studied Cecilia's face for a long moment, then gave her leg a squeeze, a small gesture that Cecilia knew was unearned. "Have your girl call for me when the time comes."

# 47
## EDITH

*Outside Puławy, Poland*
*January 1941*

AFTER HER HARSH FORAY INTO THE MIDDLE OF conflict, Edith was more determined than ever to exercise what little control she had in putting things right. She spent her days cataloging objects, duplicating her ledger, doing her best not to dwell on the fact that she had lost hope that she would find Heinrich in that desolate country beyond the walls of the estate.

As time wore on, the faces in the country estate changed. Men appeared, then disappeared. Those who remained looked as if all the life had been sucked out of them. It was no wonder that the men looked gaunt and dark. The newspapers had not reported it yet, but Edith knew from the rumblings of the soldiers in the palace that Hitler had invaded Russia. The Russians were no longer allies; they were enemies. And the estate was not far distant from the Russian border. Now, in addition to fighting a tough band of Polish insurgents, there were also Russian threats, the soldiers had told her.

After witnessing the roadside shooting, Edith did her best to stay to herself on the lower level, to drown out the worries about the hellish devastation that she knew stretched for miles around her in all directions. She could not function if she stopped to wonder how many camps there were, if there were any towns left standing, how many Polish families' homes had been emptied of their contents, how many people were packed into cattle cars. All she could do, she thought, was to record everything she saw, everything that passed through her hands, until she could figure out what to do with it that might make a difference.

Edith tore out a blank page from the back of her ledger and began to copy the details of a small oil painting.

*Subject: Landscape with shepherds*

*Artist: 17th-century Dutch, possibly a follower of van Ruysdael*

*Support: Walnut panel, .32 meters by .63. Equal members joined on the horizontal. Signs of damage from boring insects, no longer active.*

*Ground: White, very thin. Broken in places, probably during transport.*

*Paint: Oil, thinly applied with translucent film and pencil drawing barely visible underneath.*

*Cradle: Low, pine. Warped. Broken upper corners . . .*

*Destination: Shipped to the Alte Pinakothek, Munich, via train, Manifest #3467*

*Original owner: Nowak family, Lower Silesia, exact town uncertain*

"Good morning, my dear." Jakub, the lean Polish translator, entered the room, smelling of soap and the oily cream he used to slick his hair and wiry mustache.

Edith quickly stuffed her duplicate inventory page between the creased pages of her ledger. In a way, Jakub had reminded Edith of her own father, and she felt comfortable in his presence. But now, she felt the sting, the panic of her secret perhaps having been discovered. Had he seen her copying the ledgers?

But Jakub hardly seemed to notice what Edith was doing. He sat at a large table and began poring over his own stack of pages. The German officers relied on Jakub to translate a variety of things that came through the doors. Edith watched him carefully noting the contents of a letter. He was meticulous, dutiful. Just doing what he was asked because, well, what choice did he have? Just like her, Edith thought, and she wondered where Jakub's true sympathies lay. Edith walked over to Jakub and perched on the edge of the table.

"Jakub," she began, her voice barely above a whisper. She struggled for what to say or how to broach the subject. But she had his attention now, his sharp blue eyes on her.

"I wondered if you had any . . . contact . . . with groups outside . . ." she began, hesitating. She knew that Jakub left the palace at the end of each day and returned the next morning. Edith did not know where he went, or who or what he knew beyond these walls. His face remained blank, unreadable.

She tried again. "I have heard that there are people in the countryside who can get information to those who might, who might . . ." Her eyes scanned the vast horde of stolen goods stacked high in the shadows of the storerooms. "Help protect all of this. Or maybe get it back where it belongs. Do you know anything about that?"

Edith watched Jakub press his back against the chair and purse his lips. For a moment, he considered her words, turning his pen over and over between his fingers. Finally, he said, "I am only doing what I am asked, my dear." A tight grin. "What else could I do?"

Edith nodded and began to turn away, but then Jakub leaned forward and whispered, "But please . . . tell me. What were you thinking?"

Edith walked over to the ledger book and removed the duplicate she had stashed in between its pages. She returned to the table and handed the page to Jakub.

Edith watched Jakub peer down at her tiny, neat handwriting through his glasses. Silence stretched long and heavy between them. Would he turn her in? Would he tell the officers upstairs that she had been compiling a duplicate inventory until she could find a way to get it into the hands of the right resistance group? What would happen to her? "You are copying the inventories," Jakub whispered finally, meeting her gaze.

"I . . . yes," Edith said, struggling to explain herself, but Jakub seemed to understand already.

Jakub paused, pressing his fingers under his chin. "Your Governor Frank," he said. At the mention of Hans Frank's name, Edith bristled. "Perhaps you know that he has already ordered the murder of hundreds of thousands of my people? Maybe more. My brothers are missing. And their wives and children." A shadow passed over Jakub's face. "His men do not hesitate to shoot on sight. Without cause."

A sharp pain stabbed at Edith's gut and she stared at her hands. How could she explain that she herself had helped Frank get what he wanted? That Jakub might have every right to blame Edith along with all the other Germans who had invaded his home country so brutally? "I only know what is reported in the papers," she lied.

"And the German press will not report his crimes against us," Jakub said. Just as Edith conceded that Jakub would not help her, he said, "But it is my belief that not all Germans are bad. You, for example. It is clear to me that you are a lady with great respect for art. And for human life. You want to see these things returned to their owners." He gestured into the dark recesses of the storeroom, then to her inventory page on the table. "I might help you," he said finally, lowering his voice.

"Really?" Edith felt her shoulders fall in relief. "What can we do, Jakub? I feel so helpless!"

Jakub paused and examined the doorway warily. Finally he whispered, "The ladies in the kitchen. They may appear to know nothing, but they are connected with groups beyond this palace."

Edith's jaw dropped. The quiet, unassuming women who baked bread, washed dishes, and laundered their bed linens? Those who didn't appear to understand German at all? Edith had all but given up on communicating with them. Now, she could hardly believe what Jakub was saying.

"Your secret is also mine," said Jakub. Then he tapped Edith's copied inventory page with his fingers. "If we work together, I think we can find a way to put these into the right hands."

# Part IV
*Object of Desire*

## 48
## LEONARDO

*Milan, Italy*
*April 1491*

**THE PORTRAIT IS FINISHED.**

His Lordship's secretary has asked me to arrange an evening to unveil Cecilia's likeness to the court, to Ludovico's closest friends and guests. For now, the picture rests on an easel in my bedchamber in the Corte Vecchia, the paint finally dry under my thumb. I return to my drawings, the face of Cecilia Gallerani seeming to watch over my shoulder with her curious expression.

I thumb through the stacks of drawings I have made during the years I have spent in Milan. A man based on the perfect proportions described by Vitruvius. Ink-washed renditions of Our Lady turned out for various devotional pictures. A design for a public square and my failed attempt to win the commission for a cupola for Milan's cathedral. Countless studies of horses in preparation for the great equestrian monument to His Lordship's late father. Nearly all of these things, Ludovico il Moro has tasked me to design.

But the truth is that His Lordship needs none of them. On a fresh piece of parchment, I have begun to plot a series of architectural designs for improvements to the Castello Sforzesco that will bolster its defense in the face of invaders. I have spent many hours taking measurements of the old battlements and the long outdated underground system of hydraulics. I have redesigned the bridge over the moat, which is currently useless against an attack.

In recent weeks, I have watched mercenary commanders under His Lordship's employ race in and out of the castle gates on powerful horses. Two of Ludovico's closest advisers have disappeared; I do not dare to ask where they have gone. In his chambers, Ludovico il Moro surrounds himself with an ever-tighter circle of men. He seems to imagine threats from all sides—inside the castle and without.

A battle is coming, I think. It is only a matter of time.

# 49

## DOMINIC

*Siegen, Germany*
*April 1945*

A BATTLE IS COMING, DOMINIC THOUGHT. *IT IS ONLY A* *matter of time.*

The rutted road curved through the woods, the Jimmy's headlights pushing golden fingers across dusky tree trunks. They moved at a crawl; Hancock hung half out of the truck, squinting into the woods, searching. Dominic couldn't help wondering if they were lost. He hoisted his rifle a little more snugly into his arms, a nasty suspicion twisting his gut. Lost. Or being led into some kind of a trap.

The road to Siegen had been tough, but not as tough as it had been for the men before them who had pushed the German stronghold ever eastward. They passed endless evidence of heavy fighting. While the corpses had been removed from the roadside, there were still burnt-out

Jeeps, tanks peppered with holes, shell holes blown in the earth, discarded weapons scattered across the hillsides. And bloodstains. They lay in dark patches in the hills, smeared where bodies had been dragged out of them. One large stain was still bright red and sticky when they had passed, an American helmet lying half soaked in it. The sight made Dominic's heart break. He wondered if anyone had told Paul Blakely's family what had happened to him. Now Francine would be just another girl robbed of her future by the war. The wedding she and Paul had dreamed of, the children he'd hoped would have their mother's eyes—none of these would ever happen. Dominic wondered if his little Cecilia would see her father again—and if his new baby would know her father at all.

"There!" Hancock spurted the word so suddenly that Dominic's finger jumped onto the trigger, but their commander's expression was one of glee. The Jimmy crunched to a halt. Hancock pulled a flashlight from his pocket and shone it into the gloom. Its thin beam illuminated a dark opening in the hillside, an ugly gap cut roughly into the smooth soil; it was covered by the remains of a great metal gate. The gate hung from one hinge, the sharp indentations of bullet holes shining on its surface.

"Open it up!" cried Hancock. Dominic jumped out of the truck. While the other men stood warily, scanning the woods for danger, Dominic seized the cold iron and pulled. Dominic's muscles screamed in protest as he strained against the weight of the gate, but it began to budge, and to a sound of squealing metal, he and two other men managed to move it aside.

Hancock disembarked from the Jimmy and stared into the darkness, playing his torch through the opening, as Dominic and the others stretched their aching backs and picked up their rifles again. "Bonelli, grab four others and come with me," he said. "The rest of you, stay here and watch the convoy."

There was a chorus of "Yes, sir," and Hancock stepped forward, Dominic close on his heels.

"Wait!" The voice from the truck made Hancock's shoulders slump in dismay. "I come!"

Dominic saw Hancock steel himself before turning around, the rest of the men following suit. Stephany had hooked one knee over the back of the Jimmy in his attempts to get out; the vicar's robe he insisted on wearing made matters difficult as he struggled to climb out. Panting, he hoisted himself to the ground with a creak of old bones before hurrying over to them, straightening his robes.

"Stephany . . ." Hancock began.

"No, no, no." Stephany waved a hand at him, eyes shining. "I know what you will say. It is too dangerous, I must stay with the trucks. You know you will lose this fight, Walker." He reached up and gave Hancock an affectionate pat on the cheek. "Come, we find my relics, yes?" Beaming, he strutted off toward the entrance to the mine.

Hancock uttered a strangled expletive. "Fine. Do what you want, Stephany. I can hardly stop you."

Lieutenant Commander Stout was waiting for them at the entrance to the mine. He'd been waiting for reinforcements before going in; of the unit he'd left Aachen with, only five men remained, huddled around him as if for warmth. But Stout's determined posture had not changed. His mustache curved up in a smile. "Hancock!"

"Sir!" Hancock saluted.

"I heard you had some trouble outside of Bonn. Come on, let's see what we've got." Stout led the way into the copper mine, his flashlight held high, its puny beam struggling against the thick darkness and utter cold.

A long, arched tunnel had been cut roughly into the gloom. The low ceiling was oppressive, and the air would have been stifling if it hadn't been so bitterly cold. Dominic felt his hands grow numb on the barrel of his rifle. The tunnel twisted and widened with pockets and dark chambers opening off to the sides.

As his eyes adjusted to the darkness, he began to spot them. First, just the whites of their eyes; then their round faces, glowing in the weak beam of light.

Civilians.

Stragglers, survivors, who'd somehow managed to escape Siegen during the fighting. Huddling together in little clusters in the small pockets, they watched with hunted eyes as the Americans trooped past. Stout and Hancock, seeing that they were unarmed, paid them little attention. But the fear in their eyes chilled Dominic to the bone.

He assumed there would only be that handful hiding near the entrance of the mine, but the deeper the men advanced into the darkness, the more humid the air grew. Warmth started to fill the air around them, making Dominic's frozen fingers cramp. With it came the smell. It was familiar from the badly sanitized refugee camps they'd visited outside Aachen, only amplified a thousand times in the mine's closed air: the smell of humanity at its worst. Sweat. Urine. Excrement. One of the other young soldiers gagged quietly beside Dominic, and he found his own stomach turning as he checked the floor periodically to see where he was putting his boots. It was so cold lately that he'd been sleeping with them on, and he didn't want to tread in anything that he didn't want smeared inside his blankets. More pressing was the thought that for this smell to be so pervasive, there had to be many people in here. Dominic's stomach tightened.

"Be ready," Stout obviously shared Dominic's concerns. He had one hand on the pistol on his hip. Hancock pulled out his own pistol. The ugly weapon looked wrong in his lean, elegant fingers.

A thin, piercing sound rose into the air. The noise was plaintive and reminded Dominic so much of home that it made his heart pang: the cry of a baby.

Only this was not the regular scream of a fussy baby. This child was cold and hungry and afraid, and it gave voice to its unhappiness in the only way it knew how. Dominic swallowed hard as they advanced and the terrible truth came to the front. The tunnel branched and, as they followed, they saw many small cavities cut into the cave, all of them filled with people. None of them stood; they were all slumped in various attitudes of defeat on benches, stones, the odd cot. Women. Children. Men. Babies. The flashlight beams flitting through the impenetrable darkness revealed hundreds of pale and dirt-stained faces staring out at them with deep mistrust.

It seemed that the entire population of Siegen was hiding in the mines, waiting for the war to be over. Dominic wanted to tell them not to be afraid, that they wouldn't be hurt, but he spoke no German. And he realized with a shock that they were not afraid, either. These people *were* the Germans; not the minority bent on exterminating the Allied armies, but the real German people who lived and slept and ate and wanted nothing other than to get their lives back, to do what they did before the war had torn their country to pieces.

*"Amerikaner."*

Whispered by every mouth as soon as they spotted their uniforms, the word bounced from wall to wall in a susurrus of mistrust. Dominic looked into the eyes of a little girl and smiled instinctively; she smiled back, but her mother grasped her tightly and pulled her closer, her eyes filled with terror.

The tunnel opened out into another cave so big that the men's flashlights could not pick out the end. The adults who had been lying around the cave jumped up as one and shuffled back against the walls, clutching their rags more tightly around their shoulders as they stared in mute horror. Stephany tried speaking a few words of reassuring German, but even his enthusiasm waned in the face of such collective fear. They all stared silently, Germans and Americans alike.

All but one. A small boy stepped into the circle of light. His dark hair was a dirty tousle on his forehead, but when he looked up at them, his eyes were as blue as chips of jewels in the dirt. He walked up to Lieutenant Commander Stout, who froze, uncomprehending.

The little boy reached up to touch a patch on Stout's field coat. His giggle suddenly filled the mine, a golden bubble of happiness in the dark. Then he grabbed Stout's forefinger in his chubby little hand and tugged him forward. Enchanted, the soldiers followed as if in a dream as the little boy led them to a large metal door. He reached up with a tiny fist and rapped a complicated tune on the metal.

"*Amerikaner,*" he chirped.

The door creaked open. Seeing only uniforms, Dominic and his men leapt to attention, yanking the barrels of their guns up to take aim. But the eyes they looked into were not German. They were British, French, American, according to the patches on their soot-covered uniforms. And at the sight of armed Allied troops making their way into the mine, the men fell to their knees and some burst into tears.

The nearest man grasped Stout by the sleeves in shaking hands in spite of the fact that the astonished lieutenant general still aimed a pistol at him.

"Please," he begged. "Take us home."

# 50
## EDITH

*Outside Puławy, Poland*
*March 1941*

ONE NIGHT, WHILE THE GERMAN OFFICERS LOUNGED
at the dining table, happily stuffed with potato dumplings
and Polish vodka, Edith saw her opportunity.

Empty plate in hand, Edith slipped from the table and
made her way to the kitchen. Behind her, the men swirled
their glasses and laughed at one another's crude jokes. She
would do her best to appear as if she were simply retiring
for the evening, she thought. After all, her cell-like bedroom was located just down the hallway from the scullery.

In the kitchen, the three Polish women bustled around
one another, stacking dirty plates, wiping dough and flour
from the counters, sweeping debris from the floor. Edith
wasn't sure which one to approach first. She didn't know
their names; it had seemed better that way, she thought.

She only knew what Jakub had told her: if Edith dutifully copied each day's inventory, making note of the trucks and trains headed to the German and Austrian borders, the women would know what to do with the information. They could put them in the right hands. At least Edith hoped that they could.

Edith's palm went instinctively to the pocket of her field jacket. Folded into a tiny packet was the day's manifest of items that Edith had cataloged, including the original owners and locations, if they were known, all notated in her small, neat handwriting. But she hesitated. Did these unassuming-looking women really have the power to stop their allies in the Resistance from blowing up trains and trucks, as Jakub had told her? It seemed incredible to fathom. But Edith trusted Jakub, and he assured her that it was the best chance to protect these works, to perhaps someday return them to their rightful owners. What else could she do? She was only one woman stuck in a basement near the Russian border, her only contact with the outside world a regiment of Nazi soldiers, an unassuming Polish translator, and a kitchen full of resistors masquerading as kitchen staff.

Edith hesitated. Which one should she approach? The youngest of the three women stood at the sink, up to her elbows in soapy water. Edith settled on the woman wiping the counters. She stepped alongside her and placed her dirty plate on the counter. Then she reached into her pocket and pulled out the day's inventory.

The woman did not meet Edith's eyes and hardly stopped what she was doing. She simply moved her hand toward Edith's and swiped the small paper packet into her own pocket. A small, nearly imperceptible movement under the edge of the kitchen counter. Edith turned away, then heard a whisper behind her back.

*"Danke schon."*

Edith felt the hairs on the back of her neck bristle. They understood German after all.

Through a narrow opening in the dining room doorway, Edith glanced at the officers still seated at the table. A hefty soldier, one of the unit's commanding officers, tilted back in his chair and worked a toothpick into the cracks between his teeth.

Edith felt herself huff a sigh of wonder. The men had no idea that the kitchen women were listening to every word they said.

# 51
## DOMINIC

*Siegen, Germany*
*April 1945*

POWS. HOW HAD THEY ESCAPED THEIR NAZI CAPTORS?
Dominic's jaw fell open. How long had they been hiding in
this mine alongside the residents of Siegen?

Stephany was doling out more of their powdered coffee
rations to warm their frozen bones when Hancock came
running. All the men in the room flinched as one, and
Dominic clutched his rifle more tightly. But the expression
on Hancock's face was perfect joy.

"Sir!" For once, even the dapper Hancock was dishev-
eled with excitement. He pushed his helmet straight, face
shining. "You've got to see this."

Dominic, Stephany, and Stout followed Hancock down
a series of winding tunnels until they came to a door that,
judging by the splintered frame, had just been broken down.

Behind the door, Dominic only saw a cloud of fine dust. But as his eyes adjusted to the darkness, a beautiful portrait of a curly-haired lady with pink cheeks looked back at him. Then he saw what Hancock had seen. Row upon row of works of art. Paintings. Sculptures. Stacks and stacks of packed cases. The priceless works were placed haphazardly on slapdash shelves made of raw lumber, their splendor incongruous amid the dirt, the cold, and the smell.

But the truth was undeniable: Siegen's mines hid everything that old Herr Weyres had promised.

Dominic felt his weary heart beating faster as he stepped into the room. He could immediately see that this dirty mine might hold masterpieces he'd only ever read about. He wanted to reach out and touch it all, but instead, he gripped the barrel of his rifle and walked among them, gazing at the gilded frames and shining surfaces of oil paint. Some of the paintings were labeled with tags scrawled in black ink. Manet. Vermeer. It rang like a hall of fame of artists whose work Dominic had only dreamed of seeing in the flesh. Suddenly, Dominic's fingers itched to draw.

*Keep drawing.*

In a flash, Dominic was back in Aachen, kneeling over Paul in front of the ruined cathedral, watching as his friend gasped out his last breaths. The agony that swamped his body was replaced with disgust. He turned away, suddenly nauseated. It was splendid, but he would give every last piece of art in this room to have Paul back.

As he turned, dull with pain, he saw it. A huge crate, the word *AACHEN* scrawled across it.

"Stephany," he said, his voice flat.

The vicar hurried over, hope in his eyes. They widened when he spotted the crate. He rushed to it, his fingers scrabbling fruitlessly on the wood; Hancock seized a crowbar and the servicemen helped him to pry the thing open. The contents were wrapped in burlap. Hands shaking, Stephany drew it aside as gently as if it wrapped a sleeping baby. Gold and jewels glittered among the rough cloth, and Stephany fell to his knees, tears streaming down his face, as if his own family members had just been found alive. Fluent German poured from him, too fast for Dominic to keep up. Dominic's heart surged. He knelt by Stephany, putting a hand on the old man's shoulder. "What is it?"

When Stephany looked up at him, the joy in his eyes seized Dominic by the throat. He grabbed Dominic's shoulders with shaking hands.

"Thanks be to God. Thanks be to *you*, my friends," he said. "We have found them."

# 52
## EDITH

*Outside Puławy, Poland*
*April 1941*

ONE EVENING, AFTER HANDING THE DAY'S INVENTORY over to the kitchen women, Edith felt an overwhelming need for a breath of fresh air. Behind her, she heard the officers' laughter, their companionable banter at the table. Would they—and would she—ever make peace with what they were doing? And did they suspect her at all? Edith pulled her wool coat over her drab, wrinkled uniform and stepped outside.

In the moonlight, Edith could make out the silhouettes of the estate garden's formal patterns and flower beds. A crisp layer of frost had settled over the surfaces. A Nazi flag so large it hardly seemed real stood quiet in the still air, its swastika hung from the eaves of the home and draped down two stories to the bench where Edith sat, watching her breath turn into a puff of vapor. She pulled her collar closer to her neck.

For nearly three months, Edith and Jakub had diligently copied the day's inventories and transportation manifests, entrusting them to the hands of the kitchen women. Such a small act, Edith thought. Would it make a difference? If even one train car, one armored truck full of precious possessions and works of art was saved, Edith thought, then yes, it would be worth it. Edith thought of her father now, and his own small acts of resistance in the last war. With all her heart, Edith wished that she could talk to him, could tell him what she was doing, could ask for his counsel.

It had been so long without a word from her father or his nurse. Edith lowered her head to her knees, folding her arms around her head. She pressed her eyes into the sleeve of her coat and held her breath for a moment, squeezing her eyes shut against the emotion.

"Edith."

Edith pressed the heels of her palms to her eyes, as if she could push away the sting.

"Edith," she heard again, a gentle voice.

She turned to see Franz, standing in his uniform, stark against the edge of the flag hanging from the villa's façade. Even in the darkness, she could see that his cheeks were flushed in the icy air. He sat next to Edith on the bench and they both stared out into the black. Suddenly, she felt his broad hand on her shoulder. What was he doing? He knew she was engaged to be married. Was he so starved for female affection that he might try to kiss her anyway, to take advantage of the lonely isolation of this strange place, so far from home and everything they loved?

But when she turned to meet his gaze, she saw that his face was grim instead, his eyes bloodshot.

"There is news of your Heinrich."

# 53
## DOMINIC

*Siegen, Germany*
*April 1945*

THERE WAS SOMETHING SOOTHING AND FAMILIAR about the mines, Dominic thought, dank and pungent as they were. Fires built in the rooms brought warmth and light to the black tunnels. With the assurance that the fighting was over in their hometown, the refugees had started to venture into the early spring sunlight. A hint of joy seemed to come back with them, in the cleaner smell of their clothes, in the new color in their skin, and the glittering in their eyes. Or perhaps that was just hope: hope they were not all going to die down there in the mines.

But it was not the refugees that made Dominic feel at home in the mines. He stood guard over one of the many storerooms full of art they'd found, leaning comfortably against the wall as he cradled his rifle, knowing that it was unlikely he'd actually have to use it right now; he was protecting the treasures more from the refugees than from anything else. They were civilians, but they were humans, after all, and faced with the loss of everything they owned. Who could blame them for having sticky fingers, under the circumstances?

Apart from the bedraggled citizens they had found in the mine—people who were more than willing to help—they had to hire prisoners, too. Most had been arrested for petty theft and needed to be watched closely among the treasures, but the Allies had had no choice. There was too much to do. Days had already passed, and Dominic knew it could end up drawing out into weeks.

Siegen reminded him of the coal mines he'd spent all his working life in, back home in Pittsburgh. His work had been backbreaking and dirty, deep below the touch of the sun, but it had been good and hard and peaceful, and he missed it. He missed the camaraderie with the other miners and the knowledge that he was doing honest work to bring people something they needed. He missed having hard, calloused, tired hands that had chipped coal out of the earth to warm the homes of the people he cared about. Now those same hands had, for months, done little but kill.

But most of all, he missed his family. It had been nearly a year.

Footsteps in the storeroom behind him caught Dominic's attention, and he hurried to open the door, holding it aside for the group of servicemen who carried a gigantic wooden crate between them. This was one of many rooms they'd discovered packed to the roof with works of art; Dominic spotted the label KÖLN stamped into the side of the crate as the men carried it past. They'd discovered pieces from so many museums in German cities secreted away here in the darkness. Cologne, yes, but also Essen, Munster— more than Dominic could keep track of. There were altar-pieces, oil paintings, sculptures, gilded busts, all of them old and beyond pricing. Nearly forty boxes of documents and original musical scores had come from Beethoven's house in Bonn. Dominic could only shake his head in wonder.

Hot on the heels of the men carrying the crate came other soldiers, these carrying individual oil paintings with great reverence. Dramatic war scenes, lush countryside, deep-eyed portraits wobbled past Dominic in the sol-diers' dirty hands, heading for the surface and transport to safehouses.

"Wait!" The other soldier who was guarding the door alongside Dominic reached out to stop a soldier carrying a painting past him. "Is that what I think it is?"

The round-faced man stared at the other serviceman. Dominic still did not speak to his comrades much, but he knew his fellow guard, George Weaver, was a Bostonian who had arrived on the Normandy beaches along with the hordes on that same fateful day as Dominic. "What do you think it is?" asked the other soldier.

"It *is*." Weaver's eyes lit up. He reached out with a reverent hand, almost touching the painting, but hesitating when his trembling fingertips were an inch away. "It's a Rubens," he breathed. "An original."

Dominic studied the painting. It depicted a magnificent Madonna and child surrounded by saints, an image whose peace rang down through the centuries.

"Imagine!" said Weaver. "This painting stuck down here under the earth."

"Well, it weighs a ton, so if you don't mind," snapped the other soldier. He shouldered past Weaver and headed for the surface, muttering grumpily.

Weaver's enthusiasm remained unflagged. "Most people think of Rubens as Flemish," Weaver said to Dominic, pointing at the ceiling of the mine, "but he was actually born right here in Siegen."

As the masterpieces continued to parade by, Dominic recognized the mixture of wonder and dismay in Weaver's face, remembering the day that knuckleheaded Kellermann had seized his sketch of Sally and mocked it in front of all the others. It was a lonely thing to be an art lover in a world of war.

When another large canvas with a nude female passed them, Weaver barely looked at it. "Lucas Cranach!"

"You know all of these?" asked Dominic, huffing out a laugh.

Weaver shrugged. "I studied art before the war. Would

have finished my degree, but then I had to enlist." The corner of his mouth turned up in something that might have been a wary smile. "Never thought I'd find myself in a copper mine in Germany, looking at some of the greatest masterpieces ever created."

"Let's just hope we get any of them out of this place in one piece," said Dominic. "Look."

Weaver followed Dominic's pointing finger to the next painting. It depicted a family, all mounted on sleek horses with docked tails, but the paint was badly flaking in the top corner. A dark stain on the frame bore testimony to the damp that was starting to eat away at the art in the mines.

Originally, Hancock had told them, the Nazis had been controlling the heat and dehumidification of the mine from a factory nearby, but the factory had been bombed out weeks, maybe months ago. Now, the mine echoed to the sound of water dripping from the ceiling. Every surface was permeated with damp. The precious art, saved from the mass destruction that was tearing the continent apart, now faced a creeping enemy that was just as dangerous. It was a race against the damp to get the paintings out of the mine and into the weapons carriers that would trundle across the country to a collecting point. There, Dominic was told, they would be safeguarded, cataloged, and returned to their rightful owners. If any of them were still alive.

But he remembered the look on Stephany's face when he had opened that crate from Aachen, the unadulterated joy in his eyes as he touched the glittering gilded surface of the shrine containing Charlemagne's relics. It was the first time Dominic had seen that expression in his entire time in Europe. Not long ago, he had wondered why art mattered at all. And now, he felt a surge of something that he thought had been forever lost. Hope.

"Look at this!" gasped Weaver. He brought another serviceman to a halt, running his eyes over the picture.

"And that." Dominic pointed at a beautiful portrait of a stately, pale-skinned woman, the folds of her red gown so vividly depicted that he felt he could almost touch them.

Weaver stared at him. "I heard you're an artist too."

Dominic shook his head. "No, not really. I used to sketch. Portraits."

"Used to?"

Dominic turned away, suddenly sick with pain as he heard Paul's last gasp in his mind again.

*Keep drawing.*

# 54
## EDITH

*Outside Puławy, Poland*
*April 1941*

"I'M SO SORRY, EDITH," FRANZ SAID, BUT WHAT WORDS could possibly account for how a man in the full bloom of his life could be cut down, alive one second, dead the next? And for what justification?

"It happened not far from the border," Franz murmured, staring into his fingers laced between his knees, his head hanging low as they sat together on the bench in the frozen air. "There was a village, they told me. Heinrich's unit had aligned itself along a bunker just outside . . ."

Edith did what this war had taught her to do well. She brought down the veil of numbness across her head. Around the edges of the veil, images poked their way into her consciousness. Heinrich taking her hand as they strolled through the empty galleries of the Alte Pinakothek after the doors had been closed for the evening. Calling for birds as they floated in a small rowboat on the park pond. Helping her father peel an apple. Brushing a lock of hair from her face and bringing his lips to her neck.

She sucked in her breath. Her heart was already hardened against the mission of the Wehrmacht. Germans were sacrificing their lives for an undertaking that had seemed misguided from the start, but now seemed increasingly hopeless. There was one person, Edith thought, who could be held responsible for the destruction of Poland. And for Heinrich's death.

Edith imagined Governor Frank, seated at his hulking desk, sipping Polish vodka, gazing at his da Vinci over the radiator, while Heinrich and thousands of others were cut down in bloody combat. She had no doubt now that Hans Frank, Hitler's hand-chosen governor-general, was responsible for all of it, every life that had been plucked away brutally throughout the Polish countryside—enemy and countryman alike. Chills ran up her spine when she thought about his solicitousness, his false veneer of gentility.

Franz continued to give her details about the circumstances of Heinrich's death, but Edith could no longer fit the cruel information into her head. All that she could think was that she had lost the man she would have married, and it was all because of Governor Frank.

## 55

## CECILIA

*Milan, Italy*
*May 1491*

"IF YOU KNOW WHAT'S GOOD FOR YOU, YOU'LL STAY IN bed." Lucrezia Crivelli was fastening the last pearl-studded wrap around Cecilia's long braid when the knock came.

In the mirror, Leonardo da Vinci appeared, and Cecilia smiled at his reflection. To anyone unacquainted, this lowly craftsman from Florence looked as if he might be a duke himself. He was meticulously put together in purple hose and a leather doublet with metal studs that glittered in the lantern light.

Cecilia gasped. "You are a vision, signore."

He bowed.

But as she began to rise from her bench at the mirror to greet him, she doubled over, unable to straighten herself. The artist rushed to her side, and Lucrezia grasped Cecilia's arm to steady her.

"Are you all right, signorina?" the master said.

"The midwife advised her to stay in bed to stop the blood," Lucrezia said. "Such a dangerous time. But she won't listen."

Cecilia laughed nervously and stood up straight. "Please. I'm fine. It's nothing serious." Over the last day, Cecilia had felt unsteady and weak, her stomach clenching into a ball so hard sometimes that she had to curl on her bed until the feeling subsided. She hoped that she would be able to get through the sonnet and the song she had practiced without having to lie down again. The fact was that she felt terrified of the birth, but the last thing she could afford was to give Ludovico a reason to send her away. She had to uphold her place in Ludovico's court; no one else could do that for her. One song. A round of greeting to His Lordship's guests. Then she would return to her bed like the midwife had instructed.

Cecilia looped her arm through Leonardo's, and the two made their way down the corridor, he taking care to support her ungainly, slow progress toward the great *sala* where Ludovico held his most important events. Lanterns winked and flickered along the cavernous expanse of the corridors that led to the great hall. The heft of her newly made green velvet dress made a low rasp across the marble. Cecilia looked around nervously, her first foray out of her private chambers since Ludovico's wedding day some five months ago. A chambermaid bowed her head, and Cecilia was relieved that the girl remained silent as they passed.

"She can hardly walk," Cecilia heard Lucrezia whisper to the chambermaid. "Look at her!"

Ahead, in the lantern light, a cluster of court ladies and guests had gathered in the antechamber of the main hall. Cecilia felt a flutter and then a clench in her stomach, but it quickly subsided. There was a collective murmur, and then the crowd parted as Leonardo and Cecilia made their way toward them. Cecilia dared to look up and, seeing their curious, open expressions, so full of anticipation, she managed to smile. She knew that she would be expected to charm them with her vocal talents. She had done it before, and she could do it now, she told herself. She gathered her courage.

Beyond the antechamber, she could hear Bernardo's voice, and she felt buoyed enough to proceed toward the *sala grande*. She knew that Leonardo's drawings were displayed around the room for the guests to examine, but that the portrait of her stood in the center of the room, draped with a long swath of velvet that the master himself would remove when it was time to unveil his masterpiece. Master da Vinci squeezed her hand tightly against his side, and she felt that everything would be all right.

But as soon as they turned into the vestibule of the great hall, a shriek rang out. The crowd fell silent. The clipped sound of heeled shoes echoed on the marble as a woman came storming down the hallway.

Leonardo's arm dropped from Cecilia's but quickly found its way around her waist to support her.

"Beatrice," she heard him whisper behind her ear. "*Dio.*"

"*La dogaressa,*" she heard the collective whisper of the crowd. Up until that moment she had not laid eyes on Ludovico's bride, but there she was, unbelievably, standing before them.

"She was supposed to be on her way to Ferrara?" Leonardo whispered.

Cecilia was dumbstruck, and her words vanished from her as the woman stormed toward them. It was as if the world stopped the moment Beatrice caught sight of Cecilia. The two women stood face-to-face, mouths agape, as they looked upon what could have been their very own twin.

They were both dressed in deep velvet green dresses, almost identical to each other; their hair, brown and braided down their backs; their eyes dark, both burning with fire. Leonardo stood between the two women, shielding Cecilia. But Cecilia put her hand on his arm and gently pushed him aside. She had never wanted to see Ludovico's wife, but now she could not tear her eyes away.

There wasn't a sound from the crowd of guests, which had gotten larger thanks to Beatrice's shrieks of fury. Cecilia wasn't sure what she could say coming face-to-face with the woman she had wished to be all these months. Not only had Beatrice taken the position she believed she had earned, but how could Ludovico have married a woman who looked just like her?

Beatrice's eyes ripped away from Cecilia's as she scanned the crowd of guests that had assembled in her castle.

"Where is he?!" she demanded of them. "Ludovico!"

Farther down the hallway, Cecilia heard the familiar jangling of metal that accompanied the Regent of Milan when he attended an official event. The short, dark man cut through the crowd of people. It was the first time she had seen him in weeks, and she felt a lurch like a searing pike through her heart.

"What in the name of God? My bride . . ."

At the word *bride*, Cecilia leaned deeply into Leonardo's arms.

"That whore!" Beatrice stretched out an accusing finger toward Cecilia. "What is she doing here?" Beatrice's sharp voice echoed through the corridors. The crowd of guests pressed forward, enthralled with the unfolding scandal.

Ludovico's black eyes fell onto Cecilia's, then the duke took in the wide berth of her form. His eyes flickered to the crowd of esteemed guests who had made a circle around them, and he emitted a nervous laugh as if to defuse the thundercloud that threatened to explode, raining down on all of them. He grasped Beatrice's shoulders, just as Leonardo did the same to Cecilia. The two women stood facing each other.

"Well, everyone is here to see Master da Vinci's beautiful

portrait. Isn't that right, friends? Shall we go in?" Another nervous laugh. Ludovico attempted to steer his wife toward the door of the great hall, but Beatrice did not budge from where she stood before Cecilia, the two mirror images in their green dresses. Cecilia could see that a storm brewed behind the woman's brown eyes. Her hatred was almost physically painful. Cecilia winced and pressed her palm to her belly as another strong wave clenched her midsection into a tight ball. She faltered, and Master da Vinci put his weight behind her to hold her up.

"That dress!" Beatrice yelled. "A gift, I presume?" She looked accusingly at Cecilia as her voice echoed. "How charitable. Unfortunately it does little to hide your condition."

Ludovico took his wife's hand and pulled her to him, whispering in her ear. The crowd pressed forward, yearning to hear.

"Absolutely not!" Beatrice responded loudly to his whispered request, whatever it was. "She is carrying your child!"

At that moment, a strong wave overtook Cecilia, and she cried out.

"Signorina Cecilia!" Leonardo attempted to catch her, but he, too, stumbled forward as she slumped to the floor.

"Please. Let me through! She is my sister!" Cecilia recognized her brother's voice as Fazio pushed his way through the crowd of onlookers. "Cecilia!"

Cecilia felt a gush of liquid burst between her legs, and a hot stream began to run down the insides of her thighs. Blood. She felt as though she might pass out at any moment.

"Help me get her to her chambers!" Fazio cried. Two men standing nearby crouched over to help lift Cecilia from the floor. As they pulled her up from the marble, Cecilia caught sight of Ludovico's broad back as he attempted to herd the crowd of enthralled onlookers into the great hall. Beatrice d'Este continued to stare at Cecilia, daggers in her eyes, as they carried her down the hallway. *This is it,* Cecilia thought. *My final day on this earth. The last thing I will see is Ludovico's back, retreating down a corridor.*

"Make way!" her brother yelled as the crowd parted. "There is a baby coming."

# 56
## DOMINIC

*Siegen, Germany*
*April 1945*

DOMINIC PROPPED HIS BACK AGAINST A WALL AND spooned thin, watery rations into his mouth. Every bone in his body ached; exhaustion set in every time he took a minute to sit. The servicemen had been working shifts around the clock to keep bringing the art to safety; Dominic watched lines of them march through the tunnels, carrying paintings and sculptures, boxes and cases.

A shuffling beside him caught his attention; he looked up to see Stephany plant himself contentedly beside Dominic, holding a steaming bowl of his own. "You have enough?" he asked, offering the bowl.

"Oh, yeah. I'm fine, thanks." Dominic scraped together a smile for the vicar.

Stephany tucked in happily. He gulped a few bites, then sat chewing a dry, stale cracker, watching the art go by.

Dominic watched the beautiful things being carried past, the subjects of the art depicting so many feelings. Joy. Fear. Triumph. Tranquility. He was fighting to stay alive, but he was fighting *for* a world where these things mattered. He wanted Cecilia and his new baby to grow up with art, friendship, and most importantly, hope. Weaver, Stout, Hancock, and Stephany were not insane after all. They had understood it from the beginning.

Dominic placed his tin on the ground and reached into the pocket of his field jacket for a small stash of paper he had collected. With a small nub of his pencil, he began to sketch Vicar Stephany's round cheeks, his line of receding hair. Just a few lines, almost a cartoon.

"You make me look young and handsome," Stephany said, continuing to stare ahead and shovel rations into his mouth.

Dominic laughed away a bit of the ache in his bones and continued to draw. "I'll do my best, Vicar."

# 57
## EDITH

*Outside Puławy, Poland*
*June 1941*

EDITH WAS REPAIRING A SMALL TEAR IN THE BACK OF a canvas painting when Kai Mühlmann appeared at the door to the basement storage room.

Edith sucked in her breath. For a moment, she doubted it was him. She blinked in the harsh light of her lamp, then switched it off so that she could focus.

The man before her looked like Kai Mühlmann; she recognized the wide jaw, the thin lips, the hair swept back from his brow. But as he drew closer, she saw that this man was far removed from the broad-chested, confident Austrian she had seen just months ago. He was gaunt and drawn, his eyes sunken into dark sockets. His jacket hung from his bony shoulders as if on a coatrack.

Edith felt a hot wave of panic rise into her throat. Had

Mühlmann learned that she was aiding the Poles? Had he found out about her inventories, her manifests, handed off to Jakub and the women in the kitchen?

Edith pushed back the stool from her worktable and stood. "Dr. Mühlmann! What a surprise."

"Edith," Kai said, taking her hand. "It has been more than a year." He ran his eyes across the stacks of artworks stored in the rooms behind them. "I am glad to see that we are still partners in crime." Edith cringed at his acknowledgment of her role in the pillage of the Polish people.

"Well," she stammered. "Most of it is hardly worthy of note," she said, gesturing to the stacks of goods, "but there have been a few things worth . . . safeguarding."

"I am well aware," he said. "I have seen your *Wahl I* reports."

Of course he had. Mühlmann must know every detail of the works of art exchanging hands within the high offices of the regime. But looking at his knitted brow, the new lines in his face, Edith could see that the job had taken a toll.

He slumped down into a chair alongside Edith's worktable and ran his finger idly along the dusty, ragged edge of the canvas she was repairing. "I've been all over Europe. I have seen things that would astound you." Edith wondered if Mühlmann meant the works of art or the atrocities of war. She had seen more than enough of both, she thought. The two of them sat in silence for a few moments, then

Mühlmann set his intense gaze on her. "But," he said, "tell me about you. You have word of your fiancé?"

Edith swallowed, pushing down the lump in her throat. "He was . . . killed," she said. "Near the Russian border."

"Ah." Mühlmann reached out and squeezed Edith's forearm. "I am sorry to hear of it." The two of them fell into silence again. Mühlmann stood and wandered into the back storage rooms, fingering carefully through a half-dozen framed oil paintings stacked against the wall.

After Edith was sure that she would not cry, she stood and joined him.

He kept his eyes on the paintings in the stacks. "You are doing good work here, Edith. Important work. You will be rewarded for everything you've done for the Reich."

If he only knew, she thought. "I have no wish to garner attention," Edith replied quickly, holding up her hand. "I do not want anyone noticing me. All I want is to return to Munich."

Edith saw Mühlmann's face darken.

"I sometimes think the same thing," he said in a voice so low she could barely hear him. Mühlmann paced through the shelves stacked high with porcelain and small bronze figurines. "I . . . I feel as though I am stuck in the middle of something beyond myself, a maelstrom as wide as it is destructive. This is not the life I was living before the war. My father encouraged me to be a lawyer." He laughed bitterly. "But instead I insisted on working with beautiful works of art, with forgotten or ill-appreciated works of centuries past." He shook his head. "I am only an art historian. You are a conservator. We have no business being here in the midst of this death and destruction. But yet here we are and what can we do? Nothing. We must follow orders if we want to survive."

Edith shook her head to hear Kai express the words she had been thinking ever since she received her orders back in Munich some two years ago. "My only hope is that you are here to tell me that you are sending me back to Munich, that you are replacing me with someone more qualified." Edith tried to make a joke to hide her trepidation.

"Someone like that would be difficult to find," he said, and turned his eyes on her again. Edith watched his smile disappear. "Well. It seems that you have once again made yourself indispensable. And I suppose I owe it to you to get to the point about why I am here, Edith."

Edith froze. What did Mühlmann know about her? What would become of her, if he did know of her inventories?

Edith searched his face for a flicker of understanding, but Mühlmann turned his back and continued to pace among the stacks of goods piled in the storage room. "Reichsmarschall Hermann Göring, whom I have been in close contact with over the last several years, ordered me to return to Poland. He wants me to come home to Germany with several valuable paintings he wishes to acquire for the Führer's new gallery."

"Da Vinci's *Lady with an Ermine*," Edith said.

A tiny smile threatened the corner of Mühlmann's mouth as he turned to her. "Yes," he replied. "That is one of them."

Edith shook her head. "That means tearing it from the claws of Hans Frank. He is obsessed with that picture. It's not going to be easy."

"I don't imagine it will be," said Mühlmann, "but there are more pressing issues this time. Hitler has ordered more troops to hold back the Russians. And as you have already learned, the Russians are dangerous. Göring is concerned about the safety of these priceless works of art in Kraków. We are too close to the border. Our Nazi officers are no longer safe here. Nor are the pictures."

Edith wondered if that meant that she herself—and everyone in the villa—were also in danger.

Mühlmann continued. "Last time, I had to placate Göring with a portrait by Antoine Watteau. Göring was furious that the *Lady* stayed here in Poland. It took weeks for him to calm down. This time Göring has issued a command and I have no choice." Mühlmann shrugged. "I must pick up the *Lady with an Ermine*, along with Raphael's *Portrait of a Young Man*, and Rembrandt's *Landscape with the Good Samaritan*."

*The Great Three*, Edith thought.

"I will take them back by train from Kraków to Berlin myself," he said, and now Edith understood why Mühlmann looked like a hunted man.

"And you want me to come with you," Edith said, trying to hide the resentment in her voice.

Kai's face darkened. "I'm afraid that won't be possible this time, my dear. You have been given a different assignment."

Edith felt her chest fill with dread. "Please don't give me more bad news," she said finally, her voice barely above a whisper.

Mühlmann shook his head. Above them, a lightbulb flickered starkly.

"Governor Frank," he said. "He has requested you stay here in Poland. He doesn't want you to go back to Germany with the paintings. You were . . . it was part of the bargain."

Edith blinked rapidly, trying to process what she was being told. She had been exchanged for several works of valuable art, forced to stay with a vile, evil man. The man she held responsible for Heinrich's death.

"You made a bargain?" she said, her heart turning to steel.

"An exchange," Mühlmann said. "I am only returning a few pictures to Berlin at this point. Many others will stay at Wawel. And Frank . . . He wants you to be part of his personal curatorial staff."

Edith inhaled sharply. "I . . . I have to stay with him?"

"Yes, along with his wife, Brigitte, his children, and many other of his personal staff." Dr. Mühlmann shrugged but did not meet Edith's eyes. "He will not hurt you, Edith," Mühlmann said. "On the contrary. He values your expertise."

Edith turned to face him. "And if I refuse?"

"I don't recommend it," Mühlmann said, meeting her gaze. "Edith, if there was anything I could have done about it, I would have, but I have heard him brag about your art-sleuthing skills in front of others. A woman, no less. You have done your job so well that Frank sees you as one of the jewels in his crown."

"But I am just here in a basement in some godforsaken corner of Poland going through things that belong to peo-ple who have been captured or worse. And meanwhile, my own family is falling apart!"

Mühlmann smiled at her weakly. "You are doing much more than that, Edith." For a moment, she froze in terror—did he know? But he continued. "You must take solace in knowing that you are doing a great honor to the Supreme Leader and to your country. War requires great sacrifice from all of us. Besides, I think Frank likes the idea of hav-ing you close."

Edith felt as if someone had punched her in the stom-ach. She looked around at the stacks of ledgers she had completed over the months, and the stacks of artwork left to catalog. Then, she looked at Kai, realizing that he was studying her face closely.

"I leave for Kraków tomorrow," he said. "You have a

little time, but Frank will not wait forever. We should wait until some of the skirmishes die down. Then the convoy will transport you to Wawel."

# 58
## DOMINIC

*Marburg, Germany*
*April 1945*

DOMINIC STOOD ALONE ON A LOADING DOCK AND watched the approaching convoy of Allied MP escorts and cargo trucks stretch into the distance, a winding train of vehicles laden with art and the soldiers who defended it. Dominic watched it approach with a mixture of excitement and pride, his head and rifle carried high.

Dominic had been on guard duty for a couple of weeks, having traveled from Siegen with a convoy of weapons carriers packed full with art to the temporary new home of the treasures from the copper and salt mines: Marburg.

The American troops who preceded them had commandeered a massive, impressive building, formerly a state archive, to store and catalog the art. And there was a lot of art. As Dominic soon learned, Siegen was just the tip of the iceberg. Repositories were being discovered all over Germany, their contents carefully packaged and sent here. Now, Dominic felt proud and excited for his small but vital role in the mission. He only had to guard the entrance to the loading dock, a simple enough task, but he was thrilled to watch the masterpieces trundle past.

Another soldier helped him to pull open the gates of the loading docks, allowing the first of the M151s to pass. Like most of the convoys they'd been receiving, there was a mixture of American and British forces, working together to preserve the treasures of Europe. Every day they came—Jeeps, weapons carriers, army trucks— loaded with priceless paintings, sculptures, small objects, archives, and documents. Each convoy delivered another repository of precious value that had been clawed back from the greedy Nazis.

"Look!" George Weaver pointed. "It's Hancock."

Weaver and Dominic pulled themselves to attention and saluted as a Jeep carrying their commander drew nearer and stopped. Hancock hopped out, grinning with a smile that remained undiminished all these months later. Hancock had spent weeks in the field, investigating the reports that continued to pour in, detailing the locations of still more repositories: salt mines, caves, castles, monasteries, offices—anywhere the Nazis could think of to smuggle the art away. If he was back, it had to mean that this convoy was larger than usual, and was important, too.

"Greetings, gentlemen!" Hancock tipped his head back, smile widening, and strode closer. "You won't believe what I've found."

"Hold up," said Weaver. "Don't say 'da Vinci' too quickly, or Bonelli here will wet his pants."

"Hey!" sputtered Dominic, indignant, as Hancock and Weaver laughed. He smiled despite himself. "I'm still hoping for that someday."

"Keep hoping," said Weaver, clapping Dominic on the shoulder. "So what did you find, sir?"

Hancock's eyes shone. "Turns out Siegen isn't the only mine where the Nazis had hidden stuff away. There's another mine near Bernterode, and I didn't only find art there. We found caskets. The remains of a bunch of great heroes. Frederick the Great and his father. Field Marshall Paul von Hindenburg and his wife."

"Von Hindenburg?" said Dominic, irritated. "Seems we could do without *him*, sir." He knew von Hindenburg had been partially responsible for Hitler's rise to power.

Hancock shrugged. "It'll be history one day, son. Either way, somebody's gotta care." He grinned. "It's a splendid find. Come on in, I want you two to show me around all the new stuff that's arrived. Your relief is here anyway."

Dominic and Weaver handed over the guarding of the loading docks to the two soldiers who had just arrived; they followed Hancock into the building. Just inside, several desks filled an enormous entryway, each manned by

a professional pulled from one of Germany's great museums and universities. The scores of men and women were
equipped with cameras, pens, and index cards. Dominic
knew that keeping track of the growing hoard was a logis-
tical nightmare; their system of supplying each item with
a unique number was time-consuming but necessary. As
the works were unloaded, each one was photographed and
marked with an index card before being moved inside the
building for safe storage far from the damp of the mines.

Dominic and Weaver led Hancock through the building, showing him the treasures that had arrived; much of
it from the treasury of the cathedral of Metz. Paintings,
sculptures, fine jewelry, and more precious objects from
museums, churches, archives, and private collections were
neatly stacked in cataloged rows, waiting for their eventual return to their rightful owners. The sheer volume was
overwhelming. Dominic was surrounded by orderly rows
of inexpressible beauty, each piece a testimony to the value
of the human spirit that had created it; an example of how
humanity was determined to bring light and beauty into
a world that had fallen into inconceivable darkness. This
world war was not the first tragedy to strike mankind and
it would not be the last, but none of them had been able to
destroy humanity's appreciation for beauty. It was the only
thing that gave Dominic hope.

The Nazis had conspired to take everything good and
valuable in the world for themselves. But the Nazis would

not win. One day, when Cecilia was a grown woman, she, too, would be able to look upon the priceless works and know that her father played a role in a group that gave everything to save them. Dominic felt relief wash over him.

Best of all, Dominic thought, Vicar Stephany could finally return with his beloved treasures to his church in Aachen, accompanied by a full contingent of Allied guards.

"Great!" Hancock said enthusiastically as they completed the tour. "I'm off to check up on the new works arriving." He beamed and headed off.

Instead of heading to the makeshift hall that had been converted to a mess room, though, Weaver and Dominic wandered back through the paintings stacked in the hallway, chatting about this piece and that. Their new friendship had begun to heal the edges of the ragged gap Paul's death had left in Dominic's life.

Best of all, he'd been drawing again. They headed for a bust of a young woman that Dominic had been wanting to draw for days, and he settled down on the floor opposite. The moment Dominic had picked up a charcoal pencil again, a gift from Stephany back at Siegen, he had started sketching and couldn't stop. Soon running out of human subjects to draw, he'd taken to using the pieces of art for inspiration. Sitting cross-legged on the floor, Dominic pulled out one of the index cards he had taken from the stacks near the loading docks. The bust took shape briskly; first just the oval of the face, then the curves of the cheekbones, the locks of hair, the eyes. The nose. He brought it to life by sketching the eyes in, dark and vibrant. When he was done, the portrait of some long-forgotten young woman blushed prettily up at him, and he found himself doodling a couple of freckles across her nose.

"It's great, Bonelli," said Weaver when he flipped the card to show his friend.

"Mail call!" A skinny private with a canvas mailbag strode into the room, and the men snapped to formation.

The young man's voice cracked as he called out the names written on the envelopes in his hand. "Ackerman. Barnes. Bonelli . . ."

Dominic's heart leapt in his chest. The young private pressed an envelope into his hand.

Bonelli, the return address said. Greensburg, Pennsylvania. Dominic recognized Sally's neat handwriting, the careful letters with controlled loops. Dominic pressed the envelope to his face and inhaled as if he might catch Sally's scent imprinted on it. He fumbled to tear open the flap of the envelope.

"Bonelli."

His name again, but this time it was Hancock, approaching Dominic and Weaver. Both men saluted the officer as he approached, but Dominic thought he detected a hint of sadness in Hancock's eyes.

"I've got news," he said. Dominic fingered the letter from Sally, hardly able to keep himself from ripping it open. He struggled to keep his attention on Hancock. "You've both been reassigned."

Dominic's stomach flipped. He had just started to enjoy the peace and quiet in Marburg. Gripping the envelope, he tried to keep the fear out of his voice. "Why?"

"Seems that it's too peaceful here for the likes of you, soldier. You've proven yourself too valuable as a front-line man. Gotta keep moving forward toward the action."

Hancock handed Dominic a thin slip of paper, his orders stamped out on it in large impersonal letters, changing a life in a few lines of type.

Dominic's heart sank.

And just like that, just as he began to throw himself wholeheartedly into the Monuments Men's mission, Dominic was being forced to leave them behind. He and Weaver were going back to the front lines.

# 59
## EDITH

*Kraków, Poland*
*January 1942*

AT A TABLE, A LITTLE BOY WAS WORKING ON HIS
lessons, his legs swinging freely under the chair. Light
filtered through the window beside him, a luminous
reflection from the snow collecting and drifting in the
courtyard of Wawel Castle. A fire crackled loudly in the
tremendous fireplace that occupied one wall of the great
room. Several couches and chairs with deep cushions
furnished the room. Throw blankets, newspapers, and
books were scattered across the tables.

Edith had expected to be led back to the office of Hans
Frank, but instead, a soldier led her to a room where Frank's
secretary, Hilda, was straining tea leaves into a ceramic
pot, and the boy was deep in concentration on forming the
alphabet.

"Fräulein Becker," Hilda said. "Make yourself comfortable. Herr von Palézieux is on his way here to see you."

She hesitated. "Herr . . . Who?"

"They have not informed you? I am sorry. Wilhelm Ernst von Palézieux. He is a renowned architect who has come to us from Switzerland. He was appointed as Governor Frank's new personal curator. You will be working with him."

Von Palézieux? Personal curator? Was he another one of Kai Mühlmann's protégés?

But Edith did not have the chance to ask for further details. Hilda had already disappeared into the next room with the tea tray, the door swinging behind her.

Edith sat at the table across from the little boy. "*Hallo*," she said. "I'm Edith."

The boy ignored her, writing out his letters. She looked at his flaxen hair and his perfectly formed face in the snow-reflected light of the window. Edith watched the boy write careful characters in the antique style, elegant, sharply defined letters that looked as though they belonged in the German Renaissance rather than the twentieth century.

"You have very good penmanship," she said. "What's your name?"

This time, the boy raised his head and met her gaze. In contrast to his blond hair, the boy's eyes were nearly black. Just like his father's. "Michael."

"What are you working on?"

"Practicing my letters," he said. Edith spied several other pages of handwriting protruding from a notebook at his side.

"Michael." A teenaged girl appeared in the far doorway, "Come. Your tutor is waiting." Michael slapped his folio together, flashing his eyes at Edith again. Then he slid down from the chair and marched across the room toward his sister.

Edith watched two more of the Frank children make their way through the snow-covered courtyard below the window. Seemingly oblivious to the cold, the older boy and younger girl removed their gloves and began throwing snow at each other until a woman appeared, ordering them to stop it immediately, that she could not tolerate them soiling their clothes. With one hand, she dragged the younger child, who stumbled along reluctantly at her mother's side.

Brigitte Frank. The governor's wife. Edith had only glimpsed her from the window as she strode across the lawn with her five children, or in grainy black-and-white pictures in the newspaper, but she recognized the tall woman immediately. She was a picture of severe elegance, wearing a long woolen coat with a mink collar that shifted in the wind. Even from the high vantage point of the window, Edith felt as intimidated by Brigitte as she was by her husband.

Somehow, Edith had become enveloped into the family's private wing of Wawel Castle. Into their private business. How did she get herself into this position? As much as she had felt trapped in the countryside villa, she now wished that she could return there, far from the clutches of Frank and his family.

"Fräulein Becker."

Edith stood.

Before her was a slight man with large glasses. He bared his crooked teeth in a strained smile. "Governor Frank has heaped praises upon you. It is an honor to meet you finally." He extended his hand. "I'm Ernst." Edith took his hand, warm and confident, not too firm. "Governor Frank is away from the palace. We might meet in the front room adjacent to his office. We will have space there to get to know each other. Please."

Ernst opened the door for Edith and gestured for her to follow. They stepped into a long corridor lined with paintings and large picture windows overlooking the Vistula River. Along the way, Edith could not help but observe the dozens of paintings hanging along the hallway. Landscapes. Portraits. All at least a century old. Ernst seemed happy to slow his pace. He looked at the paintings silently by Edith's side.

Edith didn't say anything as they walked down the hallway. She kept her hands clasped behind her back and her spine straight. Ernst smiled at her often, but she didn't respond with a smile of her own. She didn't want to be charmed. She didn't want to make a new friend. She wanted to do her job and return to Munich with her inventories.

Maybe then she could make a difference. For now, she had stuffed the inventories under her mattress, for fear that someone might search her suitcase or the pockets of her clothing when she was out of the room.

Edith recognized a familiar picture on the wall and she stopped. "Landscape with shepherds," she said. "Possibly a van Ruysdael or one of his followers."

"Good eye," he said.

"I saw it once before, in another fine home." Edith recognized the picture as one she had cataloged and packed for Wawel. With a sickening feeling in the pit of her stomach, she realized that she was once again witnessing the fruit of her efforts: priceless works of art ripped away from their rightful owners, the most priceless of all reserved for the governor's own private collection. She wondered if Ernst could see her face turn green.

Edith had no paper or pen, but instinctively, as they strolled down the corridor, she began cataloging each work in her head.

Artist, subject, size, medium, origin.

Edith's fingers fidgeted behind her back. She doubted that she would have a way to get a list of works in Wawel Castle back to Jakub. All the same, Edith thought, she must record what had landed in the personal collection of Poland's governor. Perhaps there was something that could be done with the information.

"You are the governor's personal curator," she said,

facing Ernst now. The words *personal* and *curator* didn't seem to belong together.

"Yes," he said. "As are *you*, my dear." His mouth turned into a grin. "Your skills and knowledge are well known. Governor Frank was insistent that we bring you here as part of his personal staff."

Edith felt the hairs on her head prickle.

He began walking down the corridor again. "We are tasked with the interior decoration of each of the governor's private residences across Poland. None of them are as large as Wawel, but all the same, the task will keep us busy for some time to come, I think." He chuckled. "Thanks to the efforts of yourself and other curators working around the country, we have a lot of beautiful things to choose from."

"Interior . . . decoration," Edith said.

"Well," Ernst hesitated, his brow wrinkled. "It's much more than that, of course. Yes, we must concern ourselves with draperies and cutlery, I'm afraid, but along the way, you and I will have the privilege to handle—and hang— many other paintings for Governor Frank and his wife."

Edith fell silent, letting the information sink in.

Ernst opened another large door, and they stepped into a room that Edith immediately recognized as Hans Frank's office. There was no one there, but when Edith turned into the room, she gasped.

*Lady with an Ermine.*

It was still there, hanging on the wall, just above the

radiator, as it was when she had departed Wawel Castle some two years before. The soft, brown eyes of Cecilia Gallerani, mistress to the Duke of Milan, stared back at Edith from across the room. Edith's mouth remained open for a few seconds until she found her voice.

"Oh my! I didn't expect to see this one here again. I . . . I thought the picture went back to Berlin again . . ."

Ernst nodded. "It did. But, as you may know, this is Governor Frank's personal favorite. He negotiated an arrangement with Göring . . ." He hesitated. "And now it's back where it belongs."

Edith turned back to stare at the picture, feeling sorry for Kai Mühlmann, who had made too many trips to Berlin and back with this painting and the other two. He must have felt impossibly wedged between two selfish men fighting over a painting of a girl who lived so long ago. Edith shook her head.

"Mühlmann . . ." she said.

Ernst scratched his temple, where the hair had receded from his forehead and been swept back with oil.

"Oberführer Mühlmann is no longer in Governor Frank's service," he said, his lips spreading into a thin line. "That is why Governor Frank called me from Switzerland to handle his private art affairs."

Edith felt her heart race. She knew that Kai Mühlmann was working far afield, but now, had he been relieved of his duties? Had he crossed some kind of line with Hans Frank?

Had he been dismissed? Or worse? As much as Edith disagreed with Kai's stance on taking works of art that had never belonged to Germany, she empathized with his plight in the middle of these powerful men.

"I was pleased to hear that it was you who brought the *Lady with an Ermine* here to Poland to Governor Frank," Ernst said. "I was waiting for a long time to have the opportunity to look upon her in person."

Edith looked at him with a blank expression, not returning his charming smile. "Yes, I brought it here the first time. Apparently, it's been to Berlin and back multiple times. I understand Reichsmarschall Göring is interested in having it in the Führer's collection."

"Well, now it has been returned to where it should be. Here in Poland. It is rightfully ours. You know, all three of the Great Paintings belong in Poland, do you not agree?" Ernst asked, trying to draw her into conversation as she realized she would not be able to trust him.

"Surely the painting is put at greater risk being shuffled back and forth between here and Berlin. I believe that our greatest job is to ensure the safety of the works, not to put them in harm's way," Edith said.

Ernst grinned wide. "I respectfully disagree, Miss Becker. Our greatest job is to make Governor Frank happy. No matter what it takes."

"Well, at the very least, this picture should not be hanging above the radiator!"

"You are right, of course." Ernst shrugged. "I have mentioned it on several occasions to the governor. But that's where he wants it. Governor Frank wants people around him to make him happy and satisfied. That includes us, doesn't it, Miss Becker?"

Edith bristled. Heinrich had lost his life because of Hans Frank and his campaigns across Poland. She didn't want to risk anything that might get her killed, and more than anything, she wanted to get back to Munich and be with her father in the final chapter of his life. If only she had someone who would accept a letter of resignation.

But as she looked into Cecilia Gallerani's eyes, Edith wondered what else she could do to keep these priceless masterpieces out of the personal collections—and the clutches—of these greedy men. How could she ensure the picture's survival when the whole country of Poland seemed on the brink of destruction?

# 60
## DOMINIC

*In the woods near Dachau, Germany*
*April 1945*

EVEN THE TREES SEEMED POISED TO ATTACK. AS THE convoy wound its way between the dark tree trunks, Dominic tried to swallow his fear. The old feeling of being on edge, the old instincts to shoot, overtook him.

Gunfire did not worry him. Returning to security detail on a wooded path through the German countryside, he'd already been in a few skirmishes and he was falling back into the old routine of hypervigilance; his shooting skills had not suffered during the few weeks of peace, and he was learning to not think. Just shoot, be ready to fight, and hide the pain and fear in the sketches he made by flickering candlelight when they were stalled, somewhere quiet.

Most of all, Dominic regretted being pulled away from the mission of recovering great art, of recovering hope for the future. To his astonishment, Dominic regretted having to leave Hancock and the other Monuments Men behind in Marburg. Recovering works of art was now where his heart lay, where he felt he could make a small but lasting contribution in a world that otherwise hardly made sense.

The only thing that kept him sane was running his eyes over Sally's words, written out in her neat script. He kept her letter in his breast pocket, and in moments of quiet, he pulled it out and read it again. *I love you*, she had written. It was all that mattered, that, and a new healthy baby girl. Kathleen, after Sally's mother.

According to their commanding officers, Dominic's division was about to convene with convoys from another battalion before heading to Dachau. The men had been briefed about the large prison camp that lay within the area. The mother ship of the Nazi concentration camps, the officers had said. The intelligence reports painted a harrowing picture of the thousands of prisoners being forced to march to Dachau as it was one of the few camps left within Nazi-held territory that was still operational. Dominic was certain that many of the marching prisoners would not make it that far.

As the M151 rumbled on, Dominic hugged his rifle close to his chest, trying to comprehend the scope of the cruelty that would demand the murder of thousands. He kept his eyes on the curves of the road.

Around the next bend, the Jeep rattled out of the forest

and into a clearing, and ahead, Dominic saw several dozen boxcars standing haphazardly beside the track, abandoned by fleeing Germans. On the horizon, the sunlight glinted off barbed wire and a gate tower: Dachau. They continued toward the camp, a curve of the road leading them toward the boxcars, and that was when the smell hit them.

Beside Dominic, Weaver uttered a strangled swearword. Dominic would not have had the breath to curse even if he wanted to. He grasped at the place where his Saint Christopher medal had hung and prayed inwardly, his stomach flipping. The stench was incomprehensible. Compared to this, the smell of the copper mines at Siegen was sweet perfume. Siegen had smelled of thousands of people living and sweating and urinating; this smelled like thousands of people dying. There were undertones of excrement, but far more distressing was the smell of decaying flesh. It was sweet and cloying and it choked Dominic's nostrils.

Dominic felt as if he had been welded to the side of the Jeep. He stared fixedly ahead, his imagination running wild with what that smell had to mean. Then he heard the screaming. At first, he thought that there were living people on those boxcars, until he heard English words scattered in the yelling and realized that the voices were those of the American soldiers in the two-and-a-half-tons at the front. He had not thought that grown men could make sounds of that pitch, of that level of sheer horror. His hair stood on end, goose bumps bursting out across his body, and he still stared at the countryside, refusing to turn his head forward. Then, the Jeep slowed, and the entire convoy clanked to a disorganized, unplanned halt.

"No," croaked Weaver beside him. The syllable, uttered in a tone of such inexpressible dread, yanked Dominic from his trance. He had to look. He had to see because it could not be what he was imagining.

It wasn't. It was so much worse.

The boxcars were piled with dead bodies.

There must have been more than thirty cars, halted on the tracks. The bodies were stacked, none of them covered, just thrown naked and emaciated onto rotting heaps. Men and women. Children. Mothers, fathers, brothers, sisters, their remains thrown down and forgotten, packed with less care than Dominic had stacked sacks of coal. People who somebody was grieving for, lying bloated in the sun with flies crawling on their slack faces, walking across the surfaces of misty eyes. Blood and excrement dripped slowly out of the bottom of the boxcars. Arms and legs, faces hung out of the windows. Cheeks pressed flat, eyes pressing against the glass of closed windows with the pressure of other corpses. It was a hellish panorama of death on a scale that Dominic could not comprehend. The image was seared onto his very soul. Overwhelmed by horror, the Allied convoy could go no farther.

"I'm gonna be sick," croaked Weaver.

Dominic jumped out of the vehicle as if in a dream to

make room for his comrade as he scrambled out and staggered into the trees. "We haven't even reached the camp yet," he said faintly to nobody in particular. "We haven't even got there yet."

He took a step back and his boot made a squelching noise. Looking down, he saw he was standing in a dark and sticky stain of rotting blood. Flies swarmed around his boots, and he could bear no more. The pressure of the war, all the horror of it came pouring onto him, pressing him down like a giant fist determined to pound him into the dirt.

He relived it, all of it, the landings at Normandy, the first time he saw a man torn limb from limb by a blast from an explosive shell, the first dying breath he'd ever heard, the pop of the guns, the terror of the whistling shells blowing past, the hundreds of miles rocking back and forth in a rattling Jeep waiting for the sounds of gunfire to come bursting over the hills, the shelling of Aachen, the miles between him and his family, the torn and destroyed works of art they hadn't been able to save, the terror in Stephany's face as he emerged from the ruined pulpit, the light fading from Paul's eyes.

That was the worst: the pain he'd felt losing Paul, felt by family members of every last one of these hundreds of innocent dead dumped thoughtlessly in boxcars. The magnitude of the grief threatened to crush him. He threw down his rifle and bolted, hands clapped over his ears as if that could keep the memories out. He tripped and stumbled into a ditch, knees hitting mud, and the contents of his stomach came burning up into his throat.

## 61
## EDITH

*Kressendorf House, outside Kraków, Poland*
*June 1944*

**"THREE FORKS ARE MISSING. AND A SERVING SPOON."**
Brigitte Frank shot Edith an accusing glance.

Edith surveyed the silver service splayed out on the dining table before them. Teapots and trays, carving knives, spoons. Special forks for caviar, herring, and game. Edith and Ernst had counted them all before Brigitte and Hans Frank arrived at the newly furnished country house. Surely there was a mistake?

Ernst had been adamant that he and Edith oversee the operation of organizing the silver service themselves. Brigitte Frank, he told her, would make sure that each individual piece be cataloged and counted. Hans Frank's wife had grown up destitute, Ernst had confided in Edith, and now, as queen of Poland, she coveted each precious belonging.

And, Edith saw, Brigitte's worst fear was that someone might take it all away from her.

"It is as I have already told you," Brigitte said, looking down her nose at Edith. "They are too easy to tuck into a servant's apron. Any one of those ungrateful Poles might try to take advantage of us," she said loudly enough to be heard from the kitchen.

"We will count again," Edith said, bringing a clipboard with the catalog of silver destined for yet another fine country home that the Franks had commandeered as their own. It was true that many invaluable works of art had been transported to Germany; some of the most valuable had been tagged for Hitler's museum in Linz. But now, Edith knew that many valuable things went to furnish the newly confiscated fine homes of Nazi leaders. The truth was that many of these luxuries had never been intended for any museum; they only went to line the coffers of Hans Frank and the other high-ranking leaders instead.

While Brigitte fussed with Ernst over the placement of a picture, Edith double-checked her list of silver pieces. The noise of clinking silver made it sound as if there was a dinner party underway, and Edith imagined the elaborate soiree that the governor-general and his wife were to host in this very room the next day, after she and Ernst finished their task of hanging paintings, placing candelabra, and counting hundreds of silver serving pieces.

"Higher on the left side," Brigitte called out to Ernst from the other side of the room.

In the picture, a peasant's hut stood in the foreground, its roof sagging and its doorway filled with the broad body of a sheep. Beyond, the soft outlines of trees appeared in dim light. Edith might have classified this painting, probably the work of a German artist a century ago, as *Wahl II*, but another curator, unknown to Edith, must have sorted it into a collection that was labeled for the country estate of Hans Frank, where Edith and Ernst were tasked with decoration. From the top of his stepladder, Ernst reached out to adjust the frame. The painting leveled, he descended to the floor, decorated with patterns of different species of wood inlaid into an intricate pattern. Of all Frank's country estates that Edith had seen in past months, this one was the most beautiful. She had helped roll out rugs, put the silver in brand-new chests, and hung the drapes with precision. They kept the drapes pulled back, tied with gold tassels.

Edith was distracted by movement beside her: a staff member passed by, holding two candelabra. She had seen them before. She had assessed their value in the basement of the headquarters before she was forced to come work with Governor Frank and then Wilhelm Ernst von Palézieux. Were they a wedding gift for a Polish couple who might no longer be alive? She felt sick to her stomach. The room darkened around her. Edith glanced out the tall window to the countryside beyond. Over the past months, Edith had done her best to skirt around the edges of Brigitte and her children, eager to keep her distance from them in order to keep her distance from Frank. To Edith's relief, Frank had been away often. But now, the family had arrived, and there was no avoiding the Franks any longer.

At that moment, the dining room doors opened and Edith recognized the dark silhouette of Hans Frank in the doorway. His teenaged son, Norman, shadowed his father. A sharp pang stabbed Edith's gut, a now-familiar reaction she felt each time she was in Frank's presence. She wished she could find an excuse to disappear.

"We are missing silver pieces," Brigitte proclaimed loudly to her husband. "I tell you, they will take them in a second."

"I will check the kitchen, madam," Edith said, relieved for a reason to duck out of the room.

In the large kitchen, two of the dining room attendants, Polish women who had been recruited from the fields outside the villa, lifted pots and pans from a crate, placing them carefully into an ornately carved wooden sideboard. Over days, Edith had watched the women carefully, wondering if they might be, like the other kitchen women, resistance fighters in the guise of benign house servants. Edith had lingered in the kitchen and had spoken to the women often, checking to see if they showed signs of understanding German. Would they be able to help her, and she them?

But Edith saw no flicker of recognition, no matter how often she attempted to engage them.

Every evening, Edith recorded what information she could on blank ledger pages, folded into a small package tucked once again under her mattress. Brigitte's catalog of silver services paled in comparison to the inventories Edith had compiled, she realized. *One day*, she thought, *perhaps the records can help return the works to their rightful owners.*

One of the kitchen boys, Józef, spoke good English, Edith discovered. With an eager, playful expression, he greeted her with a "Good morning, ma'am," in the hallways and spoke with Edith about music and art, practicing his English skills. But she did not know if he was aware of the miles of devastation around them. Edith questioned Józef about his life outside the estate walls, looking for a flicker of resistance, trying to see if he might open the door to networks beyond the estate walls. But he kept the conversation to basic topics—the arrival of rain, the serving of coffee, his favorite type of dumpling.

When she could get her hands on a German newspaper, Edith scanned the headlines. SIEGE OF LONDON CONTINUES. CONFIDENCE IN VICTORY AT THE DECISIVE HOUR. THE DANGER OF AMERICANISM. THE ETERNAL BATTLE FOR TRUTH. There was nothing about the harsh realities of the Polish countryside. Her days were filled with strange, fractured, altered communications.

Suddenly, the door to the kitchen swung open and Józef

came bursting through. He looked wide-eyed at Edith and the kitchen servants.

"Józef," Edith said to him in English. "We are trying to locate several silver forks and a serving spoon. Have you seen them? Can you ask the ladies in Polish for me?"

But Józef only stared at Edith as if he had not heard a word she said. "The Americans! The British!" he said, nearly breathless. "They have landed on the beaches in France."

"What? How do you know this?" Edith said.

"We . . . In the servants' corridor. We heard it on the radio." He paused, a guilty expression on his face. "The BBC." Had Józef been listening to the banned radio programs? It was dangerous, especially with the Frank family now in residence. But Edith could see that Józef's disobedience was overshadowed by nervous excitement.

"They have landed by the thousands!" he announced to Edith again. "The Anglo-Americans! They have invaded the beaches in France!"

# Part V
## *Homeland*

# 62

## LEONARDO

*Milan, Italy*
*June 1491*

A NEWBORN BABY. A SON FOR LUDOVICO IL MORO. A bastard son, to be understood. But I do understand, for I am one too. He will never rule the duchy, but ultimately, the boy will have a future.

And, thanks be to God, Cecilia is also well. It is always a worry, when a child is born. New life and death so closely intertwined. For Cecilia's sake, I feel grateful for her good health, especially since the girl suffered so greatly during the birth.

All the same, surely her time is up now. Ludovico il Moro now has a new wife, a mistress, and a newly born bastard child under the same roof. Hardly a sustainable arrangement. One or more of them must go. What will become of them?

For my own sake, I feel grateful that my portrait of

Cecilia Gallerani is now complete. Just in time. Even better, Ludovico il Moro accepted it by patting my shoulder in gratitude, then staring at the beautiful girl in the picture with a mixture of love and sadness. As I said, it's time for her to go.

In my little factory at the Corte Vecchia, I have finally turned back to my greatest joy: the dusty flying contraption that has lain dormant on the rooftop all these long months. Time and space have led me to change the design. A seed of the idea came to me long ago in a dream and I sketched it briefly. If only I could recapture the image.

I open the old sketchbook that was in my bag during that long journey from Florence to Milan, almost ten years ago now. The worn pages open long-neglected rooms inside my mind. All the defensive designs that I had originally proposed to His Lordship. Landing craft. A type of catapult never before seen. A portable bridge.

My finger lands on a design for cannon that might be used to explode a mine full of treasures. Not a bad idea, I think. I tear the page from the book and vow to show it to His Lordship.

# 63
## EDITH

*Altaussee, Austria*
*January 1945*

EDITH STEPPED OVER THE RUBBLE THAT COATED THE dirt floor of the mine. In the near darkness, she followed the lean silhouette of a *Gefreiter*, his flashlight flittering over the rugged walls of the tunnels that had been blasted into the side of a mountain. She inhaled deeply in the thin, cold air, feeling panic slink up inside her, an instinctive fear that she might run out of breath. The soldier moved swiftly and confidently through the low tunnels. Edith and Ernst struggled to keep pace.

As her eyes adjusted to the dimness, Edith made out wooden shelves and scaffolds, little more than pieces of freshly milled lumber, hastily nailed together. Inside these makeshift scaffolds, she saw stacks of crates. And as the soldier's flashlight scanned across the jagged walls of the salt mine, Edith saw the gilded edge of a frame flash in the light. Paintings. Hundreds—no, maybe thousands—of works of art.

The sight took Edith's breath away.

Finally, the soldier stopped. "This is just one of the mines that we're using," he bragged, turning his eyes on Edith. He kept turning to look at her, scanning her body but never meeting her gaze. She crossed her arms.

"Where are the others?" Edith asked, Ernst close on her heels.

"That's classified," the soldier said in an arrogant tone. "They are scattered in various locations in Austria and Germany. We have secured them for the works of art the Führer will use to fill his new museum."

The soldier might be an arrogant fool, but he wasn't lying. The sheer magnitude of the operation made Edith's head spin. For more than five years, Edith had had the impression that she had been working alongside a handful of other art professionals, quietly spiriting away paintings, sculptures, and other works in the name of the Reich. Now, as she stepped through room after room of scaffolds and crates, each filled with works of art from who knew how far away, it became clear to Edith that she was not as important as she had been led to believe.

How many other art professionals were there across Europe, stuck in basements, in country villas, in museum storerooms, in church treasuries, cataloging and arranging transport for each of these priceless masterpieces? She was only a tiny cog in a giant wheel.

In June, shortly after they learned of the Anglo-American invasion in Normandy, Edith and Ernst had started moving. Frank had tasked them with moving all the works in Poland deemed first quality—*Wahl I*—into hiding. The arc of Edith's days now began and ended with crating, loading, unloading, arranging, organizing, and documenting works of art. She and Ernst traveled with a large case of paperwork, pages of inventories, truck manifests, careful records of shifting, priceless cargo.

Mines, bank vaults, university storage rooms, museum offices.

Irreplaceable works of art were spirited away into corners of the German and Austrian landscape where, Frank argued, they would be safe from harm as Poland became ever more volatile, with new threats from the Russians and the Allies. Edith feared that the works might be damaged, stolen, lost, or forgotten instead.

At night, in the dim light of her bedroom, her eyelids drooping, Edith made herself stay awake long enough to copy down their movements on her secret inventory, reduced to a minuscule shorthand that only she could interpret.

Most days, Edith felt that her meticulous efforts must be futile, for what could she do with the inventories now? Sending the lists to her friend Manfred at the Alte

Pinakothek seemed the natural thing to do, yet too dangerous to contemplate. What if someone intercepted her letter
before it arrived in Munich? How could she reach him?
Instead, Edith hid the copied inventories between her mattress and the metal springs of her bedframe, or in the lining
of her traveling case. It was all she could do, she thought,
until she had a better opportunity. She knew she couldn't
trust any of Frank's staff. Surely they had been vetted more
completely than anyone else for their loyalty.

And now, they were constantly on the move.

In January, Governor Frank finally had been forced to
abandon Kraków, to move his family back into German-
speaking lands, along with staff and the works of art he
held most dear. Da Vinci's *Lady with an Ermine* was rarely
out of his sight.

The first time they had moved the Great Three, Edith
had worked with Ernst and some of the staff to load them
into the back of an armored truck, along with some other
priceless works. Their arrival at a remote private residence
in Sichów, a village in western Poland where they were unlikely to be tracked, had been prearranged. The paintings
would be stored there temporarily for safekeeping.

Slowly, pieces of information had dripped to them;
Americans and British troops were making their way eastward, fighting back German lines. At the same time, Russian troops, now enemies, were moving west. In between,
the Nazi forces were being squeezed into an ever-narrower

band. Edith worried about Jakub and his friends in the Polish resistance networks. She had no way to contact him and wondered what had become of him—and their efforts.

In spite of the new threats, Edith was relieved to hear that Hans Frank would stay behind in Kraków. Eventually, though, to her dismay, Frank joined them in Sichów, bringing along Brigitte and their children. Shortly after the family's arrival, the group—and the Great Three—moved on to another private residence in Morawa, staying there for only a short time. Night after night, Edith continued to stuff her precious, now tattered, inventory of works stolen from Polish collections under her mattress, packing it again each morning into the lining of her leather suitcase. It was not easy, as their movements became ever more uncertain, their circle ever tighter. Would her inventories ever help to repatriate the belongings to their rightful owners? Edith felt overwhelmed at the magnitude of the task of returning everything to where it belonged.

Edith had a difficult time reconciling the man who, by day, was responsible for the devastation around them, and by night, doted on his children. Brigitte herself was often absent, a blur in high heels and a fur coat as she made her way out the door. It confused Edith that those who were closest to Frank treated him with affection or indifference. Could they not see what evil he brought swirling around them?

Then, a few short weeks ago, Brigitte and the children had returned to Bavaria for the holidays. Frank had remained behind, but to her relief, he sent Edith and Ernst off again with the priceless works of art, this time without him. They rumbled in the back of a truck toward the Austrian border. Each time they moved the paintings, the more Edith witnessed how devastated the Polish landscape had become, little more than a hellish panorama of rubble and dust. She stayed focused on protecting those pictures in the trucks; it was all she could do now.

It was only when they had crossed the Austrian border that Edith began to see signs of life. Her heart ached as she saw the first street signs in German. At night, she had a warm meal and a warm bed. As part of Governor Frank's entourage, she never wanted for anything, except the things she wanted most of all: her family and her freedom.

Was her father still alive? And if he was, would he have forgotten all about her by now? She had been gone for so long, and the only communications they received were intelligence reports that kept them on the move.

Throughout the salt mine and in some of the palaces and residences Frank owned, she'd seen artifacts that had come through her basement office. She had deemed them worthy or unworthy. Perhaps she'd been given more power than she deserved, more authority over the property of others than she should have. Who was she to say what was truly valuable and what wasn't? She didn't want to see these works of incalculable value lost. Master paintings and objects, each one irreplaceable.

Now, Edith, Ernst, and a few other staff and soldiers accompanying the family for security, stepped carefully through the rubble of a salt mine in Altaussee, Austria. It was the first time in nearly three years that Edith had set foot in German-speaking lands.

They passed a small room that the soldiers were using as a latrine. Edith cringed as she realized what she'd seen: paintings inside the dark, dank cell, propped against the wall.

"Stop!" she said, grasping Ernst's forearm. "You cannot keep pictures in the latrine!" she scolded the soldier who was leading them. "Have you no sense?" Edith stepped into the reeking room and pulled out two large landscapes darkened by time and soil. She wished she could take them to her conservation studio at once.

But looking around her at the hundreds of invaluable works of art piled inside the darkness of the salt mine, Edith felt desperation fill her throat. What if the Nazi officers blew it up of their own accord as they fled, a desperate assurance that it would never fall into their enemies' hands? And what if the Anglo-American forces bombed the mines without realizing what treasures lay inside? Time was not on their side, Edith realized. How could she get her secret inventories into the right hands without risking her own life?

# 64
## CECILIA

*Milan, Italy*
*June 1491*

**CECILIA WAS IN LOVE.**

As she watched her son's chest rise and fall with each breath, she curled him in her arms and thought that she might never let go. All she wanted to do was stare into the baby's dark eyes—deep, midnight pools, just like his father's.

The chambermaid dusted motes from the corners, where they came in with the open windows and the heavy, clammy heat. Now, the shutters were closed against a summer storm, the rain and distant thunder beating a steady, comforting rhythm for those inside the palace, while turning the world outside into a slippery, frightful mess. Cecilia inhaled the dampness, which smelled of trees and the country. It brought an image of running through the woods as a girl, and for a moment she longed to escape this city of gray stone and return home to Tuscany. If Ludovico turned her away, Cecilia thought, maybe she could find a way back home. Whatever happened, Cecilia was just grateful to be alive.

In the dim light, Cecilia traced the baby's perfect profile with one finger. She ran her thumb down to his hand, and he squeezed it in his tiny fist. Violina pressed her damp nose to the baby's neck, inhaling sharply and looking at Cecilia's face for reassurance before settling at her side on the bed.

In a small room off Cecilia's chambers, the wet nurse unpacked her meager belongings. There was little for the woman to do, as Cecilia had insisted on putting the baby to her own breast. No one else could love her son this much, maybe not even Ludovico.

Four days gone. Four days, and Ludovico still had not come to lay eyes on his new son. Every time the door opened she hoped to see his face, but it was only a chambermaid, a kitchen servant, or Lucrezia.

The day before, the duke's secretary, Giancarlo, had arrived in her chambers with some fanfare, presenting Cecilia with the gift of a large, flat gilded box. She had opened it to find several large sheets of parchment, heavy with wax seals hanging from the bottom of the documents. She ran her finger across the Latin words etched out in brown ink. Pavia. Saronno. Additional place names she had never heard of before. Tracts with rice and grapevines. Land deeds naming Cecilia Gallerani as the owner. More pages with ownership of cattle and horse-breeding farms in the Po Valley delta.

Her eyes flickered to her dressing table, which was piled with more gifts from Ludovico and people in his court who had never paid her the least bit of attention before now. Hand-stitched clothing and adornments for the baby. Honey cakes and sweets of almond paste made in a nearby convent. A large gilded tray painted with scenes of the life of Saint Anne. Ceramic plates and small bits of pearl for her hair and silver threads to trim her dresses.

Even her loyal court poet, Bernardo, had paid her two visits and had even composed a lovely sonnet in honor of Cesare's birth. But mostly, Cecilia remained alone in bed, curled up with her infant and her dog.

A firm knock on the door and Cecilia felt hope swell through her body. Ludovico? But as the door opened a crack, Cecilia recognized her brother's wide brow and sheepish grin instead.

# 65
## EDITH

*Neuhaus am Schliersee, Germany*
*January 1945*

**"WOULD YOU LIKE A DRINK?"**

Hans Frank walked over to the bar cart near a window overlooking a breathtaking view of Schliersee Lake. From this vantage point, Edith could see the familiar sloping roofs of fine Bavarian homes, and beyond, snow-capped peaks. Only an hour's drive from Munich. Could she find a way back home? Whatever happened, Edith was just grateful to be alive.

"No, thank you."

"I have Polish vodka." Frank grinned at his reference to their first meeting in Kraków. Edith only kept her eyes on the patterned carpet. She stood, hands folded in front of her, next to a hulking desk in the office of the centuries-old farmhouse that formed the heart of Frank's family estate.

Frank's farmhouse, Schoberhof, was enormous but nearly empty. Brigitte Frank had gone out, and Frank's children were playing outside, running in the snow on the expansive bank that sloped toward the lake. The cook and housekeepers must have been working in the kitchens, Edith thought, tucked away in the bowels of the house. She mused that they, too, must have wanted to stay out of sight. The only sound was the clock ticking loudly in the hall.

On the way to Frank's farmhouse, they had stopped to drop a truckload of treasures and armed guards at Frank's former office in Neuhaus. Frank had tasked Ernst with the secure delivery of the works as a gift to another high-ranking Nazi official in Munich.

Then, Edith found herself alone. For a moment, she allowed herself to fantasize that she might be allowed to return home. But instead, to her great dismay, Frank had insisted that Edith continue on to his private villa with the family. Now, Edith was essentially a prisoner. Her home, her father, was less than an hour's drive from those snow-capped mountains, but she could not leave the estate. She was afraid of what Frank might do if she crossed him, or dared to leave.

Da Vinci's *Lady with an Ermine* was not on the list of works to be dropped at Frank's former office. Instead, the picture now sat in its wooden crate, just a few feet from where Edith stood, in Frank's home. Edith took some comfort in having her eyes on the picture, knowing that it was safe. She worried about the other paintings—the Rembrandt, the Raphael, the many others of incalculable value that had been shipped around constantly in recent months.

All the same, Edith knew that da Vinci's *Lady* wasn't any safer here than it was traveling all over Poland and Austria, or being stored underground in a salt mine. Surely, Frank was a target for the Anglo-Americans. On the surface, there was the illusion that Frank was living as some kind of country gentleman in this Bavarian estate. But if he was a target and his private villa was bombed, the painting and their lives were at risk as much as they had ever been, in Poland or anywhere else.

Edith stared at the crate, knowing she would soon be asked to open it and hang the picture for him. Frank stood silently at the bar cart, examining a crystal tumbler filled with transparent liquid. She wondered what was on his mind. She wished that Brigitte would come back home.

"Would you please hang our girl?" Frank said finally, in a low voice, taking a sip of the drink and pursing his lips. "I'm sure you will do a more professional job than I."

It wasn't the first time she'd held da Vinci's *Lady* in her hands, but Edith handled it with as much reverence as the first time she saw it pulled from the walled-up room at Pełkinie. She stepped forward toward the space on the wall where the painting was to be hung. She stared into Cecilia Gallerani's eyes, admiring her beauty, taking in every brushstroke, the glossy surface that separated the two women by some five hundred years. The expression on Cecilia's face seemed so serene. Surely she was coddled like a treasure? Surely she could not have known what it was like to fall prey to the whims of powerful men and events beyond your control?

"Enchanting, isn't it?"

Edith felt Frank standing only inches from her back. She did her best to ignore him, reaching out to level the painting. With the other hand, she squeezed the handle of the hammer she had used to drive the nail into the wall. Frank had closed the space between them down to a point that she couldn't get away. Her fist closed tightly around the hammer.

"Are you happy about going back to Munich, *mein Liebling*?"

*I'm not your dear.* Aloud she said, "I am looking forward to seeing my *vati* again, seeing if he is doing all right. He was ill when I left. I hope he is there for me to return to."

She looked over her shoulder at him, crossing her arms over her chest and stepping away a little.

"Cecilia Gallerani was a beautiful woman," she mumbled, trying to distract him.

He looked at the painting, a proud look on his face. "Yes. It is a privilege to have her under my care."

*Because it isn't yours*, Edith thought.

"Will you be returning to your fiancé when you get back to Munich?"

Edith tried to keep the look on her face neutral. She shook her head, turning a blank face to stare at him. "He was killed in Poland."

But Frank hardly seemed to be listening. The announcement didn't change the look on his face at all. He was still staring at the picture of Cecilia Gallerani. He didn't care that Heinrich had died, that he had been killed in a battle Frank was responsible for. He didn't care about the thousands of lives he had helped destroy. He was a greedy, obsessive monster.

Edith wondered if she could hit him over the head with the hammer. Would she have the physical strength? The courage? What would happen if her attempt was unsuccessful? But what if she succeeded instead? She indulged in the fantasy for a moment before he spoke again.

"You have provided excellent service during your time with us, Miss Becker. I will see to it that you get a well-deserved post at the museum when this is all over."

Edith had her doubts that when it was all over, there would be a high post for her to consider.

"I need to go home now." Edith forced herself to look into Frank's eyes. "My father . . . He has been ill for a long time. Please," she said. "Let me go home to Munich."

She watched Frank's lips spread into a thin line. "Hmm. But my dear, we still have work here. And besides, we are at risk here right now, perhaps even more so than we were in Poland. It is not the time to travel."

Frank stepped closer to her again. He was so close, she could feel him breathing on her neck. She closed her eyes, trying to press down her disgust. Edith inched to the side and walked back around him to the couch opposite the desk.

She kept walking slowly and made her way to the balcony overlooking the lawn that sloped down to the lake. Two armed guards wore a path between the lake and the house, looking bored. Edith opened the double windows and stepped out onto the narrow balcony, feeling Frank behind her, tracking her steps. From this high vantage point, she watched the gardens, the rolling hills, cascading like ocean waves, stretch out before her to the icy edge of the lake. Bavaria. Home. It had been four years too long.

She leaned over the railing, looking down at the children rolling in the snow below. Norman and Michael, dressed in matching lederhosen and knitted mittens, were engaged in a mock wrestling match. The dogs circled them, leaping with joy. The lawn was littered with smashed snowballs and muddy footprints. Little Michael stopped then and looked up at her, his blond curls spilling from his cap. He smiled and waved frantically as if there was no way she could spot him otherwise. She grinned and waved back. Sweet, innocent child. What would become of him? How long before he would be swept up into Hitler's Youth?

"You have good children," Edith said. Frank came forward and stood next to her, looking down at his children below. "You must protect them," Edith said. The two of them watched a drift of dry snow suddenly come to life, swirling across the glassy surface of the lake.

# 66
## DOMINIC

*Munich, Germany*
*May 1945*

MUNICH WAS A FREE CITY, DOMINIC MARVELED AS the dusty Jeep rolled through the crenelated gates of the city. The battle had been brief, with little resistance put up by the few German troops that remained. Now, relief washed over the soldiers.

There had been skirmishes over the past two days, the first of them just outside Dachau the day before as the shell-shocked Americans reeled from the horror of seeing the dead bodies piled so carelessly in the boxcars. Those boxcars. All those emaciated bodies stripped of everything they had—their dignity, their society, their possessions, their identities. Just a collection of nameless flesh rotting in the unflinching sun, stripped to the bare bones of their souls and bodies before being killed and forgotten.

Stories of other concentration camps that had been liberated—starting with Majdanek in Poland the previous July—had found their way into the ranks of the Americans marching on Dachau. The figures were staggering. Auschwitz, liberated by the Soviets a few months before, was the story that haunted Dominic the most. One number stuck in his mind. Eight hundred thousand. It was the number of women's dresses the Soviets had discovered hidden in a warehouse full of personal belongings, presumably those of the inmates who had been killed. The number was more than Dominic could comprehend. But nothing had prepared them for what awaited them in Dachau.

In comparison with the rest of Dominic's unit—the men who had marched on Dachau to liberate the stricken camp—his mission now was simple; he had been sent with a small group of other soldiers to go ahead to Munich and prepare it for the arrival of the rest of the troops. He was intensely grateful not to be marching on the internment camps. The gunfights they'd had seemed a trifling nuisance in comparison with the mammoth task of rescuing the thousands of sick and malnourished prisoners.

The convoy met with no resistance as it rumbled into the city. On the contrary. The atmosphere seemed hushed, expectant. The division preceding Dominic's had already secured the city, and as they moved down the main street, people began to emerge from houses, basements, and shelters. Wide-eyed, they stared at this new spectacle: armed men who meant the civilians no harm. It was not an occupation, but a liberation.

The damage to the city seemed random. They passed whole blocks of buildings that stood untouched, the glass still intact in the windowpanes, flowers even beginning to blossom in beds and window boxes. But then these gave way to an entire street that had been turned into a heap of smoking rubble, shrapnel scattered dangerously all around.

Heedless of the sharp edges, more and more civilians came out to the streets, staring in mute disbelief at Dominic and the other soldiers. Hope began to gather behind their eyes the farther into the city they traveled; a crowd started to gather, then to follow as they moved ever slowly onward. Munich had been the target for a barrage of bombings over the past years. Those citizens who remained were struggling to believe that perhaps it had finally stopped.

The crowd gathered momentum, packing the sidewalks. Then, a handkerchief fluttered, white against the bleakness. And another. And another. Voices rose in the crowd, chattering, cheering, and suddenly everyone was there; the streets were lined by cheering, waving innocents who had had no part in the start of this war and were inexpressibly relieved by what looked to be the end of it. White handkerchiefs peppered the crowd as they waved and shouted. Increasingly, it felt more like a victory parade than a war zone. Children, then their parents, began to run alongside the tanks; bicycles clattered and spun down the streets, piloted by overexcited children who tried to keep up and dodge debris at the same time.

Yelps of excited German caught Dominic's attention. He turned to see two teenagers running behind the truck, reaching out to him with expectant hands, their eyes afire with hope. Laughing, he and one of the other servicemen leaned down to grasp their hands and pull them up onto the truck bed. Dominic recognized the tone of a scolding mother as a woman in a headscarf shook her finger at the two boys; they waved cheekily, grinning up at the armed men all around them. Excited by the idea, more and more teens and young adults rushed up to the Jeeps in a frenzy of peaceful excitement, trying to hitch a ride. They all wanted to be part of the liberation party, of the eventual peace of their city.

"Dominic!" yelled a happy voice. Dominic looked up. Weaver stood on the back of the Jeep alongside him. He held up a sign that, not long ago, had been posted at the city limits. Dominic's German was imperfect, but he could roughly translate: MUNICH: CAPITAL OF THE NAZI MOVEMENT. Weaver laughed, waving the sign above his head, enjoying the irony.

Munich's people were overjoyed. They filled the streets, packing so tightly that the convoy slowed to a crawl to avoid crushing the celebrating public. In a swarm of color, waving handkerchiefs and throwing flowers, the crowd swirled around the vehicles. There were at least a dozen German teens in the truck bed with Dominic; they bounced and hugged one another, hugged the soldiers. He had never seen so many people together all so happy to be alive.

Above the general chaos of the happy crowd's cheering and yelling, a voice suddenly rose above the rest in a yell of disbelieving joy. The convoy clanked to a halt as a wild-eyed young man ran into the street, half carrying and half dragging a wireless set that sputtered in protest as he manhandled it roughly to the sidewalk. "Listen!" he shouted, his accent spread thickly over excited words. "Listen." He turned the volume on the wireless up to the top.

From his place in the middle of the convoy, Dominic couldn't hear much. He thought he recognized the dramatic classical music that was playing—Wagner, perhaps. Hope leapt in him, and he could see it leaping into the faces of the people all around him, too.

The music stopped, then a booming German voice spoke through crackling static. The crowd was hushed as they listened to the words that Dominic couldn't understand, but he felt a ripple of excitement running through it. The voice had barely finished speaking when suddenly the crowd erupted in a yell of joy and triumph. Handkerchiefs were thrown in the air; people hugged, danced, shouted in German. A complete stranger threw her arms around Dominic and jumped up and down, shaking him until his teeth rattled.

"What? What is it?" Dominic asked. "What's happening?"

"It's Hitler." Weaver's eyes were filled with tears at the sight of the overjoyed civilians. "Hitler is dead."

Dominic couldn't believe his ears. He had barely thought of the ruthless dictator as a human being at all; he seemed more a force of nature, some dark and brooding presence bent on the destruction of the human race. He wondered, briefly, for how many deaths Hitler could be held responsible. Dominic thought of Paul. Then he thought of those boxcars, and part of him couldn't help but wonder if Hitler had been a human at all.

But his death still had to mean one thing. Berlin had fallen. Dominic pulled off his helmet and waved it in the air. "Yeeeah!"

"You know what this means?" Weaver asked him, beaming.

"It's almost over. It's got to be almost over," said Dominic.

Weaver was laughing. "It's almost time to go home."

Home. The thought pierced Dominic with a familiar, sweet agony that tore into his very soul. Closing his eyes, he touched the sketchbook that nestled in his pocket alongside a pack of the index cards he'd been given back at Marburg, now bent and ragged around the edges, but held together with a length of string.

When he opened his eyes, they lit on one part of the crowd. An old man stood hunched over on the sidewalk, his expression slack and vacant except for a confused furrow between his bushy eyebrows. He looked up at Dominic, his eyes wide and uncomprehending; Dominic attempted a smile, but it only served to make the man look more lost. He cuddled a stuffed toy dog to his chest; it had once been white but was matted and faded with age. Its button eyes peered out at Dominic with a benevolent expression as the old man squeezed it to his chest.

Dominic wondered when last this old man had seen the sun. He screwed up his eyes, deepening the wrinkles of his cheeks, and squinted up at Dominic with his head to one side. Then the middle-aged, auburn-haired woman dressed in a nurse's uniform, standing by the man's side, grasped the old man's hand. She whispered in his ear as he inclined his head toward her, seeming to try to focus intently on her words. When he looked back up at Dominic, his eyes had lit up. His slack lips twitched, then curved and split his face open in a wide grin. The old man waved at Dominic, and Dominic saw tears well up in the woman's eyes.

This, Dominic thought, was what liberation really meant.

# 67

## EDITH

**Neuhaus am Schliersee, Germany**
**May 1945**

FROM HER BEDROOM WINDOW HIGH UP UNDER THE eaves of Hans Frank's family farmhouse, Edith heard English on the radio.

She had been sitting on the edge of the bed for most of the afternoon, reviewing her tiny handwriting on the tattered pages of her copied inventories. The majority of the works on her list were marked now with small checks, each one dropped off at one of Frank's "safe havens" between western Poland and Bavaria—the many bank vaults, museum storage rooms, salt mines that Edith had set foot in in recent months.

Edith's eyes ran over the last few items that were now held in Frank's personal estate: a handful of valuable rugs and other decorative objects, several important paintings.

Edith ran her finger across the first entry in the list: Da Vinci's *Lady with an Ermine*. She felt relieved that this picture, at least, remained in her care.

Meanwhile, Edith had been left idle. Frank's old family estate hardly needed decorating. Brigitte had rumbled away in a car surrounded by armed soldiers, taking the younger children to visit family elsewhere in Bavaria. Only Norman and his father had been left behind. Norman, whose English was nearly as competent as Edith's, eschewed her offer to work with him on his lessons.

What was a "lady conservator" to do? Edith bided her time, trying to make herself invisible in the lakeside estate, hoping that Frank would leave her alone. Edith had double-checked the lock on the bedroom door before allowing herself to slide the inventories out from the creaking bedsprings.

But now, the strange sound of an English-speaking radio announcer, wafting through her open window from another place in the house, lured Edith from the bed. She moved quietly toward the sound, her feet soft on the floor. She went to the window and opened its tall pane wider, looking out to the vast expanse of spring green, sweeping down to the lake and its waters sparkling in the afternoon sun.

Edith strained to make out the words. She leaned over the balcony and looked toward one of the windows below. Norman's room. It stood directly below hers. Sometimes, she knew, like most teenage boys he liked to spend time alone where no one would bother him. But now, he was listening to the radio with his window open, the volume turned up loudly. He knew the family was gone and she was the only person here besides himself, his father, and the staff. Was he doing this purposefully so that she would hear what was being said?

Edith began to pay close attention to the words. It was British English, she felt sure of it. Edith looked up at the sky, a feeling of apprehension sweeping over her.

Hitler. Shot dead.

Had she heard that right?

The announcer was speaking quickly, but then she heard the word *Munich* and strained harder.

Munich. The Allies had already entered Munich. The Americans and the British were making their way through the streets of her hometown.

Edith's heart beat heavy and hard against her chest. Papa. Troops were probably bombing left and right, soldiers making their way through the city, leaving bodies in their wake. If the Americans were anything like the German soldiers, there would be a lot of bloodshed.

She turned away from the balcony when she heard Norman closing his window. Had he opened it for her to hear?

She needed to leave, to get home now. But how? Frank would not let her go. She knew his whereabouts, and what he had been doing all these months. She might easily turn him in.

Edith scanned the landscape beyond the edges of the lake. Were there Allied troops out there? Would they destroy da Vinci's *Lady*? Was there something she could do to save it? Edith's mind raced. Should she stay, and tell the foreign forces everything she knew? She had spent the last years doing what was in her power to save priceless works of art, but now, she thought mostly about saving her own life. Besides, she could hardly trust that these foreign soldiers would treat her like anything but an enemy.

Edith folded the ragged pages of her inventories as flatly as she could, and tucked them into the waistband of her skirt, where they were barely hidden by her light jacket. She gently opened the bedroom door and tiptoed into the dark hallway.

Her heart pounded in her chest as she considered the location of a door to the outside where she was least likely to attract notice from the kitchen staff or from Frank's armed guards who yawned and paced along the lakeside.

*The door leading to the vegetable garden*, she thought, tracing the side of the stair treads so that they would not creak as she descended. That one would allow her to duck into the trees along the wall that led to the main road.

But just as she turned onto the dark stair landing, Hans Frank appeared as if out of thin air. He stopped, grasping the handrail, and set his dark eyes on her. Instinctively, her hand flew to her waistband, then she froze.

"Where are you going, fräulein?"

# 68

## DOMINIC

*Neuhaus am Schliersee, Germany*
*May 1945*

DOMINIC HAD ALMOST FORGOTTEN THAT THERE WAS beauty in the world. Even the priceless beauty of the artworks he'd seen saved had been marred by damp and, at best, stuffed into a storehouse instead of displayed in a place where people might appreciate them.

But the Bavarian countryside thrown open before him was exhilarating, making him ache for a big sheet of paper that he could draw on with wild abandon. He would depict the incredible lines of it first; the long, sweeping, gentle curves of the green hills; the occasional view of sharp Alpine peaks in the distance, white-capped and blue-sided; the points of the conifers that clustered in the valleys. The sand-colored road that the convoy followed wound through the hills as naturally as if it had been scraped softly out of the grass by two giant fingers. And this late in spring, everything seemed to be blooming white and yellow on the flanks of the hills. Here and there, little lakes lay basking in the sun, like pieces of sky that had wandered from above and curled up to sleep in the hollows of the warm earth.

He was free to enjoy it, too. Helmet hooked over his knee, he allowed the warm breeze to push its fingers through his close-cropped black hair. He could hardly believe it was real. Only days ago, he'd been facing the horrors of Dachau and the gritty reality of bombed-out Munich. But the countryside south of the city felt like paradise. He was almost worried to look too closely in case his focus would shatter it like a dream. His rifle lay over his knees, his hands idle on the barrel.

There had been almost no fighting since they'd entered Munich. News of the Führer's death and Berlin's fall had spread through the country, sending the German army into disarray and making the German people ever bolder. The other news that had spread fast was that the American soldiers were friendly to civilians. People came crawling out of the hiding places that had gotten them through the awful shelling—barns, basements, and bomb shelters—to run behind the liberators, shouting in excited German and waving white rags. Kids quickly discovered that the American soldiers had small sugar rations, and they came begging, their eyes wide and mischievous. Many of the soldiers were fathers, and few could resist those hungry, eager eyes.

Dominic leaned back against the side of the Jeep as it trundled on. It was a blessed relief to be traveling through this sunlit countryside, enjoying a respite from the terror and desperation, but he still felt regret that he was not with the Monuments Men. Neuschwanstein Castle, not far from where they were now, had been captured by the Allies. Dominic had heard the news that inside the castle, the Monuments Men had discovered a hoard of art that, in quality and numbers, rivaled even the treasures they'd found at Siegen: sculptures by Rodin, Fragonard's portraits, masterpieces by Vermeer. He wondered if he would ever see such stunning artworks as he'd found in Siegen again and felt a pang of regret that he still hadn't set eyes on a da Vinci. If only he could have stayed with the Monuments Men long enough to have uncovered such an incredible find.

The convoy crested a little hill and Dominic looked down at a heart-lifting sight. Just ahead lay another of the mountain lakes that covered the countryside. A soft breeze ruffled its surface, making it the deepest blue he could imagine, creased like a luxurious swath of fabric. Waves of shifting grass interspersed with wildflowers rippled on either side of the road as the convoy continued toward the shimmering lake. The smells of spring rose all around them; crushed grass, sweet nectar, dust kicked up by the convoy, all with a sunbaked sweetness that made Dominic almost drowsy with contentment. If only Sally could see this.

The convoy came to a gentle halt. An officer stepped out and stretched before ordering the men to take a break and dig into their rations. The servicemen disembarked, gazing around at the beauty of the scene; a few of them simply flopped down on their backs in the grass and looked at the sky as if enchanted. It seemed like a long time before any of them had been allowed to enjoy the sun.

"You've gotta draw this, man," Weaver said to Dominic, stepping down from the Jeep.

Dominic jumped off beside him. "I will. But first, I gotta take a leak."

Weaver plopped down on the grass and opened his pack. "I'm not gonna wait. I'm starving."

Dominic headed toward a clump of shrubs he'd spotted at the crest of the hill. "I'll be right back."

He lifted his rifle from his shoulder and placed it in the Jeep. There was no need for it now. Then, he wandered toward the hill, admiring the carpet of beauty unrolled all around him. It gave him hope, hope that this war was almost over.

## 69
### EDITH

**Neuhaus am Schliersee, Germany**
**May 1945**

HANS FRANK HAD NEVER TOUCHED HER BEFORE.

Edith cringed at the feel of his grip on her forearm. Slowly, he led her down the stairs, and along the seemingly endless corridor.

When they crossed the threshold to Frank's office, Edith's eyes immediately went to the portrait of Cecilia Gallerani, as if the nearly five-hundred-year-old girl could impart some of her own serenity to a situation teetering on the brink of disaster.

"Governor Frank . . ." Edith began.

"Have a seat," he said, letting go of her arm. He sat behind his hulking wooden desk.

Edith lowered herself into the chair opposite Frank's desk.

He looked somber, his brows pulled together in a concerned frown. He sat for a moment in silence, his elbows on the desk, his clasped hands in front of his mouth. Edith thought she saw his eye twitch. He seemed to be corralling his energy, or perhaps suppressing it. Edith could not guess.

Finally, he pressed a stack of papers in front of her. "I need you to—"

Frank stopped speaking abruptly when the door opened. His teenaged son, Norman, stood there, but did not enter. He only stared at his father.

"What is it?" Frank finally broke the silence.

"*Vati*," Norman said, tentatively. "The Allies are coming to arrest you. I heard it on the radio."

Edith's eyes widened. Her hands gripped the armrests of the chair so tightly her knuckles turned white. She studied Frank's face, trying to read his reaction.

But Frank only stood calmly and turned away from both Edith and his son. Edith looked back at Norman. She tried to send him a telepathic message, thanking him for allowing her to hear his radio when the announcement about Hitler and the liberation of Munich was being broadcast.

"Papa . . ." the boy said. "Did you hear me? They are coming."

Frank removed a large diary from the shelf behind him and placed it on the desk. Next, he carefully removed a few more volumes and stacked them there. Then, Frank walked over to the window. He pressed his hands deeply into his pockets and simply stared at the lake.

Edith moved slowly, not wanting to make any noise to attract the troubled man's attention.

When she walked past da Vinci's *Lady*, she hesitated. Could she try to save the painting? Would she dare to pull it from the wall? What would Frank do? She could no longer predict. She hesitated, then forced herself to put one foot in front of the other. There was no way she could take the picture with her.

When she got to the door, Norman was blocking her way. He looked her in the eyes for a moment. She returned his gaze, unblinking. With a single, almost nonexistent nod, Norman stepped to the side and she slipped past him. The boy went into the office with his father and closed the door behind him.

Edith moved swiftly through the kitchen, where the cook and his assistants went about making pies for the next day's luncheon, when Brigitte was due to return home. They had no idea that everything was about to change. Edith said nothing. Businesslike, she walked toward the back garden door that led to a gravel path. She cast one look over her shoulder to see if anyone noticed she was leaving, but she saw no sign of the guards who spent their days lazily strolling the edges of the estate. Edith let the door click softly behind her.

In the same moment, she patted the waistband of her

skirt to make sure that the folded inventories were still there.

And just like that, Edith was outside the walls of the farmhouse. She looked up at the hillside before her, the bright sun making dappled patterns across the landscape where the flowers were beginning to sprout blooms in all the colors of creation.

Edith looked back nervously, afraid someone might be watching her from a window as she ran across the grass. She skirted along the stones at the foundation of the house. Perhaps even Hans Frank himself would see her, but surely he cared little about what might happen to her now. It was his own life on the line. No longer was he the arrogant governor of Poland who could claim the riches of anyone for his own. Now he was an enemy to extremely powerful forces, and they were about to come and give him the justice he deserved.

Edith felt glad that the Allies were coming, that they might finally penetrate the ever-tighter circle that had closed in on Frank and his closest associates in recent months. So many killed and families destroyed because of his ego, his greed.

Edith hurried across the lawn and to a small field that would take her to a winding path that led around the edge of the lake. For the first time in years, exhilaration filled her lungs with hope.

Edith moved quickly along the shoreline as it snaked

northward, in the direction of Munich. The American and British soldiers would eventually find the villa. Would they bomb it? Would they destroy all its beauty, just because of the evil man who lived there? She hoped they would have respect for the artwork and the artifacts that could never be replaced, especially *Lady with an Ermine*. Surely there would be a few intelligent, art-loving men among the soldiers?

She could only hope. But for now, all she wanted was to go home.

When she reached a narrow footpath where the lake tapered off into a smaller stream, Edith broke into a run.

# 70

## CECILIA

*Milan, Italy*
*June 1491*

"LITTLE DUKE." FAZIO APPROACHED CECILIA'S BED and plunked himself down beside her, casting his gaze to the bundle in her arms. He pinched one of the boy's tiny toes between two fingers and kissed its tip. Then he gazed at the child's nearly transparent eyelids, which flickered in his sleep. "His Excellency's only son."

Cecilia could only shake her head. "Whom he has not laid eyes upon."

She watched her brother's face fall. "No? Ah." He rose from the bed and began to pace the room. Silence hung heavy in the air. "Well. I believe he has been called away on important matters—" her brother began, but she raised her hand and her brother fell silent.

"Fazio," she said. "All the chambermaids—even old Bernardo—have held the baby in their arms. But not his own father." She sighed. "I suppose it is time I admit that our mother was right."

"Our mother?" Fazio's eyebrows raised.

"Yes. She said I would be nothing but a high-ranking whore. And now. Well, look at me." She gestured to the grandeur of the room and the baby in her arms.

"Cecilia." Fazio returned to the bedside. "Mother only wanted to secure a . . . respectable future for you. And she was trying to protect you—in her own sort of heavy-handed way—from having your heart broken. She could see how things might turn out, even if you could not."

Cecilia swallowed hard. "That horrid Beatrice! Can you believe her?"

Fazio sat and took her hand. He closed his eyes and nodded. "I know. But Her Ladyship is Ludovico's wife now. This is her home, her castle. She has every right to stake her position. She has done nothing wrong."

Cecilia wanted nothing more than for someone to take her side, but she knew her brother was right.

"And His Lordship . . . He is under a certain amount of pressure from his bride. Coming here to this wing of the palace is probably more difficult for him now than you realize. And anyway, now, my dear, there is a decision to be made."

"What decision?"

"The portrait," he said. "Beatrice does not want it here in the house any longer. His Lordship has asked Master da

Vinci to remove it."

"My likeness? I see. Well, I suppose it will be even easier for Ludovico—and everyone else—to forget me if it disappears from the palace."

Fazio's mouth spread into a thin line. "I hardly think His Excellency will forget you, my lovely, but there is more." Fazio took his sister's hand, an act of comfort that she graciously accepted because she was certain whatever came next would be difficult to swallow. Cecilia held her breath this time.

"His Lordship has arranged for the Verme Palace to be readied for you." He paused. "You cannot stay here much longer."

Instinctively, Cecilia pressed the baby to her chest. "Cesare?"

Fazio nodded. "He will go with you. As will the wet nurse, a cook, and a dressmaid. You will have everything you need. I don't know how that happened. His Lordship was keen on keeping the boy here under his roof along with Bianca. But someone seems to have changed his mind."

Cecilia exhaled. "Thanks be to God."

Cesare stirred now, making gurgling noises in her arms. Cecilia fiddled with the laces on her gown and attached the baby to her bare breast while her brother studied the ivory fan—a gift from the Neapolitan envoy—on Cecilia's bedside table.

"He could not have come to deliver the news to me

himself?" She huffed in disbelief, then thought for a long minute. "You see, Fazio? I told you our mother was right. I *am* nothing but a whore. A whore whose lover no longer visits her, however."

"I am sorry," Fazio said, then took a deep breath and met her gaze. "So, my sister. You have learned that most things—especially things inside the walls of this castle—are temporary. I do not know how long my own tenure may last. We must strive to navigate the . . . machinations . . . of His Lordship's court. And just as you discovered that your time here has been fleeting, you must understand that the move to the Verme Palace will also be temporary."

"What do you mean?"

"I suppose I should make it as clear as I can. His Lordship is doing you a favor by allowing you to retire to the Verme Palace for a time. I don't know how long; perhaps until Cesare has been weaned. At a certain point, you will need to make a decision. There is no getting around it any longer. I am certain that I could arrange for another meeting with the superior at Monastero Maggiore . . ."

"The convent."

He nodded. "It is either that, or we must—at last—find you a husband. If that's what you want, our brothers and I owe you that, at least."

*Yes*, Cecilia thought. *It is time for me to leave this house. And this man.*

# 71
## EDITH

*Neuhaus am Schliersee, Germany*
*May 1945*

IT IS TIME FOR ME TO LEAVE THIS HOUSE. AND MOST *of all, this man*, Edith thought.

From a hillside dotted with tall grass and wildflowers, she watched a small convoy of vehicles moving slowly along the road. Military vehicles, but not like any she had ever seen before.

Edith crested the top of the grassy hill where she could watch the curl of the road below. The road she'd seen from the window earlier in the day led to this place. That probably meant that it led to Munich. She stood in the grass dotted with tender spring blooms, watching as a convoy made its way through the countryside, toward the lakeside village where Frank's villa stood. She caught sight of the red and white stripes—an American flag—tied to the side of one of the vehicles making its way along the road winding between the hillsides. The tightness in her chest gripped her more when the convoy came to a halt.

Edith moved closer, wading into the tall grass growing out of the mud. Some of the soldiers were skirting around the halted jeeps, their guns ready, their eyes scanning the horizon for danger. She hoped she couldn't be seen and if she was, that she wouldn't be mistaken for an enemy even though she still wore her drab, German-issue uniform. The grass itched her ankles around her now-worn leather loafers.

Edith stopped at a tree and crouched down, her heart beating hard against her chest. If she was careful, she might be able to hear if there was much destruction in Munich. She squeezed her eyes together, holding back tears of despair. If she was too late, and her papa was dead, she could only blame herself.

But she refused to give up hope. Heinrich was gone. Her papa still had a chance. She had to hold on to that.

She was almost close enough to make out the soldiers' words. They had blunt, strange accents that made it difficult for her to follow. But what she did understand made no sense to her. They weren't talking about important subjects, like the treasures being found, the people who had died, the homes being invaded. They were talking about football. Several of the men were laughing. She had heard of football, the American game, but knew nothing about it.

The talking confused Edith. Weren't they concerned about possible threats from these hillsides? Weren't they afraid for their lives? Soldiers or not, they had to be a little bit scared. But instead, these men seemed joyous and playful. She stayed where she was for a while, waiting for the Americans to move on so that she could continue her journey toward home. But they hardly seemed to pay attention, so Edith ducked low behind some shrubs and kept moving.

When Edith rounded a tree, she suddenly found herself staring into the eyes of a young soldier in the process of buttoning his trousers. The soldier's face went white and the two of them gasped simultaneously and stared at each other in frozen horror for a couple of seconds.

Then, the soldier's hands flew to his shoulders, his chest, his midsection. But there was no rifle slung around his shoulder. He was unarmed. The soldier backed up a step or two and yelled something—a name—Weaver?—over his shoulder.

"Wait, wait!" Edith whispered hurriedly, shaking her head and raising her hands in the air at the same time. "Wait, I am not your enemy." She spoke the words in broken English. She hoped she was saying the right things. She dropped her eyes to his undone pants and quickly moved them back up to the patches on his uniform, and then to his face. He had turned beet red.

He was handsome nonetheless, young, maybe in his early twenties. He was short and lean, with an angled jaw and large, intelligent eyes. He turned resolute, steady and firm, his earlier scare behind him. He locked his eyes on her, his jaw set.

She dropped her eyes to the name on his tag. Bonelli.

"Mr. Bonelli," she said in a pleading voice. He looked startled that she said his name. Edith continued in English. "Please. Do not call to your friends. I am alone; I won't harm you. I am just trying to go home to Munich." His face softened. She went on. "Come . . . closer . . . I can tell you something."

He ran his hands along the front of his field jacket again, as if double-checking that his rifle wasn't there. He looked over his shoulder as if ready to call out to his fellow soldiers again, but she waved her hands frantically.

"Wait, please!" she said. "I . . . I have information . . . for you."

The soldier paused, but Edith's heart beat wildly in her chest and all the other English words in her head vanished. The small packet of her folded inventories suddenly pressed into her waist, as insistent as a sharp stone in her shoe, a painful reminder. Should she show the inventories to this American soldier? Could he actually do anything with them? Should she trust him at all, with her knowledge, with her safety? The last thing Edith wanted was to trade her newfound freedom for capture among the Americans.

"I . . . I have information . . ." She directed the words

to him again, wishing he spoke German. "Important information for you."

"What kind of information?" he said. "Where did you come from?"

"I . . . My name is Edith Becker," she said. "I am an art conservator from the Alte Pinakothek." She watched his gaze remain steady, uncomprehending. "It's an art museum in Munich. I know a great deal about the paintings and artifacts that have been stolen from the Polish people and others all across Europe. Many, many paintings, sculptures, other art objects." Edith hesitated, then realized that at least she had one piece of information that the Americans would want to know. "And I know where you can go to find Governor Frank."

The soldier faltered. His mouth hung open for a long moment, but he said nothing. Then, he narrowed his eyes at her. "You are going to tell me where Hans Frank is hiding? Why would you do that?"

"I . . . I am not loyal to the man. I have suffered greatly because of him, though not as much as many others. He is a selfish, evil man. I have no loyalty or obligation to him."

"You are German," he said, his eyes raking over her worn uniform. "Are you part of the Resistance?"

Edith didn't know how to answer. She had been a part of the art curating team for one of the most powerful leaders of the Nazi Party. But she didn't believe in their mission. She had an inventory of the stolen goods stuffed in her waistband. She had made an attempt to save what was in her power, an attempt that now seemed small, almost insignificant.

But how could Edith leave without trying to get these American soldiers to act in some way? Edith told this Bonelli where Frank's villa was, how to get there, and what they would find. She told him how many German soldiers were there to protect the place, how many staff, and that the governor's son was currently residing there, though the rest of the family was away.

"Please," she said as Bonelli turned away from her to return to the convoy on the road. She held out her hand and placed it on his arm. He looked down at her hand and back up to her eyes. "Will you please look out for the governor's son? He may appear nearly grown but inside, he is just a boy. I fear that he will be terribly frightened when you arrive to arrest his father. But the boy has done nothing. Nothing, I assure you."

The American pressed his lips together, giving her a sympathetic look. "I wish I could guarantee his safety, miss. But that's impossible. They are hostile enemies. I will look out for the boy but . . . well . . ." He shrugged.

She blinked slowly, nodding as the cruel truth sank in. Then the inventory tucked into her waistband cut into her skin again. Surely she couldn't risk letting it out of her possession, after all her hard work? She had no idea whether she could trust him. What if he didn't believe her? What if they lost it? If she handed it over to the Americans, it would be out of her control forever. It would never go back to Manfred, might never help get these priceless works back to their owners. Edith felt in her heart that if she handed over the inventory now, after all this time, she would live to regret it. But there had to be something the Americans could do. Edith grabbed Bonelli's arm once more, getting him to turn back to her. "What is it, miss?"

"Wait. Do you know who da Vinci is?"

The man blinked slowly. "Leonardo da Vinci? The painter?"

Edith nodded. "One of his paintings hangs in that villa. It's an original painting by the hand of Leonardo da Vinci. A portrait from the fifteenth century. A girl named Cecilia. It's in Governor Frank's office, hanging on the wall. Please, try to keep it safe. Unharmed. It's titled *Lady with an Ermine*. There is no price high enough to match its value."

"Cecilia," he said, and Edith saw that the mere mention of the name prompted a wide, beautiful smile on the soldier's face.

"And the boy's name is Norman," Edith replied. "Please. He is innocent."

"The painting of Cecilia. And the kid. Got it. I'll do my best, miss. All right? Now, where do you think you are going?"

Edith turned her eyes to the distance.

"I am going home to my father."

Edith turned back, moving swiftly out of the grass and toward the main path that snaked along the lakeside. Behind her, the soldier, Bonelli, stood watching her, a lone silhouette at the crest of the hill.

# 72
## DOMINIC

*Neuhaus am Schliersee, Germany*
*May 1945*

THE GIRL'S SOFT BROWN EYES HELD A SPARK THAT took Dominic's breath away. She stared into the middle distance, her lips curving slightly as if she had just been surprised by someone she was pleased to see. The smooth curve of her white, youthful cheek was highlighted by the sharp line of her elegant nose; her shining brunette hair was bound to her face, framing its flawless radiance with dark edges. The rest of her hair was plaited down her back and sheathed in translucent mesh trimmed with gold. The smooth expanse of her shoulders, neck, and upper chest was bare but for the graceful curve of the double strings of black beads that draped there.

Dominic leaned closer, inspecting it, almost nose to nose with the beautiful girl. Her dress was elegant yet modest, its cool blue complemented by lustrous red trimming on the sleeves and gold decorations along the hems. But it was her expression that was most remarkable. She seemed so alive, and he could not read in the skilled brushstrokes how exactly the artist had achieved that startling effect of live-liness. He wanted to clear his throat and see if the girl in the portrait would turn to acknowledge his presence, this grubby American soldier staring at her across the centuries.

A painting by Leonardo da Vinci. A real one. Dominic could hardly believe his eyes. The lady who had caught him unsuspecting by the lake had been telling the truth. Now, Dominic wished that he had not let her simply walk away. What else could she have told them? What other treasures could she have helped the Monuments Men uncover? Now, Dominic was kicking himself for letting her go. He was so angry at himself about it that he had not even let his fellow soldiers know about the strange encounter. He had only told his commanding officer that they had received word about Frank's location.

The *Lady with an Ermine*. It was a dream come true in so many ways; a dream Dominic had never expected to find here, under these circumstances, on the other side of the world, on the far end of a gruesome war, in an old house by a lake. But somehow that made its beauty all the more startling. Despite the slick and crackled paint, its emotion and realism still seized Dominic by the heartstrings and wouldn't let go. He was so tempted to reach out and touch its surface, half expecting the girl's skin to be warm. But he knew that to lay a hand on the five-hundred-year-old paint would be almost as bad as Siegen's damp had been. He pressed his hands together behind his back and drank the picture in with his eyes instead.

Around him, the enormous estate of Hans Frank echoed with the sound of American boots trampling on the floors. Schoberhof, they called the house. It stood majestically along the lakeside, with its hulking, traditional Bavarian architecture and sweeping expanse overlooking the glittering brilliance of Lake Schliersee. Dominic could barely comprehend the sheer size of the house, much less that it belonged to one man. His little brick home on Swede Hill would fit in the man's living room. The mere sight of it had left a bitter taste in Dominic's mouth. While his fellow human beings died by the thousands in the brutality of concentration camps, Frank had lounged in comfort in this beautiful old farmhouse by the lake, adorned with riches— even with a painting by the hand of Leonardo da Vinci. This house, Dominic realized, belonged to the same man they called the Butcher of Poland.

Straightening from the portrait, Dominic stared around the room. Frank had had his last day of ease in this estate. The special forces that had been called in to arrest him, one of the most wanted war criminals in Europe, had left a couple of days before with Frank bound between them. The staff required to keep the estate in pristine condition had been taken, too, for interrogation. Looking at the house, Dominic presumed there must have been many. Cooks, cleaners, gardeners—they must have worked to keep every surface so spotless. But the signs of disarray were already creeping in around the edges. Dirty bootprints covered the floors; there was a grubby handprint on the doorknob opposite, and scratches on the marble flooring where furniture had been pulled aside to search the house.

This was the task left to Dominic and the rest of his unit: searching Frank's home and especially his office, looking for evidence that might condemn this vile human being in court. Other soldiers were busy turning the office inside out. Dominic could hear their voices as they rummaged through the rooms around him. But the commander had seen the look on Dominic's face when he spotted the portrait through an open doorway.

"Off you go, Bonelli. Weaver, too." he said. "I expect a report for the MFAA by tonight."

Dominic had not budged since. He knew he should be joining Weaver in searching the bedrooms and hallways for tapestries, paintings, and sculptures, but he just couldn't get his eyes off this girl depicted in centuries-old skill. Painted by Leonardo da Vinci's own hand.

Weaver walked into the room carrying a pair of elaborately painted vases. "Still with your girlfriend, Bonelli?" he joked, setting them gently on a table.

"Absolutely," said Dominic, smiling. "Hancock and Stout are not going to believe this."

Weaver stepped toward the door. "The sooner we get this information to the Monuments Men, the sooner these things can be returned to their owners, if any of them are left."

Dominic nodded gravely at Weaver's assessment, but he found it difficult to turn away from the portrait. Weaver came to stand beside him and stare reverently at the painting. "I would love to describe this in technical jargon," he gestured. "The brushstrokes, the use of light and shadow. . . . But honestly, words seem inadequate." Weaver pressed his hands in his pockets and shrugged.

"I know." Dominic's eyes roamed across the portrait's soft lines and vivid expression. "Pure magic."

# 73
## LEONARDO

*Milan, Italy*
*June 1491*

**"PURE MAGIC."**

That is how His Lordship has described my portrait of his Cecilia. I am so gratified that I cannot find words to respond to his assessment, so I change the focus to the most obvious subject.

"My deepest congratulations to you on the birth of your son, my lord."

Ludovico il Moro nods, and I think I see his eyes wrinkle. The sign of a sincere smile. Little Cesare. Where is the little rascal now, I wonder?

But His Lordship turns his attention back to the portrait of Cecilia Gallerani. To my surprise, he places it in my hands. "Take it," he says. "For safeguarding, I cannot keep the picture here anymore. I cannot guarantee that it will not be damaged. Or stolen. You will know what to do with it," His Lordship says.

"You no longer want to display it here, my lord?"

"Beatrice. She wants it removed immediately from the castle."

Ah yes, I think. The portrait will be in danger of destruction.

"Your boy will stay here in the palace with you, my lord?"

"For a time. He is in the nursery with the wet nurse. He will have my protection if not my name. Of course I will see to his welfare and his education, just as I have for my Bianca. It is the least I can do."

"But, with all due respect, my lord, perhaps the boy is better off with his mother? If she is also leaving this place, then it might be in the best interest of all."

# 74
## EDITH

*Munich, Germany*
*May 1945*

"EDITH."

Her father's simple recognition of his daughter forced all the tears that Edith had held back for years to come rushing forth in great sobs. She kneeled on the floor beside her father's chair and let him pat the top of her head while she let the tears run down her face. She felt like a little girl again, crouched at his feet, his broad palm across the crown of her head. Behind them, several dozen leather-bound books filled with bookmarks and notes collected dust. The old clock insisted on ticking.

Best of all, Edith had found her father in more or less the same condition as when she had left, no better but certainly no worse. It was all thanks to the efforts of Rita, to whom she owed everything. Edith wished that her father might have been able to understand where she had been, what she had been doing, and most importantly, that she had tried to be brave, just like him. The loss of her father's mind was an injustice that seemed impossible for Edith to reconcile, but perhaps his obliviousness to the calamities around him had kept him alive, helped him survive this cruelest of chapters in their country's history.

Edith hardly recognized her home city. To her astonishment, some parts of Munich were left wholly intact. Viewed from a certain angle, the buildings and the trees appeared just as they had before the war. But you had only to turn a corner to find another street in utter devastation, leveled to little more than a pile of rubble. American and British vehicles and tanks lined the street in front of her apartment building. There were many more along the other streets throughout the city. The Nazi flags that had flapped across the public buildings of the city—for years now—were coming down.

Some mornings, Edith awoke disoriented, not knowing where she was, and was filled with relief to see the dim outlines of her childhood bedroom. Often, she dreamt she was still a prisoner in the home of the governor of Poland, and she awoke in a cold sweat. Other times, she expected to rise and return to work in the basement of a once-fine Polish villa, sifting through piles of treasures that belonged to others. How many lives had passed through her hands? So many families destroyed. She could only pray for their safety now.

And Edith couldn't help but pray also for the safety of da Vinci's *Lady with an Ermine*. She wondered what had happened to the picture. Had the American soldier she had encountered at the lake—Bonelli?—found the house? What had the soldiers done with the painting? Would they confiscate it, take it back to America with them after all, just as she had been warned that they would do? Would it make another, final voyage, this time across the sea? Edith supposed that she would accept that outcome, as long as the picture was put into a museum collection where it would be properly preserved. Cecilia—her portrait—deserved to be treasured.

But in the back of her mind, Edith wondered if she had missed her chance to make a difference, for the *Lady with an Ermine* and for so many other important works of art that her hands had touched in recent years. She had made a decision not to share her inventories with that Bonelli, in that strange encounter on a Bavarian hilltop. Was it the right choice? At least, she thought now, she had a better idea of how to put the inventories to best use.

# 75
## EDITH

*Munich, Germany*
*May 1945*

EDITH WATCHED MANFRED'S HANDS TREMBLE AS HE shuffled the worn, creased pages of her inventories. Then, she saw slow understanding dawn on his lined face. Edith placed a hand over her mouth, stifling a smile.

"Edith." It was all he could say. His wide eyes ran over the tiny script, the pages and pages of works of art stolen from Polish collections.

Behind them, standing on an easel in her conservation laboratory was the old, overpainted picture by Hans Werl, the same picture that Edith had been working on the day she got the assignment to begin researching the treasures of Poland nearly six years before. How much had changed, how much she had changed, she realized.

Edith touched the dusty surface tentatively with one

finger. The picture waited for her; it was just as if she had walked out of the office yesterday, and had arrived to start again, right where she left off. Was that possible? To pick up right where you left off, when so many would never have that luxury?

In the galleries and storage rooms of the Alte Pinakothek, many other treasures awaited, hundreds of paintings and objects stacked methodically in her office and the adjacent storage rooms, waiting in the dim light to be returned to their owners. Edith felt her body quake when she saw the state of the museum. During the Allied strike, a bomb had landed on the roof, collapsing one side of the long façade to the ground. Relief washed over her when she realized that her conservation lab was still standing.

Meanwhile, her colleagues were beginning to return from their far-flung assignments. Around the building, curators and administrators filed back into their offices, wandered the hallways, stopped to embrace the coworkers they had not seen in months, if not years. Manfred had returned from a long stint in Berlin. The atmosphere in the museum was a strange state of euphoric confusion, hushed excitement, and tears of joy, grief, and disillusionment. Edith realized that there would be much to do. With the devastation around them, no one seemed to know where to begin. Would her native country ever be able to recover, to atone for the many acts of evil that were now coming to light?

# 76

## CECILIA

*Milan, Italy*
*June 1491*

**IN THE NIGHT, HE CAME TO HER.**

In the depth of slumber, her heart led her. She smelled him, his intoxicating scent of the forest and horses and old velvet. His thick beard raked across the delicate skin of her neck, sending a shiver down the length of her back. Instinctively, she turned toward him and hooked her ankle around his leg, pulling him to her. Her hands went to his bare shoulders, damp in the clammy air. For a moment, it felt like the seconds before a summer storm, when lightning crackles in the clouds. She inhaled sharply, hungry for breath in the stifling air.

"My flower."

Softly, he ran his fingers along Cecilia's jaw. The feeling tingled down through her body and she remembered all the nights he had held her, kissed her, taken her, right in this very bed.

But as he moved his face to her breast and began to twist his fingers clumsily around the tiny buttons of her chemise, Cecilia began to wake. She was raw and sore from the birth. And as much as she wanted him to hold her, to see her, to acknowledge her, to love her, she could not bear to feel his weight on top of her. Not now.

And where was Beatrice? Asleep in their chambers? If she woke, would she come looking for him? Cecilia's eyes went to the door, where she saw that the duke had fastened the metal latch behind him when he had entered.

At that moment, Cecilia heard Cesare begin to fuss in the next room. She knew that the sound would only get louder. He was hungry. She sat up in bed, and Ludovico rolled onto his arm. She threw back the linens and walked into the small room where Cesare slept. The wet nurse was already on her feet, but Cecilia shook her head. She took her son into her arms and loosened his tight swaddle.

When she returned to the bed, Ludovico was sitting on the edge, tangled in the linens and running his palms over his black hair. In the moonlight, she saw the profile of his bare arm and chest. She settled herself beside him, Cesare cradled in her arms. She unfastened her night-shirt and let it fall from her shoulders, only the edges of her body visible in the moonlight. She felt the baby's delicate skin stick to her bare breast in the stale air. While Ludovico watched, she guided Cesare's mouth to her breast. For a few quiet moments, the three of them sat there in silence on the edge of the bed. She felt Ludovico's eyes on her.

For a fleeting moment, Cecilia closed her eyes and allowed herself the fantasy that everything was perfect, just the three of them together. But she knew in her heart that it was just that. A fantasy.

Would His Lordship claim this bastard child as his own?

Ludovico leaned over and rested his chin on Cecilia's shoulder, looking down at the baby. He watched the curve of Cesare's angelic face in the gray glow of the moonlight. Cecilia searched for Ludovico's black eyes in the darkness, and finally, he returned her gaze, a flicker in the nightglow.

"Ludovico," she whispered. "Your son."

# 77
## EDITH

*Munich, Germany*
*May 1945*

EDITH'S DESK WAS A DISASTER OF STACKED PAPERS, small objects, and dust. But on her chair, Manfred had left a copy of a British newspaper. She took a deep breath and allowed herself to open its folds. There were two different articles on Hans Frank. One concentrated on calculating the number of deaths the man was responsible for—now counting into the thousands. In her mind, Edith included Heinrich in that category. The second article spoke of the horrific death camps he'd opened all across Poland. His own people were put in those camps to be tortured and starved. How could a man do such a thing?

"Edith!"

Edith turned to see the museum director stride through the door. Without thinking, Edith pressed the newspaper into the messy stack on her desk, her heart pounding.

"What a sight you are! It has been so long." General-direktor Buchner grasped her hand in both of his. She felt the calluses there, but his eyes were soft and sincere. "I am gratified to see you in good health."

"As much as can be discerned from the outside," she said, returning the grasp of his hand.

"Yes," he said, his brow furrowing. "I suppose each of us is carrying our own burden on the inside."

"There is much to do here," she said, gesturing to the painting on the easel.

"Yes," he said. "That's why I'm here. Don't get comfortable just yet." Edith watched Herr Buchner pull a file from under his arm and place it on the worktable. "I'll get straight to the point, Edith. You have new orders."

"New orders?"

Edith's shoulders fell. All the wind went out of her lungs and she dropped down in the chair, feeling it spin around until she felt dizzy.

# Part VI
*Recollection*

# 78
## DOMINIC

*Munich, Germany*
*May 1945*

THE WAR WAS ALL BUT OVER, BUT DOMINIC'S HEART was heavy. He was not going home. He was only reassigned.

Dominic's footsteps were slow and shuffling as he followed a British officer around the Allies' newest Central Collecting Point. The building was massive. Its rows of doors stood between vaulted pillars, frowning down on the street with its high window ledges like disapproving brows. Brooding right at the center of Munich, the building loomed over the road, its shadow wrapping Dominic in a chilly embrace in the still-crisp spring morning.

Dominic followed the officer around the building's façade, learning the locations of all the locks and exterior doors, windows, and fire escapes. He'd already been briefed on the building's extensive alarm system. He walked along the street with his hands pressed deeply in his pockets, still feeling awkward and lopsided without his rifle; but there was no more need to carry a gun on the streets of the Allied-controlled Munich.

In exchange for turning over information about a priceless painting by Leonardo da Vinci, Dominic had been rewarded with a job at the Munich Collecting Point, where works of art would be cataloged, conserved, and eventually returned to their owners. He was a hero, Stout had told him, though Dominic could hardly imagine why. Just lucky, he thought, to run into that lady on a hilltop with his fly open.

Dominic followed the officer from door to door, listening to his explanations in round tones that spoke of English hills.

"And now you have heard everything about the outside," said the officer as they finished their circuit of the building and reached the front door again. He grinned at Dominic. "The boring part is done. Now let's take you inside so you can see what you're really here for."

Dominic dredged up a smile. "Yes, sir."

Guards saluted them as they walked down the hallways into the voluminous front room. The officer walked briskly, talking excitedly about the art that was being unloaded inside the Collecting Point, but Dominic found himself only half listening.

He knew he should be excited to be working here. Not

only had he been taken out of the fighting—and not assigned to the heart-wrenching task of cleaning out the concentration camps—he also got to work with some of the priceless masterpieces that had been collected from hiding places throughout Germany and Austria. He might even get a chance to take a second look at some of those glittering paintings that he had glimpsed only fleetingly as they were passed up into other hands, and into a line of armored vehicles back at the mine in Siegen.

But Dominic was struggling to find enthusiasm for the project. Much as he loved being around the art, he had hoped with everything in him that his performance in helping to retrieve some highly precious work—paintings by Rubens, Rembrandt, and even da Vinci—from the home of one of the most wanted Nazi leaders would be enough for his superiors. He had hoped it would be enough to send him home at last. He had seen so many stunning masterpieces and he had loved them all, but none of them could begin to compare to the hope of returning to his family.

The front room of the Central Collecting Point was similar to the one at Marburg; desks in orderly rows across the floor, professionals busy photographing and cataloging the pieces that were carried up from loading docks by American, Australian, and British soldiers. "We can't keep up," said the officer. "We've been calling in more and more staff to help. The stuff just keeps coming in from all corners of Europe. The scale of the Nazi confiscation is mind-boggling."

In Munich, Dominic sensed a change in the atmosphere compared to Marburg. Then, there had been a feeling of desperation; every piece of art had been handled nervously, with respect to the blood that had been shed to find it, and with horror at the thought that this might all be in vain. At any moment an Axis bomb could have come down on the building in Marburg and destroyed all their hard work. But now that the war was won, the entire building buzzed with excitement; new hope filled the eyes of the professionals as they photographed and wrote. They touched the art with reverence and joy, taking in the beauty of every piece.

"Brilliant, isn't it?" said the officer. "Come on, let's have a walk through the storerooms."

The rooms here had a more permanent feel than the slapdash setup at Marburg. Everything felt more settled, more organized. And though this building was easily twice the size of the old state archive at Marburg, it was even fuller. Room after giant room opened off the corridors, all stacked high with beautiful artwork, neatly arranged in various categories. Paintings hung on walls or stood on easels instead of being stacked on top of each other; some effort had been made to arrange the sculptures on the shelves in an eye-catching manner.

"Hard to believe it's all in *this* building, eh?" said the officer.

"Why is that, sir?" said Dominic.

"Because these were Hitler's own Nazi headquarters." He shuddered, his eyes far away, and Dominic wondered what he had seen. For Dominic, the very mention of the name Hitler brought back the vivid image of those boxcars at Dachau, piled high with the dead. It was an image that he knew he would take to the grave with him, as vivid—down to the smell and the sound of the soldiers' screaming—as it had been the day he had witnessed the hellish sight.

"Well," said the officer, straightening, "now it's where we sort the art they stole and give it back to the people who rightfully deserve it." He found his smile again. "Come on, I want to show you an old friend of yours."

Curious, Dominic followed the officer upstairs into a huge, square room that would have been stark and sad if its walls had not been hung with beautiful paintings in gilded frames. There was only one window—a stern, rectangular affair facing west, letting in a square of grayish light—but it was enough to illuminate the portraits that lined every wall. Skillfully depicted faces stared out at Dominic in a variety of attitudes; reclining, fighting, posing, frowning, smiling, and laughing.

But it was the portrait at the center of the room that immediately commanded his attention. The soft eyes of the girl so skillfully portrayed by Leonardo da Vinci stared past him, the placement of the painting on an easel in the middle of the floor making her even more striking. Among the other works by grand masters, somehow this girl still stood out, her beauty ringing down through the centuries to seize Dominic's heart.

"Oh!" he exclaimed. "It's her."

The officer laughed and clapped him on the shoulder. "I'll leave you to it. Duty starts tomorrow morning. Until then, enjoy yourself." Before Dominic could thank him, the officer was gone and Dominic was left once again to gaze into the eyes of Cecilia Gallerani.

# 79
## EDITH

**Munich, Germany**
**June 1945**

THAT FAMILIAR FACE—THE SOFT BROWN EYES, THE lively expression. The white ermine.

Edith couldn't believe her good fortune to stand in front of da Vinci's *Lady with an Ermine* again. But this time, she was not in a basement of the war-torn countryside; nor was she on a rumbling train or in a salt mine, or the home office of a man bent on destroying all that was good in the world.

Instead, she was in Munich, in her own hometown. This time, she was safe from harm. And the picture was safe, too. She could hardly imagine it.

"It's not bad news, Edith," Buchner had told her, and he was right. "It's an offer from the Allied forces. They want you to come join them as a civilian employee at an Allied checkpoint here in Munich. Works of art from all over Europe—including those pulled from Poland—will go through the checkpoint. The art will be collected, cataloged, and repatriated to its rightful owners, wherever they may be."

Edith had blinked at him in disbelief. Manfred. The inventories had made it into the right hands after all. Manfred had marveled at the inventories Edith compiled. He told her that he would need some time to talk with his associates and figure out the best way to utilize the important information that Edith had assembled. At last, Edith thought, her labors might bear some fruit.

"The checkpoint is here in Munich?"

Buchner had only nodded. "I hate to lose you again right as you have returned to us, but they are requesting you by name. I have no idea how they know of you, but they insisted on having Edith Becker work with them. You must have done something . . . remarkable."

The Allies wanted her services, as a civilian. She was not being ordered anywhere. She would not have to leave her father behind and she would still be able to handle and safeguard—*really* safeguard this time—the priceless treasures she so dearly loved. And at last, her carefully transcribed secret inventories might be put to some use after all.

But shortly after Edith had departed for her new job, news of Generaldirektor Buchner's arrest spread in hurried whispers and gasps that reverberated through the hallways.

He had been accused of collaborating to steal the Ghent Altarpiece from a museum in France, and the Allies wanted to question him on the whereabouts of other works of art. Edith could hardly believe her own good fortune in being invited to help return the works to their owners rather than being arrested for their confiscation.

Had she been responsible for confiscating Leonardo da Vinci's *Lady with an Ermine*? Edith stared into Cecilia Gallerani's eyes, so full of life even after five hundred years and countless trips across the war-torn countryside. *I did my best to protect you*, Edith pled silently with the girl in the picture, as if Cecilia herself could have vouched for Edith's good intentions. *So much of it was out of my control.* But in her heart, Edith knew that wasn't true.

For the first time since she had laid eyes on the picture five years before, Edith felt that she could look at the picture in a new light, in the light of a conservator's eye. After all the movement through different countries and climates, she feared that the picture might need to be stabilized. She leaned forward and ran her eyes over the surface, looking for cracks, scratches in the raking light.

Carefully, she turned it over. The picture had been painted on a walnut board. There were cracks on the vertical axis, some hairline, others wider.

"It's you." Edith heard a strange accent at her ear. "The lady from the lake."

Edith turned to see a familiar-looking man before her.

A slight man, handsome, with chocolate-colored eyes and an American accent.

"Am I right?" he asked, his face earnest and serious. "You led me to this picture."

Edith studied the name on his uniform, and her eyes lit up with recognition.

"Bonelli! Mister B-Bonelli!" she stammered. She laughed then, throwing her head back so that a wing of chestnut hair traced along her cheek. All her hard work. It hadn't been wasted after all. She stepped forward and threw her arms around Bonelli's neck. He staggered back a couple of steps until she finally released him.

Bonelli ran his palm over his hair, recovering from the surprise.

"And you are a hero!" Edith exclaimed, and she watched the corner of his mouth turn up in a sideways grin.

"Call me Dominic." He extended his hand.

"I'm Edith."

Dominic gripped her hand. His was calloused but steady. "How strange—and wonderful—to see you again, miss."

"Indeed," Edith said, not wanting to let go of the hand of this stranger who had done more to save the portrait in one day than Edith had done in five years. "I should introduce my companion," she said, gesturing toward the painting. "This is Cecilia. But I think you have already made her acquaintance?"

"I have had the honor."

Edith smiled again. "She tells me that a brave soldier rescued her from the castle of an evil tyrant."

"Yep," said Dominic. "Swept her right off her feet."

"Her prince in an armored car." She grinned at him. "But now it is my turn. It will be my job to bring Cecilia back to the way that Leonardo da Vinci must have seen her when she was sitting before him." She touched the frame of the painting with gentle fingers.

"Why do you call her Cecilia?" asked Dominic.

"People call her *Lady with an Ermine*," said Edith. "But we believe that it is a portrait of a young woman named Cecilia Gallerani who lived in Milan about five hundred years ago."

"Cecilia is my daughter's name!" said Dominic, his eyes wide. He gestured to the picture. "She was beautiful."

"Yes." Edith's eyes were dark and wide now as they searched the portrait. "And she will be again when I am done with her."

# 80

## CECILIA

*Verme Palace, outside Milan, Italy*
*August 1491*

CECILIA LOOKED UP FROM HER READING TO SEE A FA-
miliar silhouette framed in the doorway. She would recognize him anywhere, his elegant form with light flowing
around him. In his hands, he held a large rectangular-
shaped package wrapped in blue paper.

Cecilia let out a screech and jumped up and down on
the octagonal tiles.

"*Cavolo.* That all my pictures might enjoy such a recep-
tion," Leonardo said, stepping across the threshold into the
shadows.

Cecilia laughed. "Master Leo. I must admit that I am
happy to see the painting, especially since I thought I might
never lay eyes on it again. But mostly I am thrilled to see
*you.*" Cecilia pressed the painter's face between her palms
and kissed both cheeks. Following her mistress's example,

Violina weaved her way back and forth against Leonardo's emerald-colored hose excitedly, her tail a frantic mass of white fur.

"I am satisfied to see that you are still surrounded by the beauty that befits you," he said, taking in the great stairway and the darkened frescoes in the vaulted ceilings of the Verme Palace.

Cecilia shrugged. "It's not the Castello Sforzesco, but that is only a good thing. Come. You must see how Cesare has grown. And you must tell me everything of Bernardo, and of you and your own pursuits. I have missed you both so much."

They took their seats in the *sala grande*, a bright room that overlooked an inner courtyard where Cecilia was trying in vain to grow an olive tree like the ones in Siena. So far, she had only managed to grow it up to a spindly, weak-looking branch. While the artist began to unwrap the blue paper that protected her portrait, Cecilia studied his face. He seemed to have aged years since the last time she saw him. Fine lines stretched across his pale forehead and alongside his eyes. Wiry, gray hairs had sprouted around his once-youthful face. And the color seemed drained from him.

"Are you well, my friend?" she asked, her demeanor turning concerned.

"Yes. Just . . . occupied, more than usual," he said with a thin smile. "If I am honest, signorina, since your departure from the house, His Excellency has turned . . . restless. Irritable. He loses his temper. He changes his mind. I have begun and scrapped at least a dozen different projects." He shrugged. "Mostly drawing canals, fortifications, bridges, even new looms for his many silk factories." He swiped his hand as if swatting a fly.

"You are also painting for him?"

"Yes. Another portrait." He hesitated, studying her gaze. An uncomfortable silence stretched between them

"Lucrezia Crivelli." Cecilia whispered her name.

But Leonardo did not answer. He didn't have to. "I see," Cecilia said, despairing for a moment that Ludovico had taken another mistress so quickly. Her own dressmaid and would-be companion.

*What a naïve girl I have been*, Cecilia reproved herself.

The artist sighed, then quickly changed the subject. "Ludovico first enlarged the gardens around the palace. Then he changed course again, back to fortifications along the eastern edge of the city. We have revisited the idea of a bronze equestrian statue to immortalize his father; I had as much as proposed the idea to him years ago and even made a life-sized clay model. You know yourself that there are many white walls in the palace that might be painted. And the duke himself has promised me work at Santa Maria della Grazie. I suppose that I should be gratified. I did work my way into His Lordship's graces with my offer to support his military efforts. But it has become an unwieldy burden, in the end. I would only admit that to you, since you would understand what I mean about His Lordship's changes of heart."

"And Bernardo?"

Leonardo's brows arched. "If you want to know the truth, he is not himself. Spends his days in the library, reading and writing poetry. He has attempted to make friends with Beatrice. She is learned and lively, I'll admit, but it is not the same. Bernardo misses you. We both do. And His Lordship has mostly left him to his own projects in the library, which I suspect suits him fine," Leonardo said with a half smile. "Ludovico has turned his focus away from supporting the artistic life of his palace. Instead, he is obsessed with making alliances with the French throne and the Holy Roman Emperor. He is imagining threats from every corner. He has had me drawing and redrawing military plans until late in the night. I fear that he might be sharing my work with them, and I do not know how they will be used. And Beatrice, well, she seems unable to distract him."

"Please," Cecilia said, raising her hand. "I can no longer afford to fill my mind with such concerns. It is enough for me to evaluate my own circumstances."

"I have burdened you," Leonardo said. "That was not my intention. Tell me about you, my beauty."

At that moment, the nursemaid brought Cesare into the room, his black hair damp and his fat cheeks red from his afternoon slumber.

"*Amore*!" Cecilia jumped up from her chair and took the boy in her arms, covering his face with kisses.

"Young man!" Leonardo exclaimed, tugging gently on the baby's dressing gown. "I see that they have been feeding you well here." Cecilia was certain that Leonardo saw the spitting image of Duke Ludovico il Moro in her baby, but he had the diplomacy not to say so. "And I have brought you a gift," he said to the baby, smiling. "A likeness of your mother. Perhaps years from now, when I am gone, you will look upon it with a fondness for the man who painted it."

"I wish I could say that I could not accept it," Cecilia said, hardly able to contain her excitement. "But yes! Of course we will take it. We will find the perfect place to hang it. Thank you," she said, kissing the painter on the cheek. "Now come. Some air will do us all good."

Leonardo followed Cecilia, baby in her arms, into the shade of the courtyard. They walked past crumbling stone and roses tangled on the gray arches, and Cecilia's sad olive tree.

"You are settled here?" he asked, looking up at the coffered ceilings in the archways above their heads. They glimpsed one of the young kitchen maids, who quickly disappeared into the maze of corridors that fed from the courtyard.

The Verme Palace was smaller and not filled with the things that her castle had been, but it would be suitable for Cecilia and Cesare to live well. She had brought with her fine clothes, jewelry, and a few decorative boxes and vases that she was used to seeing in her chambers. To her astonishment, she had even found a trunk for Cesare waiting for them, full of everything a baby could need. As she unpacked her life and Cesare's, Cecilia wasn't sure what was worse—to be loved and unable to be kept, or to never have been loved at all.

Ludovico had also sent a nursemaid, a widow who had brought up five boys, to help her raise Cesare. Everything he had promised her she had been given. A fine place to live, lands held in her own name, horses, and a maid to help her raise their son, who would have his father's protection as he grew into a man. Ludovico il Moro had never promised his own heart to her; she had to admit it. Perhaps, deep inside, she had known from the beginning that she would never have him himself; her own mother and brother had told her so.

"Yes," she said. "It's not the ducal palace, but in many ways, it is better." She gestured for Master da Vinci to sit on a bench alongside an old herb garden now choked by weeds. "I have everything I need. A chambermaid. A wet nurse. A cook. And books! More than I could read in a lifetime."

"And there is no *dogaressa* under the same roof."

"Yes! That is what I like best of all," she said, laughing. "I do not know how long this will last, but I shall enjoy it as long as it does." She did not like to admit that the days were long and lonely, that she did not know where she would go when Ludovico decided that her time here was up.

The artist seemed to read her mind. "You know where you will go next, Signorina Cecilia?"

Posed with the question of whether to go to the convent or stay in the castle, she had easily chosen a tenuous life with Ludovico il Moro. But this time, things weren't so simple. Cecilia was no longer a naïve girl. She knew more now, she had become a woman, and she understood that her decisions had long-reaching consequences. Her decision to stay in the castle against her mother's will had been the decision of the girl who thought she was a woman, but she now had a child to think of, not just herself.

"My brother has encouraged me to take my vows at the Monastero Maggiore. That is what brought me to Milan originally."

Leonardo nodded. "A logical solution. The Monastero Maggiore is full of highborn, educated women. You would find others there who share the same interests and talents."

"So I have been told," she said. "But I cannot imagine leaving my child behind." She looked upon her baby with such love and adoration that it would be clear to anyone who saw her how deeply she cared for her son. As if he understood his mother's words, the boy patted her cheeks with his chubby palms. "I do love him, more than I ever thought I possibly could. He is so beautiful and brings me such joy. And so, it seems that the only other option for a respectable woman like myself," she said, half smiling, "is to marry."

Leonardo's eyebrows rose. "And is that what you want, Signorina Cecilia?"

"I . . . I can't go to a convent. It isn't the right place for me. I want to learn and write poetry and spend days in the library. Maybe before I lived in the castle, but I can't anymore. I'm a woman now and . . . most importantly . . . I can't possibly think of leaving Cesare."

"So then, your decision has been made," he stated. "You're going to marry."

"It is the only way for a respectable woman, no? But there is only one problem. Who will take a marked woman with a bastard child? Even a high-ranking one?" They stood quietly for a few minutes, listening to the birds flitting in the arbors of the crumbling courtyard. Cesare contentedly rested his head on his mother's shoulder and looked at Leonardo with a curious expression.

Leonardo stopped walking and reached his hand to the boy's fist. "I came here partly to extend an invitation," he said to Cecilia. "On the feast of Saint James, I am going to meet a new, potential patron who has invited me to San Giovanni in Croce, near Cremona. He is a count. A widower."

Cecilia stopped walking, too, and eyed Leonardo suspiciously, but he went on.

"Count Brambilla is an active patron of painting,

sculpture. Music. Poetry. He has requested that I bring a sample of my work to show him. Word of my work for Ludovico il Moro has spread, and I now regularly receive such promising invitations around Lombardy. This time, I thought that I might take your portrait, seeing that it is one of the best examples of my abilities. And perhaps he would also like to see the sitter, just to ensure that it is a true likeness. Would you consider coming with me?"

# 81
## EDITH

**Munich, Germany**
**January 1946**

EDITH SAT ALONE, CROSS-LEGGED IN THE MIDDLE OF the cold floor, staring at a great canvas depicting a sea battle, when she realized there was someone standing at the door. Private Bonelli. Dominic.

She saw him hesitate, then begin to turn around to leave, but she scrambled up to standing and straightened out her skirt. The winter light from the tall window poured icy and silver onto her, reflecting in the tears that ran down her reddened cheeks.

Dominic stopped. "Miss?"

Edith raised a white hand to her face and dashed at the tears. "I'm sorry," she said, sniffing. "It's nothing."

"Don't look like nothing," said Dominic.

Edith grasped her hair in one hand, pulling it back from

her face. "Paintings like this were Heinrich's favorite." She pointed to the picture of the sea battle, ships firing cannons into the darkness. "I used to bring him into the museum after hours, and we would walk through the empty galleries together. It was . . . lovely." A smile broke through even as more tears ran down Edith's jaw to meet at her neck. "He had little understanding of art, but he always loved the dramatic scenes. He could always see when something was beautiful even if he couldn't understand why. After I started studying, he would tease me for describing everything so . . . what is the word . . . properly, rightly . . . *technically*." She sniffed, half smiling. "He used to say that the best beauty was that which was beautiful without trying." Her voice cracked on the last syllable. She clasped a hand over her mouth and sobbed.

The American placed his hand awkwardly on her shoulder. Edith struggled to find her voice again. "They destroyed everything." She looked up at Dominic, no longer trying to stop the tears. "Why did they have to take it all?"

"I wish I knew," said Dominic. Edith heard his voice tighten and thought she saw tears threaten to well up into his eyes, too.

"My father always taught me that art was one of the things that gave people something to live for, and so we have to preserve it, to share it. I never understood why someone could presume to possess a piece of the past like that—a piece of the past that belongs to all of us."

Dominic collected himself. "Your father sounds like a smart man. I never thought I might risk my life for a picture. But," he said, "that's exactly what we've been doing for all these months. I'm glad that at least a few people think it was worthwhile."

"It was worthwhile, Mr. Bonelli," she said, almost a whisper. "Dominic."

For what felt like an eternal stretch of silence, the two of them stood achingly close, with only the sound of Edith trying to catch her breath. She felt a stirring in her gut, a feeling that she had not experienced since before that day when she boarded a train for Kraków. She felt strangely secure in the presence of this American soldier. In an instant, she thought, he might pull her tightly to his chest and there would be no turning back. It would be the most natural thing in the world. Part of her wanted to be caught up in the warmth, the security of his embrace. She knew in her heart that if he did try to embrace her, she would not resist.

Instead, Dominic broke the spell. He took a step backward and she wiped the tears from her cheeks with both palms. Edith followed his cue, separating from him. She watched him lace his fingers behind his back and begin pacing the dark room.

Before the portrait of Cecilia Gallerani on the easel, Dominic stopped. He took a step nearer to the painting and gestured to the white creature poised in Cecilia Gallerani's arms. "That animal," he said. "It looks like a rat."

All the pressure that had built up in the room was suddenly released. Edith turned her head, laughing, a relief from the tears. "It's an ermine." She shrugged. "But you're close. It is a kind of rodent."

"Why would a rich, pretty girl like that carry a rodent around?"

Edith shook her head. "You are funny, Dominic," she said, her smile half hidden by a swath of hair. "A white ermine is a symbol of purity. Noble people used to trim their robes with their fur. It's probably a symbol more than an actual pet, although some ladies probably did keep ferrets as pets."

"Strange pet," said Dominic. "Still looks like a rat to me."

Edith laughed and gave his shoulder a shove. "Go finish your sketch and stop bothering me."

# 82

## DOMINIC

*Munich, Germany*
*February 1946*

DOMINIC WATCHED EDITH'S FINGERS MOVE TENDERLY over the edges of da Vinci's portrait. Her touch was both gentle and sure as she detached it from its frame, inch by careful inch, painstakingly and utterly focused. When she was concentrating deeply, Dominic noticed that she tended to bite the inside of her bottom lip on one side, folding up one corner of her full pink lips. She made no sound, her hands steady, her gray eyes intent on her work. Dominic admired her unvarnished beauty for a few moments before speaking.

"Is that the original frame?"

"Certainly not."

Edith did not look up as she gently pressed the last corner from its frame. "Very few pictures from the Italian Renaissance have their own frames unless the wood was originally an integral part of the painted wooden panels." Straightening, she stepped back. Her chestnut hair curled up at the ends; it tickled her cheek now as she examined her handiwork with a critical eye. "Most likely, da Vinci designed his own frame for this picture; it probably looked different from this one. It must have gotten detached from the picture at some point."

By now, Edith answered Dominic's questions automatically. It had taken Dominic weeks to work up the courage to show her one of his sketches. Even then, it was not his personal favorite—a drawing from memory of Sally, not her entire face, but just a part of her that he could not forget: the sharp line of her jaw joining to the smooth curve of her neck. Instead, he showed Edith one of his many reproductions of the enchanting girl da Vinci had painted centuries ago. But ever since, Edith had taken his questions seriously. And he had many.

"What kind of panel was it painted on? How come the solvent cleans the painting, but doesn't damage the paint? How did you learn to restore art?"

This last one led to more questions, questions that didn't always have to do with art. At first, Edith's answers had been evasive. Quick and patient as she was with answers to his multitude of art questions, Edith had been guarded about her personal life, and when she finally did open up, Dominic saw why. Those gray eyes could turn storm-dark with pain when she was asked about her family. He knew that she lived at home with her sick, elderly father; he seemed to be the only family she had left. When Edith had told him about losing her fiancé in Poland, it had nearly broken Dominic's heart.

As the weeks, then months, ticked by, Dominic was amazed to learn that Edith Becker, this modest conservator, had not only survived as a personal assistant to the man the newspapers were now calling the Butcher of Poland. She had also personally couriered the portrait by Leonardo da Vinci on trains and armored vehicles across Poland and Germany, multiple times.

Dominic sat on one of the tables of the conservation studio. His job as a security guard was a piece of cake after everything he'd encountered in the field. He watched Edith, wearing a brown canvas apron over her plain dress, lay down gold leaf on a frame with a fine brush.

"You were never tempted to run away with it?" he asked. "Keep it for yourself?"

"No."

"But surely you deserved to keep at least one masterpiece," he joked. "You worked so hard to keep the picture safe all that time. You put yourself at risk."

Her smile faded. "All of us have been at risk, Dominic, whether we liked it or not."

"Fair enough."

"This might seem strange, coming from someone who has made a career around art, but I have never wanted to own one of these myself. I only wish to study them, to save them. And now, ultimately, to return them to their rightful places. When I get back to my job at the museum, that will be my mission. To return each work to its original owner. Those who are left."

Dominic wondered what could be said of the shattered continent, the broken world all around him, blackened by the war. It would take more than art to pick up the pieces of the conflict-torn world. But now he knew that art would play a role whose importance could not be denied.

"You yourself should see that. You have played an important role," she said.

Dominic shrugged. "We only did what we could to save lives. And to save whatever art we could."

At that moment, the doors behind them opened, and two men entered the room. Dominic jumped from the table and immediately saluted, recognizing one of them as the director of the Central Collecting Point. "Sir!"

"At ease, soldier," said the director. "I'm looking for the lady." He nodded at Edith.

Edith set down her brush and wiped her hands on her apron. "Sir?"

"Fräulein Becker is one of the best art restorers we have," the director told the other man. "She has been working on the altarpiece as well. Edith, this is Major Karol Estreicher. He is a Polish officer who has been working with us to identify works that must be returned to his country."

Major Estreicher nodded vaguely, but his eyes were not on Edith. They were set on the rising beauty of the great Veit Stoss altarpiece, now disassembled in the shadows.

The room was far fuller now than it had been when Dominic had first come here almost a year ago. Half of it was occupied by the enormous Veit Stoss altarpiece, a hulking shadow in the dark room. The multipaneled altarpiece towered against one wall, a gigantic collection of painted panels and elaborate sculptures, dismantled into several pieces. Dominic imagined that, fully assembled, it might reach some forty feet in height.

Dominic had already spent hours sketching it, and he'd only managed to finish all the figures from one of the panels. He had recognized the Virgin Mary and most of the apostles, but there were other scenes he could not interpret. He had watched conservators and curators swarming around it for weeks, examining the armatures that held it together, studying it and talking about how it might be safely packed for its return transport to Poland. Edith had told him that it was one of the greatest national treasures of Poland. It had always stood behind the high altar of Saint Mary's Basilica in Kraków before the Nazis took it.

Now, Dominic watched the Polish officer take a few steps closer to the altarpiece as if in a dream, and he reached out with one hand to touch one of the gilded reliefs. His handsome face crumpled, and tears gathered in his eyes. Turning back to Dominic, Edith, and the director of the

Collecting Point, he choked out two words in a heavy accent.

"Thank you."

Then he removed his hat and fell to his knees, staring up at the altarpiece as if he could drink it all in with his eyes. For a few long minutes, the room fell into a silent reverence that Dominic had not encountered since he saw Vicar Stephany fall to his knees before the relics of Charlemagne in the Siegen mine.

Major Estreicher finally gathered himself and rose to standing. He replaced his hat and swallowed. Red-eyed, he walked back to them, his back rigid and resolute. "I am here to take her home," he said. "I am most humbled and honored to have been selected for the task. It is one of Poland's greatest treasures. It is one of the few things my country has left. Thank you for taking good care of it all this time."

Dominic saw Edith's composure wobble for a second, but she swallowed it down. "Major, I must introduce you to Dominic Bonelli." She touched his arm. "He is one of our very best guards. He has done a fine job making sure the altarpiece and other pieces of art are kept safe here in Munich. But also, he is responsible for protecting many works of art across Europe. He even helped to rescue the da Vinci from Hans Frank's private villa."

Estreicher's eyes settled on Dominic. Dominic felt the tall Pole study him, running his intelligent-looking eyes over his short frame from head to foot. "Is that so?" he said.

"Then I will make sure that you come with us to Poland to return these works, Mister Bonelli. Clearly, you are the right person for the job. Besides, we will need high security on the train."

Dominic smiled as his heart sank. Home had never seemed so far away.

# 83
## DOMINIC

*Munich, Germany*
*April 1946*

HIS RUCKSACK WAS A ROUGH SURFACE FOR SKETCHING, but Dominic had learned to draw on just about anything—the dirt, his knees, even the stock of his bolt-action rifle. His pencil worked quickly across the paper, pulling together the shape of a young woman. His unsuspecting model stood on the train platform in the crisp chill of the spring morning, the light behind her silhouetting her curves; the gentle slope of her hip in her long wool skirt, the flip of her hair at her chin.

Edith was chewing the inside of her lip again. She clutched a wooden clipboard in her arms, heedless of the cold that tugged at her wool jacket as she checked the shipping manifests for the hoard heading back to Poland. The line of freight cars seemed endless; it stretched into the distance, the sight of the boxy silhouettes still twisting Dominic's stomach a little. Much as he had enjoyed working at the Central Collecting Point, he was not sorry to be leaving Munich. Hopefully, he was approaching his last stop in Europe.

He turned his pencil sideways a little in a grip Edith had taught him, adding light and shadow to the sketch. It was one of the last blank pages left in his sketchbook. The book contained dozens of copies of *Lady with an Ermine*, whom he had greeted privately early that morning. She was one of the very few things he would miss about Europe. She was not, however, the only lady he knew he would be missing, a thought that he pushed aside.

Instead, he thought of the letter from Sally that he kept tucked in his shirt pocket, close to his heart. The best thing about the end of the war so far was the mail running again. He had sent so many drawings to Sally, showing her his life in charcoal and paper; drawings of the men, the buildings, and mostly, the art. Tucking each of them neatly into an envelope, writing his home address on them and sending them back to America felt like perhaps home was real after all. Like it hadn't just been a happy dream in the past that he'd woken up from into a chilly and inhospitable real world, where he was shunted from place to place on the whim of those in command.

He was pleased to be leaving Munich, but every part of him screamed that he was heading in the wrong direction.

Instead of westward and home, this train was taking him east—to Poland, with a line of freight cars that would return the nation's treasures. He knew from the frantic script and teardrop stains on the paper that Sally was suffering just as much as he was.

Dominic took one last look at the quick study he had made of Edith. He wanted to remember her like this: smart, efficient, naturally beautiful. He folded it and held it in one hand as he tucked the sketchbook neatly into his pack with the other.

Leaning against a wall in the shadows of the train station, he watched as workers carried the last few items once held at the former Nazi headquarters. They had spent days carefully packing up the paintings, sculptures, books, and manuscripts into padded crates and loading them tenderly into the train cars. All these were treasures that the Nazis had cruelly robbed Poland of; all of them were headed back home. Dominic wished he could be headed home, too.

It had been almost two years since he'd landed on the beach at Normandy. Cecilia would be running around by now. He had missed all that: her first words, her first steps, her development from tiny baby to a little human being with her own thoughts and ideas and expressions. With a pang, he realized he had never heard his almost three-year-old daughter speak. He closed his eyes tightly, remembering the words of Sally's last letter to him.

*Cecilia asked when Daddy was coming home yesterday,* she had written. *I can't wait to have an answer for her.*

Dominic looked up. The wind caught at Edith's skirt, pressing it against her shapely figure; he allowed his eye to run down the curve of her hip. It was time to let her go, to leave her here in her homeland; she wanted life to return to normal just as much as he did. Major Estreicher approached her on the loading dock, carrying a manifest of his own. They consulted each other's papers and nodded to each other. Dominic knew that that was his signal to go. Major Estreicher turned and beckoned to him, then headed to the train to give the go-ahead for departure.

Dominic checked around himself to ensure none of the pages had fallen out of his sketchbook and approached the train. Edith stood on the loading dock, the manifest hanging from her hand. Suddenly the look in her eyes was desolate as she watched him coming nearer. She stood forlorn and alone.

"Don't worry," he said. "Cecilia will be in good hands. You can trust me."

"I already trust you with Cecilia," she said. "You saved her once. I know you will get her home."

Dominic's duffel bag had already been loaded on the train. He glanced west once before turning to Edith. For a few long moments, the two stood in awkward silence. At a loss for words, Dominic finally held out the folded sketch in his hand.

She took it from him, unfolded it, and studied it. She always had something to say about his sketches; for every compliment there was a balancing criticism, pushing him to do better. But not today. She smiled up at him with tears in the corners of her eyes, trapped by the soft prison of her lashes.

"It's perfect," she said.

She had been his friend in a dark time. But Dominic's heart was yearning to be back home, to a girl who had been raising two babies without him, a girl who had been waiting patiently for years. He held out his hand to Edith and watched her smile turn sad.

"Travel safely, soldier," she said. "I hope you get home to your wife and your daughters soon." Then, Edith reached into the pocket of her coat and produced a small, brand-new pad of paper. "Here's a little something to occupy you on the train," she said. "You should keep drawing, you know."

Dominic thought his voice would fail him if he spoke now. So he just nodded and smiled at Edith. Then he turned away, jumping up into the train as the whistle blew. As it rattled away down the track, the rhythmic clank and chuck of its pistons driving them ever farther, his last impression of Munich was of Edith's silhouette on the train platform. She looked just as he had found her on a Bavarian hilltop all those months ago. All alone. Strong. And brave.

# 84

## CECILIA

*Verme Palace, outside Milan, Italy*
*October 1491*

**"ATTENTO. ATTENTO!"**

From the second-floor window, Cecilia watched her mother wave a plump hand under the nose of a manservant who was loading a small crate into the back of a carriage. Her mother fanned herself, following the slinking youth back through the door of the palace, then heckled him again all the way back to the carriage. Her mother resembled a bothersome magpie, scolding and nipping at his heels as the poor man walked back and forth with Cecilia's worldly goods.

Cecilia could only shake her head and chuckle at the sight.

Even though Cecilia was leaving the protection of Ludovico il Moro with much more than what she came with, from the high vantage point of her window, her worldly possessions seemed meager. There was a trunk full of dresses, a large box filled with hair adornments and jewels, another one with shoes of satin, leather, and velvet. A shawl made of fox. A small box of wooden toys and hand-sewn animals for Cesare.

Then, the surprise. On a crisp morning, her mother.

Signora Gallerani had appeared unannounced at the Verme Palace, Fazio at her side. Behind them, an old mule had pulled a cart loaded with a dowry box, a chest full of hastily stitched table and bed linens, an old mantle that once belonged to her grandfather, and a favorite blanket from her childhood bed.

Cecilia had stood, jaw open, but her mother offered little in the way of explanation. Instead, she quickly scooped up Cesare in her abundant arms, smothering him with kisses and whispered promises. Cecilia was left speechless, her hand on the door latch, watching her mother stride into her life after so many months of silence. Fazio could only shrug.

And now, from the window, Cecilia watched her mother berate the young man who was packing the carriage that would carry her to her new life, her new husband.

"My daughter is a countess!" her mother kept repeating. "You must treat her things with greater care." Cecilia stifled a laugh with her fist.

A countess. Wife of a count. Another Ludovico.

In a tidy, elegant villa in the countryside, Count

Ludovico Carminati de Brambilla was waiting for Cecilia. A box holding all her land deeds—heavy with seals of metal and wax—had been couriered to Count Brambilla's home at San Giovanni in Croce, securing Cecilia's place. In addition, there were inventories of her sheep, cattle herds, and a stable of horses. Now, all that was left were her personal belongings, herself, and her little Cesare. She wondered if Count Brambilla was prepared for her mother, too.

He had seemed kind enough. The count had bowed to her and spoke to her quietly, with soft blue eyes. He wasn't much to look at, much older than she, with graying hair and a lined forehead. Cecilia had leaned on Master Leonardo to fill in the details. Count Brambilla was an upstanding landowner with a long family heritage in the wool trade, he had said. His young wife had suffered a string of failed pregnancies before the last attempt to deliver a live child took her life, too. For nearly ten years, he had lived alone in the large house, with no heirs to his estate. Cecilia saw it for herself: rows of manicured gardens with lazily buzzing insects; perfectly ordered, empty rooms; a large ground-floor kitchen where the cook mostly napped at the wooden table.

Count Brambilla was an active patron of poetry, painting, and music, Leonardo had told her. He had once held well-attended gatherings of guests, but now, the life had gone out of the house. He enjoyed the company of painters and musicians, but he longed to bring his court back again and he was unable to do it alone. Cecilia knew that this role would be easy for her, a new chance to sing, to write poetry, to spend time in the company of learned people. She knew in her heart that she could bring the place back to life.

Quickly, it became clear that the count wanted her as his wife. It only took days for him to dispatch his notary with a marriage contract to her brother. And to Cecilia's surprise, her position as Ludovico il Moro's mistress—and even the mother of his bastard son—was no barrier. In fact, instead of being treated as a filthy whore, she suddenly enjoyed esteemed status. In his most base desire for Cecilia, Ludovico Sforza had conferred upon her a higher social rank. Even the nuns were eager to have Cecilia join them, sending their confessor to petition her brother. But there was no convincing Cecilia, for she had had only one desire. One condition. And one doubt.

It was only when the notary returned with the marriage contract, in which the count promised to care for Cesare just the same as he would care for Cecilia, that she finally exhaled. She did not hold on to the illusion that a man, little more than a stranger, might accept the boy as his own child, but she would go nowhere without her son. The thought of a life behind the convent walls, without Cesare in her arms, was unbearable. She nodded in assent for Fazio to sign the marriage contract to Count Ludovico Carminati de Brambilla on behalf of the Gallerani family. On the news that her daughter was to be a countess instead of a high-ranking concubine, Cecilia's mother had rushed to Verme Palace with a mule and a dowry chest now cleaned of its cobwebs and dust.

And now, Cecilia walked from the Verme Palace for the last time, and out of Ludovico il Moro's life. She waded into the cool, sunlit courtyard before the palace. There were only two things she wanted: her baby and her portrait.

Inside the carriage, Cesare, content in his grandmother's arms, did not make a move toward Cecilia. And seeing his smile, and her own mother's, made Cecilia smile with them.

"Where is the portrait?" she asked the manservant.

"It's here, Signora Contessa," he said, lifting the portrait that Leonardo da Vinci had carefully wrapped for her into the passenger compartment. Then, he lent Cecilia a hand as she climbed in beside it.

The carriage driver signaled the horses to go. The smell of wet earth rose as the horses' hooves tore into it, and the wheels creaked forward until they picked up speed and made their way through the gates.

# 85
# LEONARDO

*Milan, Italy*
*October 1494*

I WATCH TWO BOYS ROLL WHAT IS LEFT OF THE FLY-ing machine through the great double doors of the stable inside the Corte Vecchia. Little more than a skeleton of splintered wood and ripped silk. This time, it drew hundreds in the square before the cathedral façade. Another spectacle. Another laughingstock. I might try a different approach next time, that is, if I can put the embarrassment behind me and find the energy to start again.

I may as well start again, I think, for Ludovico il Moro is occupied with other matters and pays little attention to me now. He is the Duke of Milan, at last, and he has more serious matters to consider. The new title changes little, I think, for Ludovico il Moro has been the acting duke for many years now, even if he has only been regent.

Anyone might have predicted the demise of poor Gian

Galeazzo, the little duke who used to haunt the hallways of this very house as a boy, finally grown old enough to pose a credible threat. Poisoned in broad daylight, Marco the harpist whispered to me in the palace corridor. Sitting at the head of the table, too. The servants are saying that His Lordship's own physician mixed the concoction, Marco had said. But there will be no consequences other than the passing of the title to Ludovico il Moro, for who holds the power to challenge his authority, after all?

Cecilia Gallerani left the ducal palace in good time, I think. I cannot help but smile to think of Cecilia, now a countess in her own right just a day's carriage ride from here. I must go and visit her, I think. I would like to see where she has hung my portrait, to know if her husband, the other Ludovico, appreciates my likeness of his bride.

Besides, there is so much to tell. Cecilia might approve of Beatrice's evening gatherings, filled with new sonnets, new entertainments, new dice games. I had my doubts, but the duchess has become a fine and skilled consort for Ludovico il Moro, in spite of her youth.

Still, Beatrice has not been completely successful in distracting His Lordship. In the corridors, the servants whisper that Lucrezia Crivelli is with child, and that Ludovico has set aside orchards and a tower near Lake Como in her name.

But as much as I might enjoy a trip to see Cecilia Galle-rani in her estate far beyond the walls of Milan, I wonder if she will welcome me and my tales from the ducal palace. Perhaps I should not fill her mind with such fodder. It is all for the better that she has left it behind.

# 86
## DOMINIC

*Pittsburgh, Pennsylvania, USA*
*May 1946*

A MONTH AFTER LEAVING KRAKÓW, DOMINIC FOUND himself on a train again. But this time, there was no rifle on his back. No helmet at his side. No paintings under his surveillance. His duffel bag held no more ammunition or rations. And his heart felt as light as the sunshine that fell in warm rays through the train windows as it clanked through the green landscape of the country where he was born.

Dominic had not thought much of America on the long journey home from Europe; his mind had been utterly occupied with Sally and the children. But when his feet hit the dirt on Governors Island, he was overcome. Heedless of the watching crowd, he'd dropped his duffel, fallen to his knees, and pressed his lips to the ground, tears pouring from his eyes.

They hadn't stayed in New York for long. Just pausing for a shave and to change into a clean uniform, he and a batch of other young men had flooded into Grand Central Station. Dominic descended to the platform where a conductor marched between two trains, one bound for Pittsburgh, another for San Antonio. Dominic paused in taking his seat as he watched the train headed for Texas pull away from the station. Without Paul. For so many of the soldiers, there would be no going home.

Dominic's only consolation was that he had gotten to play a role, however small, in bringing home not only Leonardo da Vinci's portrait of the enchanting Cecilia Gallerani, but also many other works he knew the Poles held dear. He thought back to his train ride from Munich to Kraków, surrounded by wooden crates holding many paintings and the dismantled pieces of the great Veit Stoss altarpiece. He thought of the ragged-looking people running alongside the train, so relieved and excited to see the Allies as they pulled into the Kraków railway station.

Now, a wide and distinctly American landscape—familiar and at the same time strangely foreign to his eyes—clipped by outside the train window. Dominic opened his duffel and pulled out his sketchbook, flipping through it to a sketch that he had kept especially for Sally. It was too precious to mail; his first drawing of the *Lady with an Ermine*, it was technically not his best—showing evidence of his clumsiness before he'd met Edith—but every shaky line spoke with the wonder he'd felt at beholding the face of an original da Vinci. He couldn't wait to show it to Sally and tell her everything. He knew he would never see that masterpiece in the flesh again, but he felt content. Instead, he'd spend his days drawing the timeless masterpiece that was his beautiful wife, encouraged by the words that had drawn him through so many hard times.

*Keep drawing.*

The last leg of the journey seemed to take years, but at last, the conductor called out Pittsburgh. The atmosphere was one of tremendous excitement as the train pulled into Union Station. Servicemen hung out of the windows, waving, crying as they spotted family members and street signs and shops that spoke of home. Dominic's heart was racing. He pressed up against the window, suddenly sick to his stomach with nerves. It had been so long. Would he even recognize Sally? Would she recognize him, two years and a war later?

When he saw her, it was like having a bucket of cold water thrown over his head. He couldn't breathe. He could only stare. It was her hair that he saw first, licking like flames around the edges of the navy hat that perched on her head. Then her body, shapelier than before, and her face, and her eyes, searching the crowd for him. Her freckled cheeks were flushed with excitement, her lips curving into a smile that pierced his heart like lightning. She was the most beautiful thing he had ever seen. He had gazed upon Rembrandt and Vermeer, Rubens and Fragonard—even a portrait by Leonardo da Vinci—but none of them could come close to equaling the smile of his wife.

In her arms, a toddler was reaching for her mother's face with chubby fists. And at Sally's side, her little hand curved around her mother's slender fingers, was Cecilia. The little girl had her mother's eyes, and her head of baby fluff had grown out into a raven torrent.

Dominic wanted to run to them, but he felt he couldn't move as the train clanked slowly to a halt. He just stared at his family among the swirling vortex of the crowd, and his heart swelled until he felt it might just lift him into the air and float him away toward the sun and the clouds. The memories of the war swirled around him. Landing on the foggy beach. Forging a friendship with Paul during the miserable forced marches. The sight of Aachen. Finding Stephany cowering beneath the pulpit. The bloom of blood beneath Paul's writhing body. The bombed-out museums. Fighting on the roadside as they headed toward the Rhine. The smell of Siegen. Sketching on index cards in Marburg. Parading through Munich. Finding the beautiful da Vinci in Frank's house. Edith. Major Estreicher's tears. Kraków, and its cheering crowd as he hung Polish and American flags from the windows of the train. Years of pain and loss, suffering, beholding the wanton destruction for selfish reasons, the prejudice and unwarranted hate toward those deemed unworthy of life. The reign of terror brought to an end by violence.

He gazed at his family and he knew, to keep them safe, to give them a world where there was art and beauty, the long struggle had been worth it.

The train whistle sounded, bringing life back into Dominic's limbs. As the doors slid open, he grabbed his rucksack and pushed his way forward into the crowd.

# 87
# LEONARDO

*Milan, Italy*
*February 1497*

**THE REFECTORY OF SANTA MARIA DELLA GRAZIE LIES** in silence except for the sound of clinking spoons and the occasional scrape of a chair on the stone floor. I spoon watery polenta into my mouth and watch the two dozen Dominican friars huddled around me. To my right, His Lordship. But Ludovico has not taken a bite.

Instead, the Duke of Milan sits before his plate, staring at the wall before us. The wall is mostly blank, at least so far. There, I have roughly sketched a composition, a symmetrical image of Christ surrounded by his disciples. The men are huddled around a table, much like those of us at the table now. A Last Supper. His Lordship asked me to prepare the fresco months ago, but now, all he wants to do is sit here with the monks and stare at my work in progress.

In fact, ever since the beginning of January, when Death defeated Birth, taking his young bride and their baby to the Hereafter, His Lordship has done little but sit and stare. He does not eat. Hardly speaks. Ludovico is so shattered at the loss of his Beatrice that he has ordered all the windows of the ducal palace covered in black drapes. The music, the feasting, the gatherings. All of it has stopped. Not even Lucrezia Crivelli, heavy with a child of her own, can console him. Only the chambermaids slink down the dark corridors now.

His Lordship has only done so much as ask me to finish my Last Supper on the north wall of this refectory and request that I join him for a meal here twice a week. And so I sit and eat, watching the wall along with Ludovico, and considering how I might make this image more beautiful and different from anything ever before seen in Milan.

And so, it's on to a new project. It's not an armored vehicle or a flying machine, but until His Lordship is able to think of such matters again, it is enough to keep me in his service.

# 88
## CECILIA

*San Giovanni in Croce, Italy*
*April 1498*

CECILIA WATCHED CESARE AND HER TODDLING daughter run down a grassy hillside, chasing an ungainly white goose. In her hands, Cecilia held a letter sealed with the wax stamp bearing the arms of Ferrara.

"*Attento*, Cesare! Don't let her get too close. It will bite!" But the little girl only squealed with joy and Cecilia could not help but smile, too. Her children were thriving in this peaceful estate of Count Brambilla. They all were.

But as Cecilia ran her hand over the wax seal, her brow knitted in worry. A letter from Isabella d'Este, the older sister of Ludovico il Moro's wife, Beatrice. It had been a year since Cecilia had received a formal letter from Isabella, sharing the news of Beatrice's death in the ducal palace of Milan.

At the time, Cecilia had found it unbelievable to hear that Beatrice, her former rival, was gone, she and her stillborn baby both victims of a ruthless childbirth. Cecilia had only shuddered, feeling the old fear reaching for her soul with bony fingers. Only luck, she thought, had spared her from the same fate. Cecilia had gotten on her knees to thank God for her life in this quiet, country paradise. For her own life, and for those of her son and daughter.

Since sharing the news of Beatrice and her baby, Isabella d'Este had continued to write to Cecilia and even to visit her, exchanging works of poetry and music composed in the court of Ferrara. Isabella sought the company of all the learned ladies of the region, Cecilia's husband had told her. There was no reason not to welcome her company. Cecilia should consider herself flattered by the marquess's attention, he had said. It meant that she was someone important, after all.

Now, Cecilia watched the goose leap awkwardly into the pond, then glide away. On the bank, Cesare called to it and flapped his arms like wings. Cecilia smiled, then broke the seal and unfolded the parchment.

*From Marchesa Isabella d'Este, Ferrara*
*To Contessa Cecilia Gallerani, San Giovanni in Croce*

> *Having seen today some fine portraits by the hand of Giovanni Bellini, we began to discuss the works of Leonardo and wished we could compare them with these*

*paintings. And since we remember that he painted your likeness, we beg you to be so good as to send us your portrait by this messenger whom we have dispatched on horseback, so that we may not only be able to compare the works of the two masters, but also have the pleasure of seeing your face again. The picture will be returned to you afterward, with our most grateful thanks for your kindness.*

# 89
## EDITH

*Munich, Germany*
*October 1946*

ON THE TRAM, EDITH SAW THE FACE OF HANS FRANK. For a long second, her heart stopped.

It was him; there was no denying it. There, on the front page of the newspaper. She recognized Frank's black eyes, the slick sweep of his hair across his broad forehead. But his expression, captured in the small picture of grainy newsprint, seemed strange and uncharacteristic.

Edith felt her heart return to beating, this time hammering in her chest. A man scanned the interior spread of the paper; behind the newsprint, all that was visible were his neatly pleated trousers, his polished shoes, and his hat. Edith wanted to look away from the headline, but she could not make herself do it.

GOERING COMMITS SUICIDE; 10 OTHERS HANG

Alongside Frank's picture, there were images of nine more men. Frick, Seyss-Inquart, von Ribbentrop, others, their names typed out in black, bold text beneath their pictures. Was he really dead? Hanged, at Nuremberg Prison, just as the headlines said?

The metal wheels squeaked to a halt, and the tram doors folded open. Edith grabbed her bag and stepped down to the sidewalk, leaving the image of Frank on the front page of the newspaper behind. Another image of Frank flashed through her mind, one of him breathing down the back of her neck as they stood before Leonardo da Vinci's portrait at Schoberhof. Edith shuddered and pushed the memory aside.

The imposing, familiar façade of the Alte Pinakothek came into view, with one wing now little more than a pile of rubble. *Stay focused on the present*, she said to herself. Edith did her best to think of her father and Rita back at home, her shopping list of ingredients for a pie they might enjoy after Sunday's dinner. She thought about her plans to meet up with an old classmate she had met by chance on the street, a girl who had also lost her fiancé in battle. She thought about the old painting on an easel in her conservation studio that she was itching to repair. Edith finally felt her heartbeat return to normal.

But memories and questions licked the edges of her mind. Where was the *Lady with an Ermine* now? Just a few months before, Edith had read news of the death of Prince Augustyn Józef Czartoryski, the once-owner of da Vinci's portrait, who had become ill during his family's exile at the Spanish court. Edith felt sad that Prince Augustyn would never lay eyes on the picture again. Would his young son ever return to Kraków to reclaim his family's art collection? Edith hoped that in the meantime, the provisional government in Poland would have the foresight and the care to keep the picture safe.

Edith greeted the security guard at the museum's employee entrance and exhaled as she followed the long corridor to the conservation studio. There was a picture waiting for her, a seventeenth-century still life that had been brought in from the Netherlands. The canvas was torn in transport. Edith expected to work on it for a period of weeks.

"Edith!"

Her old friend Manfred was waiting for her as Edith hung her coat on the rack. Manfred had already filled Edith in on all she had missed while she was busy working in the Allied Central Collecting Point. In spite of the fact that one wing of the museum was a mangled pile of stone and would not be open to the public again for years, many of the artworks, galleries, and offices remained intact. Edith felt fortunate that the conservation studio had remained unscathed. It was more than they could say for many of their colleagues. Two curators had been killed while traveling with German troops. Another one had died right here in Munich, the victim of excess in food and drink that had finally caught up with him. And the museum's director, Ernst Buchner, was being detained in connection with the theft of the Ghent Altarpiece in France.

When she finally closed the door to her quiet conservation studio, Edith let her shoulders fall in relief. She adjusted the light so that it raked across the surface of the still life, outlining the edges of pieces of fruit and leaves painted three centuries before. Edith looked carefully at the fine cracks across the surface. She ran the bottle of thinner under her nose to make sure it was still serviceable after having sat on her shelf for so long. She dipped a long brush into it and ran it across a small rag to test it. She must do what is in her power, she thought: saving works of art, one piece at a time.

But the once-beloved silence of her conservation lab now brought with it a new and unbidden level of chatter in her mind. Lingering questions. Uneasy self-reflections. A new examination of conscience that, Edith feared, might endure.

*Beware the beginnings*, her father had said.

Edith imagined that this burden of self-reflection might stay with her, but she resolved that from now on, she would remain vigilant, her eyes open to the city and the world around her. She would be ready to act in the face of darkness, sooner rather than later.

Across Germany, were others bearing this heavy weight

of hindsight? How long might it take, Edith wondered, for her countrymen and -women—and for herself—to atone for having served evil instead of good?

# 90

## CECILIA

*San Giovanni in Croce, Italy*
*April 1498*

*From Contessa Cecilia Gallerani, San Giovanni in*
*Croce*
*To Marchesa Isabella d'Este, Ferrara*

*I have read Your Highness's letter, and since you wish
to see my portrait, I send it without delay and would send
it with even greater pleasure if it were more like me. For
it was painted many years ago, when I was a naïve young
girl, newly arrived in Milan.*

*But Your Highness must not think this proceeds from
any defect in the master, for indeed I think there is no
other painter equal to Master da Vinci in the world, but
merely because the portrait was painted when I was much
younger. Since then I have greatly changed, so that if you*

*saw the picture and myself together, you would never be-lieve it could be meant for me. All the same, Your Highness will, I hope, accept this proof of my goodwill and believe that I am ready and anxious to gratify your wishes.*

*I look back fondly on my time spent with Master da Vinci, and with Master Bernardo Bellincioni, who, to my great sadness, succumbed to illness soon after he com-posed the ode that I enclose for you with the portrait.*

*I am also including a small sketch that Master da Vinci made of me when he came to visit me last year. How happy it made me to see my old friend. In this image you might recognize a more accurate representation of my appearance.*

*Gone is the young beauty in the portrait, now un-recognizable as myself. Instead, you will see a happy old woman with a house full of children, music, and art. I have come to accept that war is inevitable. Beauty is fleet-ing. Only love and art endure. At least that's what Master da Vinci taught me.*

## 91
## LEONARDO

*Milan, Italy*
*August 1499*

IN MY NOTEBOOK, THERE ARE SEVERAL DOZEN sketches of the creature they call a stoat or ermine. I have never seen one.

I have inferred the creature's appearance through observing ferrets in the possession of a few of the ladies I have been fortunate enough to paint, those with more exotic tastes. The ferret emits a strong odor from its nether parts when frightened or aroused. It has been many years since I have thought of the creature.

I place the sketches in a leather case, alongside stacks of other scribbles I have collected during my years in Milan. Great mechanical wings. Hands. Heads. Mining drills. Skulls. Madonnas. Wheeled vehicles. Flying machines. Saints. Demons. I have drawn or painted them all.

In the end, His Lordship might have been better off

to allow me to realize one of the many war machines that I proposed instead of spending hours replicating the faces of his mistresses in paint, those whose youth and tenure in his household were ultimately fleeting. If he had, I might not have to give up my comfortable bedchamber in His Lordship's city residence so soon.

But fortune's wheel turns. And now, the French king's men are marching southward. For all Ludovico il Moro's efforts to ally himself to the French, he has made them enemies instead. Men will always make war.

But it is art and beauty, I think, that give us something to live for.

So it is time for me to return home to Florence, to better prospects. Time to return to my father, to my brothers, my cats. My friends. My enemies. Will they remember me, after all this time?

I close the latch on my leather case and scan the landscape outside my window. Before the cannon fire and smoke appears above the silhouette of the northern hills, I will be back in my native city.

For I may not be a maker of war machines but I have proved my worth as a painter. And in Florence, I might work again.

# ACKNOWLEDGMENTS

I NEVER IMAGINED THAT I WOULD WRITE A BOOK about World War II. I have always shied away from reading books, or watching movies and documentaries covering the war. The scale of inhumanity has always left me feeling hopeless. Even as a historian, I have struggled to comprehend how something as hellish as the Holocaust could have evolved as it did.

Few parts of World War II were more brutal than the Nazi invasion of Poland. So when, a few years ago, my teenaged son Max invited my husband and me to watch a TV documentary about Hans Frank, the Butcher of Poland, my first reaction was to recoil and bury myself in a novel set during the Italian Renaissance instead. But my son (who, incidentally, was born a short drive away from Milan's Castello Sforzesco) had grown into an avid, knowledgeable World War II buff. As a small kid, he knew all the plane models and major players from the Normandy beaches to the Pacific theater. He interviewed World War II veterans as part of his Eagle Scout project. He loved to play the board game *Axis and Allies*, and yes, he always won. So in the name of family time, I joined my husband and my son on the sofa.

The 2015 documentary *What Our Fathers Did: A Nazi Legacy* included interviews with Niklas Frank, the son of Hans Frank. I found myself immediately wrapped up in the incredible story, but when Niklas Frank described how Leonardo da Vinci's *Lady with an Ermine* had once hung on the wall of his childhood home in Bavaria, it stopped me dead in my tracks. Truth is often stranger than fiction, but how on earth did *that* happen, I wondered? I did what I always do: I plunged headlong into research. What would it be like, I wondered, to be the person tasked with the job of stealing a painting by Leonardo da Vinci? The curiosity led me down rabbit hole after rabbit hole, until a story told in two timelines emerged clearly in my head. Edith and Cecilia suddenly seemed as real to me as my next-door neighbors. After that, the book seemed to write itself.

I have done my best to stick as closely as possible to the actual timeline of events, both in the fifteenth as well as the twentieth centuries. I've also endeavored to remain faithful to the known biographical details about the historical figures depicted in this book. The sources I consulted for this project are too varied and numerous to list here but I've compiled a full bibliography, images, and more resources on my website for anyone who wishes to delve deeper into the historical background of this story, both in the 1490s and the 1940s. Visit lauramorelli.com/ NightPortrait for more.

A couple of research resources deserve special mention. First, I am grateful to the work of the Monuments Men Foundation for documenting the vital contributions of these service members and for their ongoing efforts to return all manner of stolen art to their rightful owners. Also, a 2012 exhibition catalog from the National Gallery in London entitled *Leonardo da Vinci: Painter at the Court of Milan* was ever at my side during the research for this book. I am grateful to the scholars Luke Syson and Larry Keith for this fantastic reference.

Jenny Bent, my literary agent extraordinaire, saw the potential for this project and suggested *The Night Portrait* as a title that would make readers say, "Ooo! What's that about?" Jenny provided sound editorial as well as business advice for this project, and for both, I am sincerely grateful.

I am so thankful to Tessa Woodward and the team at William Morrow for getting behind this story, helping to turn it into a book, and for putting it out into the world with such professionalism.

My husband, Mark, and our children—Max, Giulia, Anna, and Leonardo—have endured many years of a wife and mother with her head in the clouds and her fingers on the keyboard. Nonetheless, they do their best to distract me and ultimately, they cheer me on. They are everything.

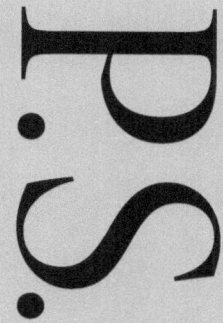

## About the author

## About the book

Insights,
Interviews
& More . . .

# Meet Laura Morelli

Davide Mandolini

LAURA MORELLI holds a PhD in art history from Yale University and is the author of fiction and nonfiction inspired by the history of art. She has taught college students in the United States and Italy and has developed lessons for TED-Ed. Her flagship shopping guidebook, *Made in Italy*, has led travelers off the beaten track for more than two decades. Her award-winning historical novels include *The Painter's Apprentice*, *The Gondola Maker*, and *The Giant: A Novel of Michelangelo's David*. Learn more at lauramorelli.com. ❧

# Author's Note

As far as we know, none of the military contraptions that Leonardo da Vinci drew for Ludovico il Moro were ever realized. Shortly after completing Cecilia Gallerani's portrait, Leonardo would go on to paint his famous *Last Supper* in the refectory of Santa Maria delle Grazie in Milan, under Ludovico's patronage. Leonardo's artistic success in the service of the courts of Milan and France ultimately allowed the artist to save his reputation and return home to Florence as an acclaimed creator rather than a criminal.

Cecilia Gallerani became an esteemed author, musician, and patron of the arts. The son she bore with Ludovico il Moro, Cesare Sforza Visconti, was dedicated to monastic life and became abbot of the Church of San Nazaro Maggiore in Milan. Cecilia also bore four more children with the other Ludovico, Count Ludovico Carminati de Brambilla, known as "Il Bergamino." Cecilia ultimately presided over one of the most celebrated courts of northern Italy, drawing artists, writers, nobles, and politicians from across Europe. She lived to an old age and even befriended Beatrice's older sister Isabella d'Este, one of the most influential women of the Italian Renaissance.

After Cecilia Gallerani was banished from the ducal palace, Ludovico il Moro set his sights on Lucrezia Crivelli, who bore him a son. Lucrezia may have been the subject ➤

of Leonardo da Vinci's beautiful portrait called *La Belle Ferronière*, though the sitter's identity is debated. However, the duke's string of power plays and amorous pursuits was cut short. After bearing him two sons, his wife, Beatrice d'Este, died in childbirth at age twenty-one. Ludovico was soon overcome by the forces of Louis XII, who invaded Milan in 1499. He died as a prisoner of the French king in a dungeon at Loches Castle in 1508.

In 1940, the art historian Kajestan Mühlmann prepared 521 works of art as a "gift" to Adolf Hitler from Hans Frank, governor of occupied Poland. Mühlmann would go on to oversee one of the most complex networks of art theft in history. By 1944, the Nazis had either stolen or tried to steal every known painting by Leonardo da Vinci. After the war, under custody of Allied forces, Mühlmann helped identify a number of important works of art. He escaped from a hospital in 1948 and was never recaptured even after a Viennese court convicted him *in absentia* of high treason; a decade later, he died of cancer.

Most other German art experts who were conscripted to the Nazi effort to collect works of art—functionaries like the fictional Edith Becker—quietly returned to their lives and their jobs after the war. A few of them later spoke about their attempts to assist the Resistance, either by documenting stolen works, saving convoys from bombing, or

4

returning works to their original owners. Others undoubtedly took these secret activities to the grave.

When the Allies located Hans Frank at his Bavarian lakeside villa in May 1945, da Vinci's *Lady with an Ermine* was among a handful of remaining masterpieces in Frank's personal possession. After his arrest, Hans Frank made two failed suicide attempts. During the Nuremberg trials, Frank pled that he had done everything in his power to safeguard the art treasures. At the same time, he was labeled "the butcher of Poland" and was held in part responsible for the death of the staggering sum of six million innocent Polish people. He was hanged, along with nine other high-ranking Nazi leaders, at Nuremberg Prison in October of 1946.

The efforts of the Allied Monuments, Fine Arts, and Archives Program to save important European monuments and works of art have been recognized by the Monuments Men Foundation and the popular book and movie starring George Clooney and Matt Damon. Thanks to the Monuments Men Foundation, many of these individuals—and their incredible contributions—have been documented for posterity. In addition, some of the men and women who helped protect, recover, and transport the masterpieces— especially enlisted soldiers like the fictional Dominic Bonelli—remain unknown to us. ➤

**Author's Note** *(continued)*

I like to think that Edith Becker and Dominic Bonelli, both figments of my imagination, might have been swept up into the great swirl of unsung heroes of World War II, and that they might have gone on to live much quieter lives after 1946.

Leonardo da Vinci's portrait of Cecilia Gallerani, known as the *Lady with an Ermine*, was returned to Poland after World War II and held under Communist rule in the collection of the Czartoryski Museum. In 1991, the painting was officially returned to the ownership of the Czartoryski family. It traveled extensively to exhibitions across Europe and America for the next two decades. In 2017, it was put on public display at the National Museum of Kraków, where it now inspires visitors from around the world.

This is a work of fiction. However, I have done my best to portray the real people I write about with respect. While researching and writing, I have endeavored to understand the decisions and choices of those whose lives have been touched by historical events that, for many of us, seem unimaginable.

*To join a free online course about the portraits of Leonardo da Vinci, and to access much more historical background, videos, images, research, and further resources related to World War II art theft and this book, visit* lauramorelli.com/NightPortrait. ❧

# Q&A with Robert Edsel, Founder of the Monuments Men Foundation

Courtesy of Saloon Media

*Robert M. Edsel next to a painting of the Madonna and Child, attributed to Cima da Conegliano, which was stolen in 1944 from the Borbone-Parma Collection and recovered in 2016 by the Cultural Heritage Protection Unit of the Italian Carabinieri*

ROBERT EDSEL is the number one *New York Times* bestselling author of several books about Nazi art theft and the Monuments Men. His tireless work in pursuit of art plundered by the Nazis inspired the film *The Monuments Men*, as well as the TV series *Hunting Nazi Treasure*. In addition to a career full of ➤

entrepreneurial and philanthropic accomplishments, Robert Edsel founded and
has devoted himself to the mission of the
Monuments Men Foundation. The nonprofit
organization honors the heroic work of the
men and women who protected civilization's
most important artistic and cultural treasures
from armed conflict.

You can imagine how thrilled I was when
Mr. Edsel agreed to answer some of my
questions about the extraordinary history
of the *Lady with an Ermine* and those who
sought to save her during World War II.

**Q: Of the staggering number of works of art
stolen by the Nazis, what was special about
da Vinci's portrait of Cecilia Gallerani?
What do you think made this picture such an
object of desire?**

**A:** Through the centuries, conquerors have
taken prized cultural and art objects from
the vanquished. What distinguished the Nazi
looting operation was the degree of planning
and dedication of resources. German art
historians created lists of works of art that
were targeted for theft prior to the invasion
of each nation. Leonardo's *Lady with an
Ermine*, Raphael's *Portrait of a Gentleman*,
and Rembrandt's painting, *Landscape with
the Good Samaritan*, were obvious targets. As
a group, they constituted the three most rare
and valuable paintings in Poland. History

continuously judged Leonardo a genius talent, from his youth until today. With just sixteen or so fully accepted works by the Renaissance master, ownership of Leonardo's *Lady with an Ermine* would have conferred the greatness Hitler envisioned for his Führermuseum.

*Q: Why do you think the Nazis were focused on possessing works of art by Old Master painters, in particular Leonardo da Vinci, Johannes Vermeer, and Jan van Eyck?*

A: Hitler used art as a weapon of propaganda, redefining through his eyes what constituted "good" art—works by German and Austrian nineteenth-century painters and Old Master artists—from that which he considered "degenerate," objects created by Impressionist and Modern artists. From Hitler's perspective, owning masterpieces by such icons as Leonardo, Raphael, Vermeer, and van Eyck evidenced his superior knowledge of art and refined taste. The rarity of these artists' works and their importance through the ages made them "must-haves" for the Führermuseum.

*Q: What's the most interesting thing about the story of this portrait's theft and restitution? Are you surprised that it didn't go missing—or wasn't destroyed?*

A: Visitors to museums today know all too well the admonitions of guards and docents: ➤

"don't use flash photography," "don't stand too close," and "never touch a work of art." Yet during World War II, millions of works of art, including many of civilization's most treasured masterpieces, were transported over bomb-cratered roads, often without crates or protective wrapping, and then hidden inside salt mines, caves, and castles. Some, like *Lady with an Ermine*, were moved on multiple occasions during the war. That so many survived, largely undamaged, is truly miraculous. Returning millions of stolen objects was a towering achievement made possible by Western Allied leaders, General Eisenhower in particular, and of course the work of the Monuments Men.

*Q: What can you tell us about the real Monuments Men who were involved in the recovery of this particular portrait? What do you think we ought to know about them?*

**A:** In early May 1945, Monuments Man 1st Lt. Daniel Kern had the task of searching the Neuhaus, Germany, home of Nazi Governor-General of Poland, Hans Frank, where he discovered the *Lady with an Ermine* and *Landscape with the Good Samaritan* paintings. Frank, who was responsible for the murder of millions of Polish Jews, had fled his headquarters in Kraków just a few months earlier, taking with him dozens of priceless objects besides the Leonardo and Rembrandt, including church vestments, ivory chests, and ancient manuscripts. Kern seized these items and turned them over to Monuments Officer Lt. Craig Hugh Smyth, director of the Munich Central Collecting Point, where the Monuments Men processed for restitution almost one million stolen objects.

Like many of the Monuments Men, Daniel Kern had an educational and art background. A lifelong Brooklynite, Kern was proficient in five languages. In addition to his career as a teacher of classical languages at Brooklyn's St. Francis Preparatory School, Kern spent time as a freelance artist, writer, muralist, theatrical set designer, and lecturer. He died in 1979 at the age of seventy-nine. The year before his death, he donated his papers to the Brooklyn Historical Society.

*Q: Raphael's Portrait of a Gentleman, which was also stolen from the Czartoryski Collection, is still missing. What is the latest on the efforts to recover this lost masterpiece?*

**A:** Each year since the end of the war, rumors have surfaced about the whereabouts of this beautiful panel painting, but the fact remains that none have materialized into solid leads. Monuments Man Lt. Bernard Taper spent nearly two years, from 1946 to 1948, searching for it. Taper, and Polish Monuments Man Major Karol Estreicher, interrogated both of Frank's art advisors, ➤

Kajetan Mühlmann and Wilhelm Ernst von Palézieux, but to no avail. Several years ago, we interviewed a man in Germany for our television program *Hunting Nazi Treasure*, who claimed to have seen the painting in someone's home; however, after the passage of so many years, he couldn't identify the home. And so it goes. I remain of the opinion that this long-sought painting will, like so many others, eventually be found. Until that day, we live in hope—and pursue every lead.

**Q: *What would the Monuments Men want us to know about their work and accomplishments?***

**A:** I have known twenty-one Monuments Men officers during my many years of research and writing about them. These men and women—heroes of civilization—were extremely proud of their military service, and all they accomplished as Monuments officers. One Monuments Man told me, "After all the war years of nothing but death and destruction, FINALLY we could do something positive!" During their last six years overseas, from 1945 to 1951, the Monuments Men and Women organized the return of almost four million stolen cultural objects and safeguarded another million objects that belonged to German museums and libraries until they could be rebuilt. Much of the beauty in our world that we admire today survived because of their efforts.

Lt. Cdr. George Stout, the officer whose thinking on the topic of cultural preservation ultimately led to the creation of the Monuments Men force, spoke about the importance of their mission. His words are timeless. They are infallible. When world political and military leaders ignore them, civilization suffers. In referring to the protection of monuments as the "right conduct of war," Stout said: "To safeguard these things will not affect the course of battles, but it will affect the relations of invading armies with those peoples and their governments. . . . To safeguard these things will show respect for the beliefs and customs of all men and will bear witness that these things belong not only to a particular people but also to the heritage of mankind."

*Q: With fewer living World War II veterans left to share their stories, how has the mission of the Monuments Men Foundation evolved in recent decades? How do you see the organization's role going forward?*

**A:** During its first twelve years of operations, the Foundation successfully raised worldwide awareness about the Monuments Men and Women through film, television, and books, honored their military service through the awarding of the Congressional Gold ➤

Medal—the highest civilian honor bestowed by the United States—and preserved their legacy through a partnership with the National WWII Museum, which enabled the Foundation's incomparable archives and artifacts to be accessible to students and scholars around the world.

Now, in its second decade of operations, the Foundation has shifted its focus to longer-term objectives. We believe in the importance of continuing the mission of the Monuments Men by locating and returning to the rightful owners works of art and other cultural objects that went missing during and after the war. It's incredible to think that hundreds of thousands of works of art and other cultural objects worth billions of dollars remain missing to this day. The Foundation is also putting its remarkable legacy to use through the development of educational programs for schools and museums. Finally, the Foundation will continue to act in its vitally important and unique role as the *super partes* organization in matters of art restitution and preservation, providing impartial and objective assistance where needed.

*Q: What would you like for readers to know about the mission of the Monuments Men Foundation today?*

**A:** No nation has the financial resources to pay for the preservation of all its national treasures. With world governments facing ever increasing budget demands, preserving our shared cultural heritage for future generations depends on building public support now. This presents wonderful opportunities to engage our youth in the preservation of art, monuments, and other cultural treasures in much the same way as they are passionate about saving our environment. It is an ambitious agenda, but one that pales in comparison to the challenges that confronted just a handful of Monuments Men officers. Their achievements not only inform the mission of the Foundation, they provide an inspiring guide for students, educators, military and world leaders, and the general public.

### Q: How can we help support the Monuments Men Foundation?

**A:** Donations of any denomination are essential for the Foundation to continue its work. Gifts are easy to make by visiting the Foundation's website, monumentsmenfoundation.org/donate. The Foundation is constantly seeking to expand its Board of Trustees and Advisory Board. We are always on the lookout for like-minded people who share our passion for this important mission. For those interested in leadership of our organization, or becoming major donors, please contact me directly at ➤

**Q&A with Robert Edsel** *(continued)*

robertedsel@monumentsmenfoundation.org.
We invite you to follow us on social media to
learn more about the Foundation and to stay
connected with upcoming announcements
about discoveries and returns of stolen
objects. ❧

# Reading Group Guide

1. Leonardo da Vinci's portrait of the *Lady with an Ermine* stands at the center of this story. Did you know of this portrait before reading this book and if so, what preconceptions did you have about it? How has your appreciation of this painting changed since reading this story? What do you think is special about this portrait?

2. Edith begins by "just doing her job," until she realizes that she is a cog in a giant wheel of Nazi art looting. At what point does Edith begin to face a moral dilemma with regard to da Vinci's *Lady with an Ermine*? What other choices do you think she might have had, and what might have been their outcome? What choice do you think *you* would make in a similar situation?

3. Cecilia's drive to become a worldly, learned woman of distinction clashes with her family's plan for her to join the convent. How do you think Cecilia navigated the narrow set of choices that a woman might have had in the Italian Renaissance? How might things have turned out differently for her? ➤

4. Throughout the story, Dominic struggles with weighing the value of a work of art versus the value of a human life. Can you think of other examples in our contemporary society where people must weigh similar questions?

5. How have Dominic's, Edith's, and Cecilia's upbringings prepared them—or not—for the trials and tribulations they face in this story?

6. Leonardo da Vinci spent much of his professional life striving to be a great inventor and engineer, while history remembers him first and foremost as a painter. Why do you think this is?

7. How does the theme of prejudice weave throughout the four main characters of this book? What prejudices do Cecilia, Edith, Dominic, and Leonardo carry with them—and how have they been the object of the prejudice of others?

8. In many of the scenes, the characters are in new and uncertain places far from home— Edith in Poland, Cecilia and Leonardo in Milan, Dominic in war-torn Europe. How did each character's adventures far from home ultimately change them?

9. Throughout this story, Cecilia and Edith often walk a tightrope in order to protect themselves from the obsessions of powerful men. Were you surprised by some of the decisions they made along the way? What would you have done in their shoes?

10. Why do you think that Edith decides to tell Jakub about her idea to copy the inventories? What does she risk? Would you have done the same? Why or why not?

11. In the final scenes of *The Night Portrait*, Edith learns of Hans Frank's fate, sees the portrait returned to Poland, and returns to her ailing father. Were you satisfied with this conclusion, or do you wish that Edith had paid a higher price for her actions?

12. By the end of *The Night Portrait*, Dominic returns home safely from war to his family, Cecilia settles into her new life as a countess and learned lady, and Leonardo returns home to make his fortune in Florence. What do you predict for each of these characters in the next ten years of their lives? ∼

# Suggestions for Further Reading and Exploration

The following reading list represents a small fraction of the sources I consulted while researching *The Night Portrait*, but it will get you started if you want to explore a particular topic in greater depth. For a more comprehensive bibliography, historical research on World War II art theft, Leonardo da Vinci, and much behind this book, visit the online research vault at lauramorelli.com/NightPortrait.

## THE EARLY CAREER OF LEONARDO DA VINCI

Bambach, Carmen C. "Documented Chronology of Leonardo's Life and Work." *Leonardo da Vinci, Master Draftsman*, Carmen Bambach, editor. New York: Metropolitan Museum of Art, 2003, pp. 227–241.

Brown, David Alan. *Leonardo Da Vinci: Origins of a Genius*. New Haven: Yale UP, 1998.

Farago, Claire J. *An Overview of Leonardo's Career and Projects until C. 1500*. New York: Garland Pub., 1999.

Isbouts, Jean-Pierre, and Christopher Heath Brown. *Young Leonardo: The Evolution of a Revolutionary Artist, 1472–1499*. First ed. New York: Thomas Dunne Books, an Imprint of St. Martin's Press, 2017.

Kemp, Martin. *Leonardo Da Vinci: The Marvellous Works of Nature and Man*. Rev. ed. Oxford; New York: Oxford UP, 2006.

Marani, Pietro C. *Leonardo da Vinci—The Complete Paintings*. New York: Abrams, 2000.

Syson, Luke, and Larry Keith. *Leonardo da Vinci: Painter at the Court of Milan*. London: National Gallery, 2011.

## ABOUT THE *LADY WITH AN ERMINE*

Brown, David Alan. "Leonardo and the Ladies with the Ermine and the Book." *Artibus Et Historiae*, vol. 11, no. 22, 1990, pp. 47–61.

Christian, Kathleen. "Petrarch's 'Triumph of Chastity' in Leonardo's 'Lady with an Ermine.'" *Coming About—A Festschrift for John Shearman*, Lars R. Jones and Louisa C. Matthew, editors. Cambridge: Harvard University Art Museums, 2001, pp. 33–40.

Christiansen, Keith, et al. *The Renaissance Portrait: From Donatello to Bellini*. New York: New Haven [Conn.]: Metropolitan Museum of Art; Distributed by Yale UP, 2011.

Cotte, Pascal. *Lumière on the Lady with an Ermine by Leonardo da Vinci: Unprecedented Discoveries*. France: Vinci Éditions SARL, 2014.

Głuchowska, Lidia. "The *Lady with an Ermine* by Leonardo da Vinci: Its Originality, its Remakes and the Problem of its Repainting." *33rd CIHA Congress: The Concept of the Original as a Hermeneutical Problem*, July 16–30, 2012, Nuremberg.

Hodge, Nicholas. "Sale of the Century." *Apollo*, vol. 185, no. 651, 2017, pp. 56–58, 60. ➤

Suggestions for Further Reading and Exploration
*(continued)*

Manca, Joseph. "Wordplay, Gesture and Meaning in Leonardo da Vinci's Cecilia Gallerani." *Word & Image: A Journal of Verbal/Visual Enquiry*, vol. 24, no. 2, 2008, pp. 127–138.

Moczulska, Krystyna. "Leonardo da Vinci: 'the Lady with an Ermine'—Interpretation of the Portrait." *Bio-Algorithms and Med-Systems*, vol. 5, no. 9, 2009, pp. 143–146.

Villa, Giovanni Carlo Federico. *Leonardo da Vinci, Painter: The Complete Works*. Cinisello Balsamo, Milan: Silvana, 2011.

Winters, Laurie, et al. *Leonardo da Vinci and the Splendor of Poland: A History of Collecting and Patronage*. Milwaukee: New Haven: Milwaukee Art Museum; [Distributed by] Yale UP, 2002.

Zöllner, Frank, and Johannes Nathan. *Leonardo da Vinci, 1452–1519: The Complete Paintings and Drawings*. Köln; London: Taschen, 2003.

Żygulski, Zdzisław, Jr. "Costume Style and Leonardo's Knots in the *Lady with an Ermine*." *Leonardo Da Vinci, 1452–1519: Lady with an Ermine: From the Czartoryski Collection, National Museum, Cracow*. Vienna, IRSA, 1991, pp. 24–27.

### ABOUT THE ERMINE

Beck, James. "The Dream of Leonardo da Vinci." *Artibus Et Historiae*, vol. 14, no. 27, 1993, pp. 185–198.

Cobb, Morgan B. "Sex, Chastity, and Political Power in Medieval and Early Renaissance Representations of the Ermine." Order No. 10085435 University of Cincinnati, 2010.

Musacchio, Jacqueline Marie. "Weasels and Pregnancy in Renaissance Italy." *Renaissance Studies*, vol. 15, no. 2, 2001, pp. 172–187.

Niemelä, Pekka, and Simo Örmä. "Lady with an 'Ermine.'" *Source: Notes in the History of Art*, vol. 35, no. 4, 2016, pp. 302–310.

## ABOUT CECILIA GALLERANI

Bellincioni, Bernardo. *Rime*. Bologna: Romagnoli, 1876–78.

Servadio, Gaia. *Renaissance Woman*. London; New York: I.B. Tauris; Distributed by Palgrave Macmillan in the United States and Canada, 2005. See pp. 51–52 for Cecilia Gallerani.

Shell, Janice, and Grazioso Sironi. "Cecilia Gallerani: Leonardo's Lady with an Ermine." *Artibus Et Historiae*, vol. 13, no. 25, 1992, pp. 47–66.

Tinagli, Paola. *Women in Italian Renaissance Art: Gender, Representation, and Identity*. Manchester; New York: Manchester UP; St. Martin's, 1997. ➤

## ABOUT LUDOVICO SFORZA

Bologna, Giulia, et al. "Milan and the Sforza: Gian Galeazzo Maria and Ludovico Il Moro (1476–1499): Documentary and Iconographic Exhibition on the Occasion of the International Conference 'Milan in the Age of Ludovico Il Moro.'" Trivulziana Library, Castello Sforzesco, Milan, 28 February–20 March 1983. Milan, Rizzoli, 1983.

*Ludovico Il Moro: His City and His Court, 1480–1499.* Milan, Archivio de Stato di Milano, 1983.

Welch, Evelyn S. *Art and Authority in Renaissance Milan.* New Haven: Yale UP, 1995.

## ABOUT THE CZARTORYSKI FAMILY

Czartoryski, Adam Jerzy, and Alexander I. *Memoirs of Prince Adam Czartoryski.* New York: Arno, 1971.

Wałek, Janusz. "The Czartoryski 'Portrait of a Youth' by Raphael." *Artibus Et Historiae*, vol. 12, no. 24, 1991, pp. 201–224.

Zdzisław, Żygulski, et al. *The Princes Czartoryski Museum: A History of the Collections.* Kraków, National Museum in Cracow, 2001.

## ABOUT NAZI SEIZURE OF ARTWORK AND HANS FRANK

Aalders, Gerard. "By Diplomatic Pouch: Art Smuggling by the Nazis." *Spoils of War*, no. 3, December 1996, pp. 29–32.

Alford, Kenneth D., and Sidney Kirkpatrick. *Allied Looting in World War II: Thefts of Art, Manuscripts, Stamps and Jewelry in Europe.* Jefferson, N.C.: McFarland & Co., 2011.

Berge, Richard, et al. *The Rape of Europa.* Collector's ed. Dallas: Agon Arts & Entertainment, LLC., 2008.

*Dr. Kajetan Mühlmann Report to Hitler on Art Treasures* (1940), International Military Tribune, vol. XXVII, no. PS-1233, (USA 377).

Edsel, Robert M., and Bret Witter. *The Monuments Men: Allied Heroes, Nazi Thieves, and the Greatest Treasure Hunt in History.* First ed. New York: Center Street, 2009.

Edsel, Robert M., *Rescuing da Vinci: Hitler and the Nazis Stole Europe's Great Art: America and Her Allies Recovered It.* Dallas: Laurel Pub., 2006.

Estreicher, Karol. *Cultural Losses of Poland: Index of Polish Cultural Losses during the German Occupation, 1939–1944.* Manuscript ed., London, Publisher Not Identified, 1944.

Faison, S. Lane, Jr. *Consolidated Interrogation Report No. 4.* US Army, Strategic Services Unit. War Department, Art Looting Investigation Unit APO 413, Dec. 15, 1945, pp. 5, 6.

*Frank's Headquarters at Wawel Castle, April–July 1940.* US Holocaust Memorial Museum, courtesy of Niklas Frank and Erika Noebel, Film ID: 2980, Accession number 2016.519. ▶

**Suggestions for Further Reading and Exploration**
*(continued)*

Housden, Martyn. *Hans Frank: Lebensraum and the Holocaust*. New York: Palgrave Macmillan, 2003.

Kowlaski, Wojciech W. "The Machinery of Nazi Art Looting. The Nazi Law on the Confiscation of Cultural Property—Poland: A Case Study." *Art Antiquity and Law*, vol. 5, no. 3, 2001.

Lindsay, Ivan. *The History of Loot and Stolen Art: From Antiquity Until the Present Day*. London: Unicorn, 2014.

Nicholas, Lynn H. *The Rape of Europa: The Fate of Europe's Treasures in the Third Reich and the Second World War*. First ed. New York: Alfred A. Knopf, 1994.

Petropoulos, Jonathan. *The Faustian Bargain: The Art World in Nazi Germany*. New York: Oxford UP, 2000.

Piotrowski, Stanisław, and Hans Frank. *Hans Frank's Diary*. Warszawa: Państwowe Wydawn. Naukowe, 1961.

Simpson, Elizabeth, and Mazal Holocaust Collection. *The Spoils of War: World War II and Its Aftermath: The Loss, Reappearance, and Recovery of Cultural Property*. New York: H.N. Abrams in Association with the Bard Graduate Center for Studies in the Decorative Arts, 1997. ∾

www.ingramcontent.com/pod-product-compliance
Lightning Source LLC
Chambersburg PA
CBHW030537020726
47494CB00005B/1404